Chasing He

Public Pleasures,

Hiding Alibis,

& Dirty Secrets

From the Life of

K. K. Foster

First Edition

ISBN: 978-1-68-922859-6

Dedicated to my LGBT+

Intro

The sound traveled in and out of her ears as she rolled her head back and forth regain some consciousness for her vicious lover. The rustling of his boots and voices carried in and out of her mind as a bright light entered one of her eyes and then the other. She could hear his sound but not his words. Her breasts shimmied on her bare chest and she felt them laying over on both her arms. She could feel his hands around her neck as he jerked her hair under the ground, pulling her head down harder into the blacktop. She could feel the inner pain he had thrusted upon her as she urinated unconsciously.

Her head slowly rolled side to side as Noah grabbed her face and shook it to wake her. He slapped her repeatedly, screaming at her, and to keep her enjoying the rape, he spit water on her face forcing her to open her eyes to the rolling bright sun. He was not finished planting his rapist seed inside her. The bright white spots with multiple lights were too harsh to keep viewing. Ally kept asking her something. Her eyes hurt badly and heavy from swelling. His cock was deep inside her vagina as the pain throbbed from him, then deep in her anus to make it throb. He put both dicks in her at the same time to make the pain more intense and the seed plant. He had beaten her eyes shut. He jerked her head into the ground again by getting beneath the blacktop and reading the instructions on her Tramp-Stamp. She tried to spread her arms and legs for him but, they hurt too much. A picked guitar backed by Mellotron flutes, and an electric piano blared into her senses. She tried again to give herself to the rapist. She wanted him to finish inside her. She heard him saying her name, and she

answered without her voice or lips moving, and he slapped her again, as let go of her hair.

She paused to interpret the music. He kept shoving his big dick in her ass making her gasp and clinch. Her wet hair whipped across her ass as Noah punished her for her sin. Below she could see Noah beating Simon as he screamed and begged for freedom. He was laying on the ground tied down with Noah thrusting into him with every punch. She could feel every blow on her body as it happened and the pain stayed with her. Noah was killing him. Killing him like his serial victims. She called out for Noah and never heard the cry, only Noah's hands on Simon's painful neck. She said his name again and could not hear herself. He stepped on her arm at the elbow and she jerked it away. Zachary was crying in his room for his Angel wings. Noah forced her arm down again and stepped on it, pinching her skin with the heel of his boot and the blacktop. Zachary cried in the distance for instructions from the music.

She reached for his pinching heel and he held her other arm down. Then he tied it down. He covered her with his body as he drove into her torn cervix warming her body, and the bright light was so intense, she kept her swollen eyes closed. He kept thrusting into her uterus and slamming into the cervix as wetness rubbed her and fingers felt her. She began to cry again from the pain. Daddy pulled her hair gently to calm her spirit and she leaned her head toward his safety. The rape wasn't over. She felt the darkness creeping over her body under the lights, and the pain masking her senses. Her vagina burned and cramped inside and she felt the soreness in her rear. Her lower back ached from laying on the padded sheet as both cocks pounded inside her. Her scalp hurt so much from the constant yanking of her Angelic locks, that she

tried to grab it, but was tied down. Her vulva responded to the arm restraints with what little natural lubrication she could give. Her breasts shook loosely, exposed to the world for the first time in years. She again tried to hold the car door mirror up for him, but she failed yet from his hard thrusting, and her lips repeated the name Emily over and over as she tried to IDentifY to escape. Zachary was crying in the bathroom for her hair when she tried to rise up, she screamed without air and jerked about in pain on the mattress.

Someone's semen squirted onto her face and responsible, she tried licking it off her lips and opened her eyes to see his silhouette hovering over her. Quickly, she struggled to drink his precious seed. His silhouette. A rapist. A husband. A friend. A Witness. Both their Alibis watched the horror of her desire. Her Soulmate, who just raped her for her needs. The father of her children watched her struggle to get the life-giving wetness into her mouth. He was blurry and shared a line across his face that moved when she looked him over. The man who just saved her soul from Simon, and he jerked her left eye open and flashed his light into it, and then her other eye. Cold sperm smashed into her face again and she opened her mouth to have him or them. She closed her eyes in pain hearing her name again. She could hear his constant chatter sounds but, not understand most of it. She rolled her head from side to side repeating the words, "Stairway to Heaven, Noey. Stairway to Heaven. Noey? Noey?" with barely a whisper.

The doctor yelled her name again and she opened both eyes to him instantly. His silhouette leaned down to her looking into her eyes. Julian jerked herself and her thickness shimmied across the emergency room gurney. She could not push him

6

away. He repeated her name and other voices carried afterwards. She nodded and tried to speak as tears raced down her cheeks. Instantly, she winced in pain and tried to grab her throat. Her wrist had to remain strapped to keep the IV needles flowing. She repeated his name by only moving her lips, "Noey? Noey? Noey?"

A skinny blonde Tomboy stuck his head over her face and kissed her on the lips passionately but, gently. He was dripping his tears onto her face blending their emotional trauma together. When he leaned back, she could see it was Andrea. Andrea immediately put her hands across both of Julian's large breasts hiding her scarred nipples, and screaming at the nurse to cover her NOW! Andrea bent down and kissed her again and Julian tried to kiss her back through the pain in her lips, and Andrea hugged her delicately as she sobbed. When Andrea backed away to look her in the eyes again, Julian could see the transfer of blood on Andrea's face and panicked, shoving her head back into the sheet. She was electrified by the rush of pain lingering throughout her battered body as her conscious slowly got clearer. Her eyes rolled back and stopped sending signals and she could no longer register sound. Andrea rushed out of the way as the grand mal seizure took Julian away from her and the doctors and nurses and the moment.

Andrea screamed as she backed away from the team trying to stabilize her until it finished. One nurse was preparing a needle and the doctor yelling calmly to get a crash cart ready. Andrea fell into the corner of the room and slid down the walls crying and holding onto herself. Julian jerked and seized into stiffness with a loud, torn grunt that carried into the other Emergency Room bays. Cringing her face as she shook, the nurses held her nude legs up on the table

7

and raised the side rails of the gurney as they injected her. She remained electrified in the darkness as a chubby woman nurse held her head gently, and others held her legs. They would have to ride it out with her.

Chapter One

-Shy Alibis Hide the Mirror

Beeping sounds filled the ICU when she woke up. She felt like her body had experienced a train wreck...two train wrecks, was more like it. Immediately, she recognized the pain in her vagina and anus. When she moved the first person to her was Andrea, and her tears trickled off her cheeks onto her face as they kissed. Andrea nervously looked at the team of investigators standing around the room, and passionately kissed her again and gave her what love she could.

So Julian could see her, Andrea held the mirror up to her own face and sounded off "IDentifY Rachael," and put the mirror in front of Jordan or Julian and she tried to speak. Her left eye was bandaged shut and only her right eye, full of broken blood vessels and completely red, could see. She tried to IDentifY but, could not make a sound without immense pain in her throat. She winced and tried to push through the pain and failed again. She looked at Rachael in desperation who kept nodding and holding the mirror for her. She tried to IDentifY again, and could not get a sound through her voice box. She rested her head exhausted by pain, and looked away from everyone.

"God Damn it. She can't IDentifY. God damn it, Julian. Are you Julian?" She slowly looked at Rachael and offered no response with her face or patched eye. "You are Jordan?" The investigators around the room shared odd looks back and forth to the situation in the mirror. Rachael asked her again "Jordan? Nod if you

are Jordan?" and she did not nod. "So...Julian. Just nod for me." She did not nod. "Can you hear me?" and she nodded twice as tears rolled down her face.

Rachael looked around the room judging her position from those who could hear her, and nervously asked the unidentified patient, "Emily?" She stared at Rachael with her one eye, without a nod. "Tessa?" she asked. And she did not nod. Rachael looked around again and lowered her voice. "Dakota?" and she waited before asking another name...Arizona?" She turned her one good eye away as she looked to the ceiling.

Rachael stepped back, covering her mouth with her hands and staring at her in the bed. "She does not have her Alibis? Honey, did you Crash?" She stared at her one blue eye surrounded by red, and asked a very important question. Likely, the most important question she could ever ask her. "Do I need to find your Crash Key?" Her blue eye stared back at Rachael as she barely shook her head ten or twelve times to get her point across. Gently, she raised her hand and signed the letters N.O.

Tom, one of the investigators spoke up, "What's this 'IDentifY' stuff, we have her purse and ID from the scene. That is Jordan Taylor, Jon Taylor's wife, SANICS Team Leader."

Rachael quickly spoke up, "It is important that she speak...SPEAK...her IDentifY Cover. Otherwise this conversation will not stand in court. She must IDentifY Alibis before her statement. God damn it, Julian! What were you thinking?" Rachael stepped around the bed and began tucking the sheets under the Blue Eyed woman's feet to rid herself of the frustration.

"This is stupid. Danny said rolling his eyes. Who made up this rule? We all know her from work...her hair."

The Patient tried reaching her arms around her head and Rachael rushed to her hair. Rachael immediately starting jerking it for her, and the blue eye closed to the controlled pain relieving her stress and Rachael started giving instructions.

"Rape cases can be filed as Jane Doe, file her as Jordan Doe until we get this 'Identity.' I know who she is." Tom blurted out, and Rachael quickly rebutted him.

"The District Attorney will not recognize her statement without IDentifY testimony. This is how it works. Put an APB out for Noah Taylor aka Jon Taylor. He is on the run."

"Why do you think Jon did this, Officer Briggs?" asked another officer, this one in uniform.

Rachael glanced back at the blue eye to make sure it was closed and lowered her voice to give instructions. "Jon was the last person with her. That itself is enough to start the investigation. He is on the run. I did not find his body at the crime scene but, his Under-Cover clothes were there. I found her strung up naked to the side of the car. He is nowhere to be found. Find him and bring him in for questioning. Notify me when you find him."

The blue eye opened and looked around seconds after the room got quiet. Rachael was standing over the bed leaning on the rail with her hands spread out to the side. "Think we will call you Jay until you can IDentifY. DA is a fucking idiot." Jay carefully nodded her head while staring at the Bob Ross style painting on the ceiling tile. Quickly, Jay jerked in great pain and pulled herself up with the handrail. She immediately felt the catheter inside her swollen urethra and tried to lift up her vagina when she sat. She started jerking the hand rail to get it out of the way so she could get up. Rachael hugged on her to stop her from getting

11

up. Jay held her balance and by the look in her one blue eye swimming in red, her Texas determination was kicking in.

"Lay back down. Are you hurting? You are on Dilaudid not morphine. Morphine makes you sick." Jay started shaking the guard rail to get her to put it down. After Rachael did, Jay tried to rise out of the bed and Rachael screamed for the nurse to help her.

Wincing in pain, they worked Jay back into the bed, and lifted up the back so she could sit up. Every time she moved she felt the wrath of her Stranger-Danger Rape by her own husband. Frustrated she could not speak, and get to the shower to wash away the evidence, Jay struggled. When she got functional, she motioned for her cup of ice water, and after a little sip. Her chest jerked and shook and the painful expression on half her face remained hidden. She gently let the water run out of her mouth and onto her gown. Rachael watched her, and slowly removed her dress to reveal herself, and her 'SLUT' tattoo to the hospital staff.

Jay shook her head and pointed at her friend's pussy and flat chest and shook her head repeatedly. "Jay, I am your Beard. You were just raped by Noah. Jordan is not here to protect you and it is my responsibility to you that I would always beard for you. Simon or Noah will not ever rape you again. Noah has done it long enough, if you ask me." Rachael tossed her dress on the bed and spread it out over the woman she loved, and stood there with no panties and no need for a bra. Only a strap with her gun and badge around her thin thigh, was all she needed.

Jay shook her head and then touched Rachael's hand for her immediate attention. Jay made the phone gesture with her thumb and forefinger to her ear and mouth, and Rachael perked up and got her purse and

12

dragged a chair over next to the bed. When Jay got her phone from Rachael, she immediately called her Momma. Jay pointed to the ID name and gave it to Rachael to talk while pointing at her.

"Voicemail Jay...hi Julian's Mother, this is Rachael...umm...Julian was in a car accident tonight. DoctorLands West. She is fine. A few bruises. Um...the driver beat her up and Noah is on the run. She needs you to take care of the kids. DoctorLands West. She's getting a few stitches inside her lips and unable to speak at this time. Thank you."

When Rachael handed her the phone, Julian signed 'I love you' to her mother and kids. She saw the time on the phone and was shocked it was nearly four in the morning. She immediately called Noah and handed the phone to Rachael.

Smirking, Rachael took the phone and pretended like she cared. "I have been calling his phone all night, Jay. He is not responding. He is on the run, Jay. He raped you. Beat you. On the run."

Jay shook her head staring at Rachael. Then demanded her phone back without a word...if she could have spoken, she would not have. She immediately started texting.

Text to Noah: ♥♥♥ *Notre amour livrera nos circonstances ensemble* ♥♥♥ *I love you. I'm sorry. Please come see me in..."*

Jordan showed Rachael the text and she answered it, "DoctorLands West. Just told your mother that."

Jay continued Texting: ...DoctorLands West. I love you. You were wonderful baby. I l♥ve you so much. I need you. ♥♥♥

After sending it, she immediately started texting Rachael.
Text to Rach: HE DID NOT RAPE ME! STOP THAT! WE MADE LOVE!

Rachael pulled out her phone and after reading, gave Jay a stupid look and spoke. "Making love? Is that what you call beating your wife into seizure? Do not get stupid. Simon raped you and you didn't want to testify against him...what now, Noah? He raped you so he gets a pass because you're married to him. WTF JAY?" We take Rapist down."

Text to Rach: Damn you Rach. He did not hurt me or RAPE me. It never happened and you need to make sure it didn't happen in any report.

Rachael read it and gave her the look from hell. "I had to put up with Simon crossing the line and I protected you since that day." She leaned into Jay to make sure she was heard. "I WILL NOT LET NOAH GET AWAY WITH DOING THIS TO YOU! HE HAS BEEN ABUSING YOU FOR YEARS!"

Text to Rach: PLEASE ANDREA! THIS CANNOT HAPPEN! NOAH DID NOT RAPE ME!
Rachael rolled her eyes at the text and answered her. "The hell he didn't. AND HE WILL PAY FOR THIS JULIAN! SIMON GOT AWAY WITH IT FOR YEARS! NOAH WILL NOT!"

14

Jay immediately went for her hair, twisted it, and pinched it between her lips and let out an exhale while staring at her friend, then texted her while sucking hard on it.

Text to Rach: I'M SORRY! I LOVE YOU! SHOULD HAVE TOLD YOU! TRICKED NOAH INTO THIS! TOLD HIM MAKE IT BAD! SIMON'S SEED LIVES IN ME. NOAH TAKES IT AWAY WITH HIS ANGEL SEED. DO NOT TAKE MY NOAH RACH. PLEASE. YOU'RE MY BF. MY GF. HIS SEED COMPLETELY TAKES MY FEAR AWAY. PLEASE?

Text from Jay to Noah: Notre amour livrera nos circonstances ensemble. ♥♥♥

Rachael read the text, and didn't look at her for a moment. When she finally made her decision, she got up and lifted her dress off Jay's legs and told her outright. "I'm prosecuting him for Domestic Violence, attempted murder, sodomy, and rape, Julian. It is what Jordan would do for any woman in your bed. Or..." Rachael stopped to put parts of the puzzle together for Jay, and after staring into the distance, looked over at her beaten woman, and asked, "Is this the first time or is this the first time he has gotten out of hand?" And she walked out of the bay naked carrying her dress over her shoulder and her Ruger EC9S 9mm subcompact semiautomatic pistol between her thighs. "He won't get away this. I want him gone from out life."

Jay pulled up Rachael's IDentifY mirror and looked at her face. She could only see one black and purple eye and assumed how the other side of her face felt, and that he had beaten her there, too. Her entire pale face was a purple shade of bruising down her cheek bones and into her split upper lip pinching her

15

twist of hair. Dried blood was still visible in her nose and she picked at it hoping no one was looking. She looked over at the bathroom and felt the catheter again. Honestly, she didn't think her legs would get her there, so she beeped the nurse.

Lifting her gown forward, she looked down her chest and could feel the immense swelling inside her breasts. She equated it to how she felt when she was breastfeeding and very late to the breast pumps. Looking around, she cupped one of them and felt how heavy, large, and sore they were. Gently squeezing it as she would to spray milk for Noah to drink, she felt the warm wetness fall onto her stomach. Unprepared, she looked at her nipple and squeezed it again, only to see more liquid come out. Upon inspecting the other breasts, it leaked as well. Her thoughts went to her last period, and it was too recent for a pregnancy, diagnosed by the beaten up Medical Doctor Patient.

When the nurse arrived, she tried to communicate in sign language, she wanted to go to bathroom. The nurse reminded her of the catheter and that she could not have a bowel movement unless it was an emergency. Jay nodded over and over that it was, and she called for an orderly to get a wheel chair to get her to the bathroom. Rachael, with her dress on, with one of the doctors, walked in, and the nurse asked Jay if she could wait, and Jay nodded. She signed for a washcloth but, the nurse did not understand. She imitated washing her face with her hands, and Rachael said 'washcloth.' The nurse happily went and got one with warm water, and handed it to her. Jay laid it gently across her face and relaxed as she quietly pulled her own hair under her gown and listened.

Rachael quickly lifted her dress off exposing all of her goods again and laid it across Jay's legs. The

doctor just stood there looking at her...in shock. He finally spoke up after admiring her petite assets with a complimenting swallow. "Ma'am, I am sorry but hospital policy will not allow you to visit in the nude. You must put your dress back on." Rachael was prepared this time and pointed to her vagina for him to see her pistol and her badge. He only noticed the vagina, as most men would.

"Please keep your...uh...okay...vulva...just...stay in the bay and keep the curtain closed." He relented. Walking over to Jay, Rachael reminded him they were both MD's and he acknowledged them with a nod and moved next to Jay, as he imagined her petite ass leaning on the other side of the bed. Gently, he peeled her eyelid back and put the light into it to watch the pupil dilate. He checked the other eye and came back to the left one. Jay followed him with both eyes feeling better that she could still see through both. Her left eye had a scratch in it.

"Well Jordan Doe, your pupil was fixed and dilated when you arrived. I was looking through it when your grand mal seizure activity started. Cerebral edema, MTBI, and the MRI shows fluid from swelling. Your bowel is torn, your cervix is torn deeply, and you have a crushed uterus, blood vessels broken in both eyes..." He looked over at Rachael taking a seat, and jokingly asked, "...Anything to add, Doctor Gun?"

"Yes. My wife was brutally raped, and your caddy attitude is riding me something mean." He looked at Jay's one pretty blue eye, and she winked at him shaking her head. She hoped he got the idea. "It is called Bearding doctor. My wife was raped once before, and this is her second time as a victim. It will not happen again. My nudity helps her heal and feel safe." Rachael reached over for her purse, and the doctor went on looking at Jay's damaged eye.

"The cornea is scratched. Will your wife be making the medical decisions for you until your vocal chords heal?" Jay nodded as well as Rachael, who was writing something. "All meds will be intravenously given tonight and by noon we will be doing both. You have a lot of infection leaking into your system so antibiotics are key." Rachael handed him a written prescription to help him comprehend her authority.

Staring back at the Doctor, he read it and smiled. "Now that is a first," he said, looking down at Jay. "Your wife just wrote you a prescription for her nudity. Well, guess I can't argue with that Board violation. Good luck getting the pharmacy to fill that bottle, Doctors."

The Doctor casually walked out and Rachael rolled her eyes at his privilege. Jay reached for her phone and text her mother to tell the children she is alright and loves them very much and hopefully Noah can pick them up from school today and they can all come see her this evening. Rachael was still waiting to talk, when she pressed Send.

Looking square at Julian's one eye, Rachael was blunt. "Did Noah and Jon rape you, Jay?" Jay shook her head staring back at her. Was Jordan raped? Jay shook her head. "Was Julian raped?" Jay shook her head again. Rachael leaned over to her and grabbed her hand and leaned on the gurney rail. "You must tell me what happened, Jay. The truth. I love you." Lowering the anger in her voice, "We need each other Jay. You not being honest with me is only going to trouble our friendship. Us and him, Jay." Jay shook her head again.

Rachael let out another brave exhale and asked. "Are you having Simon flashbacks from the night we attempted to peel the false memories blanket? You have not been the same since that night." Jay just

shook her head and looked down at her feet for a break in the stare. Rachael held the pause, since only she could speak.

"You said you asked Noah to rape you?" Jay did not offer her a confirmation of what transpired. "So who asked Noah to do this?" Jay stared back at Rachael. This was indirect questioning of a police officer, not a friend and both knew it. Rachael waited and Jay made no motion or gesture to validate the crime.

"Julian cannot ask for sex in your...uh STUPID...religious marriage, Jay. So this could not have been Julian asking to be raped. Jordan was designed...designed by US, might I add, to protect you from Simon and Noah, and to deal with your internal and external wounds. So..."

The nurse rolled in with an orderly and announced they could go to the bathroom. Rachael immediately told her she could not go into the bathroom until a 'Rape Kit' was completed. Rolling her head back at Jay, she looked at her. "...Not until the rape kit is done, Jay."

Jay looked over at the nurse, and relented with a nod. The nurse pushed the wheelchair to the side and walked out with the orderly as he took second glances at Rachael's long nipples.

"As I was saying, Julian or Jordan did not want this rape. And I have an idea who did...Noah." Jay rolled her blood-red eye and shook her head. She was getting annoyed that her best friend was pushing for evidence. "You can't IDentifY or won't IDentifY. I've been with Emily, Jay. All through college when you lost control of her. Asking for Stranger-Danger rape, was your-Emily's big fetish." Her blue eye rolled everywhere as she shook her head.

19

"Jay, stop shaking your head at me and listen."
She got very insistent, "If Emily has resurfaced, we
can deal with this. Do not shut me out Girlfriend or try
to bury Emily again. Jordan is already accenting like an
ignorant Hillbilly, thus fragmenting the Alibi. I have
been warning you about the fragmenting. Your Helix is
in danger now and you could lose all your secret Alibis
with Jordan, or worse."

Jay raised both her hands spelling the word NO
in sign language letters and shaking her head. *How
much clearer* she thought, *could she be*. Rachael stood
up and slapped her waving hands away and raised her
calming voice to frustration. "Emily, wanted to marry a
rapist and, it looks like you did. What is with this shit,
Jay or Emily? You still love being raped? You did in
college as Emily, and your IDentifY Alibis are
fragmenting. We are going to see bits of each of
them...as they collapse onto each other."

Jay shook her head with a rope of her hair
across her shaking lips. With only one eye available,
she could not get her point across. Grabbing her phone
she texted Rachael again.

Text to Rachael: "I was not raped. Noah did not
rape me. Stop saying Emily. Stop mentioning those
names. NEVER MENTION EMILY AGAIN! YOU MADE
PROMISES ANDY!"

Rachael looked up from her phone, and asked
her, "Were you trying to get pregnant?" Jay quickly
responded to her shaking her head, as she answered
her texting.

"Yes. Not with rape. I want another baby with
Noah. Another more ten if I could. Soulmate Angel he
is to me Andy. Please."

Angrily, she barked at her, "You already had one rapist's baby, why not three or ten? And stop the stupid Angel crap. YOU ARE NOT AN ANGEL! Angels do not let Rapists run free or want to breed with the SICK FUCKING PIG MEN ARE!"

If Jay could stomp right now, she would. Instead, she punched her phone screen fast and hard with her fingertips.

"Ally is not Simon's child. Emma was. STOP THAT!"

"Simon was your rapist and you had his baby. Noah is a rapist and you had his child. This is why I suspect Alibis are bleeding into your character banks, Jay. 'INTO YOUR BASELINE, JAY! You are going to need the crash key." Her voice reared up again in mid speech, "You are fragmenting in your Helix! What is it?" Rachael demanded to know, and slammed her palm on the bedrail. Jay answered her with her fingers on the phone as fast as possible.

"Stop saying that. YOU MADE PROMISES ANDY! DO NOT THREATEN OUR RELATIONSHIP OVER THIS! NOAH IS NOT A RAPIST! YES I GOT PREGNANT! ALLY IS NOT SIMON'S BABY! DON'T DO THAT TO ALLY OR ZACHARY! I LOVE YOU! YOU ARE MY GF! DO NOT PUSH THIS RAPE ISSUE WITH NOAH AND SIMON! SIMON IS GONE! I LOVE YOU AND I LOVE NOAH!"

With her thumbs sweating and holding her breath, Jay finally took a break, and Rachael read it, and Jay could breathe again.

"Emily. Emily said this once to me after two guys finished off in her. I hope I get pregnant. I want to live

21

my life devoted to rape. I want to catch rapist, I want to be raped, and I want to counsel rape victims, and show them it can be a good time if they look at it from the right angle. YOU SAID THAT, JAY! EMILY SAID IT!" Jay was shaking her head as hard as she could without aggravating the pain too much and started texting in frustration.

Jay immediately began texting Rachael again.

"Emily said that, Andy, not me. I have devoted my life to helping rape victims after Simon raped me. I needed to. I may have done some bad things. But that is the past. PLEASE LEAVE MY MISTAKES IN THE PAST? DO NOT BRING IT UP ANDY! PLEASE! PROMISE NEVER TO MENTION EMILY AGAIN! PROMISE ME! HELP ME! I LOVE YOU! EMILY IS OUR SECRET!"

Rachael put one hand on her hip, and tilted her head as she spoke. "Noah doesn't know about Emily. YOU ARE EMILY! I wish he was here to see her. You're fragmenting multiple personalities, Jay, and can't remember who said, she said. YOU ARE EMILY! EMILY IS YOUR BASELINE AND JULIAN IS JUST AN ALIBI!"

Jay's eye opened as wide as she could, when she heard that...again, and shook her head in disbelief.

"I need your Crash Key. If not, I will go through the channels to get it. This case can get passed on to another team." She leaned toward her pointing her finger now. "You either let me crash your Alibis to Emily, or I will get authorization to do it. I am your Psychiatrist and your Doctor and second in Command of our team. I give you your annual Evals and I say your Alibis are fragmenting the Helix. You will eventually Crash and be fucked for life, Jay." Resting her pointing hand back to her hip, she lowered her demanding tone. "It is time to end your assignment

22

in...shithole...Ohio." Rachael put both hands on her hips and leaned in again. "YOU KNOW RAPE FUCKS UP THE DIDC! SIMON FUCKED YOURS UP WHEN HE RAPED YOU BACK THEN!"

Finished, Rachael gave her the stare of authority, as she stood there nude with a gun and badge strapped to her thin thigh. Jay started crying and covered her face and Rachael pounced on her breaking chance. "And another thing, I am going to arrest Noah for this rape...Emily's favorite new Rapist...as your Dissociative Identity Disorder Covers bleed into your conscious, affect your conscience, and your REAL Dissociative Identity Disorder." Jay just continued crying holding her hair over her face. "And I will remain nude for you until your Crash Key or a rapist named Simon or your Angel, a rapist named Noah comes back to get you and rape you again." Rachael worked the fear on her, as she had done for so many years.

Flashes of the rape whipped into Jay's mind, as she saw Noah fucking her up the ass and hitting her in the face from behind. His hand grasped tightly around the front of her throat. She could feel his fingers pulling onto her esophagus, and the immense pain inside her anal cavity. She could also feel her swollen clitoris tingle when she re-imagined the violent sex. When she came back to the moment, she was no longer crying but, staring. Carefully, she put her hair back in her mouth and thought about her fear and how it made her feel, physically.

Rachael now stood at her feet, at the end of the bed as nurses walked by and stared at her naked rear end. Jay looked up at Andy in a stare of desperation, and slowly, with intent, shook her head to her again. She may have lost Simon's fear; taken away by the man she loved but, gained a new one that felt right.

23

Rachael was honest with her, this time from a different position, "You played with rape in college, Emily. Men fucked you and you never saw their faces. We both did it. We let strangers have sex with us and we covered our heads with pillow cases so we would never know who they were. We did it, and I love you, Girl. But if you asked someone to violently rape you again. Something is wrong inside your mind." Jay went back to crying looking away and Rachael stared her down.

"Something is wrong if you asked for this and refusing to admit that you wanted, or worse, needed this." She paused as she let the crying take a good hold on her. "Senior year. You needed it so much you almost didn't graduate. You spent your senior you're on your hands and knees with a bag over your face and Strangers using you. It has come back on you. Denial will not hide what you have done. Your God has seen what you enjoyed. I can only save you, Jay, not your husband, and certainly not your God." Jay repeatedly shook her head to her, as she cried in bumbling pain.

Leaving Jay in tears and cuddling herself, Jay pulled at her own hair for mercy with her eye closed, as Rachael pulled her dress over herself and walked out of the bay letting her brief, but intense, psychotherapy do its job.

Looking over the open window of the driver door, into the car, Jay could see her hands cuffed to the steering wheel and felt his cock deep in her vagina. She looked down at her wrists, and rubbed them as she felt the stimulating rush of emotions. The bones in it were very sore. A man was fucking her from behind screaming at her and punching her back and fat Texas ass, with his fists. She knew it was Noah. She realized the pain inside her vagina and her

24

sore body as the emotions rapidly changed. She wiggled her hips a little to feel it again. Her vagina and bottom ached, and so swollen, she had to keep her legs spread apart. The pain, in the right spots, made her smile.

Chapter 2

-Synthetic Lovers Bid a Stairway

Jay heard the sound of a food tray being placed on the table. Immediately, she felt Andrea laying against her chest. Lifting up the blanket to make sure, Andrea snuggled to her breasts. She was her best friend, co-worker, former lover, occasional lover, and submissive partner, and still, completely nude with Rachael's gun and badge strapped to her thigh. She held Jay's left breasts against her face like a suckling baby that had filled its hunger and rested softly. Jay smiled and felt the love they once had and how it had turned into a strong sisterhood that one could not exasperate. She only wished Andrea's over-protective Rachael Alibi inside her, would not interfere with her marriage. This was how it was supposed to work. Jay figured Andrea would get her work personality, Rachael, off her back when she could talk again without angry emotions leading to over-protection. Having fallen asleep, IDentifY would reset her from the Alibi Rachael to Andrea.   Her children came to mind, and then Noah, and then her fear of consequences swarming around Noah. She laid the blanket back down and grabbed for her phone to text him. She fumbled with it due to her loss of depth perception and reached over and straightened the food tray that was not square with the table. When she saw the cup handle was not symmetrical to the rest of the dishes, she adjusted it with a feeling of relief.

Text to Noah from Jay: I hope you are safe. God be with us baby. I love you. I need you. DoctorLands West. Thank you my soulmate. You own me. Notre amour livrera nos circonstances ensemble. ♥♥♥

Toying with the apps, she finally heard the sweet sound of a slow picked guitar backed by mellotron flutes, and an electric piano. Her heart sank into her chest as it always had since she was a child. Her Daddy's song played every day in their home as a child. It was playing when her mother gave birth to her, it played next to her crib, and at age eight, her father sat her on his knee and explained to her, who she really was and that the song carried the sound of God's voice...if she could hear it. Closing her eye again, she sat on his knee, her hair was roped across her lips, like her Mothers', and both Father and daughter tugged on Julian's long locks, gently.

The song continued as Julian took on a slow familiar rapture inside. He told her to listen very carefully to the music and the words of the Seraph that followed the musical notes, and to understand what he was telling her and why. The man singing the song was one of them, bound to the earth with wings, such as her mother and father. A Cherub of the highest order serving God, as she would do. Like the singer, she was gifted by the heavens to provide those in need with comfort, protection, patience, salvation, unconditional love, and purpose. She, like her mother and father, and the singer of the song, were Angels, cast down with duties.

"The Angel is conversin' with God, tellin' you the mystery as God whispers it to him." Her father told her. "The Angel tells you the story usin' words with double meanin's."

"I hear the Angels listenin' and cheer and clap for him, Daddy." Julian said to him.

"Blessed she is," said her father, and the sermon will help you understand your purpose, as an Angel." Daddy gently brushed her long hair with his fingers and played the song with her to provide her with inception. "Such is the story of Hope, and the duties of an Angel that be bringin' forth everlastin' graces. Once you understand the musical notes little Angel, yer' hearin' God tell the Angel what words to sang to Angels like you, and me and Momma. What an Angel must do is understand the riddle the sangin' Angel is given by God. Only Angels of God's earth can understand what he and she is bein' told to say, and one day, you will understand. Most importantly, you hear the voice of God actually speakin' at-cha'.

"The Angel is moanin' here Daddy, is he hurtin'?" "He is expressin' yer' duty of pain and the pleasure it will bring you to take it from others. An Angels duties are often painful and necessary, my blessed child of God. Yer will come to understand yer need for pain as your wings grow. If you listen, the God's words are the musical notes. It takes Angels of our order, many years to understand."

"What part is God talkin', Momma?" the young Julian asked looking at her mother whose hand she held with Momma's hair and her hair, between their fingers.

With tears in her eyes, her Mother answered her with a soft tone. "The Singin' Angel tells the story of what has happened to one of heart, and that a day comes when God speaks to his Angels, like you, upon which the Angels debated their duties with him, and changed their path to follow their duties. Right here. Right here. Listen. The whispers of God are spoken through the music-like the sound a songbird makes."

28

"Songbirds sing music, Momma?"

"That's right, Angel. The Songbird is announcin' God's whispers that even Angels have doubt about bein' Angels. The whispers of the music, are of God's voice, my Child."

Eager, Mother did speak. "Now, listen to him whisperin' to the Singin' Angel, what message to sing to the Angels. The Angel warns you of a Piper...often in bright, patchy colors." Her father stopped to hear the whispers to the Singing Angel. His head slowly nodded up and down as he interpreted the notes to words.

"Do you hear the whispers, my Deary? Between the song's lyrics, Honey?" Her mother asked quietly.

Julian shook her head, looking at her father become entranced in the rapture. "I hear music between the singin', Momma."

"That my Bluebonnet Angel, is God's voice, and only real Angels will be able to understand the words when they grow their wings." Her mother explained joyously. "Millions of people, Honey, even outside of Texas, have heard this converse of God, and never understood what it was. Texas has more Angels than anywhere." The young Julian watched her father, and how everything about him had changed before her. His spirit rose and his aura balanced. She didn't understand it at the time but, she saw his rapture in the moment.

"Listen to the words about yer' duties Julian, as you shine light on things in life to show the people a better way." Her mother pushed.

Julian got up and straightened the crooked book lying on the table in front of them and sat back on his knee to look at it again. "Why do the scary shadows follow the souls and get bigger Momma?" Julian asked, as her father came back into the moment.

29

"It shows how far down the wrong path they have travelled and runnin' out of time to change their evil ways. There is always time for salvation before yer' judgement." Her mother said in kind, for her to understand.

"It sounded like music not words Daddy, what is God sayin'? Julian looked into her father's windows and witnessed his beautiful soul. She may not have known what she was seeing but, she would never forget it what purity looked like.

"That is what yer' have to find out, my Child." He told her looking into her soul for the purity he had always seen in her.

"Daddy, am I really an Angel?" Julian asked, hoping it was true.

Her father was finishing looking through her windows and smiled when he answered her. "You be my Dear, as yer' mother and I be. Only Angels can have Angels. When you can understand the musical notes of the Song, you will know you are a real Angel."

Andrea moved a little, and the memory faded, as it had her entire life. Jay put her phone down and pulled her hair down to her vagina and pushed it between the right and left swollen labia and her thighs. Roped and twisted, she put some in her mouth, and the rest in her hands as she began to pray. Only then did she realize she didn't have her boots on and wiggled her feet as they dangled outside the blanket. She smiled at them and looked to make sure the boots were in the room. After seeing them, she promised to add to her prayer that she needs to be forgiven for not wearing her boots. This Cowgirl, loved her boots.

After her long prayer, her hair didn't get stuck in her wedding ring, only to see it was missing. Immediately, she started patting Andrea to wake up and shoving her hand in her face. Andrea crawled out

from under the blanket, and sat up to wake up. Her skinny stick figure actually fit between Jay and the rail. Andrea suckled Jay's breast one last time and climbed down bumping the table and mumbling about coffee, as Jay flailed her arms in the air without a sound. Her torn vocal cord would take much more time to heal.

Andrea walked into the hallway and turned left rubbing her face, and caring less about being in her birthday suit. Jay sat there staring at her finger and looking all over the bed, and feeling around her wide hips and gently under her crotch. Panicking, she took a photo of her finger and sent it to Andrea. She heard Andrea's phone beep and located it in her chair on top of a pair of jeans and work boots. Jay did not recognize them and looked around again. It was not on her tray table. And she assumed the staff had removed it. The cup handle was turned in the wrong direction again, and she delicately put it back in the correct position.

Jay Text to Noah: Need you. 911. Julian

Rachael stumbled into the room carrying a cup of coffee and a bit more alert than Andrea was. Jay immediately pointed to her finger and then to the jeans. "What Jay? Those are my clothes. I went home last night. I am done with dresses and being so feminine for Michaels." Jay kept pointing to her ring finger and glaring, when Andy sat in the chair by the jeans to get warm and drink her coffee. Two Orderlies walked by and gawked at her nudity as she sipped. Andy slid down in her seat and spread her legs apart and rubbed her vagina fresh, and sat back up to cross her legs. She went back to sipping the warm, real cup of joe.

31

"I don't know where your ring is. Calm down, Bitch. I will find it. I think they take it off when you come in unconscious. Or the MRI lab or CT scan. Your wooden cross necklace is missing, too. Just let me sip the morning." Jay reached over and knocked everything off her tray table and Rachael's bare feet hit the floor like a good soldier being called to attention. Jordan was pointing at her to leave the room and go find them NOW!

Nude Rachael casually walked out to the nurse's station rubbing her hair back into place and sipping. Gently, the nurse reached up and touched Andrea's arm and turned pink with her smile. Rachael returned the smile, and a wink and maybe an offer.

Nurse Theresa admired Rachael as she walked back to the bay, as most of the staff did in the moment. Nude, she had the power, the walk, and the beautiful thin body, and certainly, the experience. Jay was texting her mother again asking if she had seen her ring and wooden cross.

Rachael sat back down and told her angry friend. "They will contact the lab and find out. Even the ambulance you rode in on. If it is at the crime scene Jay, it is impounded already. Locked up. Safe. You do have marks around the front of your neck from Noah the rapist."

Jay angrily tossed off her blanket and proceeded to try and scoot passed the handrail but, her large asset was just too embedded in the bed. With each painful grunt, she pulled herself exerting pain everywhere, especially in her nether region. When the catheter jammed into the bed she reared back in pain slamming into the bed. The painful expression on her face was much louder than her moans. She was sweating and angrily stuffed a twisted rope of hair into her mouth and jerked on the other side to calm down.

Instinctively, she reached for her cross dangling from the braided rope around her neck to twist between her fingers. Missing, that annoyed her even more.

Nonchalantly, Rachael said "No bathroom until the rape kit, Jay," between her sips, as her crossed ankles dangled back and forth impatiently. Jay flipped her off with the hand short her wedding ring. She could not reach anything else to throw so she shoved the tray table away from her to make it crash into the chairs. It didn't. She pouted and winced from the pain all over. "I will cuff you, Girlfriend. Right to the bed. NOW STOP IT!" Jay didn't even look at her with her one eye.

Instead, she texted Rachael.

Text To Rachael: Please go to the house for me. See if Noah is there. I need him. Do not tell him I lost the ring. I need some things. Please Andrea. Please. I need coconut oil, headband, Noah. Your Matrix Formula?

Ignoring her requests in the moment she asked, "Have you tried to IDentifY again? I need you to for my investigation, Jordon Doe." Rachael looked up at her coffee as Jay reciprocated the ignoring, and texted her again.

Jay continued with her text: my Bible, my pink IDentifY mirror, hide my sex toy next to bed-orange white plastic dog bone. PLEASE! Bible living room or dining room. Coconut oil next to dog toy, headband bathroom in bedroom.

Rachael heard the beep of her phone, and dug it out of one of her shoes and read it. "If I go, will

you...no. Do the rape kit for me now and I will go for you."

Jay shook her head with her hair still in her mouth, and waited her out. Jay held up the hand mirror so Rachael could see herself and Jay tried to grunt "IDentifY."

Rachael looked at the mirror and murmured, "Rachael." Jordan turned her head to one side and stared at her pleading without words and only an eye to give credence.

Text from Jay to Noah: Mustangs always come home. ♥♥♥ Please straighten that chair next to you.

Rachael got up balancing the chair with the others and pushed the tray table back to her and asked if she would promise to do the Rape Kit when she came back. Jay nodded and crossed her hands in prayer. Rachael grabbed her jeans and pulled them up and continued to stare at Jay. "I have to get my hormone shots anyway, so it will be a while. Text me if your list grows."

Rachael smiled after getting her work boots on, and walked over to hug Jay and kissed her on the lips, gently. Rachael took Jay's hand and put it on her left nipple and rubbed her fingers across it repeatedly. Jay pinched it between her fingers and pulled on it with a smile, just to appease her. Rachael leaned in and Jay licked it before sucking it into her mouth. Rachael's eyes rolled back into her head and Jay pinched her other nipple. Both of them felt the tingle between their legs, yet only one of them could get wet at the moment.

She leaned down and French-kissed Jay and shared her spit and tongue with her. Rachael gave her a quick kiss afterward and started out the door with a

shirt in hand, reminded Jay not to masturbate without her witnessing it. Jay rolled her eye. *As usual, intimacy was going to be a medium of exchange with Rachael, to get help for a wounded friend*, Jay thought.

Jay sat back and tried to think of anything else she needed from the house. Quickly, she pulled the blanket off and the gown exposing herself completely. She watched the nurse's sneak peeks at her from the station and they saw Jay spread her legs and take pictures of her vagina. She kept her breasts covered with her left arm and took as many pictures as she could of her swollen area, then waited for the nurse to walk away from the station, and she snapped photos of her bruised breasts. She held each one up and snapped pictures so her nipples were clear in the shot. When the Nurse Theresa walked in, she quickly covered her breasts again.

"Can I help you with anything? I see you're trying to take nude selfies. Is that for evidence or..? Jay nodded her head to say evidence, and motioned for her to get the wheel chair. When they nurse brought it over, neither of them could pull her Texas ass out of the bed, and she had to get help. Jay struggled in pain trying not to express it verbally, and finally got to the edge of the bed exhausted from the millions of nerve cells screaming at her brain. As she pulled the wheel chair around, Jay dropped her phone to the floor trying to keep her breasts covered. Instantly, she stopped and waved at the nurse.

Pointing to her nipples covered by her arm, she tried saying nipples but, without sound. Jay signed the letters but, the nurse did not understand.

"Are you deaf ma'am? Your chart didn't say..." Jay continued to point to her boob and the nurse asked to look at it. Reluctantly, Jay uncovered one of her breasts to show her large areola and tried to put

her short stubby fingers around the edge and cover the areola with the other hand. Quickly, she covered them again.

"Your nipple. Does it hurt? Is it leaking? Frustrated, Jay dropped her tits down and covered both nipples with her palms. Both nurses looked at each other confused.

"A bra. You want your bra. Ma'am your clothes were taken by your wife," one of the nurses said politely. Jay started to sign again, and quickly pointed to the bandage over her left eye.

"You need a bandage over your breasts? Are you bleeding?" Jay shook her head no. She saw a band aid on the woman's finger and immediately pointed to it with glee.

"You need a band aid for your breasts. Is it leaking?" Jay shook her head again, and kept making a circle with her small hand large enough to cover her scarred areola. Jay kept pointing at her band aid, and then circling her areola and back to the band aid. Then she exposed herself again to put her fingers together to show a big circle and pointed to the band aid again.

"You want a large band aid for your breasts?" Jay gleefully nodded and covered herself again. "I will see what I can do. I'm not sure we have round ones that large. Pardon me for saying." Jay smiled as the nurse slowly working her catheter out of her urethra and sighed with relief when it came out, and landed on her feet with joy. Her knees wobbled and nurses grabbed her and tried to turn her around to sit in the chair. Naked, she held their hands as she tried to plop into it gently. Her wide ark couldn't fit, but she made it squeeze in there. The nurse read the 'Ark' tattoo on her ass and smiled to the other one before wheeling her to the bathroom.

Pulling her out of the wheel chair to get into the bathroom, she realized walking bowlegged was the trick. In pain, she noted to herself, it felt like a basketball between her legs. As she held the doorway shuffling barefoot onto the tile, the nurses noticed her labia from behind.

"Do you need a donut for your labial hypertrophy?" Jay stopped with her big rear-end facing them, and slapped both her sore butt cheeks with her hands to show she already had enough cushion. She slowly closed the door with her back to them and rushed to the shower. The nurses put the wheelchair outside the door and went back to their station.

Jay clambered into the warm shower forgetting the bandage on her eye until the water hit it. She peeled it off and began rinsing herself off. She had to lean on the wall to stay standing and holding onto the handicap bar, she reached down to her vagina and painfully inserted her finger. Jerking up and down from the pain, she worked her two fingers into her vaginal canal to try and rinse out any semen that could be swabbed. Bobbing up and down as she tried, she finally got two fingers in and breathed, spitting from her mouth with a grunt. It was not pretty.

Looking down she could see the shower water flowing red, and she frowned almost shedding tears. She grabbed the mobile shower head and switched it to powerful small stream and sprayed up into her vaginal opening as much as possible. The pressure felt good on her labia and vulva mound and clitoris, and moved it closer and closer and moved it up and down her thick labia majora. She bent over and sprayed at her anus with her ass on the wall and the other hand trying to spread her butt cheeks apart. When she stopped, she sighed exhaustion from the pain, and

37

stood there breathing it away. The water felt wonderful on her face from the mounted shower head.

She felt relief for her and Noah, and washed under her breasts and under her arms, and put the mobile shower back. She felt so much better now getting rid of evidence. She gathered the shampoo and put her five feet of hair across both handicap bars and washed it foot by foot.

When she opened the bathroom door, she pushed the wheelchair out of the way and hobbled over to her boots under a chair, and slipped them on. *That felt wonderful*, she thought. The nurses watched her covering her breasts with the dinky towel, and one got nervous with her putting her boots back on and rushed over to stop her from leaving.

When Theresa got there, Jay motioned for the bed, and they walked over to it so Theresa could spread fresh blankets over the blood stained sheets. The nurse helped her get her short body up on the bed again, and slid her back so she could sit up. Jay breathed again keeping the towel over the breasts. Forced to keep her legs apart Theresa started to pull off her boots and Jay abruptly bent her knees and rolled her eyes back in pain.

"I will get you another blanket." The Nurse said to her. Jay nodded as the pain subsided and sat there exposing her prized Texas gift to the world but, she had her boots on and a good shower.

Another nurse came in and shied away from Jay's vulva exposure but, inquisitively took a gander at the size and color of it. Jay watched her look at it in disgust and didn't really care. The nurse handed her the pill cup and water, and glanced at Jay's Texas gift. After Jay harshly swallowed, she sucked down the cold pain-relieving water as much as she could, as the nurse noted she was going to get a blanket. The water

was her salvation in the moment. *Hopefully, two blankets arrive,* she thought.

Waiting nearly twenty minutes and every person in the world walking by to see her big Texas labia that was now yellow, purple, red, and looking like it was in its twenty-fifth month of pregnancy. She put her water bottle down in front of it just in time for the Gynecologist to arrive. Jay was used to her gift's normal size of being in the fifteen month of pregnancy and happy to be abnormally large labia. Even though, she probably would not mind it staying larger since everything in Texas was bigger.

Reading the chart, she noted to her the vaginal medical issues, as Jay's tiresome nodded at the situation. "Swollen vagina, uterine rupture, vaginismus-blocked penetration, closed urethra, nine stitches in the cervix, six stitches in your perineum and closed uterus, from partial collapse and crushing…and even a tear in the bowel." Jay just nodded politely to what her education and experience had already told her. "I'm very sorry this happened Miss Doe. We have you on several antibiotics to heal things as fast as they can. Can I get you anything?" Jay shook her head, not even attempting sign language for a blanket. She was exhausted.

"Miss Doe, your vagina is so swollen you can't leak blood and excess fluid which will concentrate and bacteria will form. When was your last menses?" Jay held up two fingers. "So you are ovulating. This is a good thing and will allow you to heal. We are going to insert a tube to help keep it draining. Your labia majora concerns me. With respect…" Jay started nodding, "…were you labial hypertrophy before the accident, or is this size from swelling." Jay put her thumb up and kept rising her hand upward. "Higher labial hypertrophy?" Jay used her hands to show her

the word big. "I see. I can recommend a plastic surgeon for Vaginoplasty procedure if you like. You may need it to retain a more manageable size." She was very professional when she spoke. "With the swelling at this level, it is likely to produce stretching, sagging, and permanent resizing." Detailing the complications, the Doctor spoke as delicately and respectfully as she could. Jay shook her head at the lady. "I see. If you plan to have children, the chances they will stretch more is high. I just need to tell you these things." Jay signed, the letters MD and pointed to herself and the Doctor had no clue what she was saying.

"'Catheter for two days to keep urine flowing otherwise you could get a bladder infection, and yeast infection, and or a burst bladder. Keep up on your fluids, please. The nurse will by soon to place a vaginal catheter." Jay shook her head no. "You don't want us draining the fluid? We must keep it draining." Jay grabbed her phone and search for MD. When it popped up, she showed her and pointed to herself. The Doctor got it now. As your Physician, I recommend it." Jay smiled and pointed to her Texas Labial Hypertrophy and pointed to the bathroom. "Okay." She told her she would note it in the record that she recommended it but, the Patient refused. Jay nodded politely and put her hand to her chin and dropped it forward to say thank you.

Her cold water cup went right back to her swelling hot vagina and she covered it with her hair. Neither blankets had arrived yet, so she texted Rachael again:

Text to Rachael: Copenhagen-fridge, chalice from bedroom if any in it. Do not spill seed. Blue bandana headboard of bed, eye liner. Noah boots with

40

spurs-bedroom. Check again need to hide any sex toys. TY

A nurse finally arrived with four blankets and spread it out over Jay and she gave her the small towel used to cover her scarred breasts. Offering to remove her Shyanne Exotic Pirarucu Western boots, Jay declined shaking her head. A second nurse arrived hooking up her Dilaudid to her IV and the patient-MD sat back and waited for the synthetic heroin to work. With a rope of hair in her lips, her breasts covered, and exhausted, she was waiting for the lights to go out in her mind.

Chapter Three

-Smirk the Bitching Kinfolk

When Jay's medication high lifted, she awoke to a mouth full of hair, a few gawking nurses staring at her from the nursing station and Andrea sound asleep snuggled to her breasts...completely nude...again. Jay took the rope of hair out of her mouth and covered Andrea with all the rest of it since she was sound asleep on the blankets. Jay gently cuddled and kissed Andrea on the head and snuggled her baby. The nurses smiled their approval from afar as they played on their computers. Jay lifted her blanket to see Andrea's hand palming on her breasts for feeding. She smiled and shook her head reaching for her phone and trying not to disturb her Woman. The smile was from seeing Andrea fall into their old routine of suckling; a counseling of her Mother Issues, during Medical School, a few years ago.

Text to Noah from Jay: My husband. My Dominion. I love you. ♥ *I hope that God is protecting you. Please text me let me know you are ok. God is watching us. DoctorLands West ICU* ♥♥♥

When she finished she rested, admitting to herself it was nice having Andrea snuggle her and give so much love to her in her time of need. She whispered to Andrea without a sound, "Luke 6:38. I share with you, my love."

42

Text Noah again: My seed is plenty for you. 1 Corinthian 7:3-5. Rodeo Permission? I am sorry I am asking. Witness Andrea. Punish me later please. Pick my boots for me.

Andrea rolled her eyes open and put her hand up to rub Jay's hair and face and kissed her breasts under the blankets. Jay snuggled her with affection and asked how she was feeling. Andrea chuckled and snuggled Jay's hair more as her own blanket, and pulled Jays head down for an intimate quick kiss. Afterwards, Jay asked if Andrea would put the band aids on her nipples.

Andrea got up and got them from the tray table, and Jay looked at the nursing stations and saw only one nurse was watching and she squeezed her nipple to see if it still leaked. It did but, not as much.

When Andrea saw this, she was shocked. "Are you pregnant...finally?" Jay shook her head and squeezed more out of it onto her fingers. And tasted it. Her expression was not of satisfaction. Andrea watched, curiously. Having never had breasts, she was curious. Jay pointed at the band aid and then her nipple, and Andrea brought them over. The Self-titled Wife grabbed the small circular one to cover the leak, and Jay pushed her hand away when she brought it up to her nipple. Jay wanted the big round band aids. Pointing, Andrea got the hint and Jay stretched her breast to flatten the areola area and Andrea put it on her. Huge they were, Jay's extra-large areola extended past the diameter of the band aid, leaving a fading brown ring around it, but it covered most of the scar. Together, they were more efficient on her smaller right breast. She immediately got her phone to communicate with Andrea.

From Jay to Andrea: Can you call Noah's number? Please? Call him for me.

Taking a strategic step, she used Jay's phone to call. When she got a voicemail, she just dangled the phone back to Jay. "Voicemail Jay."

Jordan pushed her hands to say carry on a conversation with the voicemail and after the beep, Andrea left a message from Rachael and Jay.

"You presume this to be your battered, raped wife in a hospital bed. DoctorLands West. She would like to see you now. She is in bad shape." Shaking her head, Jay did not have a happy expression on her face and read more like 'stop fucking this up.' "So you need to come see her NOW you RAPIST SON OF A BITCH! I WILL HUNT YOU DOWN YOU FUCKING RAPISTS SIMON BASTARD! I WILL ARREST-" Jay yanked her arm attached to the hand holding the phone and then ripped it from her in anger. With both her blood colored, blue eyes, she stared down Andrea's green eyes and without breaking the standoff, reached for Rachael's IDentifY mirror and held it up to her without blocking the staring contest.

Andrea caved when she was forced to look into the mirror Jay was jamming at her. "Rachael," she confessed. Jay did not stop staring her down. This manipulation of a friend, in desperate need, through an Alibi, was getting out of hand.

Jay immediately called Noah's number again, and when it was time to leave a voice mail, she sat back to stop Rachael from seeing it, and typed the numbers: 7224 58327 and hung up, staring back at Rachael staring at her.

Then she texted him Psalm 41:9 Rach=Judas

44

Rachael stared at her, making decisions for herself, yet only she and Andrea would know what those were. Finally breaking the stare, Jay softly pointed to the bag Rachael brought from Jay's house. Rachael stared at her still without moving, and Jay toned down her angry stare but, stared back.

The clock on the wall ticked as each of them scrambled for a strategy to get what each one wanted or needed. The nurses shuffled in the hallway. Alarms could be heard down the hall and they stared. Trays clanked in the hospital. The earth spun. The clouds drifted by and the sun continued to rise.

The moment when friendships and relationships and IDentifY Covers collide and only one baseline gets what they desire, and the others forebode. Portend IDentifY Dissociative Identity Disorder Covers, they must. Decisions were being made without words and no one was letting the others know by speaking or signing, and only one under IDentifY. *Where did loyalties lie?* Each one thought.

Jay broke the tension by looking down at herself and slowly tearing up, and Rachael continued to stare and decide. Jay text her without looking up.

Text to Rachael: I'm sorry. Please bring me the bag and Noah's boots. Please Rach. I'm sorry.

The sound of her alert did not register her senses or stop her from staring Jay down. Simply, Jay looked down trying not to be imposing, since she wasn't. Her eyes never left her boots. Recognizing Rachael wasn't even looking for her phone. Jay gave her a quick, glance of guilt and signed she was sorry, and looked back to her boots. Jay had tears in her eyes and Rachael did not. Rachael had realization that

in the end, she and Andrea and Emily were going to lose again...IF...Noah ever came back...again.

Text from Jay to Rachael: Please stop. Go work on the Matrix Formula. ☺

Jay palmed her breasts to push the band aids on tighter and slowly pulled her blanket off her chest, and exposed them to Rachael, and rested her head back as she looked at her, with her arms pushing her breasts together. Finally, Rachael looked down at Jay's large mammary glands, and walked away to get Jay's gifts from home. A peace offering everyone seemed to accept.

Jay had to point to Noah's boots and Rach grabbed them from the floor and sat it all on the bed between Jay's boots, on top of the blankets. Jay tried to reach Noah's boots, but could not get them, and Rachael knocked them over toward her without a word but, handfuls of non-appreciation, and Jay snuggled them against her bare chest and rubbed them on her face inhaling the smell of Texas leather. If anything would make her clitoris tingle, it would be Texas leather. Rachael and Andrea rolled their eyes and sat down in a chair farthest from the bed.

Jay pulled off both boot spurs and tucked one boot on each side of her in the bed, and started tying the spurs into her long hair hanging down the side of her head. One on each side to dangle down near her belly. When Jay pulled the end of her hair through the knot, she noticed it was shorter. Blindsided she started grunting and shaking her hair at Rachael to show her it had been cut. Now panicking, she gathered her hair into a rope and tossed it in front of her on the bed to measure. It was shorter. She began punching the bed on each side of her legs and shaking her head violently

46

and slammed herself backwards into the mattress. SHE WAS PISSED OFF!

Rachael just thumbed with her phone as if it made no difference to her. Jay yanked a feminine pad form the bag and through the box at Rachael. Without looking up and reading her phone, she answered her. Your hair was tied to the headrest of Noah's car when he BEAT YOU and RAPED YOU AGAIN! EMT cut it off to get you free for the ambulance. With a long purring exhale as she thumbed through her email, Rachael spit out her diagnoses, "BATTERED WOMEN SYNDROME, JAY!"

Flustered, she began jerking her hair with both hands on each side of her chest, and gritting her teeth as trichotillomania kicked in. Rachael yelled at her without looking.

"STOP IT EMILY! JUST STOP!"

Rolling her eyes back, Jay felt the pain take away the anxiety and began to rescind her pulling slowly, but still jerking it for comfort. When she finished her tantrum, she aggressively finished tying the spurs in her hair, stuffed some of it into her swollen vaginal opening, some in her mouth, and the rest in her hands. It was time to pray for forgiveness from God, Noah, and Texas for getting her hair cut without permission from her husband. She slammed back into the back of the bed, adjusted to fit like a lounge chair.

Rachael just smirked and scrolled as Jay prayed. Not really giving a damn, or hiding her own damnation of it. When Jay finished, she got into the bag from home and opened her blue bandana. She wrapped it over her bad eye and over her hair as she tied it in the back. She was back to being one-eyed yet, fashionably cute in a crooked skull cap. She picked up her large drinking cup filled with water and through it into the

bathroom door. It splashed from the ceiling on down but, nobody seems to care accept Jay. Nurses didn't bother to come see what the ruckus was.

She pulled out her eyeliner, coconut oil, brush, phone charger, Tru-Fragrance Rock & Roll Cowgirl perfume that Rachael loved on Julian, black headband, and an orange and white dog chew toy she named Venus, and held it up to show Rachael and smirked for bringing a sex toy to the hospital. Rachael looked up from her phone and crossed her legs as she slid forward in the seat. She was nude. "Thought you might want a good dog toy to play with...Freak. Buy a dog." Jay stuffed it in one of Noah's boots with the coconut oil, and pulled out her own IDentifY mirror and tried again but, could not speak thus, could not IDentifY her Alibi. Out of the silence came Rachael's response. "Don't worry Emily. I already know. It's in my report about your IDentifY hiccups, and recommendation for Crash." Jay offered her the smirk back, and Rachael continued, "I tried to IDentifY as Emily. She was occupied."

Jay's smirk did not change for a brief moment, and she got back to her goodie-bag to find her can of Copenhagen Straight Longcut tobacco, mascara, brush, and a steno-pad with pens and markers. Jay knocked on the guard rail to the bed and showed Rachael the steno-pad when she looked up. "Thought you might want to right a statement about your husband, Simon raping you...oh I mean Noah raping you." Jay tossed it at her hitting her in the leg and Rachael just ignored her, and Jay's middle finger.

She pulled the spurs out of her hair and bandana off, and proceeded to brush the tangles out of her hair and making sure the bristles dug into her skull for frustration release. *What a wonderful feeling it is to brush it after days of this crap-shit,* Jay thought to

48

herself-*Ass holes cut my hair.* She continued, *forgive me Texas, and Noah, and God. I shan't keep it shorter. I promise to let it grow a foot taller than I...for God and Texas.* Her autonomous sensory meridian response was in heaven, where one day, her hair and Bible would take her with her boots on. Only which pair for eternity, would be the hard decision.

Jay's phone alerted before she was done brushing and, she immediately got hold of it to see if it was Noah. It saw Rachael, so she finished her brushing, tied her blue bandana over her head and left eye, and tied Noah's spurs back into her hair before responding. Stirring her anger was expected 'Pokes' from Rachael.

From Rach: You married a rapist after being a rape victim. You let men rape you for money in college, Emily. You know it. I know it. Noah might know it from your diaries. Hugs to Emily. I will arrest him in a day or two. Just waiting for him to show up here.

Jay gave her the evil, bloody eye, and got back to responding on her texting app.

From Jay: NO RAPE! I need Noah and you. Our children Andy??? NO RAPE GD I FELL DOWN!

From Rach: I DON'T KNOW who you are or WHY YOU ARE LYING TO ME! NOAH IS A SIMON. IDENTIFY!

From Jay: I cannot IDentifY properly. To say who I am violates policy under DIDC Regs. I'm protecting you and Noah here...and me. Trying to cover our asses so we don't get re-assigned...apart.

From Rach: NOAH RAPED YOU! Remember anything? Tell me now! Rape kit NOW!

Before responding, Jay roped her hair to suck on and manage herself. That cup laying on its side on the floor by the bathroom door, was driving her OCD mad.

From Jay: What is wrong with you Rachael? Really. Something is not right with you. Don't you care about my life? My kids??? My husband???

Rachael, tired from texting blurted it out instead. "He is on the run. Can't find him. APB already. No sign of him at the house but, this was in the fridge." Rachael pulled out a small glass food container with a red lid, and held it up for her. It has a shot glass in it with a small lid taped onto the top to keep it from spilling.

Jay's eyes got wide, even if she couldn't see with the other one. Noah's morning chalice of semen, which by God, she owned, and responsible for, was right in front of her. She immediately put her hands out to get it and yet, Rachael just toyed with it. No sharing. No offering. Just toyed with it. "It's warm now from me carrying it. Probably warm like when Noah jerked off. You remember demanding he do it every morning for your sick habit...right Emily?"

Jay aghast at her friend, sat back letting the tingling in her clitoris fade. She glanced over at the cup on the floor and stared expeditiously. Rachael popped the top of the container and peeled the top off the shot glass exposing the essence of his seed. Jay watched in fear and anticipation as her mouth watered. She was not expecting this kind of treat from her goodie-bag. Jay's heart pounded and her clitoris began to throb for it. Dominion Noah, putting it in the

fridge for his Angel, made it her responsibility, in the eyes of her God.

Rachael sat there naked, letting everyone who passed by see her bare chest. With her legs crossed, she really was non-binary in every way. Jay took in every move she made, and anxious when Rachael smelled it near her nose and expressed her repulsiveness for it.

"I can never swallow this shit. The taste is horrible, Emily. Medicinal cum aftertaste...like...like tasting medicine one should not have tasted when trying to swallow it. Yet, you get nearly a full shot of it today, Emily. Why do you let him make you drink this shit over that stupid book...every day? He uses this seed and his Bible to make you his slave. To make you his victim, Emily...again. To make you his rape victim...again."

Rachael's phone alerted and she slowly read the text and responded to one of her many lovers, while still holding the shot glass. Finally, she spoke up, "You have to offer better than that, Emily. I also want you to confess that he raped you and you are living as Julian and even though you really are Emily. And Emily, you know there is plenty more seed out there in the sea...a limitless supply of it. I'm sure you remember slutting for it." Her warm, disingenuous smile followed as she looked at a nude picture of another Trans Lover on her phone.

Jay just looked at her in contempt but, certainly not of his seed and contemplation held the silence between them. "Be a shame if I spilled it, Emily." Jay glanced up at her and nodded a defeating confession. Rachael got up and poured half his cum on her right nipple and rubbed it around her small areola and drenched her other nipple with it. She powerwalked

over to Jay smiling her achievement, and let her lick it off.

Jay sucked them clean with enthusiasm and satisfaction. Rachael rolled her eyes back and held on to the bed rail and forced her nipples into Jay's mouth. One of the nurses at the station tapped the other one to watch. Everyone was getting something they enjoyed. Jay was thinking boundaries had been crossed, and somewhat lit a small fire on the bridge that connected their friendship.

When Jay finished lapping up the semen, Rachael tried to drain more and she rolled her long erect nipples around the inside of the glass. Jay sucked them hard and Rachael put the shot glass on the tray table and rubbed her wet clitoris with her four fingers. She fingered herself deep and let Jay finish licking her tits. *It was time for Jay do her diligent duty as a Witness,* Rachael thought. She graciously licked Rachael's fingers clean every time Rachael offered it. When she finished, Jay licked the shot glass and fingered all the wetness out. It was her vitamins. Several nurses had gathered to watch from the station to share in the tingles as Rachael got back in command of her Bitch.

"You should rub some on your clit to feel the burn, Emily." Jay scooped out the last bit of seed and painfully inserted it deep into her labia with great satisfaction. Rachael smiled like a lying FBI Agent at a Senate hearing. She would be more than happy to walk out of there pregnant, again.

"Now Emily, the rape kit?" Jay immediately shook her head. "You promised Emily, if I gave it to you that you would comply. BITCH! Do not try and back-pedal your way out of your promises after asking me to keep my promises about your whoring past. YOU let men rape you, repeatedly in college. You keep

promises, and I will keep promises. You are mentally ill, Julian. You have been abused so much by men, you don't know that it is abuse."

Jay stared at her with a poker face, and slowly lifting her chin up, she rolled her head around for the big fight. After suggesting she insert Noah's DNA into her vagina, and then demanding a Rape kit, was strategic bullshit to her. She was sick of the lies and the interrogations.

A short, thick cowgirl carrying big round hips with a Texas ass on them, short thick legs, and big bosom, came shaking forty-eight year old long black and gray hair touching the floor behind her Texas Star cowgirl boots, walked into the room with two happy children. The poker match changed when Momma entered the game.

Springing to life, Jay quickly drank her diet soda and swished the seed out her mouth. The satisfaction in her smile and one bloody eye reminded her again of the joys that motherhood had gifted her with. The hugs and tears were endless with the ebullience of the children. Momma stared at Rachael standing there in the nude with her 9mm pistol strapped between her skinny thighs, and the word SLUT tattooed above her vagina, Momma offered her a warm Texas greeting.

"'That cattle brandin' seems fittin'. Put yo' damn balbriggans on 'round my kinfolk. Kin don't be needin' to see yo' piddlee'o love purse with piddlee'o feedin' bags. Men milk cows, not prairie posts, Gunsel."
When Andrea turned to get her jeans and t-shirt off the chair, Mom made another suggestion, "And grow some ass while yer' at it, men don't like makin' love to chaw-bone. Hit the fixin's more than once." And mom flipped a can of Copenhagen to her lovely daughter in the bed, healing and asked for her own spit can.

Rachael struggled to get her jeans up as fast as she could, forgetting to remove her gun, when Momma sat back in a chair and took out a pinch of her finest powder snuff.

"Ain't no longhorn gonna tag you for Momma duty, Andrea. You be half-a bubble off plump. Shotgun her to the chow line like yer' Daddy, Julian. 'Him went slim to plump happy. Bless my Angelic Cowboy." Rachael gave her a dirty look but, dared not stand up to her on her turf.

Momma prepped a line of sniffing powder across the back of her hand and took a fast snort. "So my Buckle Bunny got lawn-darted? Lookin' good, my Deary. Right back on the horse. That blue rag be bringin' out the color in that snake eye I gave you." Rachael and Andrea tucked tail and walked out carrying her shoes and her shirt and yelling at anyone who would listen.

"BATTERED WOMEN SYNDROME, JULIAN! BOTH OF YOU HILLBILLIES!"

Chapter 4

-Anger. Rape. Jealousy. Sanctuary.

Seeking a game elsewhere, Rachael pasted on a new poker face and got off the elevator three floors down. *This would be fun*, she thought, as revenge filled her heart, and destiny took on blinders. Decisions had been made to gamble it all for real love.

Rachael stopped to ask the nurses about the 'Illegal Un-document Person' she had checked in that morning. Thankfully, Columbus was a Sanctuary City that allowed assistance to needy Illegals. When she walked in the room, her prisoner was messing with the cuff on his right wrist that bound him to the bed.

"I hope your stay is comfortable, Noah." He quickly looked up at her.

"Where is Julian, Rachael?"

"Well Noah, she is still unconscious. Life-flighted to the Cleveland Clinic-Trauma Unit. You did a hell of a number beating and raping her. Didn't know you had the violent sexual side for rape...but I guess all men do. Right Simon?"

"Are you kidding me? Life-flighted? Come on, Rachael? We were making love. She asked for things to be rough. Nothing new with her. I don't remember it all. I would not hurt my wife. I love Julian. She is an Angel of God...remember? A Little fun Stranger-Danger. She is the mother of my children...my soulmate. Rach. You have to believe I would never hurt her...not on purpose. Where are my clothes? Get these cuffs off me?" Rachael just stood back reviewing her phones text messages.

"Yes, it is a good story. If she dies, you understand...I know you lack a quality education being a man...if she dies, you will be charged with murder. I mean but...what is that compared to Rape, Sodomy, Felonious Assault, Domestic Violence, and a Wife beating Rapist. I can just keep adding to the list, RAPIST!"

Noah was silent. Taken aback really. Observing her, the situation, their history, and his plight, before speaking up to her. "Get over yourself, Girl. The jig is up. Get these cuffs off me so I can go home and see Julian and the kids. I know she needs me. My kids need me. You too, nearer my heart. Nice one. Ha ha. Let me out of here. I think the funny is over, I have been here all day." He lifted his wrist up to her and stared, waiting.

"Do not worry about the bill, my Illegal Friend. ICE will not find you here, Simon." She loves to poke.

"DO NOT CALL ME SIMON, RACHAEL BRIGGS! Do not run your mouth to me. This is not funny at all. Un-cuff me now!" Noah said with series inflection.

Rachael looked up at him from the phone. "Want to see the damage you have done to my wife, Simon?" Rachael walked toward the bed carefully showing him the photo of Julian's swollen and discolored vagina. Noah looked the best he could but, Rachael knew not to get to close. She let him have a good look, zoomed in to it, and watched him look away ashamed.

"Hold on, let me send this text to Julian from your phone."

Text to Jay: Hiding on run. I'm a drug addict. I'm a rapist. Please Rodeo with Andrea many times a day. I hate your Religion. Angels are not real.

Rachael gave him a big smile and said, well, "Let me tell you about the woman you thought you

56

married. I'm sure this may come as a shock to you so you better stay lying down." Rachael put his phone just out of reach of his bare feet and any chance of him grabbing it. Before sitting down in her chair, she stripped off her clothes completely and freshened up her pussy at him, and tasted it staring him down. He looked at her pussy and nipples, and then her eyes in complete shock.

"Thinking about raping me, Noah?"

"No Rach. What they fuck is wrong with you? IDENTIFY NOW!"

Rachael adjusted herself a little more and slid forward and spread her legs to show him her wet, shaved pussy. She watched him stare at Indigo, and she stared at him. He glanced at her nipples and she slowly fingered her clitoris for him. *Her sluttiness could make a faithful man sweat,* he thought.

"I hope you do." She whispered to him.

Slowly, she started circling her clit and rolling her head back as she masturbated for him. Noah just watched not sure this was really happening or not. With a quick glance he looked around to see if anyone watched him, watching her. As her two fingers entered her opening, he could hear her wetness. Feeling the need, she worked them in and out for him.

"IN and OUT!" She smiled at him and to the pleasure taking her.

"Officer Rachael Briggs what the fuck is wrong with you? I will not fuck you. I am faithful to my wife and children. You sick bitch. I will never leave Julian for you. That man-body makes me nearer pukin'," and he spit at her landing on her flat chest.

Gently, Rachael rubbed his spit into her pussy, and then to her left nipple and finally, she sucked it off her fingers. "I love fucking Julian, Jonny boy. Maybe I should have you taste my seed since your Bible says

she has to taste your seed. Your wife taste my seed every day, Jonny boy." Rachael lifted one eye brow quickly and dropped it.

Text from Jay to Noah's Phone: I love you baby.

♥ *By God I love you so much. DoctorLands West. Please. I love you. I want to have more children with you. The rape worked. I am losing my fears Baby. We can fix this. Please Noey. DoctorLands West ICU 626.*

♥♥♥

"Jonny boy Noah, your woman set you up and I helped her." She waited for him to respond but, he just stared at her. So she went on to tell more of the story. "You see, SANICS needs more arrests, and since you raped Julian, that makes me look good. And since you raped other women in unsolved raped cases that Julian has been covering up for you, I guess I can make the entire calliope crash to the ground."

Her cynical smile at him spoke volumes, as she continued to rub her clit with her fingers.

Pleading like an angry man, "I did not rape anyone, Rachael. You are so fucked in the head. What is your game here? Save SANICS? Am I your Patsy here? What the FUCK?" He looked at her with stupid expression. "I'm telling you, if this is some bullshit joke, waving your nasty used up cunt in my face is taking it too far you FUCK FREAK BITCH! I have never liked you. I don't know how or why Julian puts up with your slut bullshit?"

Rachael crossed her legs and leaned forward elegantly sucking the pussy juice off her fingers before she spoke. "Because I'm married to your wife Jonny boy, and she is a true ratchet. Rubberdick...Rubberdick is how I always said it. And...what you got under that blanket, Noah?" Looking at his crotch area, "Julian

says it's very small. Can't get her satisfied like me? Maybe she needs some more big black cock." And she followed with faked shock expression on her face. "Yes, I said some more." She leaned back and rubbed her clit some more, and to give him a better view, and put her knees up to her chest and rested her feet on the seat. "I want you to fuck me, Noah. Give me some of the Christian seed, Boy. Seed me like you do Julian. Like when you raped her. I like in the ass. Have since I was seven. Daddy fucked me short of every night with his big dick." Noah's expression changed to a serious concern. But, he watched her spread the wetness all over her fresh tasting vagina.

Rachael leaned back and bucked from her orgasm, as he heard the sound of her soaking set fingers force their way in and out of her glory hole. After she held her breath to enjoy Daddy's memory, she soaked her hand real well and flicked it across his face.

"I don't know what has happened to you. I don't know but, you have done wacked on this operation. Julian is going to hear about this shit." Rachael was near finished sucking her fingers clean when she played with her nipples for him.

"I'm charging you with rape Noah James Taylor. And not just your wife. You raped me as well, Stupid. You raped other women...since I have access to your DNA...after I get your cum inside my sweet pussy, Simon." She gave him an evil smile when she stopped speaking.

"I saw your lab results from your blood test today. I waited around all day for them to find the PCP, sildenafil, breath mints. You hopped yourself up on drugs and sailed away into raping MY WIFE!" She licked her thick wetness off her fingers again and swallowed every drop. "That dick hard yet, Simon. I

59

think I need a squirt. Now I may not swallow it like you force Julian to, with the stupid religion you put down her throat in your cum but, I like getting squirted right here in my pretty, slutty pussy." In an appreciative high pitched voice, she added. "Julian licks it for me all the time." Rachael reached down and inserted all four fingers and flung her wetness at him again. This time, he pulled the blanket up and covered his face. She liked that.

"I have video of the rape, thanks to Julian picking the spot for her final real male rape. I always wanted to know if you were any good in bed. I can admit it. Julian and I always share, and after how many times you fucked my wife and put that white sticky privilege inside her, I would assume you would have ten kids by now. Guess them there balls are a little small, huh?" She started flicking her long, luscious nipples and quivering from the intensity. All the rapist you have worked to catch. You turned out to be one yourself, Simon."

"Do not call me Simon. IDENTIFY!" he screamed.

"Pretty good cover if you ask me. Julian told me about your secret IDentifY as a serial rapist and killer. She told me a many of things, Simon. We know about your gay sex and your gay brother. I know about your trial and fail in the porn industry as a man who liked to be fucked in the ass as a Trans-phobic Cowboy." Rachael put her feet to the floor, and leaned down on her knees too speak. "I'm going to get some of that seed in me tonight, Simon." And she cattily pointed at his package popping her blonde eyebrows up and down.

"It will be your privilege to let you rape me, Simon. I'm answering your Craigslist add that you posted from your work phone. It's nice to have a paper trail to enjoy your rape game. OH! Remember

the counseling sessions at the Girl's School and you played the rapist, Simon. I saw that boner in your jeans each time you chased those girls down."

"You are stupid Rachael. Plum fuckin' stupid. I don't get turned on by little girls. As you can see, I married a thick Woman...and not some guy like you." He kept the blanket up to his chin praying her vagina didn't send him any signs to raise the flag.

"Let me take some photos of my pussy for you." She pulled her phone out of her boots on the floor and starting taking pictures of her wet vagina. She even offered her a few slaps to swell it up. Gently pulling her lips apart, she snapped a close up of her wet vaginal opening and stiff clitoris. "My pussy is pretty sweet. Her name is Indigo. Now let me send all the photos to your phone, Simon. You can print them off and hide them in your Bible."

"I don't have a Bible...stupid." He kept on alert as he argued. "Julian owns all of our Bibles, not me. I'm not the religious one in our family, Rachael. Damn? You haven't learned that after all these years?"

"But you do Thumper. I saw it at your house today when I was gathering evidence. I saw it. Rubbed my wetness in the pages of it. My wife sent me there to gather everything we planted to convict you. You are lucky I didn't shit on your Bible-brainwashing crap. The bullshit you use to program Julian into a submissive slave that serves a man. Shoving your fucking seed down her throat. Up her ass. Cumming in her mouth." She jerked forward, falling to her own anger. "I HATE MEN LIKE YOU! YOU ARE A FUCKING RAPIST TO MY WIFE!"

Noah leaned his head back when she shouted. "Why the fuck do you keep saying your wife, Rach? Like Julian would marry your Dyke-ugly-ass." Rachael stomped to her feet in anger.

"Don't you ever call me that you toxic piece of white male shit. I married Emily first year out of college. YES! Your wife is still married to me! Your wife is a lesbian—." And she rolled the rest off her tongue with pride. "—pussy licking, cunt sniffing, woman tasting, fat-ass lesbian. We have been sleeping together since we first met. You keep feeding Holy cum in her mind to control her. You control her by keeping her fat, by pumping that bullshit religion into her head, and pumping that idea that if she doesn't get your seed, Simon will get her." She leaned in again with her emotions barking. "YOU FUCK! YOU ARE SIMON AND YOU RAPED HER!   AND GOING TO JAIL FOREVER!"

Noah leant back with his eyes wide open shaking his head in complete disbelief. He wasn't really sure this was really happening. He reached down and adjusted his sack for protection with his un-cuffed left arm. Rachael watched him do it. She knew once he got hard, she would ride him good.

Smiling flirtatiously, she picked up the phone and sent Jay another message.

Text to Jay from Noah's phone: Rachael will show you how to pussy therapy. I like idea of her fisting you for me and you must Witness for her. Goodbye, Noah.

"Well, if Julian is fat, you're somehow pretty. I guess you hate short and thick country women now, who are not short, boney, and flat chested like you. Julian stomach is flatter than yours, Fatso. What fucking drugs are you on Andrea? What happened to you? IDENTIFY!"

"JENNA! She screamed at him and the room fell silent and held in place by the tension and the rage

covering Jenna's face. He searched his mind and could not recall a Jenna in the DIDC. So, he played along, like a man.

Sarcasm dripped from every word he muttered, "Oh Jenna. That's right. Jenna. Yeah. Nice to finally meet you, Jenna. Hey tell me, WHO THE FUCK IS JENNA? Jenna." He smirked when he said it. He was either getting horny to her pokey nipples, since Julian would never share hers, or the pheromones were activating his neurotic sex desires...again.

Jenna sat back down and crossed her legs, and her mannerisms seem to change with it. She was now blocking his view of her lady parts in question. I'm the woman who married, Emily. Your wife, Emily." She winked at him seductively and with a curling smile. "Didn't know that one did ya farm-boy? Julian is only an Alibi DIDC...stupid. Her real personality is Emily."

Noah just laid there, not really sure of how to proceed with the conversation, so he sat up and put his feet to the floor and Jenna admired his chest, as he covered up his manhood. "Confused yet, Noey?"

"Actually, I know Emily. I used to fuck her back on Park St. Guess she was blonde and I was eighty-eighty years old then. That girl was bad in bed." Rachael maintained her seductive pose with her legs crossed and leaning down on her knee with her right elbow.

"You are making me soooooo hot, Jenna. Un-cuff me and I will rape you too...if you still like that rough dirty stuff from the Park Street case."

"Genesis 19:36. Daddy is allowed to fuck his daughter so long as Mommy is gone." And she winked at him before calling him "Daddy." Noah didn't know how to respond and chuckled a little. "I know you are already touching Ally. Julian told me she was starting to see the signs, Noah. She hates your fucking guts

63

and this is how we get rid of you." He offered her a grave look.

"Fuck you! Don't accuse me of that crap. I don't take that shit lightly Bitch and I don't know any Bible quotes. That be the wife's department...and I'm not sure which wife you are talking about...mine or you're imagiNARY WIFE YOU FUCKED UP, YOU CUNT!" He leaned in toward them to make sure his inflection was felt by all her Alibis. "Don't ever accuse me of touching my daughter again. I will snap your twig, BITCH!"

Mimicking Julian's voice with a sneering for effect, "Stitches in her vagina, Noey. Stitches in her ass, Noey. Stitches between her ass and pussy, Noey. Stitches in her face, Noey. Crushed uterus, Noey. Torn cervix, Noey. Ugly fucking tits, Noey. Drink my semen, Noey. God will be mad if you don't fuck me and be your slave wife, Noey. Let me lick your balls, Noey. Rape me, Noey. Beat me, Noey? Did you bring friends, Noey? Emily has to be Julian to tolerate you. You have never had the privilege of Emily and you never will. Emily, the woman you know as Julian, was my first true love, Noah. Texas, Noah. Tasted me, Noah." She switched back to Julian's sneering for one last bite. "Simon will get you Julian if you don't let me abuse you." Jenna sat back in her seat like a true tomboy, instead of the Tomgirl, Rachael.

"STITCHES FOR BITCHES, IF YOU WANT SOME!" Noah screamed and waited. He meant it. "Bitch, if you want equality, come and get it. WHO THE FUCK IS EMILY?" He added just to push those buttons, and hoping to get his hands on her. "Burn that feminist bra and step into reality, CUNT!"

Noah looked at her without another word. He was pinned down with very little ammunition for this fight. He could not find any to use or use to sort this one out. He just went with it and in his manly

expression, put his hands together in front of him, and spread them out and up a little while dragging out the one word he could find, "Yeah. I'm a serial rapist. That is how I do it. Remember? I'm Simon."

The stand-off of stares began. His brown eyes, her green eyes. Her power smirk. His widening of his eyes. His rattling off the cuff holding his right hand to the bedrail. Her shifting in the chair. She moved her tongue over her teeth and she started again by using the phone screen for a reflection.

"IDentifY, Rachael," she said to the reflection, and uncrossed her legs for him. "You are going to get forty years, Jonny boy. Forty years for this rape, the rape you will get convicted on from that seed you are going to squirt in my pussy tonight. Indigo is thirsty. It isn't big black dick but, it will do." Back to the reflection, "IDentifY Andrea." And she looked at him and spoke with a kind, soft voice. "Noah, I have always admired your love of the Bible, so could I study with you sometimes and maybe you rape me, too." She put the screen back to her face again, "IDentifY Emily, can you get me some Stranger-Danger sex tonight, Noah? I will wear a bag on my head and bring them in and let them rape me. Let everyone watch me get fucked. IDentifY Noah..." And she made a deep hillbilly voice for him, "I need to get some steer lube to get in that fat 'gully' Texas pussy, Wilbur."

He chuckled at her imitation before speaking. "Doesn't work without a mirror, Rach...I know it. You know it. Dumb ass. Too bad you never understood humor without judging for control." *This shit was too weird for him,* he thought. So again, he winged it, "No mirror, No IDentifY...Stupid. Doesn't work that way...Stupid. 'Flat chested jealous Bitch. You are jealous that I have Julian and you are trying to be every person on the planet to have her. You dumb

Stickboy. She don't want you. I got the dick. I make the rules. I got the seed. I make the rules. You ain't learnt that one yet, Dude wannabe."

She gritted her teeth at him, almost snarling. *He called that one a victory slap* and smiled when she didn't immediately respond. *Maybe I touched a nerve moving that pawn,* he thought.

"I will be the best little boy you ever raped, Noah. And the best girl. Julian said you were not that great. Of all the men she has been with, that is pretty bad. She knows what good dick feels like. You are not it."

"All the men. Are you kidding me, Rachael? Everyone knows you are the biggest slut this side of New York. My wife has been with like five men and two woman her entire life. I don't remember the Texas chick she grew up having sex with, and then there was your nasty ass. And you fucked that shit up being a big time Slut on campus." He upped his bolstering, "Rape culture my ass. You were getting it in the ass because you have insecurities about Daddy. Fuck your Daddy issues. EVERYONE HAS ISSUES! NOW LET ME OUT OF THESE CUFFS ANd I will give you my seed...in your pussy. Just let me see Julian one time. I will fuck you and cum in you as you ask. I can even just jerk off and cum inside you at the end. But for Pete's sakes, let me go. Please Rach...Jenna?" He started adding some honey to his vinegar words.

"You're not going to just cum in my pussy. I want you to rape me too, Noah. Like you do Emily. I want you to fist me. Fuck my ass. Beat me. And cum deep in my pussy like you do Emily every fucking night for years. MY WOMAN! I want that Angel seed in me, tonight Rapist. So I know how much abuse you give Julian to escape to Emily." Rachael was biting her teeth together when she tilted her head up making her

eyes appear centered downward. "And I will shoot you if you do not cum in me, Noah. I want that Angel seed inside this wet pussy." She slapped her boney Venus mound to get her point across. "Now get your dick in your hand and get it hard for me and I will prove to Emily, you are not a real Angel."

Chapter Five

-Emily of Wine of Jenna's Essence of...

Noah violently dragged her from the car by her hair screaming his rage, ripping away the clothes she had in her hands to cover up. Viciously, he backhanded her across the face and she went down to the ground. She started screaming for help in her tears of fear and refused to defend herself to him. He dragged her around the car and slammed her face first into the driver's door as the drugs took over his system. He immediately jerked her hair back and grabbed her by the throat. When she told him to cuff her wrists to the steering wheel. He did exactly as she said, letting her wet desires prepare her for satisfaction. She feared she may have given him too much sildenafil and breath mints but, poked at him for the rush of fear.

"Rape me Noah. Please Baby. Rape me. Fuck your fat Slut. Make me take it, Baby." He jerked her hair back and instantly she stuck her ass out behind her and spread her legs. Moist was too gentle of a word for her meat curtains. She wanted his seed and his rage. Noah grunted and growled at her and screamed into her ear as he head-butted the side of her head and then the top of the car. She instantly fell screaming and crying and dangling by her wrists, outside the car. Noah grabbed her hair and tied it inside the car to the headrest, and jerked her right leg up into the door window over her hair. She was pinned now with her meat hanging down for the world to see. Her seed dripped down the inside of her left leg.

"Fuck me Noah. Fuck my fat pussy. Fuck me in my fat ass. Cum in me. Own me. FUCK ME! I'M YOUR FAT GIRL! FUCK ME LIKE SIMON! RAPE MEEEEE! His standing erection kept bumping up against her back and she tried to get it inside her but, he kept panting and pacing. Her fat pussy tingled from the fear and his warm penis. "STAIN MY SOUL NOAH JAMES!"

From behind he slapped her pussy upward marking it for himself. She jerked and screamed with it and spread her legs apart more. She needed it. She needed rape. She could feel the burn of moisture in her pussy lips as they dangled and waited for him. He rubbed the head of his dick against her ass hole and lowered it to her wet pussy and slammed it in. He immediately started pounding her from behind and choking her through his rage. The fuse of his loins was lit and he was determined to blow it in her fat Texas pussy.

He rammed his eight inches of thick hardness in every time driving it deep into the heart of Texas, and she cringed at the pain as it jammed up into her uterus and into her cervix with each thrust. She separated her ass and pushed into him. It had to hurt. It had to leak inside her to succeed. She felt her own wetness landing onto her leg as he drove it into her.

He reached down her chest and grabbed both her tits and leaned back to get deeper with his thrust. He was screaming sounds every time his penis hit flesh. She had never seen him so violent and out of control. Her eyes were rolled back into her head and she opened herself up to his rage in every way. The pain was wonderful as he tried to drive his cock through her pelvic bone.

"FUCK MY DICK BITCH! FUCK ME FAT BITCH!" and he reared his hand around and slapped her in the face. Blood gushed from her nose and into the car.

When she saw blood, the fear really hit her, and her pussy dripped even more. He slapped her across the face again and again and again. Then with the other hand. She began screaming Simon's name to stimulate more fears.

He pulled his cock out and kicked the side mirror twice before it ripped off the car. He hit her in the back with it repeatedly until she started screaming in pain. Then he kicked her in the pussy with his boot repeatedly. When she buckled, he put the mirror in her face screaming, LOOK AT YOURSELF, WHORE!"

He reached under her shaking ass and jammed his fingers up her cunt and twisted it until he got all four inside her. Then he jammed it in and out until his arm tired in his rage and pants. Her perineum ripped from her pussy to her ass hole and she jerked and kicked in pain and tears. She needed it to stop now because it was going too far. Her screams grew tremendous as she had orgasm after orgasm on top of his fist. He yanked his hand out of her pussy and rubbed her blood and pussy juice onto her face. She immediately opened her mouth and sucked it. He rammed his dick back in her pussy and pounded her screaming at the top of his lungs. By this time, his screams of pain were louder than hers. Something was wrong, and she couldn't stop him.

Noah pulled out of her and started to jack off really hard and screamed in pain and pleasure as she beat the top of the car with her forehead and mirror. He squatted down and with both fist, started punching her ass cheeks and kidneys and back and finally, her head, like a punching bag. He hit her with all this strength and rammed his head into her screaming. Julian shook and screamed with every punch. She held onto the mirror and put it up to her face. Instantly, she screamed "Julian," to IDentifY. Her pussy was now

70

dripping with thick, silky, natural white lubricant and blood.

He got lower and started punching her pussy with his fist and she screamed in agony as her natural white essence covered his hands and the car door. Her huge labia grew larger and larger with each punch and screaming, she bent her knees and spread her legs farther apart to punish it more. She screamed "RAPE ME SIMON" over and over. The pain from each punch stopped her from breathing momentarily as her nerve endings rushed the signal to her brain to orgasm. He stood up and squeezed her neck with both hands from the sides and her eyes popped open as wide as they could be. She could not resist him. She would not resist him. He could give her what Jordan could not give her in the basement. She looked into the mirror she held and tried to IDentifY again, as the light of the parking lot faded to pitch black. He continued to choke her screaming and gurgling his own blood and spit. She tried to look at him, and did not recognize the look in his eyes at all. Like a religious wife, Julian waited for him to choose her fate. He humped up against her shivering ass like a dog and screaming in his pain. When her eyes shut, her body fell limp.

Dripping blood from the tears in his own uncircumcised foreskin, he grabbed her hair and shoved his dick in her ass raging in screams. She immediately regained consciousness and began screaming and wailing her body to get away from him. Her right leg was tied up in her hair and hanging down the side of the door. Her screams turned to blood curdling nightmare cries and she rushed into her mirror to escape. "IDENTIFY EMILY! OH MY GOD NOAH! OH MY GOD YOU'RE HURTING ME! RAPE! RAPE!" She had to get someone to stop it. Her screams brought out the cries even faster as he ripped

her apart inside with each pounding thrust into her interior wall. His cock leaked from the tight grip she had on him. She lifted off the ground and her ass shook for him. She held the mirror up again and screamed "IDENTIFY SAVANNAH!" to escape. Her view slowly faded farther and farther backwards until she could slowly rise up and watch herself be raped.

He fucked her ass getting all eight inches into her and beat her in her sides and face. She collapsed under her weight and dangled by her hair and her leg over her hair. His cock came all the way out and rammed all the way in with his scream stretching her colon deep against her vagina. Their blood was now their lubricant, and he reached around front and lifted her up by her vagina. His rage and fear blended with her screams of fear and pain. He began to brutally punch the sides of her large breasts and her pussy dripped with milky-pink pleasure.

Shoving her upper body into the window well, he punched her with his left hand and his fingertip went into her eye and she jerked up and hit the top of the inside of the car. He punched her in the back of her skull with his fist and then her neck. Immediately, she held the mirror up with his thrust pounding her into the side of the car and as screamed "IDentifY Lowana," he grabbed her throat with a death grip with both hands as his semen squirted deep inside her bleeding ass.   His scream was like a train's roaring loud engine and Lowana fragmented and collapsed into Arizona and then into Tessa and them into Cheyenne and into Jordan and Dakota and Casey and Savannah, and Lowana and into darkness again where their false memory blankets corrupted and crashed onto Emily. Simon kept pounding each of them getting every last sticky drip of seed into their souls. Her dead weight leaned into him as he ripped her colon more. Before he

could pull out and beat her with his terrible rage, he collapsed backward on the pavement unconscious. His arms were spread outward, and his lungs continued to rise and fall inside his chest. Both of them were still wearing their boots. Julian watched them both from above the scene as his heart pounded his chest, and she hung backwards off the side of the car unconscious, by the handcuffs, and her right leg still up in the air hanging over her hair as it stretched inside the car and tied to the headrest.

Jay jerked forward panting, sucking the rope of hair into of her mouth when she fought to breathe, drenched in fear and sweat. The pain was not near what it was the day before. She tried to shuffle her large ass in the bed-recliner and realized Andrea was fast asleep snuggling up to her chest. Her breasts were rising Andrea's head up and down up and down at a fast pace, as she looked around in fear. She could feel the tingling as her clit swelling and the wetness grew. Gently, she leaned down and kissed Andrea in fear, on the head, and exhaled her nerves. She shook all over as she slowly laid back and cried alone. She began to shimmy so much from her fears and sobs, Andrea woke.

She heard her and immediately crawled up on her straddling her and sitting down just below her belly. She held Emily's face in her hands and stared into her blue eye and watched her cry. Jay shook even more as her sobs grew out of control since Andrea would protect her. Andrea hugged her, squatted naked on top of her and prepped for a long moment. The nurses took another look and could see what was going on.

Jay finally looked up at Andrea and she kissed Emily with the love of a good woman. Their tongues softly touched and the wetness blended together. Jay

got forceful and kissed her like she had not kissed her in a long time. Jay was holding on to her rescuer. Her cries continued and Andrea shared tears with her as she petted her hair to calm her. They tasted the salty emotion filled tears and kept their tongues touching and holding each other as the tears blended in their mouths. Andrea sat forward with her knees straddling Jay's sides as they embraced each other in love. Their moment would last in their hearts. "Emily?" Andrea asked, and Jay nodded sobbing. "We need to get rid of the IDentifY, and Julian. We will be so happy after that, Emily." Emily kept nodding to her with her cries.

The nurses enjoyed the view of the sexy couple embracing and the thin one showing everyone, the best view. As Jay calmed down, Andrea hugged her and slid back down beside her and curled up to her under the blanket. Jay was regaining herself and took a deep breath and let it drag as she regained some composure from her fear and guilt. Andrea slid her hand down to Jay's pussy and instantly felt how wet she was.

Andrea quickly dug through her thick vulva and onto her swollen clitoris. It took the length of her middle finger and some of her hand to get deep enough to reach it. Jay pulled her knees up and opened wide. She gave herself to her. Andrea gently worked her finger over her clit and Jay jerked and laid her head back and closed her eye to the terrible and arousing moment she just relived. Her lover slipped her entire little hand down the center of her labia and it was swallowed into the wet warmth of her large lips. Andrea made a fist and pulled it up between her lips and slid it back down without touching her clitoris as Jay jerked in pain and pleasure.

Whispering in a voice even Andrea could not hear, Jay commanded her. "That feels so good it hurts.

Don't stop. It hurts. I'm so sore. EASY! OH MY GOSH IT FEELS WONDERFUL! Keep fistin' my labia ONLY! Yeah like that." Holding her breath between statements, she had to control her sore vocal cords. "Oh my Gosh! That feels good. It hurts so freakin' much. She is so swollen." Andrea slid her entire head under the blanket and with her other hand she peeled at Jay's nipple band aid until she got it off. Gently, she started sucking her left nipple and licking her entire thick areola as she used her hand below. Jay shook from the intense pleasure that rolled up her spine mixed with the pain and endorphins and pleasure. Her nipples had not been sucked in so many years. Even her scars were extra sensitive with arousal.

The sound of her wetness carried and Jay could hear it slopping. She pushed her legs apart more and invited Andrea to give her more pain. Still sliding her fist up and down between her soaked swollen labia, she gently slid a finger inside on the down stroke and out on the up stroke. Jay jerked in pleasurable pain each time her finger crossed into wet Kitty's mouth. Andrea brought her hand up and smothered her bare breast and Jay ripped the other band aid off exposing herself completely to Andrea for the first time in years.

"You need a vibrator to work the swelling out." Andrea said as Jay slammed the back of her head into the mattress repeatedly. Enjoying feeling needed, she slid her fist up and down again and smothered the other nipple with Jay's seed. Jay quietly shook burying her face into Andrea's neck and shoulder and held her breath as she cried succumbing to her huge and intensely painful, orgasm. Andrea kept on fisting her labia, and rubbing the juice all over the outside and onto Jay's thighs and stomach. She grabbed a hand full of one meaty labia and Jay bobbed her head and moaned in pain and more importantly, intense

pleasure she needed with her pain. Andrea kneaded the swollen curtain between her thumb and four fingers, working them up and down making sure she included the long root of the clitoris that hide down each side of her fat vulva. Jay was jerking her entire body to manage the intensity, and held on to Andrea for safety.

Jay quivered with her head back and held onto her breath bouncing her head into the mattress supporting it. Another orgasm slowly peeled out, soaking Andrea's hand and her mattress covers. Andrea immediately started sucking her cum off her fist and fingers and back to sliding her fist between the wet labia. *Texas was so wonderful* Jay thought. She immediately bucked again, and Andrea thumbed her kitty's joy button and Jay silently screamed her orgasm into the room for mercy. *Sore nerve endings can be wonderful punishment,* she reminded herself. There could not be any echoes. The nurses all watched from their desks, and enjoyed their own wetness. Jay whispered as loud as she could, "Thank you, Texas."

She started kneading the other labia and Jay jerked her head back grinding her teeth, to escape into the mattress. She could not believe how intense it felt being so battered. Andrea slid her thumb across her clit again and Jay grabbed her sore breasts and squeezed. The wetness slid down into the blanket under her soaking her bottom more. Andrea immediately pulled the blanket off and climbed between Jay legs onto her flat chest with pointy nipples. Jay slid down and Andrea buried her face into her dripping wet swollen pussy that was rushing with blood flow to make it even larger.

"She is very warm from the swelling." Andrea told her.

When Jay palmed the back of Andrea's head, the rest of the nurses gathered from behind the desk across the hall, and stretched their necks. Jay jerked up fucking Andrea's face and everyone could hear slurping and her mouth licking at the wetness flowing from her huge mound. Jay bucked back again and jammed Andrea's face into her clit as hard as she could and held her breath and pushed and pushed and pushed her deeper as Andrea slit her entire fist inside Kitty. Jay finally let her breath escape as she panted and cried when Andrea pulled her closed fist out ever so slowly. Her best appreciation only included the word Texas but, Andrea had always heard that. Her entire vagina shook and the enlarged nerve endings responded in kind for her with tears. Jay pulled Andrea up and locked her lips to hers and passionately sucked her own wetness off Andrea's tongue and lips. The kiss would last for tantalizing minutes as Jay fought off the nausea of too many endorphins.

Andrea stood up over her lover's chest dripping from her own pussy and Jay palmed Andrea's small ass cheeks and pulled her pussy to her face grinding it into herself. It had been too long coming for Andrea, and she tossed her head back in wonderful rushes of pleasure. Jay started drinking her as Andrea's juice ran down her chin and onto her bruised, sagging breasts. Andrea started grinding her pussy into Jay's mouth and jerking from the slurps to orgasm. Jay sucked it in, flavoring as much of her essence as she could and slapped her on the ass over and over.

Her face was soaked and Jay sucked her hard clit into her mouth and throbbed it like a little cock. Andrea screamed quickly and her head and shoulders bobbed back and forth as she spilled her orgasm onto Jay mouth and chin and chest. She swallowed as much, sucking every drip from her eager, swollen labia

minora. Andrea was all labia minora and skinny on majora. The opposite of Julian. Andrea quivered again and sprayed the warm wetness into Jay's mouth as their hearts raced with chemistry. The warm, fresh cum tasted as rich as the finish and Jay's clit swelled up fast and harsher. She licked her pussy from the opening to the clit and back until Andy came in her face again inserting her tongue into Andrea's stretched urethra. Only Jay was allowed to give her this secret pleasure that made Andrea feel dominated and humiliated at the same time. To Andrea, it was her only virgin hole, and only Julian had ever been in there. This was a side effect of her long time Daddy issues.

Andrea slid down crying with a rush of emotion and locked a kiss with Jay and tasted her own juice. They sucked on each other's tongues and fought over the mixing rights. They had just made love like they did ten years ago, and its chemistry stirred fears and tears in Andrea, unimaginably. Two of the nurses started clapping from behind the desk and the older ones dashed to act like they were not there. The women embraced each other when Andrea panted into a nestle between Jay's breasts, like a little girl. This was a maternal comfort Andrea had to have.

Holding each other, Jay succumb to the synthetic heroin of her IV and Andrea to the love of her best friend, and the only woman she felt unconditional love from. Something she never got as a little girl after her mother past away. Andrea, snuggled into Jay's chest, and warmed by the bosom of her tainted motherly love, both of them completely naked and showing themselves to anyone who wanted to challenge their love. They're lost link was captured in the moment, providing healing for one of them changing, and the filling void of the other, wanting a different change.

Jay finally woke up with the urge to pee, and wiggling Andrea to the side as she struggled to get Noah's Ark out of the dip in the bed. Pushing and pulling the hand rail, Andrea reached over and pushed on her back helping her make it out of the dip. Jay had a painful expression as her large labia dragged across the rough blanket. Andrea smiled as Jay slid her boots to the floor bowlegged. It was only one or two steps before her hair snagged into the side rail and pulled Jay back and onto her well-rounded ass and labia on the floor. The pee came and Jay just sat back against the bed frame and didn't give a damn. She covered her face as the urine soaked everything beneath her. *That was not supposed to happen,* she thought, as she felt the synthetic heroin doing its job.

Andrea chuckled and when Jay didn't attempt to get up, she rolled over to the side and unhooked the caught spur in her hair. The spur fell down and hit Jay in the head, and she just sat there completely naked of band aids and clothes and concern. Jay waved her hand up and Andrea who was openly chuckling without a sound and made the hand sign over her ear for her phone. Andrea rolled back around, got her phone off the tray table and handed it to her. And scooted over so she could see over Jay's head.

Text to Noah: God has blessed Texas with my swollen gift. I sit in urine on the floor. You own it. Bath it. Andy gave me Big O. You raping me was best decision of our Accord. Fears changing inside me. The correct chemical changes in my brain. Let my fear of losing your love never go away. Psalm 51:2-4 Bath your Tomboy.

Rachael scowled as she read it, and got up angry that Jay could intentionally betray her. She walked around the bed and stared at Jay sitting on the floor giggling at herself with some tears, and causing slight shocks of pain in her nether and back regions. Rachael went into the bathroom and slammed the door behind her. Her unconditional love moment ravished, in front of her, by the only motherly woman who had ever fulfilled the role with her. That slam was a sound that would echo through the entire floor and change chemistries forever. Looking at the slammed door, Jay whispered to herself, "Bipolar Mommy and Daddy issues. Oedipus Complexity."

Chapter 6

-Combative Orgasms with odd Names

Jay waved her hands in the air trying to get the nurses attentions to help her off the floor. This was not working and she would have to wait on her Bipolar Vixon in the bathroom, so she started texting.

Text to Momma: Love you. TY for getting kids off to school. Kisses hugs for them you. Bless Daddy. Bless you Momma. See you tonight. Please be nicer to Andy. I love her very much. She is one of us with real issues.

Text to Noah: My love shall not fade for you. ♥
We will work this problem. I will quit job if need. I want your name tattooed on my Kitty-all over my body. I want the physical realm to know I have fully committed to my cowboy. Simons Rape made me feel owned by the enemy. It has now been our tool to bring that ownership home to you. I submit to you Noah. You raped my rape fear. Your conjugal rights shall never fade in my heart nor in Kitty. You raped me. You own me. Texas and I are thankful. I had my boots on for Big O. I need more. TY letting me have Andrea. I want another baby Angel for our union under God. I miss Texas. I miss kids. I miss you. Home soon. Be there. For my soul, all pleasure and crown is of your power and I submit to your will husband, as God has prescribed. I submit to you and our rape is but a powerful love making tool that has brought us closer through my fear freedoms. I feel your seed inside me.
Your humble Tomboy Cowgirl ♥♥♥

Nurse Laura came and helped Jay get off the floor when Rachael walked out of the bathroom smiling like the Devil's Angel. Jay disconnected her IV and tossed it on the bed and the nurse pinched it off. Wobbling to the shower with her basketball vagina leading the way, she felt pretty secure in her public nudity form and maybe, another orgasm in the shower would be needed for therapeutic reasons. She stopped at the bathroom door and told Rachael she would need a Witness, and Rachael merely acknowledged she was alive. Jay immediately asked Nurse Laura to help her sit and finish urinating, and then help her up.

After the nurse radioed for a cleanup, she joined Jay to happily help her. Jay grabbed her arm to keep her in the bathroom and told her to lock the door so they could talk.

Jay pointed to herself and then to her bulging vulva on display and made a rubbing in circles motion in front of Laura and she pointed to her Venus mound again.

"You want me to wash your vagina? I can do that for you. I need a courtesy witness." And she started for her radio again and Jay stopped her.

Jay leaned in touching the woman with her dangling breasts and got to her ear with her teeth clenched, "Witness me shower, please." Laura stepped back in what little room she had and politely declined with her eyes wide open. Jay leaned in to the now uncomfortable woman to whisper again, "My religion must have witness." The nurse leaned back farther and took a deep breath. She gently untangled Jay's mess of a hair and worked to untie the spurs in them for her.

"I don't think I will do that. I will be happy to stand outside but, I will not watch you. 'Can't your

wife watch you?" Disappointed, Jay slowly turned the nob on the door to let her out and the nurse exited in a hurry mentioning her plan. "I will have an Orderly change the sheets and get new bedding material."

Rachael was pulling a needle out of the IV tube injector of the new IV she was hanging. She was moving quickly to get a bottle and injector back to her jeans on the chair. When the door opened she pretended to be fluffing the blankets, and smiled at the fleeing nurse.

Jay knocked on the door to get Rachael's attention and waved her over to the bathroom. Her only piece of clothing was the bandana and even that came off. She shook her moderate ptosis as she shook with her legs, and stood there naked, proudly. Rachael stepped over smiling and Jay stepped back to let her in the room. There was no need to close the door, after all, it's not like Jay could scream at all.

Both of them nude, they stepped in the shower and Rachael lovingly pushed her under the water so she could soap her up. Jay turned the shampoo bottles so they labels faced front evenly. Handing Jay, her long, wet rope of her entire hair, Jay put it in her mouth and dangled it in front of her as she placed her hands up on the wall in front of her and let the warm water relax her aches. She gently spread her feet apart comfortably and Rachael washed her with her hand and a liquid soap. Starting at her back Rachael massaged her sore muscles with her fingertips with care and love, as Jay let the moans of small pains escape. Giving her the acupressure she needed for her back muscles, showering together had not been a thing since Med School.

Pushing her SLUT word into Jay's shaking Texas ass, she reached around and rubbed her sore neck with lather and down to her breasts and repeatedly

under them. She could not see it but, Jay really enjoyed the breasts rubbing. Slowly, she reached down to Rachael's left hand and put it back on her dangling breasts. Rachael pulled back and squirted more soap on her hands and re-applied it to Jay's nipples and size D breasts. Jay's pussy began to respond in kind. Rachael focused on stimulating Jay's neglected, sore nipples that had not seen daylight in almost ten years.

Jay could not remember the last time they felt so good being touched without fear of showing them. Even Rachael only got to touch them a few times over the years. Now Jay had to get them touched. Her knees jerked a bit as it made her tingle all over. She kept her hands up on the wall and her mouth occupied with her rope of hair. She quietly submitted to Rachael's dominance consciously and both clitorises tingled and desired one another. She felt the burn coming and spread her feet out wider to drip. She was not wearing her boots. Lathering Jay's beautifully curved rump, and wide round hips, Rachael slid her fingers between her ass cheeks and gently underneath between her labia. She tickled her stitches on her perineum with painful pleasures and Jay immediately felt a desire she had not felt in years...an Emily desire. It was enough that she looked up and closed her eyes hoping to hide from it. She was with the only other person who knew about the desire, besides Rachael and Andrea. And maybe, that is why one or both of them, delivered these consequences. And maybe, for different reasons.

Jay quivered and Rachael smiled to herself from the power gifted and put her long, sagging nipples into Jays side and started up and down the crack of her ass again with her soapy fingers. Jay began to cry to herself as her dark fetish roared at her. Rachael

immediately had her under control. When Jay's knees buckled, Rachael squirted more soap down between her wet cheeks and slid the edge of her hand up and down, just to see Jay buckle at the knees again and her ass wiggle as she moaned and cried. She knew Jay was crying, as she pushed her big ass harder against her hand. This was both their roles when the fetish was played with. Jay pushed her breasts into the wall in front of her and raised her hands up higher on the tile. The Cuckquean would have her way with her...like Simon did...like Noah did...like Strangers did. Only Rachael knew her shameful past, from years of serving her.

Rachael reached under Jay and slid two fingers into her Master's pussy and she jerked from the momentary pain and then pushed into it for more. She used her fingers to clean her pleasure pocket as the firmness of Jay's thick hips quivered tight at her waist. When she slid her finger between the labia and over the clitoris and into the dark recess under her mountain of Venus her body shook it all for her with pleasures of pain. Both felt the ownership, the dominance, the swelling of their engorged senses, they needed to find balance. Rachael slid her stretched out fingers up and down between her labia on her clit and inserted her thumb each time. Jay's big breasts shook with her into orgasm and Rachael owned her and held her up. Both were taunting the secret fetish, and knowing Emily always cried from it. Rachael needed this moment for the new beginning of their relationship to work, the other needed to confirm her Angelic fear.

Sliding two fingers deep into her pussy from behind, she put the tip of her thumb onto Jay's dark anus between her chubby cheeks and stopped to read her. Shaking with fear, Jay slowly lifted her head up to

show her a grimace of tears, her chest panting and bent her knees outward, Rachael slowly moved her thumb around, spreading her backdoor open little by little. Both their pussies caught on fire when the sobs came to Jay. Rachael got behind her and put her forearm across the back of Jay's neck and jammed her face into the wall. Jay turned her face so her right cheek would brace the impact and Rachael could hear her sobs through the steam. Rachael poked her in her backside with her hard nipples as Jay raised her hands up the wall into complete submission, and the Cuckquean whispered into her ear. "Emily?"

Rachael slid both fingers deep into Jay's vagina and curled them back inside her to hold Fat Kitty hostage, and slowly began inserting her thumb in Jay's ass, waiting. "Pillow case," Rachael whispered. Jay arched her back as much as possible, slowly covering her eyes into submission with her left hand and nodded slowly over and over confessing her desire, and Identity. "Do you miss being raped, Emily?" Holding her hand over her face, hiding her sobs, Emily barely nodded for her. The hot shower poured down her backside and softly, she begged Rachael in her fear, "Please don't rape me, Rach."

Rachael pulled her fingers out of Emily's pussy and all at once slide them in deep with her thumb going into her shower soaked, trembling rear. When she pulled out she put three fingers into her pussy to add to the pain. Then four fingers to make sure it hurt too much.

Emily jerked and moaned in pain and quivered to the burn she felt trying to secrete her pussy juice faster, and her lowered jaw dangled as she confessed her painful, desire, in a silent scream. Trying to get away, she slid into the corner to get away from the stimulating rape trauma syndrome. Forcing herself into

Jay's backside and holding her in the corner like a prisoner, Rachael slowly worked her fingers and thumb in and out and in and out, and she spoke loudly to her victim, "I missed my Cuckquean, Emily. I am raping you, Bitch!" Emily instantly bucked back into Rachael's thrusting thumb as she squirted her love juice, and orgasm, confirming her fears. Rachael rushed her with her body slamming into her and yelling. "Come back to me, Emily! I OWN EMILY! Chlick. Chlick."

Crying loudly and shaking at the knees, Rachael slid her rapist tools out of Emily and let the hot shower rinse them clean. Emily stayed where she was, leaning her face into back corner, shaking in stimulated fears. Urine dripped down her leg as her brain drowned in reward and her arms slid down the wall dangling. Rachael slammed her bare chest up to Emily's back and held her Ark up with both her hands to keep Emily stable to the wall and whispered to her. "You want to be raped, Emily. I can be your only rapist, Emily, and satisfy your desires with my love. Leave him, Emily. Take my unconditional love." One of them gathered her strength, and the other, her desires, but together, they held the wetness and the sound of the rushing shower.

Emily finally turned around stumbling, after getting over the rush of chemicals. She looked up at Rachael waiting for a nod, and kissed her softly under the water and crushed her breasts against her, as she turned her around and put her into the same corner. Smiling, Rachael hugged the corner smiling with anticipation of Emily's acceptance of her Cuckquean position from their old relationship, and stuck her flat, little butt out behind her for attention. Lathering up her thick, short fingers, Emily started sliding her hand up and down the crack of Rachael's ass and her pussy burned as wetness released in a slow instant. Her

heart raced as the Emily personality began to take control over Julian...again.

Pushing her breasts against Rachael's back she held her there sliding her middle finger down her anus and under into her soaked labia on the other side, as the juices flowed from inside. Rachael arched her back to receive more of her and Emily worked it up until all four fingers were in and out, in and out of her thin, dangling inner labia. Rachael reached over and fingered her clit as Emily forced three fingers up into Indigo and curled them back, taking her hostage. Rachael quickly held her breath as Emily forced her middle finger two inches deep into her urethra. Julian was the only one to ever penetrate her there. It was important to Rachael that Emily take her virginity long ago, and that was all she had to offer. It was a wonderfully disturbing pleasure she came to need. It always gave her the tears she needed from the emotional rush of the feeling of virgin purity. Something her abusive father took long ago. Emily began moving her finger in and out to defeat her from resisting. Gently her thumb slide partway into her waiting rear and Rachael's face curled as she began to cry from the emotional rush. Emily leaned up to her shoulder and whispered, "Kendall?"

Rachael nodded over and over without looking at her and chlicked twice to trigger Emily. As Emily brought her left hand around to the front of Kendall sliding her fingers across her dangling nipples and grabbing her by the throat while still holding her pussy hostage. Kendall creamed with anticipation as she spread her ass as wide as she could. Emily slammed her thumb deep in her ass with all four fingers going into her skinny pussy. Emily's hand slid to Kendall's throat, like her Daddy's hand always did.

Kendall gasped as Emily choked her and fucked her from behind and underneath with damning thrusts holding her up on her toes. Kendall quivered as those thick fingers drove inside her and Kendall's scream fought to come out. All their Alibis watched, and listened to her suffocation by force and pleasure.

Emily slid all four fingers up Kendall's abused cunt and slid her thumb down and rested her fist inside her vagina lifting her up on her toes in wonderful pain. Kendall's vaginal opening sealed around Emily's wrist as Kendall grabbed on to Emily's love and abuse. Kendall's thin midsection shook from the spasms and even her nipples grew until they hurt. Emily tightened her fist inside her and slowly pulled it partway out and slowly back in. Kendall tightened neck and face turned red as Emily tightened her grip on her throat to make her point. Her eyes were stuck back in her head as her mouth hung unable to let every scream out.

"Daddy's little Kendall!" Emily said as loud as her whisper could get, and Kendall quickly nodded with her face curled in pain and tears. Emily sped up the fist-fuck staring up to Kendall's face with rage, and Kendall started rocking her head and chest forward and back as her face past red and into a shade of blue. Emily was getting her point across regarding relationship statuses through Andrea's, secret Kendall fetish.

Pissing herself without knowing it, Kendall held on as Emily fisted her all the way out and jamming it all the way in without tolerating resistance. She bore a serious Cowgirl look of determination as she stared up to Rachael's bluish, painful scowl. As her vagina tightened and cramped, Emily knew when it was the right moment. She had fought with Kendall many of times in the past. Quickly, Emily jerked her fist around inside her deep pussy and watched Kendall's chest rise

and her head reach maximum dangle backward, just before her shade of blue turned purple, Emily jerked her fist out with force and slid her fingers and hand up Kendall's ass with mean attitude. Kendall yowled for her Daddy, like a bitch in heat from the orgasm as her own fingers tried dancing on her clit and she quivered crashing into the corner in front of her to escape the immense pleasure raging through her orgasmic muscles and stimulated mind. Drool dangled out of the side of Kendall's mouth onto her shoulder as Emily pulled her hand out and shoved back in as fast as she could and didn't stop until Kendall slid down hugging the corner in defeat, and crashed to the floor. Poised over her in a fighting stance, Emily let the shower rinse her thick fist as it slowly opened.

She felt herself near orgasm again, and Julian beat her sore Venus mound with the bottom of her fist until her orgasm peeled away. Both of them were panting but, only one was still standing. The Master would not lose to her Cuckquean.

Julian's long hair leaning over her face masking her innocence and rage, but holding her decision firm. She stood over Kendall with her barely sagging breasts rising and falling, nipples hard and pointing forward and down, at her victim with Emily, their secrets, and her Alibis. Together, they stared her down like a fighter looking down on her fallen opponent. Her round shoulders and chubby arms puffed out her sides with her soaked, curvy hips. As her nude curves completed the scene, her fists held stiff at the ends ready to give her more, and the water showered her victory, as she glared at the challenger to her life decisions. The sexual tension had finally been broken. Kendall weeping from the pleasurable defeat, cuddled into the corner sobbing the Daddy's shouldn't touch little girls. Rachael was realizing she was losing the battle

through Kendall and Andrea, for her long-term gain and control of Julian, through Emily.

Every Alibi knew better than to stand up to the real Julian. Her blue eyes stared through her wet, long, dark hair while she panted, with her lower jaw forward and at the ready, as the rain poured over her voluptuous body and battle-scarred breasts. This cowgirl would not submit anymore...Not for Simon...not for Rachael...not for Jordan...not for Emily or Kendall. Only for God, Texas, and her husband. There was no need for Witness or a witness, and Julian whispered to her fallen lover, "You will not rape Emily, anymore, Rachael."

Chapter Seven

-Doctor Deuteronomy

Walking up the nurse's station early this day, she wanted to remind the staff on hand. Rachael tried to be casual and showed the head nurse her badge as she glided to a halt in her new work boots and jeans.

"I want to talk about John Doe in 345. He is under my protection. Sanctuary city law allows me to keep him here provided, he needs medical care."

The nurse smiled at her with a politically correct expression of fake concern and handed her clipboard to another nurse. Rachael continued on.

"I am also his Doctor, it's in the register. He has anchor babies here. Been here for 20 years. We need to make sure no one gets in to see him, talk to him. And do not get near him. He has a hatred of our corrupted system and knows ICE is on the hunt for him. Let's make sure he is cared for and fed so we can return him to his family. It is the right thing to do." Rachael smiled and walked away never letting the head nurse get a word in. But, she did like seeing Rachael's ass in her saggy jeans and cat-called her with a quick raise of one eye-brow to show her appreciation.

Rachael walked in on Noah fumbling to get his wrist through the cuff and she smiled warmly at him as she removed her clothes to let him see what he could have today. After undressing, she brought the chair back to the same place near the side of the bed at the foot end, with two smartphones in her hand. She freshened up her pussy with a slap to it. He stared at her, wondering if this was the Rachael he could

reason with. She sniffed her fresh clean pussy and sucked her finger dry.

"So, how long have you been physically abusing Emily...my G, Simon? Huh?" He just stared at her as he shifted her blanket over his groin area. ""I asked you a question, Simon. How many times have you raped Emily, not Julian? Julian, wouldn't know it if you raped Emily. Is that why you keep her pussy mound black and blue? So she won't know when you have raped Emily? Is that how you do it, Noah? You use her big disorder against her and push her to argue with her own hair and play on her loss of memory when she converts to Emily? Hide her Diddy meds to get Emily to appear?" Rachael waited and sniffed her finger again. "Well, no words today, Simon?"

His answer started out professional, but sarcasm was his only defense. "Three times a day over nine years add holidays and anniversaries for each rape? Whoa? That number is a growing." He said very snarkily. "That blonde hair really does go the roots. Doesn't it?" He grinned from his quick Wyoming shot hitting its mark.

"What the hell happened to you, Rachael? You were a valued-."

She cut him off, "I asked you questions, Rapist." This time she was being calm. This had to be Rachael. "She told me about you thumping the Bible in face and then thumping her face with the Bible. Beating her with it constantly. Making her recite every stupid word of it." She exhaled, before she started again. "Pseudo my uneducated friend. Pseudo Orthodox." And she rolled it off with a high pitch tone. "Brainwashing with guilt and patriarchy, Simon. Us modern women are just a beginning and are too high on the IQ scale today for men. Feminism is on the march. Fuck your fake God, Country Boy."

"What do you want Rachael? Why am I still here? How is Julian doing? I wish you would let me call her just once. Hear her voice. Is she conscious yet? Please."

"So let me respect your Pseudo God for a moment, and not even mention the forty years you will spend in prison wandering the desert...hopefully getting raped. Had you men just stopped and asked for directions from a woman. All men should get raped once in their life time. And I digress into your Pseudo God. Deuteronomy 22:25-27. Does Emily cry for help when you rape her?" Rachael picked at her nail on her thumb.

"What?" Noah asked.

She enunciated each word to get her point across. "Does Emily cry for help when you rape her? Its simple questions. Did her, now destroyed voice box, make noises Little Boy? Scream?" Staring him down, she paused for a second. "Are these words too big for you?" Noah was trying to read the angle here. "I know she did, because all the butt-fucking I watched her do through college, in the name of Religion."

"I don't know what you are talking about. I didn't rape anyone...nice try though, Cunt." He answered politely, only with harsh words. "Neither of us like 'Butt-fucking'-as you termed it. Cunt. You probably do."

"Damn you are brick. Be careful with that word when you describe my pussy, your wife licks my 'cunt' almost every day behind your back." Acting agasp for affect, she partook in his ignorant acting, "How for shame of me. I may have forgot to mention that over the past years, as I pretended to be your friend, and we set your ass up to be her sperm donating Baby Daddy and monthly cash flow. Might you know, she

only chases rapists that HAVE raped her." Leaning forward to get her metaphor working, "Yes, we may have been talking the guy into it but, she can say NO after you have sex with her and it is still rape-EVEN if she asks to be raped. It is still rape, Boy." Rachael pulled her knees up to her chest spreading herself to share the beauty of her skinny pussy with pink roast beef in the middle. All her body was a hue of yellow to go with her blonde hair, and just a shade of pink between her legs. Her labia minora was the only thing large about her.

"Deuteronomy Noah. You will be put to death, by your own Bible thumping book, for rape. My good Boy. You will never get out of this. We already got the rape kit from Emily, her statements, and crime scene photos, and a video...yes a video. And she doesn't even know, I already got the rape kit done." She smirked again, and licked her fingers to rub her clit for him. "This hustle is turning me on."

"Guess I don't have anything to worry about it since I ain't met Emily yet...Stupid Cunt." He nearly growled as he rolled his frustration away from her.

"By the way, thank you for the semen you put in her ass. There was so much of it, we plan to solve multiple rape cases with it. I give credit, you may have a little dick but, you do put out much seed. Thank you for that. Seed in my pussy will feel good, Angel Boy, and when your squirting it in me, I will just simply change my mind about having sex with you. Instant rape charge." She smiled really big as her clitoris swelled with power and twirls.

"Sadly, your time in our little plan has ended, and you will be replaced for her needs....by me...finally." And she slapped her pussy for him and gently rubbed it again. "Indigo had just finished working out with Emily's tongue, yesterday." Racheal

said it seductively as a bad girl. "I like Indigo to hurt when I ride Angel's in Cowboy uniforms from queer-folk Florida." Her ever so familiar grin never failed to appear with her pokes.

"Rachael..." and he sat up showing his strong bare chest. "I was raised an un-practicing Christian. We never even owned a Bible. I never read a bible. Religion came with Julian. I accepted that on our first date, when she asked me to pray with her. I don't believe all this crap about her slutting around college, and with you. She knows the rules about Witness, and that is all you are allowed to do for her. Likely, that was you tramping your way through college. Julian brought her Bible and sat it on the table next to her plate on our first date. I got the message. She still does it today at dinner. You should know all this by now, since you have known her longer. She was raised in a very religious family and community and I will honor my wife's beliefs. She has known for years how you despise religion and worship Government. We are much smarter than that. I'm sorry. You are not living reality here."

Rachael leaned her head back to orgasm and told him to jerk off for her. She looked at him quickly as her orgasm approached and screamed, "Jerk it Boy!" and her sore nerve endings electrified and she quivered in her chair as she rubbed herself. Every finger disappeared into her essence, and she rubbed it on her face letting the chemicals in her mind reward her. "Noah watched, as just about any man would but, his expression showed a real lack of desire for her.

♫ Text message alert

"Some gap you got there. Been fucking a horse, Rach?" he said trying to poke her.

Leaning forward through her brain fog, "Actually, Emily is the one that likes sex with horses. 'Started

96

when she was a teenager, Boy. She liked to jerk horses off onto her tits and lick up the cum. Just like she did for so many strangers as their 'Witness,' in college."

Noah burst out laughing, and jerked around the bed bringing it to a chuckle. "My God, Rachael, you are one twisted projecting chick. Julian already told me your comments about how large some animals' junks are. You have the fetish for big genital organs...whatever the hell that is called. And you were the big Slut in college, not her. I met you right after college, and you're the same old Ho today. You are just getting used. Gettin' used by internet prowlers and loving it. You are just fearful the alone time is coming."

Oddly, she smiled before speaking. This must be a good one. "Doesn't our wife have big genitals, Boy? Unlike you. Cow-size pussy lips?" She said it reminding him that perhaps she was not the only one with such a fetish.

"I think you are so fucked Rach...so fucked in the head...after all this time with Julian as your best friend-TOLERATING YOU! YOU SHould know, she turned me onto religion with her love and that big Texas ass and that long hair she worships. She demanded our children be conceived in Texas, born in Texas, demanded we Accord in Texas, and I want the GOD-FEARING LIFE OF MY COWGIRL TEXAN!" He quickly took a breath, "If anyone is programming anyone, its Julian programming me...and I want it."

"Megalophobic, Boy. Read a book sometime instead of porn. Texas, huh? You don't know half her true story of Texas. The days of Luckenbach and Julian's famous cow pussy. She discovered her semen addiction in Texas...horses have a lot of semen COWBOY! And you twisted her addiction to control her

97

and use Simon's rape fear and your Bible, and we know his semen DNA got into her brain because of Emma. You got control of her rape fear and enjoy its power over her." Her eyes were glaring viciously as her jealousy stirred over that, daily.

Noah looked around the room as his brain searched his memory banks for that name. It was not registered. "Who the hell is Emma?" Quickly, he stopped his question to answer it himself, "Don't tell me, another IDentifY. You are Emma today. Right?"

Rachael chuckled as she put her feet back to the floor. "I am still so fucking horny, Noah. I need some dick today, Cowboy, with your eight pack abs. I see you are still jogging and working out. Nice." She ran her fingers through her hair, as she looked down in wonder. "I wonder where I can get some dick today from a disposable male. Any ideas little Boy?" She reached down and nonchalantly pulled at his blanket. It was an obvious gesture.

Then she started working on him mocking Julian's accent, "I mean real dick, Noey, not that itty 'thang.' I be needin' to stop and see an old friend here in the hospital for some real dick. If it ain't black, it isn't real dick. You know what I be sayin'?" And she smiled at him for some comradery, and raised her eyebrows repeatedly, as she checked his phone.

Text from Jay to Noah: Notre amour livrera nos circonstances ensemble. ♥♥♥

She jumped to her feet without signaling, and gave him some advice. "Leave her or go to jail, Noah. Just like I'm leaving you now to get a real dick shoved in my beautiful little va-jay-jay." And she did the air quotes to help his hillbilly education comprehend. Simon got Emily pregnant for me. Together we were

going to raise her as our own. Her name was Emma. Julian aborted her for you, Noah and stopped sleeping with Simon. Emily woke up the next day NOT pregnant; heartbroken and confused. The day before she was pregnant with our child. The next day, Julian claimed she finally met one of her own stupid Angel people-you. From Hickyville, Florida." Rachael pierced her lips and held them at him. "Leave her now or go to jail for life and maybe the death penalty depending how much of your semen I can spread and get women to help accuse you of rape. Na' mean? It's pretty easy amongst us liberal sisters. We stick together against the Patriarchy."

She turned and walked over to the other chair to get her clothes. "I will be back. 'Got to get my nut busted. Someone is real thirsty for her daily vitamins, and this time-AND...it ain't Emily...or maybe it is for Emily or Julian." She laughed at him wondering if he could in any way, put all that together, and winked at the clues she gave him, before turning around and getting dressed. "You are making me laugh trying to make me think you don't know Emily's alternate personality is Julian." Putting her pants back on, she watched him for clues.

"By the way, that text was from your Julian to me, shall I read it?" He was eager for any news of his wife and nodded appreciatively. "Notre amour livrera nos circonstances ensemble." His eyes opened up wide, and she could see them start to tear up.

Feeling the satisfaction as she put her shirt on, and shoes, and offered her one last riddle. "Oh what webs you dumb males can't weave, even when you are in it."

Chapter 8

-Leaks 'They,' BBC and Phobias

Rachael eyes stayed rolled back as she pulled on her long, sagging nipples stretching them three and four times their usual lengths. His big black cock jammed into her pussy with ease and she kept her knees back to get every inch of it.

"Fuck my white pussy with our big black dick. 'Fucking make me your dick bitch. Fuck me. Fuck me for being white. Fuck me Fuck me hard. You have five minutes to fuck my white privilege." She jammed her finger down her throat and gagged herself as he slid it in and out slapping his brown bag against her chaw-boned ass.

He spoke up, giving her more of what she wanted. "White bitch loves that black dick. Fucking you Kendall. I fucked your white pussy yesterday and you back today begging it. Bitch you need some brothers on your list." He leaned over the edge of the bed to ram it in her harder.

"Gag yourself white bitch."

Moaning to his pleasure offer, she kept stimulating her mind. "I need your cum inside me. Cum in my white pussy. Black cum inside me Daddy. Cum in my pussy, Daddy. Fuck IT! FUCK ME DADDY! FUCK MEEEEEE!" Her juices made their way down and got slapped by his balls and he got harder. I'm your white girl! FUCK ME! FUCK ME! FUCK ME LIKE A BITCH DADDY!"

Her disposable man gave it to her as good as she could get it and pounded hard as his thick black cock squirted into her bald, white pussy. "FUCKING

WHITE WHORE!" he screamed as he repeatedly squirted every drop into her. He squeezed off everything in his urethra listening to her moans and she reached down and pulled him up over her and he sat on her chest as she licked his dick clean. He leaned forward and shoved his big dick into her mouth and all of it slowly vanished. She reached up over his thighs and pulled him down her throat as much as possible. She wanted it all cleaned off for tomorrow.

Finding her way to her clit, she rubbed it as he gagged her. He could see in her eyes she was struggling but, he learned the routine yesterday, so he shoved it in harder trying to choke her white privilege. She rolled her eyes back and buckled under him as her orgasm dipped her uterus into his thick semen. She pushed for him to rise and he shoved it down her throat trying to get more. She immediately put her hand under her lower back and tried banging her red face into him.

His balls, divided by her chin loved their new home. Her throat muscles and her esophagus began jerking in her neck. She struggled to get his dick out as he looked up at the clock in the empty hospital room and counted down. She gagged without a sound in panic and started hitting his legs and trying to push him off and he kept that big dick deep in her deep throat.

Text Alert from Jay: Bring the Matrix Formula with you. I want to see it. Another body found.

She tried moving her head to the side thrusting out from under him and he just relaxed and watched the clock. He must have been on break, and her attempts at screaming were not important. When her eyes rolled back into her head and dangled there. He

felt satisfied, "White bitch. Welcome to real black dick."

She reached down nearly unconscious and started trying finger her clit again. She pinched it and ground her nails against it and could not get herself to orgasms. When her arms did its last jerk to her sides. He smiled, slowly pulling his big dick out of her mouth. She immediately gagged and gasped for air rolling over on her side as he stood back and stroked his cock for another hit.

Nearly drowning, she tried to tell him. "Thank you. Tomorrow...okay." He smiled and got out his cell phone and videotaped her trying to regain air and consciousness. He walked around her getting her face really close as she tried not to vomit. He got real close to her pussy and filmed it, and her tits didn't matter, she didn't have any. Same time tomorrow?" He asked her.

Holding her fetal position, she nodded and dry heaved. "Longer tomorrow. Gag me..." panting "...longer." Respiring, "White girls need big black cock." He pulled his pants up satisfied at his free score again, and left her to recover. She didn't matter to him, and that is what she enjoyed most, besides the almighty orgasms.

Still trying to regain her oxygen, she got up and scooted over to the edge of the bed near the table and grabbed the shot glass. She sat up quickly, still dry heaving and scooted to the edge of the bed. Flexing her vaginal walls she put the shot glass at the bottom of her vaginal and squeezed his semen and her cum into the shot glass. She squeezed it over and over as she stretched her lungs. Together they nearly filled it up. Rachael quickly got her electric toothbrush out of her bag and stuck it too her clit.

She sat up and put the shot glass under her pussy again, squeezing every drop into it. When her orgasm melted her, she moved the glass up and down her smooth labia to get all of her wetness. Holding it up and grabbing her throat to rub it, they had nearly got it three quarters of the way full. Rachael smiled with pride. "I love you so much, Emily. I will feed your Paraphilia using my own pussy." was the only thing she said, before spitting into the top.

Jay was fast with the remote and nothing on but news, news, and more news. She rolled her eyes at the stories hoping something about the Stiff'em body being found. She did not find anything, so mute was her frustrating choice. When her nurse walked in, she was not sure if it was a he or she. She smiled and even after he or she spoke, she wasn't sure. Peeking for breasts and an Adam's apple did not bear fruit, so she had to sit back and wait for clues. Boring to a woman who investigates crimes and minds for a living.

"By the way Mrs. Doe, I love your non-binary Partner. He or she are so funny. Does your partner prefer a Gender? I prefer 'They' myself." Jay nodded with a smile and signed him a thank you...*pun intended* she thought. He put her pill cup down and Jay poured water into it. After checking her intravenous needle for infection, They told her how much they loved Jay's hair and that everyone in the hospital spoke about it and how "Rachael and Jordan Doe" are the cutest couple they have seen in a while. And heard they were the most entertaining and fun to watch. They winked at her when They said it.

Jay only smiled and signed. They asked her if she needed anything and she pointed to her empty died soda can. They nodded and said They would be back. Jay watched They walk out and she packed her

Copenhagen for a pinch. The nosy nurses station seemed to be crowded lately, having five nurses in her view at all times now, instead of the usual two. When she pinched a hit, the women got a surprised look that didn't try to shy away or hide.

Jay pinched the last of it from the can, just to entertain them. Her empty can would make a great tool. Quickly, she roped her hair and pinched it between her lips and sat there rattling one of Noah's spurs to herself with her eye closed. That sound touched her soul, like Noah did. Delicately, she tried to match his walking sound when he wore them and rested her head back as she rattled. Grabbing the other one for her other hand, she worked to get the time and volume correct. She closed her eyes again to think of her husband and her kids and Luckenbach.

When the nurse returned They brought her a diet soda and one of her doctors. The Doctor asked her to let the nurse replace her bandana with clean gauze and she shook her head at him. She wanted to say, 'You are lucky I am actually wearing this' but, that was too much work to sign for a group likely not to be able to read sign language. She only knew letters, numbers, and a few words.

Rachael walked in with a smile carrying Jay a shot glass of semen. Jay's blue eye, beaten red, lit up and Rachael immediately told her she stopped by the house again and it was in the fridge. "Noah must really love you if he keeps leaving these for you, Emily." Jay nodded as she admired how full it was and placed it on her tray table in the perfect symmetrical spot even from the corner on both sides. She ignored the Emily comment.

The Doctor advised her that mixing alcohol with narcotics was not recommended and Jay started shooing him away. The Doctor respectfully smiled and

reminded her she could not drink alcohol on hospital grounds. Doctor Rachael cut in and lifted her yellow t-shirt off in front of him and said, "I am her personal physician Doctor, her wife, and that is her vitamins. Vitamins for her to enjoy with me. It does not contain any intoxicating alcohol. Thank you." The Doctor gave her a short stair, admired her flat chest, and smiled.

"Lucky her," he said nervously, smiling at Jay and Rachael both.

Jay put one of the spurs under the blanket and began riding the spur up and down her swollen labia. The Doctor cleared his throat a little and told her he needed to inspect her vagina and anal cavity to observe how things are healing. Rachael offered to assist as she removed her pants and folded them nicely on the chair. He advised her that policy would only allow her to observe if it was alright with her wife. Jay spit into her empty can and shrugged her shoulders. *My drink is waiting, DAMN IT!* She thought.

Pulling the blanket up, Jay was able to slip down and a two nurses entered to observe his work. Hospital policy no doubt. Using a small light from his pocket. He looked closely and asked her how it was feeling. With his blue rubber glove on, he gently inserted his fingers and pushed along with walls and pelvic bone.

"Have you been draining your vaginal opening every hour on the hour, Mrs. Doe? He asked without looking at her. She nodded and Doctor Rachael answered for her,

"Yes she has. I have been assisting her." Rachael added.

"I'm seeing signs of minor infection. Perhaps a light salt-water cleanse for your vulva would do the trick. Metronidazole." He added to the list of medicine. Jay just shook Noah's spurs as everyone looked at her vagina...again. It was really more about pulling her

hair since OCD was biting at her. "Any discomfort or bleeding?" he asked and Jay shook her spur sideways. "Anal bleeding or bloody stool?" Jay rolled her eye and shook her spur sideways.

"How about Ketamine or 3-Quinuclidinyl benzilate or cholinesterase inhibitors?" Rachael glanced up at her long enough to see Jay stop spurring and scan the pharmaceutical registry in her mind that she pounded into her brain in Med School. Still holding the spur, she slowly looked up at Doctor Rachael with her own medical knowledge, lover's instinct, and investigator's intuition, and felt the subtle poke. The Doctor didn't actually respond to Rachael. Jay spit into her can stuffed with a tissue and grabbed her phone. *I guess yesterday's ass kicking was to gentle,* she thought.

Jay stared at her with her with one eye and wore the blue bandana to enhance that one eye's color, marking intimidation, Cowgirl style. Her heavy black eyeliner and mascara exploded the red of her eye, and blue of her poked soul.

Text to Rach: You need Prozac!

Rachael stopped to see her message and look up at Jay, and not paying attention anymore to the Doctor on duty. Nude Rachael stepped over to a chair and sat down without breaking eye contact with Jay. Jay spit into her can like a Cowboy about to rope a longhorn just for the fun of it.

Text to Jay: You need Diazepam Emily!!

Jay waited for Rachael see her staring before responding.

Text to Rachael: You need Zolpidem!

The Doctor and the nurses walked out after not getting responses to their questions and Rachael rushed to press send.

Text to Jay: Vitamin K Big Pharma Style Emily!!!!!

Text to Rachael: Mind your own business pills!!!!!!!!!!!!

Text to Jay: Diddy Meds MENTALLY ILL BITCH!!

Rachael glanced up at her and adjusted herself in the seat for a sturdier sit on her chaw-bone of an ass as Jay pulled her hair around in front of her eye, and gleamed through it for the fight.

Text to Rachael: You need Anti-androgens.

Text to Jay: Get back on antipsychotics meds!

Text to Jay: Vipassana!!

Text to Rachael: Qualia

Text to Jay: Emily! Emily! Emily!

Rachael smiled as if the riddle had been solved

and watched Jay read it.

Text to Rachael: EMILY RAPING BITCH!

Text to Jay: STRANGER-DANGER RAPE LOVER.

Jay pounded out her response.

Text to Rachael: TRAMP! Rachael was quick.

Text to Jay: SCARLET!!!!!

Jay nodded slowly when she read it sucking on her rope of hair and her Copenhagen long cut tobacco.

Text to Rachael: DUMPSHELL!!!!

Text to Jay: I WISH EMILY HAD KILLED HIM BACK THEN!!!!

Text to Rachael: SKINNY A LA CARTE!!!!

Text to Jay: INTERLOPER SEMENOLOGIST!!!!

Jay reached over and downed her shot of semen flamboyantly. Staring at Rachael, she put her tongue to the bottom of the shot glass and licked up every swimmer. Rachael smiled at that victory.

Text to Jay: SHORTY AND FAT!!!

Text to Rachael: RELIGIONPHOBE!

Text to Jay: Bible Thumping RAPIST HUSBAND!!!

And Jay shook a spur to thank her.

Another text to Jay: YOU'RE OBSTINATE!

Text to Rachael: Enigmatic!

And Rachael got up and walked to her bedside and the tension got thicker immediately. They would only look after hitting send to read their responsive expressions. Perhaps since she was closer, the text would magically send faster. When educated women argue, common sense seems to get put aside to get the point across. Men, just beat on each other and have a beer afterwards.

Text to Jay: YOU'RE ABTRUSE BITCH!
Text to Rachael: UNREQUITED LOVER!-COLLEGE!
Text to Jay: UNREQUITED LOVER-NOW!
Text to Rachael: INSOUCIANT SITUATION!
Text to Jay: ZEALOT!
Text to Rachael: KVETCHER!
Another text to Rach: GREEN-EYED ASTERISK!

When Rachael looked up after reading it, Jay stuck her tongue out at her.

Text to Jay: FAT ASS BITCH!
Text to Rach: TWIG VAMP!
Text to Jay: ATYCHIPHOBIC!
Text to Rach: ANDROPHOIC!
Text to Jay: LILAPSOPHOBIC!

Jay whispers: Sociaphobic.
Rach yells back: OBESOPHOBIC!
Jay whispers: Gamophobic.
Rach yells: VENUSTRAPHOBIC!
Jay whispers to her: Micropenisphobic Lover.
Rach yells back: MACROPENISPHOBIC!

Rachael stormed out of the room angry or hurt, or both perhaps, offering her last accusation, "Bitch

with a cow cunt. Go fuck a ranch-hand behind the barn. It's what you are best at. Nasty hillbilly tobacco snuff."

Either way, truths had been spoken and sometimes, that is what needs to be said. Jay shook her head smiling, "Bitch could pick a fight in an empty house," she whispered and spit into her chew cup.

Chapter Nine

-Angel Tapping Indeed of Need

"Hello Noah. Comfortable?" When he sat up to respond, she continued. "I don't really care. You are getting three meals a day and a clean bedpan when you need it. Television, and a comfortable bed. Hell Noah, just think of it as your last vacation before incarceration." The smirk that followed glowed of power and satisfaction. "Ready to feel a normal pussy, Noah?" She smiled again and put both her hands on her hips.

Noah stood up scratching his testicles, and looked into the bathroom mirror about eight feet away and whispered something to himself. She liked that distracting cock getting to the ready position. He was easier to train than she thought. Holding his nice size cock in his hand, he spoke up. "I want to turn myself in, Rachael. To you. I want to be arrested. You're right. I raped her and enjoyed it and be doin' it forever and I deserve to go to prison. Take me in." He put both wrist together near the cuffs holding him to the bedrail, and waited. One cuff is already attached so, I am half way there."

Rachael took her shirt off to show her cute, effective nipples to him, and walked around the other side of the bed. The side he was not cuffed to.

"Lay back down and extend your arm. Give me your wrist so I can cuff to mine. I'm arresting you on attempted murder, domestic violence, and sexual assault." Jon stared at her in doubt. He only had one chance and he was on her chess board. He laid down and extended his arm and she cuffed it and then

111

started to cuff him to her wrist and she watched his eyes widen. Quickly, she slammed the cuff to the other guard rail, and he lost that move.

Rachael grinned as her less-than one hundred pound body landed across his shins facing his feet, and she quickly began wrapping rope around his ankles, binding them together. Jon was kicking and screaming but, the she slowed him down enough for her to tie them together. She quickly rolled off him and fell to the floor on her skinny butt. He immediately curled his body over and tried kicking her with both feet. Almost to her feet, she lurched back holding the end of the rope and falling on her ass again, and unexpectedly, pulling the rope tight, from her position. He lost that move too. "Ha ha! Not bad for a little girl from Texas. Right, Noah?"

She got up and pulled the rope to the end of the bed and tied it underneath. "Not bad for a Tomgirl from Luckenbach, Texas." His Jesus pose was permanent now. Rachael dashed over to her bag and pulled out a roll of duct tape and with him kicking and screaming, she wrapped his ankles with it, and tore off a big enough piece to open his ears, by shutting his mouth. He jerked away from her trying to dodge the tape, but after sticking somewhat across his mouth and face, she got another piece and finished the job.

Standing back smiling now, she wiggled a little side to side hip action and her jeans slid down her legs as her expression grew seductively evil. She walked one foot in front of the other over the door and placed a sock over the door handle on the outside and shut it. The leer she offered when she turned around was precious. A slutty, shy little girl, naked for a boy she had a crush, playing coy, and daringly sexy.

An Angel, fallen to earth and tainted by Satan himself, Jon thought. She knew pussy had power...she

just never really had the boobs to go along with that power. Now, the Queen, moved anywhere on her chess board.

In her power walk to him, her fingers slid down her silky chest pulling her elongated nipples to attention, and both hands slid down to Indigo. That non-binary pussy was still itching for a fight, and both hands slid across her wrinkled up labia minor and crossed onto her thighs as if she was posing for a photographic moment. Seductively she spoke to him. "How and when did you find out about Emily, and all her Alibis, Noah? How did you find out about Emily? The Envelopes, Noah? The Diaries? How many did you open? I need to know this because Julian would never tell you about other Alibis." She was sexy and, deadly in her tone.

Jon leaned his head back, and stared for protection. *This would be the ugliest PTSD moment he would ever have,* he thought. She was coming to get it, and talking about things he never heard of. And he was not going to be able to stop her. In his life, he never thought a hundred pound woman would beat him or rape him.

"HOW MANY!" she screeched at him, making him jump.

She sat a phone on the table next to his bed, and pressed the video record button. Rachael carefully dragged her finger down his chest and across his tight abs, sticking her tongue out of the corner of her mouth, she watched closely for the cock to just hint a little movement at her. She had waited to feel this for years. Her mouth watered, and her pussy went on full alert with anticipation. She was finally going to get what Emily had been getting-Angel Seed from Noah's cock. Teasing herself, she put her finger just to the edge of his shaft, and softly touched it.

"Emily is not the only slutty Angel, Noah." She whispered with evil delight and his limbs began to get cold. "That is why she picked me to own her."

Smiling with delight, she climbed over him and sat on his legs. Instantly, she laid down on his thighs and rubbed her lips against his warm, soft cock and balls. His grunts and wiggles behind the duct tape turned her on even more. Jon tried bucking that pony and she enjoyed rubbing Indigo right into his kicking shin. She needed to make sure she did him right and check his wings. She wanted him to remember fucking her for the rest of his life. She wanted to make sure his memory of Emily's sex was secondary to hers. She rubbed her lips on the head of this cock and circled the shape of her moist lips. By the third lap, her tongue touched him and he started to grow for her.

She ignored his pleas behind the duct tape and mimicked what she thought he might say. "I know...I know...Rachael is the real Angel. She takes me seed and gives my seed to other Angels who need seed to get pregnant." He uttered rolling his eyes back and forward as she teased his warm cock and grunted viciously. Mimicking Julian's accent again, she taunted his mind. "No one be havens it widout' mise' permissions, Rachael." Changing back to her seductive tone, she debated with him. "Well, Noah, Emily gave me permission to get your seed and use it against you in a court of law. Rapist."

She used the heel of her hand and shoved his balls up against his body and quickly he grew with her smile. She heeled him again and again until his full length and girth got really warm and finally, she pushed his dick into her mouth and all eight inches of it disappeared. He could feel the head get swallowed into her throat as he jerked a little and enjoyed her skills. He was full hard and had to enjoy it now, as she

came up for air smiling devilishly. It was his turn to be a victim of rape. He had to agree to it in his mind, to control it, if that was possible.

She stared at him in desire and hatred rubbing his dick all over her face while she spoke. "Julian told me how you love fucking Black women regularly...how you keep coming up with excuses to fuck them with that fake Angel brainwashing crap you do to her. You really did sell her on that with that Stockholm Syndrome programming. She truly believes you are an Angel King, as this Slutty Angel sucks your dick for you." She slapped his balls to get her point across and his dick quickly girthed. "Maybe you are a King, since you managed to get me to suck your dick. I hate White men." She said it, as if she was asking herself the question.

She bobbed up and down on him and then stroked him as she licked it from top to bottom. Both of them staring at each other's eyes, he felt like a tether ball with no ability to fight back. Glaring at him, she could see she was winning this struggle and finally, his eyes rolled back and with the head of his dick in her mouth, she smiled with power over him. This power juiced up her pussy even more...nefariously rubbing his hefty cowboy cock across the front of her teeth.

In her shy, little girl voice, she asked him. "Why haven't you wanted to fuck me, Noah? You hurt my feelings that you never put the moves on me- knowing you could have me...even right in front of Emily...she is the perfect abusable, Cuckquean for me." She switched back to the angry tone. "The Bitch personality, Julian, is not. She gets in the way with her complications..." Now back to the innocent girl, pleading voice, "...but Emily would let us fuck. We share men occasionally. WHY?" She screamed at him

115

jerking his foreskin down to his body enough to bend the head of his pretty cock and gave him a wry stare. Jon got stiff and arched his back to fight the sensations rushing him as his foreskin under the head stretched painfully. His dick loved it, his reward system debated it, and his eyes feared it.

"I would love to see you to have seen your face, every time you saw that design on her right butt cheek." Jon, immediately looked at her. He knew what she meant. She got up and climbed on top of his manhood and rested the head inside Indigo. He watched her, hoping she would sit on it. *Pussy isn't the only magical tool with power,* he thought, as he moved across her chess board.

Spoken like a caring woman, "You might as well get one last piece of ass before prison, even if it is with a Tomgirl, Noah." She kept watching his brown eyes. He was easy to read, as his brain searched for every time he spotted that design drawn on Emily's ass cheek. Before stealing his first time with her, she said "Let's talk about...Emily," and gracefully, she sat down on him and let the wet warmth of her pussy give way to the head of his throbbing dick and purposely grinding her bones down for Indigo to have it all. His eyes were still rolled back as she held her breath. Finally, after all these years, she was sitting in Julian's seat. It was a nice feeling, inside her and out.

Slowly, she worked herself in a circle soaking him good. He banged into her uterus with each rotation and she haled that. Finally, she thrusted her hips forward and back on him in a very slow pace. Jon mumbled sentence after sentence to her with his disapprovals masked by tape. She assumed what they were by the tone of them and swam in her power of the man who had pussy-blocked her for nearly ten years. Reaching up and ripping off the duct tape, he

stared at her. He was enjoying the wet warmth that wrapped his busy manhood, while moving his Rook.

Finally, he was able to speak. "That symbol drawn on her butt, was one of Julian's IDentifY lovers, because I don't have the right to tell any of her IDentifY who she can sleep with," he said. "And she doesn't have the right to tell my IDentifY who he can and cannot sleep with. But nice twist...Stupid." She smiled at his ignorance, and spoke up as she rocked his cock.

"How easily, her secrets hide from you, just amazes me. So, I'm going to tell you a story Noey, about a woman." She bobbed her head forward with each sentence. "A woman who has desires. Has passion for me. And has to have all of those needs met for her. Unfortunately for you, one of these needs is kissing my pussy." She paused for a few seconds, as if he was supposed to guess who the woman was. "Our wife, Noah. Our wife. Our wife has needs and kissing Indigo is one of her permanent needs in life. Even in Med School, she would come to me begging me to sit on her face. Last year, last month, this morning. Your wife ate my pussy...by the way, your dick is in me right now...you Cheating Cowboy."

Rachael kept up the slow pace. She had a long story to tell and busting his nut before she was through just might make her words never be heard. "In college, Emily was the biggest slut on campus, and not just because she was the fattest girl in school. Not just a literal term here. She really was the thick slut on campus, and the most popular. I'm telling you, she isn't some pair-shaped fat momma. She has got the curves in all the right places. All measured just right. Just so perfectly matched all around so...so...thick and not fat...thick like a...your cock feels wonderful Boy..." She closed her eyes and jerked forward and back real

117

fast a few times and said in a whisper, "Oh Emily. You are right. This does feel right for an Angel," and she busted up laughing.

He spoke up to her with a serious look on his face. "What fucking drugs are you taking, Andrea?"

Opening her eyes, she ignored him and saw him from Emily's view. "Noah, my real name is, Jenna. I'm from Texas. We have been lying to you about me all these years. I was Emily's first love." She gripped his cock with the walls of her vagina and lifted up on his warm member smiling. "Emily and I met when I was fifteen, and she was thirteen. I came upon her in the woods outside Luckenbach." Jerking to a stop, her mind thought of something important and spit it out. "You haven't fucked Lowana yet, have you?" She busted out with it, and then laughed.

He gave her a confused look, "Who is Lowana?" and Jenna just laughed at his male ignorance and went back to her story.

"Emily's horse roped off to a tree and there she was, fingering herself leaning against a tree completely naked. Emily even had ugly boobs at that age. Obviously, bigger than mine. She was all areola though. Big brown circles that hid the rest of her little boobies. Looked like tubes sticking off her chest with big brown balls on the end-Keep that dick hard for me, Noah." She looked at him as he stared back actually paying attention. She jerked up a few times letting him know he needed to be inside her really well. She didn't know it but, he could feel semen leaking out already. Her Queen to his Knight sounds right.

"I watched her, so beautiful, so thick, so well curved-she jerked and shook as she inserted one finger after another and I sat back and touched myself. I had always wanted someone else besides my father, touching me. I thought this might be the one.

118

Taking the rest of my clothes off, I walked out like so and over to join her." She put her arms out to show her naked self. "It was a match made in Texas, Noah. We hit it off, and watched each other. I taught her how to taste herself. And most importantly, how to taste me. I brought her to orgasm in seconds. Natural born lesbian...like me." She sped up just a little. "We would be lovers to the end of time."

"For years we made love every day. Every hour. We got on the same cycle and..." Jenna looked out beyond her victim and stared into her memories. She kept pace though; kept him rock hard inside her, slowly transferring his DNA. Those memories would keep her well lubed in the moment.

"She was my first love, Noah. My first love was a dumb Angel from heaven. Can you believe that? I was her first love. I'm another Angel according to her. In the backward world of Texas, we planned to hide our shame like other lesbians, only being a teenager, it's confusing and as simple as Emily is, she couldn't balance it. She couldn't just hide it. Angels do not hide the truth, right? Guys talked about girl-on-girl and she liked that idea...to get their approval. Sure, we let a few boys watch as long as they promised to masturbate and let Emily taste it. We called her nipples bullseyes for the guys to stare at and cum on. Fucking ugly is what they were. Even Rachael hates them. Have to agree with Simon on that topic."

She slowed her rocking back down, never mind him, just keep it hard. "I stole a vibrator and a dildo from a friends mom. 'Think maybe I was sixteen. I would slip one in her and in me. She talked about how much it hurt and felt right. I put that vibrator to her button and she never complained again. I even held it up like a dick on my little Indigo so I could yell at her like a man and in a deep voice say 'suck my big dick

bitch' and she would suck it. I liked that. I loved looking down into her eyes. I fell so hard for her. She named my pussy Indigo, Noah. Emily's blue eyes have everything in them that shows her real self. You know- Mesmerizing eyes of beauty. I knew then and now, I would do anything to keep her. This is why you are going to prison Noah James. She is my Girl. She is so easy to understand when you see those eyes and hear her voice." She stopped rocking and talking to get his attention.

"I would kill for her, Noah. Kill...for...her...again. Four ranch hands her Daddy had-Loser's like you. They had their way with here...once...just once. But, then she wanted more ranch hands-two and three guys at a time. She let them have her after her first rape or two. I buried their asses outside of town. Never told Emily." He grunted at her as she lived far off in her memory.

"My Daddy was the town Preacher man under an assumed name. We had moved here-there-everywhere, all over this racist country. He would rape a few girls and boys, everywhere we lived. That's why we had to move on from Texas when I was sixteen." As if she was in shock of an answer that hadn't come yet, she asked, "Who wants freezing snow and swamp-ass summers in Texas? I hated Luckenbach. I hated it.

♫ Text Alert

"He wanted to rape Emily, Noah, and I couldn't let that happen to the girl I loved. So I got naked and pulled at his cock to let me suck his dick. It was the first and last time I sucked a white boy off...until today with you. That was all it took to distract him from getting her. He raped my Chickpea nearly every day." Staring down at him to clarify her own words, "That is what he called a fresh little girl." Jon watched as her

120

body lost focus and her eyes stared afar. She was seeing something that required her attention.

"I gave Daddy me, instead of her. And, Emily never thanked me. She paused to think about that. "Why did she never thank me?"

Jon shrugged his shoulders and thrusted his stiff, thick cock into her and she rebooted. "Maybe 'cause all of this story line is bullshit. Ever think of that? Stupid."

Deep in herself, she never heard him. "I kept Daddy satisfied so he would not touch her. I loved my little girl." Looking down at him as if she just remembered he was there, "Don't you get that? That long hair, her summer dresses, she would smile at me and tell me she loved me as I watched her have orgasm after orgasm next to a Weeping Mellow tree. Weeping Tree was our meeting spot next to a pellow...mellow...pellow, right? A pellow tree? A mellow tree?" She stopped rocking and sat there trying to remember the tree. "I think that was a mellow tree. Anyway, for present men...you specifically stupid...not smart enough to keep up with the pillow tree. Dellow? Mellow? Nellow?"

When he opened his eyes, she had an angry look on her face, as if he wasn't going down memory lane with her. Slowly, she started rocking again, "Keep that dick leaking, Noah. With our fake-Angel baby, from your rape of me, she will never ever leave me and our child. We are going to name her Emma. You raped me and she will feel obligated to stay with our baby. Especially, since you tricked me like Daddy, saying..." In Noah's voice, "I won't rape Emily anymore if you sleep with me, Jenna." She giggled at her mockery, and smiled at him to join in the festivities.

"Emily's fat mother found my dildo and vibrator Emily kept hidden in her room. Bitch probably had ten

of her own from hypocrites and bigots at the church. She dragged-"

He interrupted her, "I love having threesomes with her Momma. She can fuck really good. I fucked her the night I met her...just like Julian. I fuck Momma every week and last year, I killed her and buried her and she came back to life for more of my big dick, Bitch. Even old Momma fucks better than you." He smiled really big.

Rolling her tongue across her teeth, she pushed her palms into her abdomen and yelled at him. "DON'T RUIN MY STORY!" and she stared to get her point across.

Finally, she started again, "Abigail dragged Emily down to the church yelling an abomination and Emily needed saved. The 'wicked Devil had taken her Angel to the dark side, she said." Jenna paused everything in the memory and the moment before she let it out with fear in her voice. "He was...He was Kendall's father...my father." Noah picked up on her sadness, only he didn't know who Kendall was.

She was slow to start speaking again, "Leviticus 18:17 Noah, do not have sex with a woman and her daughter. Daddy wanted her and scolded my Emily in front of the church, her fat mother, and anyone else there to hear it. Daddy shoved the toys in her face letting God know what she had done to herself." She seemed to be cautious when she spoke to him, as if Daddy was going to hear her. "He...he...put her on her knees and had her pray with her mother as he stood over them salivating the words of the Bible. That's what he did every time before raising my dress and raping me." Jenna looked down and to her left, relaxing her body weight on his dick and staring away. "The word of God." And she went silent. She played her Bishop, diagonally across his chess board.

122

Watching her closely, watch her memory, she started rocking again and sounded like Rachael. "Come on horsey, leak those vitamins into me. I'm ovulating just like my Emily, Noah." She squeezed her pussy tight and sat up and slid it back down a few times to pump it out. "Give it to me...My Daddy was a wise man. He took Emily into his office and talked to her without fatso momma being in there. He told her the truth. Women fall victim to sluts just like men. She would violate the word of God if she put things in her pussy. Fat Kitty was not allowed to have visitors unless it was a Preacher." She took silent and pounded down on him and rolling her eyes back with him.

"Emily had that huge, odd, black labia back then too. I mean, she is as pale as a Ghost on Sunday, and the tips of her fat outer labia are black...and HUGE! Her pussy always looked like a very pregnant woman's vagina. I swear she was part Longhorn and she grew that ass bigger to support it."

She worked herself up hard as she rammed her uterus into his thick, warm cock and chattered the story at him. "Daddy told me the same things when he would watch me masturbate. I hate that Emily calls it rodeo." She jerked his dick with her pussy as hard as she could and tried to keep her breath as she rode him. "YOU! And that stupid word. Calling it rodeo...making her call it rodeo." Jon grunted at her but, she didn't care. "Normal pussy feel really good. Right Noah?" Jon nodded. The pleasure kept his words out of the one-sided story that was more like a discussion one had with themselves when they were, bored, scared, living alone, and crazy.

"Daddy told her God provided women with a relief button when they felt the urges. 1 Corinthians 10:13. He taught us that women were allowed to masturbate so long as they did not waste their seed by

123

Witness, or enter their vagina. Genesis 19:36. Let me carry my father's children and that we could rub our button-that's a clitoris to you Hillbilly men who can't eat pussy and make a woman happy." She kept slamming down on him, and he felt the short burst of semen coming out. "It takes another woman to get it done right. Ask Emily. Honestly, she is not that great at it either. Everything is short about her like her tongue." She stopped chattering from ruining the moment, and focused on the schlicking down coming out of her vagina.

Exhausted, she slowed back down and rocked her hips back and forth to catch her breath. "We are...allowed to rub our clits and orgasm...so long as nothing gets inside until we are married...to which...the husband owns our vaginas...As stupid as that is. 1 Corinthians 7:4. Husband owns her hair, her body, her vagina...just not the button. Yet, she needs permission to touch it after marriage. And any woman is allowed to let any man have anal sex with her because the husband isn't allowed...some shit like that." She respired over and over as her chest expanded. "Julian knows the stupid rules better than me." She stopped rocking his cock and stared at him to catch her breath.

"Who wrote this shit? Who made it up? Obviously some male patriarchy setting the ways for thousands of years. She moved her Pawns, her Knight and the King; chess rules did not apply to those with the pussy.

She stopped her anger from bubbling. "BUT! There is always a 'but' in the man's world. She could never masturbate without a Witness. I know why Daddy did this. Like me, he wanted to watch and be the first in her holes...like me. That is enough to make a daughter feel special inside. He was the first in mine...both of mine...all three of mine. He never let me

cut my hair so he could pull it. He needed it to control me when he fucked me. He could only get his dick in my ass pulling my hair and calling me his son Kendall. Emily had that mane then, too. Much longer than mine. She was ripe for his touch. He wanted her more than his own child...me. As a Daddy's girl, I didn't take kindly to losing to Emily, so I kept her away from him and through myself at him. I took his seed from him. I made sure of it. I never wore clothes at home, around the house, the barn...this country gal never wore a shirt in town. I liked it. We only got a few complaints." She leaned back up and focused on his pleasure by accident.

"He scared Emmy with the words of God. Her heavy do-gooder-ness from the Bible took hold in her early from her parents, and when she found out she could never waste her seed, or allow others she Witnessed, I was happy as a clam. She and I licked and sucked and drank each other like country queens. We drank each other's seed to keep it from being wasted. Daddy always put his seed in me somewhere. He said it could never be wasted. I promise you Noah, like Emily, I will NOT waste your seed."

Jon could tell when she was drifting into her memories because she lost rhythm or stopped all together. He figured, she gave it to him good because her mind lost track of time. He started thrusting her hard to cum for her. He wanted to cum for her. It was beginning to hurt inside his ballooned shaft.

Jenna slowly pulled him out and you could hear him exhale relief...either from getting out of her before he came inside her, or the balloon was just too full. "Having Emily love me let me know God has given her to me." She said, staring off into a distant mind, before taking away her magic muscle from his magic wand. She reached over and got her phone and

offered a smile that betrays innocence, as she leaned down to take a picture of his wet, erect cock covered in her juice, she let him know she was sending Emily a text:

Text from Rachael on Noah's phone: I know about Emily and I don't want to be with you anymore. You are mentally ill. Go away! I want a Divorce.

Catching him off guard, she slammed her mouth down over his cock and it vanished completely. He jerked and kicked at the pleasure, and as fast as she could took it all the way out and all the way in again. She would give him what Emily could not, in hopes of getting from him what Emily got. His eyes sunk back and total pleasure had come to him. This was too good. She was good in bed. He hated that she was almost a man, and yet so much better than just a woman.

She held it deep and gagged on it for him and gave him quick glances. She reached up and shoved his balls one by one into her mouth and he felt the orgasm coming. His sperm drawing out of his epididymis, and her throat locked his long foreskin down his shaft. It was coming. She knobbed up and down and ripped it out of her throat and stared at him with a delectable smile. "I will always be a Daddy's girl, Noah. I hope you liked it...Daddy." She woman-handled his shaft and sucked the leaking semen off the tip, and got back on. "I don't taste cum for any man, unless he is Black. Consider that a treat, Boy. Drinking that nasty shit. I don't know how Emily enjoys the taste...the texture. Daddy got his dick down my throat and I was thankful he did. I never had to taste cum again. But Emily. She is truly one semen addicted woman. She got addicted by Witness. My fault there. I

should have stopped it but, the pay was too good. Wish I had balls to feed her too. You know, after we got married, I could not stop her from offering to Witness every guy in Med School, just so she could swallow him. Her withdrawals are horrible. Manic depression. Suicidal thoughts. Horrible. Classic...I digress. Maybe that is how she got so thick, Wife Beater."

♫ *Text Alert*

She stopped, but changed her mind and started up and down his long thick shaft of manhood pleasures, and leaned down and sucked on his nipples. He laid his head back, and like Emily, let her have her way with him, even as he slid his Knight, when she had her mouth full...which he really liked. Emily never sucked his nipples...she was all about that seed.

"I remember the words of your God as Daddy put his dick in me over and over and seeded me each time. 'Leviticus 18:17 lets Daddy fuck me.' Mom died bringing me into this world. Thanks Mom. Fourteen abortions before I was seventeen, Noah. FOURTEEN! All from my father. Not a single woman that I knew or met in church, cared. Emily did. Emmy was everything kind to me and what I loved-I needed. She gave me unconditional love. Daddy couldn't' get to her so he took me away from her. My father dragged me out of Texas kicking and screaming her name and I prayed to your God to save her and let our love have grace. One city to another when he raped and raped and raped me. I actually began to enjoy it after a few hundred times. The anal sex was hard. Very hard...but it got really enjoyable over time...like Emily in college, she got to where she needed it. The Bible does not allow men to get anal but, says nothing about women." And she chlicked as she picked up her phone to text.

127

Text to Jay: Sure wife. Anything else?

Jon's dick stood firm, and she sped up to give him a wet treat. She reached down and gathered as much of her seed as she could on her fingers and sniffed it. Then she wiped it across his two day shadow under his nose. He tried to dodge it but, she got it there, and wiped her fingers clean on what little part of his short mustache she could get, while smiling at him.

"Those pheromones will keep you hard Boy. Works on my wife and Julian and Jordan and Lowana and Casey and Cheyenne. Shall I go on? You won't remember much of this tomorrow, anyway." He grunted at her a long question or statement that he could not interpret, so she told him, "I will get to the wife part soon, Boy. Keep that seed leaking in me for now, Daddy." That was moving one chess piece, and then moving it back to move another chess piece.

"Noah, now you know why she is always comfortable with me being naked, and takes my side when you bitch about me bearding for her. She punks your ass...your so-called submissive Wifey only stands up to you to keep us together and stimulated. Understand that Noah? Emily is completely sexually submissive-worse than Julian, and will argue to get sex. Any other day, Julian would get Jordan to argue it, not Emily. That is how I can read Emily so easily. She never wears clothes at my house. Never covers up her ugly scarred-up boobs to me because she knows we have real love. She lets me suck her nipples." She tossed her hands in the air to add effect to the story. "I accept her the way she is, a midget. Even with that midget mound of Venus bovine vagina of hers. I learned to love her thick side. And that doesn't mean I don't guilt her about being fat to help her. I do my

128

pokes to keep her in submission. She calls it nagging but, if you're fat, you are going to get poked. She is so easy to poke." She busted up laughing rocking him a reward. "Get it." Her face lit up with excitement. "Emily-My lifetime Ho, is easy to poke." She busted up laughing again as he just stared at her.

He tried pulling his legs up to buck her off and the rope held him down, so he jerked his hips up in to the air and just fucked her harder. He was trying to flip her onto the floor. That didn't work but, she enjoyed it. Finally, she leaned down and rubbed her cock-rubbed face on his and licked his lips

"FUCKING BITCH!" He barked.

"Man up, Florida." She barked back as she delicately tried to get him positioned directly on her External OS, just at the tip of her cervix. Intense orgasm could be found there and she loved it jarring her ovaries. Jarring the ovaries gave a woman the added pain necessary turn an orgasm into an explosion-orgasm, when the timing was right.

He finally spit it out, as if making another move on the chess board. "You know what? If you love her so much, why do you call her a midget? She is five feet tall, Stupid...and an eighth of an inch. She insist on having the eighth of an inch in there, even if it isn't true. And I have yet to agree with you on anything ugly about that Angel. New York Cunt."

"Fuck you, Noah. I got her naked at age twelve, Noah. She rubbed her button but, she never rubbed it long enough to orgasm." Chuckling before she said it, "She was like-'I thought I was going to pee-pee.' So I got on my knees that first time we met, pushed that cow pussy into my face-YES she had a big ass then too, and licked her into my world." Jenna reared her head back and shook herself into orgasm all over his cock as he thrusted his manhood deep into her wet

recess. Panting and glowing, she looked down at him with big eyes.

"Did you feel that? That story gets me every time. Big black cock pounding me and I just go back to that first taste of Emmy and her screaming...me holding her down...forcing her to let me finger her, and it gives me orgasm every time...and the black dick fantasy always helps."

"Hate to tell you but, you're on white cock...Stupid. From Wyoming...Stupid." He said with satisfaction.

"Fuck you again, Noah. I forced that pussy into my mouth ten times a day after that. I knew I was a lesbian, and I had to convince her that my pussy was much better than any dick. Every day after that, I had her stand against the Mellow tree with her hands behind her back and licked her into bliss. I...I...would make her sit on my face with that big pussy and hold her hands so she couldn't change her mind. Is it Nellow tree? That doesn't sound correct."

Text from Jay: Chipotle. Usual. No rice.

"*I made* her be my satisfied victim and made her love me." Jenna reared back and leaked on the base of his dick with that story. "God your dick feels good, Noah. That was huge orgasm. Maybe you are a real Angel." She took a deep breath and kept riding him. "You see what I am saying, when she lets me have my way with her. Your God is so powerful, he sent me an Angel and I defeated her. In college, I worked her into Slut mode, and let my friends enjoy her...for the right price. Some Angel." She pumped his dick really hard and squeezed it
as she moaned out the pleasure of her abused little, vagina. "Stupid Zealots."

130

Chapter 10

-DP Makes the Rules

"Our wife was the biggest Ho in Luckenbach County, Noah. Not just the shortest but, like college, she never said no to man...Well to be honest, she did but, would offer to Witness them masturbate. She never fucked them...so she said...But somehow, she always got their seed in her." Her eyes went up to the left as she thought, "I think maybe I could forgive her for that." She chlicked at him with a smile and a quick glance. "After all, she is my wife, and I do like watching men use her. AND! Our bodies do need male seed."

"I mean really? How hard is it to suck a guy dry when you both masturbate together? Let me tell you, it's easy. She loves watching men masturbate and always offers to lick it up afterwards. She watches you whack-off daily for her dumb 'Chalice' game-and that is part of your religious control over her." She reached out and smacked him across the chin, playfully, but intentionally to emasculate him.

"Simon, by the time I left Texas, she was the best call girl in Texas-JUST like college and Med School. She didn't charge a dime, drinking ten-fifteen-twenty teenage boys a day after class. A DAY NOAH!" She stopped rocking his cock and held both hands up to exaggerate her maybe, exaggerated story. Guys would circle jerk at the Nellow tree into a cup for her and she drank it dry. 'She would finger it into her pussy. She called it the 'nude Bible study.' Guys and girls...even me. She would lap up every girl who wouldn't lap herself up." She chuckled, but didn't seem

to dwell in the memories like she had before. Noah watched for the clues in her projecting.

"Yes, I know. I was jealous but...I loved her. I needed her. She could do no wrong ever again. She rescued me from my father making me feel her motherly love. She always, always, ALWAYS made me hold her hand with her hair in it. I kissed her ass for her and never have stopped. I worship her Noah...in the name of your God.

"'That's about the time she started rubbing her clit with her hair for God's praise and promise. And in Texas, that long hair is worshipped by men and women and your God. I knew that and you didn't." Taking a pause from her crazy story, Jenna started bouncing on him harder. She knew he could not keep it hard much longer. To stimulate his mind with his thick, hard cock stimulating her wetness, she rubbed her natural essence on her fingers, tasted it for him very slowly as he watched, and rubbed it all over his face as he twisted to get away from her. She repeated this until her pussy was dry. He grunted and growled like Julian when she is angry, and Jenna chuckled to tell him. "Emmy did that growl as a teenage whenever someone wasted their seed. And she still does it today when I tease her about wasting my seed at home, when she is not there. In truth, I always have a dick or bitch or two for me in the waiting room." She looked at him curiously, and asked, as she squeezed her cervix against his pole. "Do you like pain, Noah? Like...like Emily does?"

Jon was ready to get this shit over with, and after eye contact, he looked away without any words or subtle clue. "Don't pull that trigger yet on your Florida meat, I haven't even talked about Simon and how many times she let him rape her. How we shared his seed regularly, Noah." She sat back up on him with

132

a shitty smile. Like a woman who had the gossip on someone she was jealous of, and was ready to tell everyone in front of that someone.

"Every summer Noah, she went back to Luckenbach County and the ranch-hands lined her up. She was fucking those Mexicans in the name of your God. She brought me to their guest house and the word had spread she was back in town. I admit, it was nice to be used with her again." She chlicked again to him, moving those chess pieces around his King.

"Luckenbach, is not a county...Stupid." The expression on her face changed quickly, as his King slipped away from her chess pieces, and she realized her fumble. Professional on cock, she kept up her pursuit with more stories to help him let go of the woman they loved.

"College was no different. She couldn't stop masturbating outside like when she was younger, and the crowds grew. What devotion in a Slut that claims she is an Angel? Huh? It's no different than most of us women, to be honest. We try to hide our dirty desires and truths, even our numbers, and sometimes, religion is the perfect way. I get it. She tells the world she is Angel, so when she spreads her short, fat thighs, it's in the name of religion." She laid her flat chest down on his tight stomach and worked her hips up and down. Feeling the pressure inside her love canal, she watched his eyes roll back as she shook his thick confidence. Her seed had thickened up, and began building up at the base of his shaft. She loved how she could feel his thick urethra working against her perineum.

"I know she kept all of this a secret from you, because I helped her hide it. Julian is nothing more than an IDentifY personality, and Emily is the real woman, and Emily would have 'Bible studies' without

133

the Bible, in dorm rooms and just masturbate with everyone that is how she was the Callgirl on campus. PRAISE JESUS! That some of the boys masturbated in front of a computer screen or she would be even more thick today from all that protein. And she was a Callgirl for any Black guy. Especially Black guys. She got wet anytime she met a Black guy, like she does when she sees Marines in their Dress Blues uniform." She watched him closely as she worked it faster, and new he was hurting. She kept her tight bun working the center and bottom of his shaft to keep him hard, but avoided the tip to push him closer to orgasm. When she saw the pain on his face, it made her smile.

"Bible Studies were a nightly routine for her...you know...to help people."" She grinned really big when she said it. "Sure she quoted the Gospel while feeling strangers pumps his seed in her. I could have cared less of their sexual needs. I had my own needs to get fulfilled."

He tried jerking away to make his eight inches of warm, sticky cock pull out, and it slipped right into her ass, and she jerked forward before it got in too far. "WHOA! Cowboy. Not that hole, Boy." She sat up on his thighs, as he gave a deep sigh of relief instead of release, and took some deep breaths as she watched her fingers not fit all the around his shaft. She liked that, and stroked him before letting him back into her wet world.

"This is a fascinating story, Rachael. It really is. Stupid fucking LIES! ALL OF THEM! Julian has never been a dirty HOOOOO! Like you and-"

She precipitously punched his balls and instantly, his mind went abrupt and sucked on the oxytocin it released, and he was unable to further his denial or communicate it. She smiled out of the side of her mouth. Power over men is intoxicating and even better

134

when oxytocin drips slowly into the mind of a woman riding thick cock demonstrating her power. When she hit them again, he screamed out his pleasures and throbbed his cock squirting small puddles out of his tip. She punched his nuts three more times and he recognized her Girl Power.

♫ Text Alert

Sitting back on his dick, she lifted her knees to her chest and spun around. He screamed out in pain, and she let her legs fall off the sides of the bed facing away from him in a reverse cowgirl position. She started tapping his balls and hoping he liked the rear view. She would get every drop from him now. "Cowgirl positions could be put to good use when necessary...like raping a man I have always hated, Noah. Do you like sucking dick, Noah? I think you're a closet Catcher, Noah. Emily told me about your gay period in Florida, Noah. You like it in the ass too, like me? And uh...She told me you did, Noah, so don't be ashamed." She smiled knowing he couldn't see her. She was attacking him from the rear now, literally, and reached for her phone.

Text to Rach: I love you so much. I hope you are having a good time GF ♀.

After reading it, she had a very big smile. It was befitting the moment, as Rachael had slept with every guy she dated before Noah, and used it as the wedge to end the relationship. "Pretty good excuse using the Bible to feed her love of semen-her public nudity-her sluttiness-being a Callgirl for religious reasons-all her fetishes that forgot to be mentioned in your stupid

Bible. But, I do thank God that the Bible doesn't forbid Lesbian Love." She chlicked at him with a wink over her shoulder. Now me Noah? I didn't sleep around like her. My Dad was a gifted orator with the Bible and a damn good fuck." She took a deep breath and let it out and held his balls between her thumb and finger and flicked each one with her middle finger to hear his painful moans.

"I actually believed he had the right to fuck me. That it was my duty to please him because my mother had died. He fucked my like a boy one night in my ass. Fucked me like a bride the next night in my pretty little dress." She reached down and fingered her clitoris and held onto his big balls, and rolled her eyes back. "DADDY DADDY DADDY FUCK ME DADDY OHHHH—" She sucked in her last breath and bounced on his cock and let Daddy rock her world...again. Jon, leaked repeatedly in her as the sound of her satisfaction made his natural instincts want to seed her.

Letting go of his balls for her own needs, she quivered and pulled her nipples as hard as she could bouncing on him, and finally screamed when she let them go. Jon instantly realized why her nipples were so long. He liked it. She got those about five inches long that time.

"OH that was sooooo good Noah. Daddy stories fuck me up. I love them when I'm wet. Not so much when I'm sleeping alone." Her hands rubbed her face as she worked to regain herself, and took some deep breaths.

"Where was I? DADDY! Like you, he was gifted with a gallon of seed each day. To be honest Noah, his tasted better than any man. If there is anything about him I miss, it's his dick and his seed...and his roughness...and preaching during sex." She punched

his balls lightly and timed herself with each gentle punch.

"To make you feel my love." By Garth Brooks, Noah. Emily said that was our song. I fucking hate that country twanging shit." Getting her cognitive function back, she lifted her legs and turned around to face him again.

"I loved the way Jordan used to speak before she started fragmenting and bleeding into Alibis. She didn't have an accent. Accents are racist and she sounds so...uneducated in the moment. You know? Jordan has been crashing for a time now, and we have patched her over and ov- YES I KNOW! You are just a man, and haven't a clue what Emily and I are talking about. Julian will fragment to and have to baseline to Emily. We will have to start with a clean slate in her mind."   Seeing he was staring at the ceiling and not her, she reached around and slapped his balls. "GIVE ME more Florida seed, Boy...MORE! I need me an Angel Baby." As if she was in a conversation with God, she threw her arms into the air, "PRAISE JESUS! HALLELUJAH! Give me that Queer Angel seed, Noah. PRAISE THE LORD AND FIND SALVATION RIDING COCK!" She put her palms back on his stomach and leaned on him as she fucked him.

"Black cock can't seem to impregnate me. Unlike our fertile Emily whom has had so many abortions that I lost count. I really did! Black guys still knock her fertile eggs up, even when she is on birth control. She doesn't want any more kids I guess. She got on birth control right after Zachary. I write her prescriptions." He rolled his eyes at her and she smiled as he steered them away.

"College was the best time of our life, Noah. Endless sex with men and women...more intense sex. Sunbathing nude-especially Emmy. She won the camel

toe of the year award every year she was there. Every one saw that pussy. She let people take video of her and photos like it was a Ho party. If they were Witness, she did not let them fuck her....sometimes. I give her that credit. I recall her letting guys fuck her at Witness...sometimes-the Black guys. Many of them squirted in her fat cow pussy and she would pull them big lips apart and get it in her. The Black guys she let shove their dick in her to finish, though. And she let them in God's name, and guilt over her White Privilege but, mostly they jerked off and put the head in her to finish. And to be honest, I would give anything to put a dick inside her and feel what that monster pussy of hers feels like." She fell back to her memory for the moment when she imagined being the man in Emily.

"My Emily...most caring women in the world and blessed them with her pussy. Bitch, thanked them for their cum. 'Encouraged them nerds not to be shy. She was a real cumdump, Noah. I didn't need the Bible as an excuse. I am an empowered modern woman, Noah." She looked at him to make sure he heard her.

"Ten guys would cum inside your sweet innocent wife and she would finger it out to eat. I prefer to leave it there. And I got jealous of it. I admit it. That semen kept her high as a plane. She would cuddle me, make love to me, and answer the door to Witness anyone, and go down on me with Simon's seed in her mouth." Jon stammered in disbelief. *That is total bullshit* he thought. *Total projecting.*

He had enough and began thrusting her to end the fucking story and she started slapping his sack screaming and he tried to fight it but, her slaps were too painful.

"Do not do that, Noey. You know, she started having sex with anyone as long as they were not white men like her Daddy...like you White Boy Taco blend.

138

Indian, Iraq, Egyptian, it was okay. Not really that good. But Black...that shit rocked my pussy and ass. It is the right thing to do after years of racist oppression. You don't know this because of your White Male Privilege but, my Emily-your Julian, does. Our big secret is, we will fuck any Black man that asks. Our rule is we will never say no to them. Sound familiar, Noah?" She twisted her hips on him again and put the bottom of her feet on the bed and her knees up and worked his dick deep into her sweet spot. "I hope that cock is hurting like hell, Noah James." She said with an evil grin and he spoke up.

"Fucking anyone other than white, eased our guilt, huh? You have guilt for being White? I love your self-imposed, ignorant guilt. While you chase Julian, who is as white as a ghost." He said it, feeling he swung back a little before he lost the fight.

"Noah, Emily never says no to you about sex...and never says no to dark, Black men either. I never say no to a Black men or men who remind me of Daddy. YOU! Told her she could never say 'No.' But YOU! You forgot to tell her that only meant you and I." She smiled and chlicked with a wink at him. "Emily loves Black dick, Noah, and I Bet you held that Bible to her heart and asked her if she ever fucked a Black man, and she smiled and lied to you. She fucked all the Black men in Luckenbach, Noah. She would visit the homes and each man in the family nailed her fat ass then made her fuck the horses."

Noah began chuckling at the stupidity of her insanity, so Jenna began grinding her ass bones into him to remind him to stop laughing. She needed to see some emotional pain from him, and if she couldn't get it, physical pain would have to do.

"Emily and I started doing this 'thang'...we started letting guys have their way with us...In the

139

name of God, of course. Hell, Emmy held her hair and her Bible between her legs when they fucked her from behind. She said it kept her pussy and ass tight for them. I didn't but, she did. God is what she cried when they fucked her in the ass. She literally cried the whole time because it felt so good." Jenna turned sideways and dangled her feet off one side of the bed. That boney ass would put some grinding pressure on his balls and squeeze out the juice. "I will never understand why God would bless an Angel with her beauty if she wasn't supposed to use it?" She stared away in wonder, like a child staring at a balloon that floated away.

"Funny story Rach, Julian does not like it doggie style...Stupid. Or being on top...Stupid. Julian doesn't like anal sex...Stupid. But, Woman-up and keep doing your job of pleasing this man. It is what you're used for, isn't it?" He paused for the moment to let her prepare her remark, only, she didn't respond with a poke. She came back feeling gloomy, and he picked up on it.

She was looking down at the ground now as something saddened her. "I was used to getting it in the ass." She shrugged her shoulders, "I like getting it in the ass." With her bipolar moving back up, she looked at him quickly with and rushed to speak with excitement in her voice. "Tomorrow, you are going to fuck me in the ass, Noah. Wonder if I will be your first since my wife refuses you access to her big sweet pale ass. Your name is on it but, you are not allowed to touch it. She doesn't deny me her 'ghetto booty,' Noah."

She purposely ground into him and he started squealing and adjust himself to relieve the pain. "We so love double penetration, Noah. I praise Jesus when two men fuck me at the same time...like Emmy. Hell, it

was last month when we said we had some research study to go to." She chuckled at his ignorance. "Holiday Inn time and Emily and I both got us some DP. Black dudes are very easy to get if you're a White woman, Noah. Emily has gotten picky with them lately...the darker the better for her. Me, as long as it is Chocolate, I will give them a vanilla shake. OH MY GOD! I LOVE THAT SAYING, NOAH!"

He cut in quick, "I guess that is part of your White Female Privilege, Jenna...or do you fail to see that? Getting Black men so easy is Privilege...Stupid." That was a good chess move.

Staring at him from the side with a stale expression, she bounced a few times to crush his balls. "Why am I telling Noah all this? Well it's simple Noah. Your marriage is over. You don't even know your real wife or her real name. I've kept her medicated since college, Noah. Dissociative Identity Disorder, Noah. Multiple Personality Disorder, Noah. Majoring in Psychology, I picked up on her not remembering things I watched her do, and constantly talking to herself. Confusion and anxieties. When I read her diaries, I knew right away, I had a new toy to play with. Started having fun with her. I fucked with Emily so much when I learned to recognize her other personality, Julian."

"Now, I keep her with just enough anxiety to need me there to keep her medicated. Learned that trick in school when suddenly Rachael was getting ignored for Tango. He was the Mexican she was doing...one of those Catholic Mexican boys she was drinking. He was a favorite...well hung that boy. Pre-Med student like us. Damn he could get deep. He started to get control of her and like a good wife I am, I put an end to that. One good pounding from him and a rape kit with a few tears and he was gone. One rape

141

accusation and he was gone." She snapped her fingers to show how easy it was

"He fed her needs-he would tie Emily down and rape her over and over and she wore her favorite red pillow case. Emily got hooked on that shit BIG TIME!" She exaggerated it with her hands again. And the semen addiction I carried over into Julian's programming. It kept her needing to drink my seed too...had to really." She looked back to the floor and kicked her feet out and watched them. "Her addiction to semen was-is so bad it had to be used to control her anxieties-her depression. I worried about trying to divide 'his' and 'hers' modular but it was not possible."

Looking over at him, without a grin or combative expression, she seemed to say something honest. "Rape fucks this shit up though, Noah. Really fucks up the Dissociative Identify Disorder Cover, we use to create our work personalities. Simon crashed Emily's real world, and now you crashed Julian's-her real multiple personality, and for that, Noah James, my magic cunt is going to crash Jon. We have worked on it for years, Em and I. We can't get things stable...or embedded into the mind strong enough to tolerate the chemical change, in the mind, that rape brings. The traumatic effect is just too, PTSD."

She spun around and put her knees up to face him and rested her chin between her knees got serious, with a dick deep inside her. It was almost as if the dick was boring and memory lane was better. "Double penetration ruled Emily's life for years, Noah. You never knew it. Emily, nearly flunked out of college because of it. Even Med School she had to get men to rape her. It was every now and then, then every week. She dropped the Bible Witness bullshit and took it in the pussy and ass at the same time, straight from the tap. Simon was one of those regular 'Strangers.' Of

course I helped her get into it. Thank you. That was how I proved she wasn't a real Angel. Just a stupid hick from the backwoods. Easy to play, easy to use. Even I encouraged her to act like she was in Texas again and not wear clothes in public on campus to get men to talk to her and I would offer her up for DP. She was stuck in the woods, I guess." She stopped looking at him as regret seemed to walk in on her. "I went topless occasionally when we laid out in the sun for everyone to get horny and come chat and get the invite...Emily would see the guys coming to admire me and we saw their erections...funny story, she called them 'the Waiters.' GET IT? And she smacked him on the belly and bounced laughing at herself. He took a horrible feeling to it, because Rachael doesn't kid and Andrea was almost modest.

"Get it, Noah? Guys bringing us drinks as we sunbathed. It was funny, you had to be there. I love her so much. Bless my Emily." He stared at her eyes above her smile and she raised her brows up and down at him to interfere with his diagnoses. "Emily is her real name, Noah. Bet Mr. Angel didn't know that one either. Did you? No seriously, did she tell you about her multiple personality disorder?" He shook his head and she stood up and sat over his legs to suck that sore and very patient, dick. "Some fucking Angels you two are?" She loved the taste of her own warm pussy juice on a stiff cock. She started by deep-throating him to suck it dry and used the heel of her hand to lightly pound into his sack. When she pulled up, and playfully shaking and smacking herself in the face and rubbing it all in her face, she winked at him and her eyes glowed with real passion for sucking cock. "Julian was her DIDC to shut Emily down so Julian could take control of her- the real multiple personality disorder she has had all her life. But, you

raped her. You traumatized her cover and PTSD fucked it all up, and in comes the Crash as a result."

"Welcome to Stranger-Danger sex, Noah." And he perked up watching this new stranger, named Jenna. Those words sounded familiar to him. *The words of a wife looking for a good time,* he remembered. She slid it down her throat over and over and came up smiling joy for her self-punishment, and his moaning approvals. "I am much better at giving head than Emmy."

"I remember, I came home from class one day...skipped by Emmy for a day of pleasure, and there he was...Simon fucking her up the ass, a cute African dude under her pounding that cow pussy and her screaming and begging for mercy and begging them not to stop. Simon was good fucking. I had that a few hundred times-like-many hundred times myself. He seemed to buy that story because she slowly stopped stroking him as she drifted off into space to watch the memory. "God Damn he could fuck and last-like you today. Indigo is drowning from that memory."

Taking back to stroking him she spoke up with a grin and rubbed his leaking seed around her mouth, "Emily had a...a...pillow case...her red pillow case over her head. The trick was, she didn't know WHO was fucking her and that made them a real Stranger. Sure I invited anyone and everyone I knew. SHE ASKED ME TO. She asked me to get men from the internet and not tell her anything about them. No Angel would ever Ho like that and that is how she was a Callgirl, and I got paid. Simon choked her with his blue bandana during DP." She slid his throbbing cock back down her throat real slow, and tightened it as she went up and down, making sure the bottom of his head got rubbed

144

really well. His entire body winced again, and again, making her tingle.

Her throbbing Boy-toy inched closer to the point of no return as she worked his balls with her palm and when his lungs couldn't hold on, she came up to give him air. "Emily found heaven in this Stranger-Danger double-penetration by complete Strangers. The guys on the dating apps loved her. Suffering from his blue-balls, he was getting pissy, and worried she would leave him tied up and no happy ending.

"So dumbass, she posted ads and you made money pimping her. Sounds like no one wanted a Stick to fuck, like you, and only her fat ass...Stupid." He smiled at his own poke, and looked at his cock, trying to lead her back to sucking it.

"NO! Guys wanted me, but I preferred women, and Emily needed Stranger-Danger to rape her stupid Angel-pretending ass. She had found her place in life and God had provided her with everything she was getting-on her knees. I usually ended up getting DP, too. 'Kinda cured me of my jealousy. But now, we need your seed for one more Baby. My Baby, and away to prison you go. Or leave her and the kids AND take her mother with you. Hell, fuck her mother a few times and maybe you will like her better. After all, you like them fat chicks."

"I'm sick of your control over Emily through her other personality, Julian. You are disposable in every way-all men are! Emily and I have planned this, and we want to be a couple again, and men as the occasional third wheel." She stroked him minimally to punish him. "We will Crash her back to Emily and Diddy meds will keep Julian away." She sucked one of his balls into her mouth and he kicked in pain as she forced it around her mouth with her tongue. "Pain is good, Noah. Pain is always good."

145

"Simon fucked it all up though, when he violently raped her. Emily crashed hard after the rape, and Julian's other personality gained control-and then reading her diaries, I understood her real disorder and now you have fucked that up violently raping Julian. This now gives Emily the chance to regain control of her mind and body." She smiled really big at him, hugging his cock to the side of her head, "Emily and I set Julian in motion to have you do to her what Simon did...AND IT WORKED!"

"It will take time to work her Diddy Meds, like after Simon. We took a year off before Med School and counseled every day. We worked to rebuild IDentifY to protect Emily through Jordan and Julian kept appearing. And this will sting but, let truth be said today since you are impregnating me. Ally is Simon's Baby. Emily refused to abort her when she learned it was from her favorite Stranger-Danger Rapist, and Simon was going to be a sperm donor for me, without him knowing, and my tits would finally grow. Emily would be our mom at home, and I would breasts feed and pump with her."

She climbed back up and put him back inside her warm wetness, and he started thrusting her to ease the pain inside his cock. "After our Baby Noah, which you will put in me today, I'm going to Transition to a man after the child is born. I need to be the man that she wants. What do you think of that?" Her Queen would soon, capture his King.

He was finally returning the pleasure as she worked to give her what she wanted. He couldn't drag it out any longer, and with hands cuffed to the bed, he would not be able to jerk-off his blue balls after she left. Like a man, he took it when he could get it. She began to babble, and stimulating his cock, most, if any of her words, would ever be heard.

"Yeah, I abused her at the beginning to prove she was just an ignorant brains-washed-zealot-fake-fat-Angel-dumb-Hillbilly but, she won me over by junior year. I started to move on and couldn't go without her. I really finally figured it out, I was meant to be her man, only I wasn't born a man, and as I a man, she really is my soulmate. I deserve to be her man. She will not have to hide her Lesbian shame anymore to her hick mother and family and our kids and her stupid religion. She hates people knowing she is a Lesbian. Fucking Bible upbringing guilt's her." Her bipolar flared into her again as she looked at him with pure hatred over the religion angle, and he she started riding in rhythm with him to give him a great fuck.

"I really hate your guts, Noah. Raping her, you trigged' false-memory relapses, and worse, YOU FUCK! YOU BASELINED HER IDENTITY BACK TO JULIAN! GOD DAMN YOU! YOU ONLY CRASHED HER A FEW TIERS! MOTHERFUCKER! YOU FRAGMENTED HER ALIBIS AND I DON'T HAVE THE SONG KEY FROM HER YET! GOD DAMN IT NOAH! SHE MAY NOT EVEN REMEMBER IT NOW!"

"You destroyed years of false memory blankets from Emily sessions after the first rape. 'Least you can do is give me a Baby for her. Rape trauma will bleed memories to false memories and eventually overcome them and BAM! Instant Julian." She nearly growled her words out now. "I want the Emily I control, Noah." Shaking in frustration, she reached under her, and wrapped his balls around the front of the base of his thick shaft and began hitting them with her fist. His girly voice carried his moans as the painful pleasure pushed him to a milking orgasm on her uterus.

"Emily still wear that blue bandana on your headboard during sex, Noah? That was Simon's choking tool. He rode her. He didn't call her fat like

you do. Always telling her how fat and ugly her tits were and her fat cow vagina. You always humiliate her about her weight. Her big rear. Her drooping breasts, her fat arms and legs..." She watched him clinching his teeth and grimacing in severe pleasure pain, as her anger rushed her and punched with every word. "YOU MOTHERFUCKER I HATE YOU! EMILY IS NOT FAT NOAH! SHE IS MY TRUST AND MY LOVER!" She pumped his dick and squeezed it with everything her worn-out pussy could give to steal from him. "YOU MOTHERFUCKING WIFE BEATER! FUCK MY PUSSY NOAH! FUCK ME FOR JULIAN! FUCK ME FOR MOMMY! FUCK ME LIKE A WHITE BITCH DADDY! GET ME PREGNANT YOU FUCKING RAPIST! DON'T EVER TOUCH MY WOMAN AGAIN!" Jon jerked back into his bed screaming in pain as his gift finally, squirted into her powerful pussy. Of all the people, she got to have his seed. She shoved his face back by his chin and milked him dry squeezing her cervix and grinding the head of his cock against her amazing Indigo.

When his screams died down, she let go of his balls, and fell next to him exhausted and he jerked his hip knocking her off the bed.

"You Bastard Goat Fucker," she yelled. "That hurt." She flipped over on the floor and got on her back with her knees up to her chest to help the semen find her egg. "It won't be long now, before I get my baby and my rape kit done...unless you want to make a deal now?" Noah lost that chess match.

Noah's head laid back, unable to escape his reward system. "I wouldn't fuck your mother, Sticktwig."

When she jammed a hypodermic needle into his thigh, he jerked up at her trying to kick himself away screaming as her thumb pushed the drug into his system. He was still tied and cuffed to the bed as he

jerked and screamed in real fear. Smiling at him, the sedation worked its way up to his heart, and with real fear in his scared eyes, they slowly faded away and closed.

Chapter Eleven

-Lovers IDentifY Only Seen

Jay sat on the toilet with the door closed and the lights off. Sitting there nude with her IDentifY mirror and staring into it. She kept quiet, not even moving her lips as she focused on the reflection. Peering into her own windows, back and forth and back and forth, she searched for her real identity, and never spoke. Deadpan expression. Not even smirks, she gave herself for fun. She could only figure out that she did not recognize herself anymore. That was her face, but in her eyes, sprouted someone she feel she didn't recognize.

Finished peeing, she just sat there staring at herself in her IDentifY mirror, again with her age old question that came to be necessary from time to time. "Am I really an Angel?" she mumbled it at the mirror and the person in it. "All my life, Momma and Daddy have told me I was, and I guess I need to know...for real. Or reassure me that I am." She looked up and spoke, "Please God, answer me."

Gently touching her face, she could see the physical results of her demise. Both eyes sunk in purple and black around the bottoms and one more bruised than the other, above her eyes. Her left eye was drowning in red around her blue iris. It was a very blood red. When she looked at her other eye, it was the same. Both scanned down to her breasts and she palmed them and caressed them testing for pain. Gently, she pulled her large band aids off to see the scars again. She rolled her fingertips across her nipples and tried to remember them before the knifing.

150

"Crooked, uneven scars," she whispered in OCD frustration.

She was thankful she could still breasts feed, though one worked much better than the other one. Her fingers dragged along the shape of the bottom rubbing across her areola scar and she appreciated that her nipples still pointed somewhat forward. Regret filled her heart, having denied Noah access for so long, because of her insecurity. At best he got to feel them in the dark. She remembered seeing porn on Noah's computer of women with similar sagging breasts and he seemed to really like the natural look. She smiled a little after the thought. She liked looking at porn herself. After all, nothing in the Bible said she could not look at internet porn. She especially liked watching amateur couples do it or men masturbate with the camera placed just below their erection. She chuckled because she could not watch the end as most men wasted their seed for the camera. Her memory brought back a video of a man who laid back on his bed and curled his own cock over his face and drank his own seed. That made her smile. She wondered if she could get Noah to do that for her. *"Noah?"* she thought, remembering how much she missed his voice. His manly scent. His mild manners at home that secretly let Julian be in charge of him, yet he was the boss. His loving smile in front of other women.

Realizing how much trouble she got him into, she slowly teared up, and watched her tears puddle in her own eyes in the mirror. *The same eyes Noah beat when he raped her,* she thought. *The only time, he ever hit my face.* We will spend a lifetime together now, she thought as she nodded to the mirror in agreement. *He really owns my soul now, and I will show him the woman who had always been inside me but, bound with huge fears from a man named Simon.*

I want him to have me. Instantly, she felt the power of not feeling the fear of Simon, but realized, maybe she feared Noah, now. She began to worry about the first time she would see him again, and how important it would be to recognize what she felt. "I will not let our world end," she whispered. "And if I fear him..." She looked deep into the mirror, "...than I..." she read what her body reaction was telling her, "...than I will give myself to him. He is my soulmate and it turns me on so much to fear him and control him." She smiled at herself for saying it so she, Emily, Julian, and any Alibis, would know.

Standing up to look in the big mirror, she placed her hand on her stomach and imagined herself pregnant again. "Some Angel? I can't even get pregnant, again." And she looked back up at God. "This Angel is tryin' her best..." She grinned quickly..." and thanks for makin' Noey try so hard, so often. It is my favorite part." And she gave God a wink looking back at herself in the mirror for reflection simpering. The full nudity exposure took away her smile as she waited.

The smile would slowly come back as her mind worked her future, she didn't need words for witnesses. She knew how she felt. This would be their summer now. Her smile faded to a smirk as she added nine months to this day, and bounced over to other days with the math. She was figuring out nine months prior to the Texas Independence day. She wanted every one of her children born in Texas, and maybe, Texas's Independence Day. "It is very important for Angels to be born in Texas," she said to herself in the mirror.

The nurse knocked on the door, and Jay opened it for the nurse and stood back and just stared at her.

"Are you alright Miss? It's Theresa, your nurse." the Nurse asked. And she opened the door the rest of the way to see what was going on in the little dim room. "Ma'am, are you alright?"

Jay just stared at her putting the IDentifY mirror up in front of Theresa, so she could look into her own eyes. Bent over looking around, the nurse stood up and glanced at the mirror and then looked at Jay in confusion. Neither one moved, they just stared into each other's eyes. Julian began gathering data through Theresa's body language and reading her windows.

"IDentifY," Jay whispered to her and shook the mirror quickly.

"Excuse me, Miss?" Theresa asked, as if Jay said something offensive.

Jay whispered to her again quickly shaking the mirror, "IDentifY now." Theresa stared at her after hearing the instructions, and interpreted her command. She looked into the mirror to play and stared for a moment as it crept up on her. In seconds she leaned back with a look of unbeknownst expression on her face, and looked up at Jay's glaring eyes again in question. Jay instantly knew, she had seen it.

Theresa looked back at the mirror and spoke softly to them, "Oh dear God." She backed out of the doorway and trotted out of the room. "The Piper will not lead her to reason," she whispered to herself leaving the bathroom projecting the nurse's furtive grimace.

Climbing back into the bed she was beginning to despise, and laid on her blankets and grunted at the nurse at the station. Jay ended up rattling Noah's spurs to get her attention and finally waved at her. The nurse clicked the radio on her lanyard and called for someone to come.

Digging her precious Noah's Ark into the bed, she was completely exposing herself again, and put one of Noah's boots down there and began pushing the tow against both sides of her swollen labia. She purposely avoided the button gifted to her by God. "1 Corinthians 10:13" she whispered to Noah's boot.

When a different nurse walked in, she stopped quickly and just stared at Jay. She didn't look at her working Noah's boot into her sore crotch. She stopped to admire the woman wearing a blue bandana over her left eye, and a very colorful red and blue one open for reading, and a mouth full of all her hair, twisted into a rope. Jay was looking down at her boot and making the best of her tool with both hands. Her workable blue eye hid behind her long, gorgeous black hair reducing her cute pale freckle-less pale-blue face, marked with a dark bruised eye under her red and blue eye. Her long black hair streamed down across her pale, white glowing breasts and stomach, and divided by her thick, pale thighs hiding her thick pale and wide rear, as her knees kept apart to work her therapy boot. Samira was struck by her beauty and stared at her openly, even though she was normally shy. Jay glanced up at her and warmly smiled from behind her hair with her eye as much as her mouth. The feeling was instant...for both of them. Samira shook herself with embarrassment and looked away removing her own twisted rope of hair from her mouth as she stepped into the room. "I...I...I...um...sorry that I...I...st...stared at you like that." She glanced back to look into her eye again for confirmation of hearing her apology. Looking away when she spoke, "I'm Samira, w...w...w...one of your nurses today." After feeling more comfortable having introduced herself, she glanced repeatedly to watch Jay rub herself in her labia with a cowboy boot. "Are you...um

154

mast...mast...masturbating?" And she stepped back to leave the room, as she watched Jay's eye for an answer. Jay shook her head and waved the nurse to come closer so she could hear her whisper through her clenched teeth. Jay leaned over and spit into her empty diet soda can.

"In case I accident orgasm...I need a witness." Jays said, whispering through her teeth, and smiled and nodded hoping she would understand. The nurse looked down and watched for a second before looking around and seeing if anyone was watching her watch. Smiling at Jay very warmly, she nodded to her smiling and blushing, and walked to the edge of the bed to block most from seeing her do it. In a quick thought, she turned and closed the door, and nervous, she stood at the edge of the bed again.

Jay laid her head back and spread herself farther apart for more than one reason and starting bouncing the toe of the boot off her swollen vulva. She tried to make sure she kicked her labia and avoided her opening. *I'm so glad I don't have labia minora,* she thought to herself...again. The painful look on her face matched the look of painful pleasure.

"Does it hurt?" the nursed asked pulling her face back a little as she watched. Jay wobbled her head from side to side and then shrugged her shoulders. The expression on her face told a very different story. She was not making her way to the land of Big O's. Samira looked around and leaned in closer to give her an assessment.

"Are you usually this...f...f...f...full in your vaginal area? They are enlarged and much discolored. Is this normal for you or from the 'accident'? The vulva and lips...are they usually full." Jay nodded. "Wow," the nurse responded...." My compliments to your...day," she stopped herself from offering a personal

155

compliment, and "...strategy. She is very plump and a uh..."she cringed when she said it, "...ver...ver...very nice Vulva-that is a compliment." She rushed to speak of something else, to shut herself up. "I'm sorry about what happened to you." She leaned in to get a better view. "The bruising extends to your, mons pubis, hypograstric, umbilical, and inner thighs." The nurse looked around quickly and whispered, Yo...yo...you...your wife...told me what hap...happ...happened. I won't tell anyone." She smiled to apologize and sympathize.

Jay said thank you with her lips, and started to kick herself hard with the boot toe and hit the wrong spot and stopped abruptly. She exhaled her breath after holding it the entire time. She palmed her mound and moaned in pain-and wishing she could moan sound. The nurse looked at the window to the hall and grabbed a rubber gloves off the wall box, and walked over to the side of the bed and put it on. "I'm going to check your urethra and if you don't mind, look under your vulva hood. Your vulva is very purple."

Jay nodded warmly accepting the inspection, and put the boot beside her on the bed. The Black nurse needed both hands to spread the top of her curtains apart just below the mountain. "She looks good under there, and...avoid the urethra above your vaginal canal. That dirty boot could give you a U...U...U...UTI....I'm going to insert my finger under your mound to check for yeast infection. If...if...if...it hurts please tell me. I am not inserting my fingers in...in...in...in to your vagina, but at...at...the very top under your mound-there should not be any pain." Julian nodded recording her manners, thick, dark hair that hugged her shoulders, her very white and pretty smile with full lips, wide shoulders, brown golden skin, and her very beautiful brown eyes with eyeliner that

156

worked. When she leaned down to stare into her Texas gift, Jay admired her dark cleavage and how big her breasts were. It was as if she was honey colored with a layer of powdered hot chocolate sprinkled over her undertone. *She is very beautiful, and kind,* Jay thought.

Slowly, the nurse's finger went in and her knuckles from her other three fingers stopped against her labia. She made a fist and inserted her finger the rest of the way. "Do...do...do...do you have any pain or burning right now? She asked being very careful. Jay shook her head no. "Well...hum..." Samira was trying to find the right words for the situation, "I'm sorry, my finger is not long enough to reach the back." She glanced up to Jay and back to her bruised vagina. "I will need to use my hand. If you have any discomfort let me know." She smiled nervously as she nodded at Jay, and slowly inserted all four fingers in a straight, vertical line. Her eyes widened as it swallowed the knuckles of her fist and half of her palm. She finally felt under her mound and asked Jay if there was any discomfort. Jay stared at her eyes, reading her expressions, and when her fingers rubbed Jay's clit gently, she noticed Samira blush and glance at her. Jay was smiling and nodding, even when she didn't glance at Jay. Both of them knew her clitoris had hardened, as Jay acknowledged to herself, her attraction to her.

Samira carefully pulled her fingers out and smiled and pulled her glove off and tossed it to the trash. Jay exhaled, not mentioning that Samira's presents had increased the blood flow back to her vagina. "Very interesting method you have to physical therapy...um...um Doctor? I'm sure your wife will be happy when she is back to work.
When...when...when...when..." Samira blushed and

looked away and pretended to mess with the equipment to help her say it. Standing very stiff, she got it out quickly. "...You're back to work." She was more nervous than the patient, Jay recognized. Samira smiled politely and let the air remain silent in the conversation. She was appreciative Jay was not acknowledging her stutters and quickly, Samira turned around to ask, "Are you really a Doctor, like your wife?" Jay nodded her head with a big smile. "I have a friend...my friend's brother is taking meds to transition, and you...you...your...wife is the first woman I have met transitioning. I think you make a very cute couple."

Jay's expression went from smiles to concern, and waved at her to come close and talk to her. When she got next to her, Samira seemed to shake nervously and avoided eye contact. "Rachael is transitionin' gender?"

Without looking at Jay, but looking at her spurs, Samira answered her, "The small...small..." Samira put her hand out to demonstrate Rachael's height, "...blonde non-binary?" Jay reached up and put her hand on Samira's hand resting on the side rail. Samira avoided eye contact again, when there should have been some. Jay waited for her to look at her and did not let go of her hand.

Finally, Samira looked at her and did not remove her hand from Jay's soft touch. "You are very beautiful, Samira. Very beautiful woman. Thank you for taking care of me. Please be my regular nurse?" Jay purposefully looked into her eyes searching for her soul.

Samira glowed nodding and put her other hand on the hand Jay was holding her hand with, and shared her bright smile through her dark full lips. Jay returned the loving warmth with her hand and smile.

158

"I love your manners and how genuine your speech is to me." Samira smiled even more, and finally spoke.

"OKAY! I like that idea." Samira was blushing red through her brown skin, and her glowing spread all over her body movements. Jay glowed back with appreciation. "Can I get you anything else? Water? Diet soda?" Jay nodded and pointed to her diet soda and smiled. Her new friend Samira walked around to the side of her bed and leaned down to quietly be heard. "I respect your sexuality and the rules of your relationship that you and your wife have set. If she can't 'Witness' you touch yourself, I will be happy to. My name is Samira...and...and you know that. Just ask the nurses for me but, don't tell them why." She smiled feeling more confident in herself now, than she did ten minutes ago. "I really do like your relationship rules. Maybe you can tell me about them when your voice comes back. Maybe tell me...me...me...more?" Jay gave her smiles and nods...in real appreciation. "Now let me get that diet soda...Oh and more band aids for your breasts? I saw those you had them on and I know where they keep them." Jay nodded really fast for that answer to be seen. When Samira walked out, Jay smacked her thigh forgetting to ask for breakfast burrito and brownies.

When Jay woke up with the spur between her legs and to Rachael kissing her on the lips. "How is my Emily girl?" Rachael went down for another kiss and Jay just gave her a quick peck on the lips. Rachael felt slighted, and stood up reading her eyes. She was trying to reach for the spur and whispered to her.

"Emily is good. Please get the spur." Rachael handed it to her and Jay started to tie it in her hair and Rachael stopped her.

159

"I'm going to pigtail you and brush those luscious locks we have." Rachael started petting the top of Jay's head and brushing her hair with her hand. "Give me a minute in the restroom and suck on it before I brush it because you know the rules Emily, no sucking on it while I brush it." Rachael leaned down for another kiss and Jay let her have a solid press.

When Rachael walked away, Jay grabbed for her Copenhagen and packing it with her forefinger smacking the lid, and making a popping sound. Six packs with her finger and it was time to pinch. The pending taste that always reminded her of Texas made her salivate. When she put the can down on the table, her water cup handle had been moved, and turned it so the label faced her.

Rachael came out of the bathroom nude and Jay could see the track marks on her left arm near the elbow. There were five of them. When she got next to the bed and presented her nude-self, Jay whispered, "Jenna always curtsied for me." Rachael smiled and curtsied for her in an oddly feminine way. "You are shootin' up, Rach. What is it and don't tell me some stupid lie. That is not 'shots' Rach. That is injection sites." Rachael covered the inside of her elbow and rubbed it. "You only had a few the other day, now many more. Talk to me now!"

"Alright Emmy. I have decided to transition a little. I have to get blood work done just about every day and shots every day. It's not fun." Rachael looked away and showed concern for one of Noah's boots in the bed and adjusted it. "I'm trying things out...slowly."

Jay stared at her with one pretty eye, and slowly peeled the bandana off revealing her damaged eye. Both could now take in the reading. Rachael spoke up after not really doing anything to the boot, "I wanted it

160

to be a surprise. I knew for a long time I was in the wrong body. In Med School we agreed that one day I would do it and be a couple. You remember. I used to wear the strap-on toy to class and dress as a man."

"I see you dressin' down now. Yer not wearin' dresses. You have always worn dresses as Rachael and Jenna. Jenna would not do this to herself. You are wonderful and beautiful Tomgirl, don't wreck yourself for somethang that can never really be." Jay hoped she could feel her love through the raspy whisper. "Get your breast done Rachael. Get them bigger than mine but, do not mess with your chromosomes. I love them just the way they are. I want a pretty girlfriend. Not a manly girlfriend. Am I making myself clear?" Rachael turned and walked away to gain distance so the whispers would not carry far enough to hear them.

"I know what I am doing. I'm a doctor, too. I know what I am inside." Rachael felt her flat breasts with her palms and spoke. "I will never change these because I know how much you like them. You need them to stop Simon more than ever since he will be up for parole in a few years, and now I keep you safe from Noah coming and raping you again. My tits are your beard, Emily. Understand that." Jay looked at her flat tits and then down to her exposed vagina. Rachael fingered herself and slowly brought her fingers up to her mouth. A ploy to make Jay's eyes come back to hers, and it worked. Rachael tasted her juice and reminded her, "And she is for your pleasure."

Jay stared at her slowly shaking her head, and Rachael moved to unlock it and got her brush and went behind the bed and pulled all her hair through the top rail and started brushing it. It was the best way to avoid the conversation. Jay untied the spur from her hair and submitted to her. "If you had breasts, you would not feel this way, Jenna. I love

161

kissin' your long nipples. Get a boob job instead and wipe away that insecurity you have been managin' your entire life." Rachael jerked her hair on purpose.

Jay grabbed her phone and quickly sent Noah a secret message.

Text to Noah: Rach singing for code. No wings.

Quickly, she covered it up by laying it face down between her legs. Rachael saw it and assumed it would be to Noah yet, made no effort to really get close enough to see it. "Why don't you use the mirror for me, Emily? The mirror is right there. I can make a few calls. Get a few friends to hold us down tonight. Get some good college boys for DP." and she chlicked at her twice. Jay pinched the side of her left breasts twice to cancel out the chlicks poking her OCD, and enjoyed the stimulation of the hair brushing. This was a lifelong ritual, and a very intimate gift for her to let someone brush it for her. A gift only few people in her life now, get too enjoy.

Reaching for her Bible, she listened for a degrading comment from Rachael and did not hear one. Jay opened it up and prepped herself to pray. She reached for some of her hair and brought it around. She inserted some of it between her right labia, her mouth and her fingers as she prayed over her Bible. She was happy she could whisper so she could be heard by only God.

"I thank you Lord for your salvation and gifts. I pray for your guidance and those of the world. Protect Noah from harm. Protect the children from evil. And please give guidance to Andrea. I can't praise you enough for your gift of Texas and Wyomin' and the love they share on earth through Noah and I. Bless his seed shan't I waste it. I will work harder at my Angelic

duties blessed upon me. Thank you for all the men who have privileged me with their seed. Your gift of life is our happiness." She smiled to herself with that one. "Please protect the children and the parents whom struggle to feed and clothe them. I shall obey my husband and the word of-"

Rachael yelled out, "Thank the Lord for double-penetrating and your love of RAPISTS, Emily." and she jerked her hair to get her point across. "Chlick. Chlick."

Jay stopped and looked to the side without moving her head and a scowl on her face, and continued, "I shall obey the commands of my husband, provide for my children, please care for baby Emma in heaven, hide Emily from everyone, and I will follow my duties of God. 1 Corinthians 10:13. Let my crown grow again for his honor and to be closer to you, and let my Envelopes remain sealed-and please, please help me find my Daddy's wooden cross and weddin' ring. I don't want to be wrong and Noah know it. In the name of God, Amen."

Whispering to herself, Jay confessed as she closed her Bible, "Crowded in my head, now it's gettin' crowded in here."

Rachael tugged at the base of her new pigtail, and asked if it was too tight. Jay shook her head and Rachael retreated from hiding and finished up the other pigtail. Jay was already peeling her round band aids off her nipples to let them breathe and wash them. She gripped her breasts like an experienced breastfeeding mother and presented her nipple as if she was feeding the baby. She felt the warm fluid leak out and onto her belly. Slowly, she looked up at God again and put a rope of hair into her lips to whisper and not to Rachael, "Genesis 1:28. Don't be teasin' me Lord."

She felt the need to talk to Noah, so she sent another text hoping for a response:

Text to Noah: Notre amour livrera nos circonstances ensemble. ♥♥♥

Rachael gave her pigtails another look from the front to make sure she was at her cutest. She adjusted the one on Jay's left side and stepped back for another glance. When she went to sit down. Jay tried clearing her throat with much pain but, enough to get her attention. When Rachael looked back, Jay snapped her fingers at her, and waited. Jenna and Rachael were confused as Jay was sending out another text.

Text to Noah: Please snowball with me, my I♥ve.

Jay stared at her angrily and held silent as she put the phone down. Rachael was not sure what she wanted so Jay snapped her fingers again, and pointed to the floor. Rachael looked down and still had no idea what it was. "Do you want me to sit on the floor, Emily? I don't want to sit on the floor. It's cold."

Jay snapped her fingers one more time and stared. When Rachael put her arms out having not figured it out. Jay reminded her, "Curtsy me before you leave my presence, Jenna." Rachael was horrified she had forgotten and quickly gave a Courtesy dip. Jay chlicked at her twice. *This fake roleplay as Jenna to get control of my feelings, is going to be fun today*, Jay thought.

CHAPTER 12

-Master Uncucks the Cuckquean and...

Jay got her spurs and tied them into her hair again leaving her bandana off her eye. Exposing herself to everyone intentionally, she sat there with her knees up and started kneading her own labia of the swelling and massaging her mound and squeezing. Unsatisfied, she slid down and turned over on her belly and laid her face against the upright mattress. Rachael looked at her oddly and sat down to check her messages with a smile. "Take a picture of my Texas ass, Jenna. I want to see it." Jay slid her legs apart and dangled them off the side of the bed. The nurses quickly came peaking. "I want to see how bad it looks after fallin' off the horse and sittin' her for days. I hope I didn't get a flat butt." Jay shook her ass and it jiggled. "Can I twerk in this position, Jenna?"

"I have to get out of here tomorrow. I am not stayin' here any longer. I am out of here tomorrow, Jenna. Will you take me home tomorrow? Mid-day, Jenna?" Rachael stared at her. Public nudity just wasn't Julian or Jordan's forte but, was Emilys'. She was aroused by it but, this definitely was getting extreme. She had not even gotten up from her chair yet when she noticed a couple nurses making their way to offer assistance...lesbian nurses as Rachael's gaydar started firing and getting defensive.

"Emily. Stop showing yourself to everyone. This is not a dorm." Rachael looked down realizing she was also naked and changed her approach. "I will take one picture of you and then a blanket, Emmy. These people think all we do is fuck." Rachael got up and

took a picture of Jay's huge ass and girl parts from behind.

"Can you see my hole?" Jay asked trying to look over her shoulder.

"No Em, your holes...you never see your holes in that position...which hole are you asking about." Rachael said quickly, and took another picture.

"My pussy Jen. Can you see my pussy hole?" Jay asked again and intentionally used the word pussy to not sound like herself.

Rachael leaned crooked for a second and took another picture. "Emily, your kitty is so fat you can never see your pussy hole. In any position. You never see it until she is spread and because you're so fat there, they never separate unless you're getting some. Why are you laying like that for everyone to admire your Fat Kitty...as you put it?"

Jay slid down spreading herself farther apart to show everyone. "How about now? Can you see my pink inside my black stripe? Or my back door?" Rachael looked around uncomfortably and took another picture. "You skinny cowgirls never know what us big girls know. Fat Kitties give a man more pleasure. Instead of just your hole rubbin' him all around. My huge lips rub his shaft all around...helps pull the foreskin back. Keeps his dick warm and wet even when he is pullin' out of the hole." Rachael's eyes got really big, when she said all of that.

"We get a long stroke and longer nerve ending stimulatin'. Your clitoris extends down into your labia like roots of a Texas live oak. Men can't get enough of a fat vagina. Fat va-jay-jay's are the queens." Jay reached down underneath to try and spread her lips apart for everyone to see her pink wetness, and Rachael gasped. She immediately saw Emily.

166

"Take a bunch of pictures. Especially my ass and thick thighs, I want to see what all my men get to see. Get close-ups of my holes to put online. I want to see how they look now. Get my pink and black in it. 'Come on, my hand is gettin' tired. Finger my ass hole with all your fingers, Jen-Jen." Rachael's hand slowly rested the palm on the center of her chest as she felt validation of her diagnoses of blending characteristics of personalities and alibis. Jay laid flat on her chest and pushed her mountain of Venus into the mattress.

Rachael got close and started taking pictures, and told her, "Em, I can't see your rea hole unless I'm using our strap-on. Your ass cheeks are so fat, they push together. I can see it, and I' m not going to spread...okay, I will to see the bruising Noah did to you, Emily." Rachael reached in and helped her labia peel away from each other and take some photos. When she tried to pry her ass cheeks apart with one hand, she was not able to do it.

"What are you doin'? Spread them apart. Get your toy in there Jen-Jen or grab a male nurse." Jay said unexpectedly.

"I can't do it with one hand, Emily, and your perineum stitches look good."

"Get a nurse to help fuck me. Please...get other nurses to watch, Jenna." Jay said with an annoyance in her raspy whisper. When Rachael turned, two nurses were already watching from the doorway. Both of them came into help.

"Here," Rach said giving one the camera. "Take a picture when I spread her cheeks apart. AND we are doing this only so she can see the damage." Rachael pushed and pulled and the phone just kept clicking. The nurses were chuckling quietly, so Jay would not hear them. When Rachael was finished, she let the two

cheeks crash together, and her ghetto booty jiggled to a rest.

"Jenna. Fill that there soda bottle with hot water and lay it up under my pussy mound."

"Say what?" Was Rachael's response.

"Shove it UNDER my mountain." Jay repeated.

Rachael filled it and slid it under her from behind as one nurse left the room and the other enjoyed the view.

"GENTLY!" Jay screamed and Rachael stopped forcing it forward and more downward and forward as it divided her labia.

"OH MY GOSH! OH MY GOSH! OH MY GOSH!" Jay started wiggling her hips and rolling her mound over the bottle. "OH MY GOSH! OH MY GOSH! I LOVE THIS!" The nurse felt a tingle in her clitoris calling for a rubbing, as Jay's thick ass wiggled.

"Are you cumming, Emily? I'm watching. We Witness." Rachael asked then said.

"NO! OH MY GOSH! OH MY GOSH! THIS FEEL SO FUCKIN' GOOD!"

"Are you going to cum?" Rachael asked a second time.

"NO! OH MY GOSH THIS FEELS WONDERFUL! OH MY GOSH IT WAS ACHIN' INSIDE ME! THIS! THIS! THIS BE WONDERFUL! I HOPE THE NURSES SEE MY SLUTTY PUSSY! OH MY GOSH! JEN-JEN!" Her role playing was obviously taking a back seat to the muscle massaging warm bottle working out the soreness.

Rachael stood back and took a few pictures of Jay humping it and rolling back and forth. Everyone at the nurse's station smiled wide eyed at them. They were not going to miss seeing Jay shift her body one way and her ghetto booty shift in the opposite direction.

Embarrassed, Rachael looked over at the other nurse and spoke nervously with reservation, "She always uses weird stuff to...do things like this. It's her upbringing-Hillbilly, you know. Growing up she used sticks and rocks...trees...just weird stuff." Her voice was shaky and her cheeks turning pink, as she watched and looked away and watched and looked to see if anyone else was watching her watch, and looked away and watched again, embarrassed, aroused, and trying not to laugh. Emily's hillbilly pussy was leaking the clear sweet stuff as her labia wrinkled back and forth to her moans of intense pleasure of oddity.

Jay stopped and tried to get up and slid forward a little and couldn't get off of it. She couldn't even get her boots back on the bed. Rachael and the nurse each lifted one of her legs and Jay rolled over to get her breath and red as a sunburn with a huge smile of intense satisfaction on her face. She was exhausted for some reason...like after doing all the work for a guy in bed, and needing to find the pillow. But if the guy is that cute, and that endowed, doing the work isn't a bad thing.

"Did you orgasm, Emily?" Rachael asked her immediately.

Whispering as loud as she could, with some pain, she said, "No! My Gosh! That gave my mountain de Venus a work out...OH MY GOSH! She was so sore-deep inside her chubbiness. That was the next best thang to an orgasm." Jay smiled panting a little and collapsed on her left side on the bed with just her head and shoulder resting against the back rest. "That really worked out the soreness deep in there. Go blood flow! I thank I could just sleep right here." Rachael facial expression was still one of embarrassment.

"I don't think my little vibrator will help, Emily." Rachael turned to the nurse, "Do you have one in your

purse we can borrow?" The nurse shook her head no and spoke.

"I wish I did." She winked at Rachael and Jay and started to leave. Rachael asked her for one more toy, "Do you have any massagers...very strong ones to vibrate the soreness out of her...areas." The nurse said she would 'looksy.' Rachael stepped over and started taking pictures of her laying on the bed, completely nude, nipples unbandage, breasts laying down her chest sideways, and a satisfied look on her face...just like Emily in college. *Might as well been an orgasm. I love how much fun Emily can be. Not a care in the world, and my Cuckquean is coming back,* Rachael thought.

"Let me see the phone." Jay commanded.

"What?" Rachael asked stupidly.

"Let me see the phone. I want to look at the pictures. Let me see it." She put her hand out for it and Rachael walked around behind her to hide again but, make it look like she was just coming around to the other side of the bed.

"Uh okay, Emily. Uh...let me see here. Uh...here it is. You lay there and be the Princess for me and I will show them to you. I...uh...don't want you to drop the phone since your laying on one hand." Rachael shuffled over to the other side of the bed facing Jay and started showing her one by one. Jay gave her the reading stare...even after Rachael started showing her the pictures. Jay was exhausted from that torment but, not handing over the phone was unnatural in their relationship.

"What?" Rachael asked mildly annoyed.

Jay snapped her fingers at her, and Rachael curtsied to her. It was a role test without words.

"WOW! Is she really that big?" Rachael nodded talking about her curtains. "I love my ass in this

one...it is huge and pretty. Damn girlfriend, my ass looks good...and this one. She is huge. I love my ass. Thank you Texas." Rachael chuckled with her, happy she was distracted by seeing the pictures instead of reaching to get to the phone and seeing a Noah video.

"Emily, when you wear jeans people can see your fat lips pushing out the front and back of your jeans. And you just now realize it's big?" Rachael told her candidly. "Remember, you wear see-thru pants without panties to get men into our dorm room."

Jay ignored her brash comments. "That is bruised there..." she pointed to her ass hole..."I can see it. It's still swollen shut, too. Going to have to fix that soon, Girlfriend." Rachael smiled a little and read into the body language for Emily. "You got one of me on the bottle, too. WOW! That was better than sex. That was-look at her! WOW! Look how thick she is. 'Oh I wish Kitty would stay this fat forever." Jay reached out and zoomed in to see her gifted labia even closer. Taking her own speech away, she nearly failed to whisper it. "No man would ever say no to that, Jen-Jen." And she looked up at Rachael, "or woman. THANK YOU TEXAS!"

After the last picture, she asked Rachael for the phone, and she immediately stepped away and fumbled her response. Jay stared at her, reading into what was and what wasn't happening and why. Quickly, Rachael began to cover her up just where she lay and quickly climbed in with her to snuggle under the blanket. Somehow, the phone was left on a chair near her clothes.

Without a word, Jay let her snuggle in with her. The two actresses found some peace in their war for the moment, and one had her boots on and the other did not. Only Jay had more answers and Rachael had more questions.

The nap only took about ten minutes when Jay heard the sound of her tray table being shuffled. Fresh diet soda, fresh water, ice, and lunch. "Ice is nice" she said to herself. Rachael was not awake so Jay played with her nipples under the blanket waking her up to a smile and they just laid there, awake. Things were too comfortable to move about and oddly, quiet. It was always quiet when Rachael was asleep.

Rachael finally spoke up from under the blanket, killing the mood. She looked at Jays nipples sitting in her face when she spoke. "Are you going to get back to Witnessing for strangers and public masturbation, Emily? You have been getting more control over Julian, and I like it. And we are married, and Julian is married to Noah and Andrea. We may not appreciate you Witnessing and masturbating for strangers, again."

Jay spoke up and Rachael looked at her nipples as if they were Jay's eyes. "No Rachael, this is my husband's Texas Woman's body. He owns it. He owns my body. My hair. My pleasure. My ass. I would need his permission-" Rachael interrupted her.

"I am your wife, Emily, I own it too. I like the public stuff. I love being naked outside like you do. I really love people looking at our bodies, and knowing I am a slut...YOUR slut. I get wet from seeing people's reactions...especially men who can't have what you own...my pussy, my body, and my pleasure." Jay looked down at her head, recognizing the almost Baby talk she did, during Psychotherapy for her Mother Issues.

Jay completely ignored her trying to steal the moment through Narcissism, and went on leading the strategy into a different topic and munching on her burger and fries with one hand. "I am nude and rodeoin' so much to help myself and my vagina. 'Tis very therapeutic and kinda humiliatin' in a good way.

And Noah texted me that I should ask you for help. That is Golden. I could not ask for a better lover than you to help me when he cannot. We help each other in every way, Sister. That shows he really loves you enough to give me to you and trust you to give me back." Jay looked off in the distance to give her concentration to her acute hearing of the response.

Rachael scowled under the blanket. This is not what she wanted to hear. "Will you rub some coconut oil on my Cattle Kitty? She needs it." Jay asked her, redirecting the answer before Rachael could give it, and leaving Rachael frustration unresolved and lamenting. This was intentional.

"Sure, I do this for you all the time. Want a fisting, too?" Rachael got up unsure of what she was feeling and Jay and sat up slowly, and scooted her big butt forward to give her lover more access. The Country Girl from Texas, did not put her beef burger down. Boots on, she pulled her knees up and spread herself wide. The nurses at the station stared at the free show in the midst of their boring day.

"Look at you Emily. You are showing your pussy and your carved-up nipples to everyone...all day. Julian thought you were too fat?" Rachael said in a snarky tone.

"I have permission. And if anyone needs a Witness, I like it." Jay added chomping down the burger as fast as possible.

Rachael started with a hand full of cured coconut oil over Jay's mound and pushed it up to puddle and melt. Carefully, she worked it down her outer labia and to the bottom. Jay closed her eyes and relaxed as she let the last of her burger rest on her plate.

Rachael gathered some of the melting oil behind the mound in the sunken lower stomach and fingered it down under the mound above her clit. "I am going

in," Rachael said to her, as her four fingers vanished completely under her mound. "Em, I love that you have two holes up front to play with. Do guys actually have sex with it...you said they did?" Jay kept her eyes close and her head tilted back against the bed.

"Yeah. Noah uses it as punishment for my sins. I love it. He slides it under my mound, above the pelvic bone, and crushes my clit when he does it. I don't tell him how good that feels. He pounds it and it hurts when he is done and I orgasm about ten times when he does it. That Angel thanks my screams are pain and that is the punishment. I cover my face sometimes when he does it. It makes me cry sometimes because it is so intense...like when I..." Rachael looked up at her as she spread it all through her thick labia.

"Like when you get two men inside you? Is that what you were going to say, Emily? Like when you get double penetration?" Rachael smiled cunningly before chlicking twice. Jay just lowered her head and looked away to not have to answer her.

"-And what do you mean punishment? You always talk about these stupid Bible punishments and I don't really understand your logic of wanting or even letting a man judge you and punish you. How does he punish you? Is this something from Texas or something?"

"Being from the backwoods of Luckenbach Jenna, you should know. All women are sexually punished for their sins. It's wonderful. Thank you Texas." Jay smiled for so many reasons.

"Did you just cum?" Rachael asked because of the Texas appreciation.

"No. It feels really good just rub some oil on my clit. I don't want to cum. This is too relaxin'. Push hard on the outside." Jay instructed her.

174

"Punishments?" Rachael reminded her re-redirecting back to her topic.

"I just do things to make sure I get punished. That's all. I over-hint for sex and when I want him to 'mine my mound.' Works like a charm. I expose myself for him too much and to punish my desires, he 'mines my mound.' Ten minutes of torcher and ten orgasms. I scream most of the time-cover my face in shame. It really does hurt but, in a very good way. I really want Noah to suck up his seed from inside my vagina and kiss me. I don't know how to ask for it. Back off the clit there, Lover Girl"

Having thoughts when the reward system was being stimulated was too much work, so she hushed to enjoy the oxytocin getting dripped into her brain from the light massaging, but intense pain.

"I need a taste of her." Jay told her still sitting with her eyes closed and her face relaxed, as she washed her palette with her diet soda. Rachael slid two fingers into Jay's labia and touched them to Jay's lips. Without opening her eyes, Jay slid her mouth down on her two fingers like Noah's cock going into her third hole. Jay sucked it clean and laid back on the pillow enjoying the taste.

"Much better than yesterday. YUMMY COUNTRY PUSSY! HALLELUJAH!" she said being facetious. Rachael reinserted her fingers and tasted her...and agreed. She gently inserted and swirled them around and fed Jay again...and again...and again...and again. Rachael sucked the fingers each time after Jay. Without opening her eyes, she handed Rachael the end of her hair. Rachael inserted it with her two fingers deep into her pussy canal. Finally, she swirled her fingers inside Jay and sucked a big one for herself. Jay pulled her hair up to her and roped it and sucked on the flavor.

"I don't hallelujah...unless it is raining black men or thick hillbilly women." Rachael said to anyone who wanted to challenge her Politically Correct position.

"Welcome back Rachael," And Jay smiled at her, letting her know, the game was over. "Can I ask you something? Texas Goddess to New York Goddess?" Jay asked her. Rachael responded with an uncomfortable sigh but, expecting a humor based question.

"Sure."

Jay gently took her rope of hair out of her mouth and started, "Why you be so FUCKIN' STUPID sometimes? Your outlook on life changes with the fad of the day...even worse...political fad, and you screw yourself so bad worryin' about what everyone else thanks of you. That is your lack of Constitution and your judgy-ness of everyone else." Instantly, Rachael stopped pleasuring her and tried to think how to respond to the direct confrontation. She knew it was planned, but not what she expected.

"You want to transition to a man, yet keep men as you just noted, givin' you sex. Thus I conclude, you are either really stupid or lyin' your ass off to me and yourself. Good luck gettin' an African-American Man who likes fuckin' little beta White guy that used to be a woman-who only weighs twenty-five pounds and FAKES BEING JENNA!" Jay opened her eyes to read her. "I will not Cuckquean a woman who has surgery to be a man. I won't Andrea 'Rachael' Marie Briggs."

Rachael pulled her hands away from Jay, looking at her, just not in her blood red, blue eyes. She wasn't quite sure what to say to the truth. Without even glancing Jay in the eye, she spoke softly. "You are a masochists Julian and I am too." Rachael dropped any defensive stance she may have had, and lowered her shoulders and arms and chin. Her own words woke her

up. Julian watched her closely, reading every hidden and obvious cue.

Rachael turned away tenebrific, and ambled over to her chair and sat down without any system defensive posturing or griping. She didn't even look up. Instead, she put her hands on her face and leaned over to bury them into her closed knees.

Julian watched closely, as she covered herself with the blanket, and avoiding any shuffling sound in the bed. She quietly slid her boots down and pulled the blanket up to her neck before speaking. "Most women are Andrea. Don't be ashamed of it. Get control of it. Like I did with Noah when he...abused me for me." She paused to let Rachael's thinking give itself time to be heard, and processed. "Noah, is my clutch and you are my Cuckquean. Married to Noah, with two children now, I can't give you the management of your pleasure-pain like I could years ago. You be out of control with the pain tryin' to alter your body to search for new ways to be givin' yourself pain and humiliation. You get naked in public now for the humiliatin' like I did back then. You didn't get breasts implants because you enjoyed the sexual humiliatin' of your flat chest." Jay finally shuffled and started whispered as loud as she could, "I love him, I had to marry him to escape Simon and myself...my fetishes. I was there with you beggin' for more pain with...all those guys and girls. You are a Slut and you want people to know it for the arousin' humiliation. You got that tattoo to feel humiliated and it makes you wet. I'm there with you, Girl. I want everyone to know I am a HUGE slutty southern woman without havin' to say it. I be needin' them to judge me as a tramp to get me aroused, yet still have to show me respect. The Bible helped me escape to the controlled environment of Noah and his rights to own my pleasure. I Cuckold

him to Cuckquean me!" She was a bit frustrated with her friend and the stupid role playing bait they had to play, to finally speak the honestly. "NOAH DID NOT RAPE ME! HE DOES NOT BEAT ME! I FELL RACHAEL!" Jay pierced her lips to see if Andrea wanted to speak and slammed her fist into the bed between her legs to stir up the fight. "If you take Noah away from me, I will take me away from you, BITCH CUCKQUEAN!"

Not a word came out of Rachael open mouth, and she looked back down to the floor. So Jay started again, just more calmly. "You really need to find someone and let them have some control. It can be wonderfully humiliatin', and I know that fucks your feminist brain up. 'Doesn't have to be a man, Rachael. You love women. You love Trans. You love African men. Why can't you have a Black Trans Master and a girlfriend Cuckquean? However you want to mix it up but, it will only work if you give up some control to limit yourself, Girlfriend. You gave that control to me. I kept you urgin' and humiliatin' and I have resisted satisfyin' you and let you go find satisfaction for the night elsewhere...all these years...occasionally I abused you just the way you wanted. But, I kept you cuckin'- kept you humiliated and aroused, hoping you would find a Michael to gain control of you."

Jay started to get a little louder, to get the point across. "I have to go back to my husband Andrea! I want to go back to my husband! I need his ownership over me. I need him to Cuckquean me. I love him. I love him because his heart is good. It is what...it is who I want to control me...and that itself is humiliatin' and such a turn on for me. I am using this incident as a way of submittin' to him, completely." She paused to see if Rachael wanted to respond, but she didn't.

"I love it in public when he man's up and demonstrates his ownership of me in front of people.

178

The humiliatin' gets me wet like nothin' else. I...I need him to keep me in my place. I have evolved and so have my fetishes. I'm gettin' out of control here in this hospital with my public urges again pretendin' to be Emily. I actually want the nursin' staff to come in and watch me rodeo. I need my Noah clutch to keep me in my place." She paused again, knowing she was giving her too much collateral information, and decided to finish and make her respond. "I'm a masochist woman Andrea, and so are you. You need to find someone else to Cuckquean you, and we need to end our sexual relationship...FOREVER THIS TIME...to save our friendship. Get a Master to get Cucked, and find a Cuck to keep. We did it for nearly ten years, Andy." She paused again giving her a chance, before the real heartbreaking started, "I will never give Noah up for you. And right now, this minute, I am lettin' you go for him-AND I HATE IT! And I'm sorry." Jay took silent and watched her keep her face hidden as she cried quietly.

Jay just watched as she reached for a tissue to help keep her own tears back. As Rachael's crying grew stronger, she started rocking and sobbing. As Nurse Samira walked in, she noticed Andrea sobbing inside herself, and Jay gently wiping away her tears to signal her. Jay quickly put one finger to her lips and Nurse Samira nodded quietly and checked the monitor and whispered she would be back.

Rachael reached over and took a large liquid capsule out of her bag and plopped it in her mouth and chewed it, prompting Jay to get curious fast. "What is that medicine? What did you just take? Why did you chew it up?" Rachael sat up in the chair and glanced at Jay through her tears. She had stopped sobbing.

"Nyquil, I have a cold." She said softly while whipping her face dry.

"No you don't. You do not have a cold. What did you take?" Jay demanded with concern.

"Nyquil. I need to sleep. Leave it alone." She sat back up taking her hands away, and leaned her head back on the wall, avoiding looking on Jay's side of the room.

"Do you think you can rub my clit for me one last time Jay...now. Taste me one last time. Please. One last time as your snuggling Cuckquean." Rachael finally looked at her, but stolid for a brief second.

Jay thought about it for a moment before answering, and nodded to her. Rachael dragged herself over to her letting her tears out and climbed up on her and stood on the bed, and rubbed herself in front of Jay. Jay smiled really big, and told her, "I love your 'slut' tattoo. You really are a good slut and I'm jealous." Rachael smiled and Jay pushed the blanket off of her to let her sit down. Rachael sat between her legs with her back leaning against Jay's pale sagging breasts, like a child getting her hair brushed.

Rachael covered them both up with the blanket and whispered. "This is about our own humiliation, not for the nosey neighbors to enjoy." Jay cuddled her across her left arm like a baby and reached down with her right hand inserting it into Rachael's wet pussy. Looking at Rachael, she told her, "I want to see Andrea for this, not Rachael." Rachael nodded and closed her eyes to the intimate moment.

Andrea felt warm, and when Jay pulled out, they looked into each other's eyes as Jay slowly inserted her wet fingers into her mouth and smiled at Andrea. She inserted her fingers again, and let Andrea taste herself. Andrea smiled and they kissed for the last time exchanging saliva and the individual essence they had falling in love with for so many years. Jay embraced her and slid her hand down to her clitoris

180

and began their final journey together as Cuckquean and Master.

Andrea's eyes rolled back and Jay slid all four fingers into her pussy and lifted her by her pelvic bone, and Andrea smiled from the pain. Leaving her four fingers inside her, Jay put her thumb on her clit and worked her fingers in and out and pushed her Cuckquean's button. Both could hear the slopping of wetness and both smiled from the humiliation.

Andrea kept her eyes closed and offered herself to her by lifting her bottom up for Jay. "I love the smell of your perfume and your hair, Julian." Andrea said without opening her eyes.

"Immediately, Jay jammed her fist into Andrea's pussy and she jerked in pain and settle back down on it. Jay fisted her over and over and Rachael kicked her left leg in pleasure and more importantly, pain from her Master. Softly, Jay began to whisper to her while her fist tried to force its way out and back inside. "You are a slut Andrea. Men use you. Paraphilia infected. I love your slutty cunt. I love you eating my cattle pussy. You're a slut Andrea, and everyone knows it. Let Black men use you. Let me fist you. Let people watch you get used. Strangers with big black cocks squirt their cum inside you."

"I'm going to scream." She whispered, barely finishing her words. Andrea squirmed into her last orgasm and Jay covered Andrea's mouth with her other hand to hide her last word. "African cum in your pussy. Black Strangers cum inside your slutty cunt. Let the Daddy cum in you. Can you feel Daddy cumming in you again, Andrea?" Andrea's scream vibrated Jay's palm as her body shook in her arms and instantly, she went limp and fell unconscious. She could not scream her humiliating pleasure anymore.

Jay smacked her in the face with her wet hand and Rachael did not respond. Jay immediately lifted her up and listened to her chest for a heartbeat and then she felt for a pulse. She was still alive yet, her pulse was racing. She slapped her in the face several times and whispered her name, and Rachael dangled dead weight in her arms. She immediately hit the nurse's button repeatedly, and threw her soda can at the nurse's station.

When the four nurses looked up, she waved for them with urgency, and one came moseying in. When the nurse got close enough to her, she whispered, "My wife has passed out for some reason. She took a liquid capsule, said it was Nyquil." The nurse called out on her lanyard radio-phone "Code Blue 626." Jay began to cry as they carried her to the end of her bed. Having shared their last intimate moment together, Rachael always had a knack for stealing the scene.

Chapter Thirteen

-Piper & the Dominion Angel Confessions

Zachary came storming into the room for his Mommy. Behind her was Ally and Mom, carrying flowers and homemade gifts. Jay scooted to the edge of the bed with her blankets under her arms to cover her nudity. Her spurred hair dangled in front of her. The Momma's glow covered Jay's face as they warmed her heart. Zachary was wearing a pirate eye patch over one eye, along with Ally and Momma.

"Can't be seein' the distance in this thang. Here you go my darlin' daughter, be that make everyman smile at your ditties." Momma kissed her on the cheek and then her forehead and between her pigtails. She sat the flowers down and gave her eye patch to Jay, and immediately put it on. The black eye patch matched her hair color and really brought out the blue in her right eye. She smiled big and Zachary was already reaching for his Mommy. "Uppy Momma uppy." Momma picked him up and gave him to Mom and Jay reached out and ran her fingers through Momma's long beautiful black and gray hair. A scrunchie held the thick ponytail on the very top of her head. It was easy to manage and spun around with efficiency. Jay wondered why she hadn't done it in a while before remembering it was more of an at-home look but, maybe it was time to try it again.

Ally ran over and hugged Mom and "R-R-RR-RRRRR" offered her best pirate sound. Zachary and Mom soon followed. Momma took a seat and joined in the Pirate charade.

She pulled out a can of Copenhagen Red and tossed it up on Jay's tray table and got her silver powder box out and pinched a few sniffs and snorted it. Jay rushed to position it correctly, so the label was legible to her position.

Momma held it up before sitting it on the tray table, "Give yerself a sniff. Belonged to yer' Great, Great Grand Pappy in the Civil War. Bless his soul." Jay smiled while playing with the kids. Not like she hadn't heard that story every other day over thirty two years. "This be the right place if yer' goin' be sniffin', the emergency room is close by, Deary." She laughed out loud chuckling to herself...as usual. Momma was always jolly and jubilant. A trait she branded on her only child. As Jay hugged and snugged the children, Momma arranged things on the tray table so it was better balanced.

"Where yer' britches Chicalina? Done run off on the wagon without ya? I can brang you some on the morrow. How 'bout yer' weddin' dress? Listenin' to yer' queer folk, 'might not be goin' back to yer' Noah."

Jay stopped tickling with the kids and looked up at for that one. "What did you say? Not going back to Noah? What did she...when did you talk to Rachael? Why did you talk to Rachael? What is her scuttlebutt? Tell me Momma."

"Your Stallion needs to be gelded. Mare's don't take kindly to whippin's without askin'. If you get my definin' young Chicalina. We don't tolerate mules kickin' the Angels."

"Yes-um." Jay responded. Mom smiled noting the behavior of the kids so they did not pick up on the conversation. "Ally drew a picture of yer, Momma. Gone on put yer' eye patch in it too. Such a lovely little artist, Jaybird. Complete with halo for her Angel Momma. "

Julian immediately spouted the scripture for her Momma, "1 Corinthians 11:10, Momma."

Momma smiled at Noah's spurs in her hair, and pointed as she spoke. "'Been wearin' yer' Daddy's spurs for years now. I took them out before we came in. They are on the truck seat. Nothin' like the sound of man's spurs to bring on matin' season. Never go anywhere without my Angel's spurs, and I still sleep with his shotgun and boots."

In her well-practiced Momma's whisper, "That's so sweet, Ally. Give Momma a kiss. You are the Princess of Momma and Daddy. Your hair is gettin' long girl. You will be a Texas Angel before you know it. Look at this Momma. Passed her Texas caboose now. Thick too. Like me and Momma, Ally. Texas blessed. Let me curry that mane before you get it in your little wings back here." Julian reached for the horse brush to share the love.

"Yes-um." Ally responded. Jay scooted back in her bed to hide her bare backside and Ally climbed up and sat between her legs for a long brushing. The family tradition that inspired Momma to get behind Jay in the bed and start working on her and giving her ponytail crown like her own.

"Are you gettin' your Diddy meds here, Julian? Make sure you are taking them, Deary. You got many of bloomers growin' at the ranch. Who is Mr. Simon? You got a set from him, and a set from Emma. Who is Emma? I know who Noah is...and he best be sendin' more flowers if he wants to be takin' my daughters hand again. I see you took off your rang, Deary?"

"Yes-um, Momma. Thank you. Ally is taking her Diddy meds daily, too. I'm goin' give you a ponytail top like my Momma, Ally. Seems to work for Old-er Angels. Hand me your pocket scrunchie."
Remembering a thought, Jay quickly reached over and

185

grabbed her cell phone and sent a text to Agent Karen Ritzman.

Text to Karen: Give me a chat tomorrow. Temp assign. Columbus Ohio. Get together again Code 9. Thanks. Jordan Taylor

"Did I tell you Jenna got elected sheriff in Gillespie County? Beautiful girl. Her mane is dandy like ours. Husband bought another Gypsy Vanner. Black one with white spots. Like your old Missy Trail."

"Yes-um. We need to get Ally some ridin' lessons." Jay said.

"Get that girl on some piano lessons, too. She told me you haven't been keepin' up with them. Momma got her playin' today. Angels must know music to recognize the Lord's instructions." Momma added.

"Yes-um." Julian offered her verbal courtesy as Ally started brushing Zachary's hair as he scooted to sit between her legs.

"I've been havin' some serious kiddy withdrawals not bein' home with my babies." Jay leaned down and snuggled both of them and gave them kisses on their heads.

"Where is your Daddy's wooden cross he carved you, Julian?" Momma was looking at her chest for it.

"I don't know Momma. It's missin' with my weddin' ring. Rachael is lookin' for it in the labs and ambulance. And I need to call Jenna and see how she is doin's. Last I heard she thought she was gettin' married and she was proposin' with her Smith & Wesson in hand. I love her, but we could never afford to go to the weddin'. But we are goin' back to Texas someday Momma, and you be comin' back with us."

"I just told yer', Concho. Her husband bought a Missy Trail." Momma reiterated.

186

"You are dang tootin' I am. Right Ally?" Ally responded with a smile.

"Cowgirls belong in Texas. Right Momma?" Ally said.

"Yes we do." Jay responded.

"Keep pulling my hair, Momma, it feels good." Ally added to the mix, making the young Momma, give the older Momma that look when they recognize themselves in their daughters. Momma kept tugging it, as older Momma kept pulling Momma's hair. Poor Zachary just wanted to make sure his doll got his hair brushed and was using his Hot Wheel truck to do it.

"Angel Ally, what is the Piper doin'?" Julian asked to show her Momma she is following Daddy's word and teaching her children what they need to know as Nephilim Angels.

"Sure Cowgirl Princess, let me finishin' her shine for ya." Momma started jerking it, getting Ally used to her future needs.

"Being bad, Momma." Ally said while brushing Zachary's hair.

"What is in the tree by the brook, Ally?" And Ally turned to answer her.

"A songbird singin'. Right Momma?" And Momma clapped for her Dearies.

"Pass that spittoon, Lovely." Momma requested and without looking, Jay held it up and back for Momma to spit. Jay sat it back down on the tray table without thinking. "Can't be lettin' the menfolk be knowin' 'round her. Them's the big city hospital and don't be respectin' a patient's right to sniff."

"Where is your girlfriend, Tomgirl?" Momma asked.

"Rachael got sick on some medication. I thank it was an off-brand cold-medicine. She had a bad reaction to it. Rachael said it has happened before. I

187

don't know what is wrong with her lately. Spreadin'
lies to you about the car accident." Jay was interrupted
again.

"Car accidents don't typical requires stitches in
yer' love taco, Bluebonnet." Momma always had a fine
way of getting the honesty rolling.

"MOMMA!" Jay waited for the silence to set, as
she brushed Ally's hair and jerked it. "A stallion and
his mare were drivin' down the road. Maybe the mare
was causin' the stallion to smile too much and steer a
little off the road. Beins' a good Mare wife." Jay
stammered the last sentence out to her. "Could I be
any clearer?"

"Tone my daughter. Of course Deary, Mare put
that Longhorn rear up and blocked the windshield two-
steppin' with four legs is goin's to make you crash in a
hurricane. Deary." Momma explained in simpler terms
as Jay rolled her eyes.

A night of brushing and dodging Momma's hints
and inquiries, the kids filled up on pizza and finally
settled and asleep on their Momma. Zachary was
snuggled onto Mom's chest with both hands filled with
her hair as he sucked on it, and Ally was sunk between
Jay's legs in the cavity of the mattress caused by Jay's
huge caboose. She was holding a handful of Momma's
long black hair to her face as she slept. She had
twisted her own lasso of hair to suckle.

"Momma, will you help me get them to the other
end to snuggle. Momma Jay has to pee?" Momma got
up and dragged Ally to the end and put her own hair
into her hand to sleep, and laid Zachary in front of her
facing Ally, and gave him some of Ally's hair to
snuggle. She immediately roped some of Ally's hair
around her finger, and put it in Zachary's mouth to

suck. He grabbed it and after a few sucks, fell right back to sleep.

Momma Jay worked her way out of the bed and shuffled to the bathroom naked. When she came out, Momma tossed her a hospital gown. "Thinkin' yer back in Texas again? You and Rachael both. You always were one for lettin' God and everyone see yer' goodies. Cover yer' longhorn Johnson hugger. Yer' rear would still make a horse happy to have you ride without a saddle. 'Milkers look very pretty...very healthy. They ain't been gettin' enough exercise, Deary."

"Yes-um. I'm a tryin' Momma." Jay said with curtsy. "I want more babies."

Momma knew her daughter's insecurity about her scars and always encouraged her. Jay smiled when she said it, and covered up the front and turned to let Momma tie the back. "Damn! Noah needs instructions too? Dominion's never seem to be able to read a woman or a book. Makes sense-it's a picture book. Your entire derriere is purple, Deary...and I don't be likin' the tattoo. 'White as a ghost don't be hidin' them bruises at all." She added, to embarrass Jay about her tattoos that her generation didn't see fit on a woman. "Saint Peter may not approve of such brandin'." She added to get her dislike across. "The Good Book does not approve of markins'."

"I have your big Texas ass Momma....and hips...and thighs...and hair...and boobs...and I assume everythang else. Daddy didn't have an ass." Jay flipped her hair around and roped it into a twist into her mouth to manage the anxiety that was coming on strong.

"I need to tell you somethan' about my Dominion, Momma." Jay said to her before sitting

189

down next to her. Keeping her rope in her mouth as she spoke.

"Let the excuses trot, my Deary, 'Trot does the rumor in the night." And Momma, roped her hair with a twist into her mouth to hear the hogwash.

"No Momma. I tricked Noah to get rough on me, Momma. Badly." Momma didn't give her time to continue the story before she gave her an un-shocked expression. "I'm sorry, Momma."

"Deary, I thank you better start thankin' straight if you want a future for my grandbabies and more future grandbabies. That is not the work of an Angel. Beat'en a Texas wife ain't usually a wife's idea...mind you so many of us might be needin' it or wantin' it. Don't be makin' excuses for that lame mule Dominion." Momma rattled on and Jay stopped her.

"LISTEN! Momma. When I was raped before, it was bad, very bad....you know. New studies came out that male DNA lives in the mind of women who receive the DNA through seed." Momma roped her hair again and put it back in her lips to keep her from smacking her with it. "I had Simon's DNA livin' in my brain from his seed. It scared me, Momma. Scared me bad. I talked it out with myself and Rachael, and I couldn't sleep at night. He already scarred me for life and scared me for life. And the truth that he was livin' inside me...for life, scared me. I asked Noah to do to me what Simon did and plant his DNA the same way and kill off Simon's DNA. To plant it on my soul. Do you understand, Momma? Everyone could see the stain through my windows, Momma. You said my windows changed after it happened." Jay asked looking for validation.

"Yeah. Shotguns solve problems in Texas. Otherwise they wouldn't exist. Who sent you sprang bloomers, from Simon or is this a different Simon?"

190

Momma said in her own kinfolk's way. Jay nodded and told her the rest.

"I'm sure it was Rachael. Rachael is so angry she is threatenin' to prosecute my Noah, my Dominion. He is off hidin' from her. She was there when Simon raped me, and I needed her. And now she is coarse as the hair on a hog, that Noah did this to me. I should have told her, but it was kinda a last minute decision on my part. I have told her it is not what it looks like, Momma. I was tryin' to face some personal fears with Noah and Simon's fear got me puttin' me to the backseat floor and I was huggin' the ground cryin' and beggin' Noah to get Simon away from me. Pissin' myself in irrational fears again. You remember my episodes after college-night terrors-screaming and hidin'. I guess it was in my head for a while. Here I am...and let God Bless my Angel. Noah has done somethin' wonderful to me. It worked Momma. He altered my brain chemistry for the better, Momma. I am tossin' around naked here and testin' my Simon fear and it is fadin' about him comin' to get me. It really worked, Momma. I looked in my windows, and the stain is covered. I be needin' to get to Noah before Rachael." Jay stopped to listen and see if she understood her situation.

"Rachael is in love with you, Bluebonnet. Fergot' to mention that part, Deary. That sexual affair gay-gal stuff comin' back to bite you in that Longhorn ass of yers'. Isn't it? You deserve it, Bluebonnet. I warned you to kick her off the wagon years ago. I could see her tryin' to un-shoe your Stallion that last timin' thanksgivin' visit."

"I don't sleep with Rachael, Momma." Jay demanded she believe her.

"Jaybird. Jenna was your first galfriend. Rachael became yer' new galfriend. I saw you and Jenna out

there in the barn. Ridin' off to the wounds gettin' naked. I saw ya kissin'. Touchin'. I could hear love chatter through your bedroom door. I prayed for you and you went back to her for more. I'm sure you did the same with Rachael." Momma smiled with the same pierced lips Jay had. "The Heaven's warned me yer' be haven' a different set of wings."

"STOP—! So back in college we-" Momma interrupted by grunting her throat at her until she stopped the lies.

"OKAY! I had a thang with her and I broke it off." Momma cleared her throat again six or eight times. "STOP! Okay Momma? Yes-um. I had an affair with her and she is really hurtin'. I really screwed up Momma. But it's not what you thank Momma. I just...just...I guess you could say dragged her along with suggestions of promises and occasionally didn't say no to the promises...when maybe I should have. Are you followin' me here?" Jay looked at the kids to make sure they were still asleep. "I love her but, I want it to stop. She is not the Angel I thought her to be, Momma."

Momma gave her opinion, like she had for years, "She is not an Angel."

"I was tricked by the Piper. I thank God has opened my eyes again, Momma." Momma looked at her with her eyes slowly rolling around before clearing up the hogwash in the story, for Jay. As she adjusted her gifted round hips, she glanced up at the Heavens for a hint of candor.

"You and Emily, slept with her occasionally and you were friends. Right, Jaybird? Wastin' seed under God, fails a married woman-you and Emily. Now she has her brandin' kit ready, only you have another brand on your longhorn derriere. Makes sense...outside Texas. Is this the work of the Modern Angel...even a

192

Texas Angel with her Texas gifts, wearing her boots, won't get a pass at the Pearly Gates. No don't look away from me, Julian Michelle. If anyone needs to feel yer' guilt it is you. And yer' Momma needs to clear the hogwash to help you say it to yerself. You were bred to be an Angel of God. Why is that so roughin' with you?" Jay interrupted her, breaking Southern traditions.

"Yes-um-I'm afraid Noah already-"

"DON'T BE TWO-STEPPIN' ON MY TRAIL, MISSY!" Momma burst out against her disrespect.

"Yes-um, Momma." Jay said with a whisper, and immediately shut her mouth remembering her place. Momma, held the floor, and she held it quiet. She pulled out her snuff box and pinched a sniff, staring Jaybird into her social timeout spot.

"Julian takin' her Diddy meds?" Julian nodded at her. "Any arguin' with yer' hair?" Julian looked down to the tile and nodded. "Get yer' meds updated Doctor, then arguin' will take to pasture. Raisin' one daughter is hard enough, so I don't want Emily to trottin' up on me. Savvy, Doctor?" Jay nodded to her in shame.

Momma looked down her nose at Julian, and from her tenure, gave courtesy to speak with a nod.

"Yes-um, Momma. Thank you. I've been havin' our arguments with Noah about Rachael, lately. I hope the good Lord will guide me through this Texas tornado. I have regrets, Momma. Andrea is not one of them but Rachael is. Lettin' the affairs continue is my regret. Design flaws in Andrea's 'Rachael' attitude, has become my regret. I thank she is pushing Emily on me, like she did in college." Momma interrupted her intentionally.

"Is Noah one of them there regrets? Angels should not have regrets? Arguin' with him should certainly be one of yer' regrets, Julian. A wife, even an

Angel-a Nephilim Angel, shall not hinder her husband. 1 Corinthians 14:34 and 7:4." Mom looked at her with experience while flapping her big Angelic wings.

"No Momma. I let somethangs from college and Med School creep up on me, and they are hoggin' at me." Jay said, hoping not to elaborate on things. "Emily thangs, Momma."

Momma rolled her head back and licked her front teeth as she got nervous. "I guess I always knew you were a lesbian, Jaybird. You may not see it but, that Slut branded Tomgirl is a spittin' image of Jenna when Jenna was a teenager. Skinny stick without milkin' bags. Maybe you kept her stayin' because Jenna's DNA lives in your brain. Trailin' me, Missy?" Momma finished showing her handle on her daughter's scientific logic.

"Momma, I assure you, I am not a lesbian. 'Bi' Momma, and I only offer myself to other Angels with Noah's consent. I must multiply Momma...with other Angels, such is Noah, Momma." Jay bravely corrected her.

"Perfidiousness is a better term, Julian. 'Can't spawn with another woman, and neither can our Emilys." Momma tilted her head holding her twisted rope just outside her mouth, and stared to get the point across..."And you must ask yerself, are you Bi tomorrow and the day after? How Bi does the Bible allow you to be? How Bi does your Dominion let you be...when you are not hidin' some of it or all of it, from him. That is a sin my daughter. You need his permission to share your heart, conjugal, and crown and Emily is married to Noah as well, Missy. Somethang tells me, you and yer' Emily, left yer' Dominion in the dark about Rachael, Deary. A subject of the Great Deluge, perhaps? Get your Diddy meds

updated before that sluttin'-trash Emily gets control of you again."

Jay took an exhausting deep breath and let it out slowly. "Okay Momma. Emily and I was datin' her in college and we kept...thangs...goin'...along...only occasionally." Jay stumbled it out looking down to the ground. "I have slowly been lettin' her go, Momma. I swear. She keeps gettin' to Emily, I thank."

"Sound like yer' unsure'in' after ten years? A very slow salvation under the eyes of the Lord, Bluebonnet. And..." Jay rushed in, to speak to keep the words she was hearing less painful.

"I really do want to stop doin' what I'm doin'...I love Andy, I just don't know...I can't understand...Why can't I just say it?" Jay got tears in her eye and smiled at her as Momma drew the clarity out of her.

"Get breathin' and get yappin', Angel." Momma said lovingly, "My contempt is gettin' heavy...Since yer interrupted me again."

"Yes-um. Sorry Momma." Jay looked down accepting her etiquette error again, but had to go on. "Simon's rape really woke me up about my life...how much I got away from the Bible and my purpose. I was really bad, and sometimes I feel like Simon saved me from that life...and I resent him for bein' the one who woke me up and saved me." Jay's red eyes could no longer hold back the wash of tears. "I thank lately I was gettin' out of control again, and maybe...I don't know...maybe...oh my gosh, I can't even say it Momma." Momma stared, slowly pulling the emotional line along.

"Oh my Gosh Momma! My babies, Momma. My baby Emma, Momma." She let herself cry. "I thank...I thank...OH MY GOD MOMMA...I had Noah rape me...like Simon." Her hands rushed to cover her face as she broke down.

195

"I did it to make him put me back in my place, Momma. To wake me up, like Simon did. Like you said about you and Daddy growin' me up. I always do thangs strangely." Momma handed her a tissue for the sobs and handed Jay her long black and gray hair to hold as a lifeline, and waited her out. Jay grabbed her own hair and blended the two together and held them tight, as she had been raised to do. It was what a little girl did in their house when tears had to shed. "May God forgive me, Momma. I tricked Jordan to trick me, to get Noah to be Simon, to stop myself, Momma."

Momma's experience told her a hug would only end a confession. "Ephesians 5:22, my Bluebonnet. 2 Corinthians 11:3-I am afraid that just as Eve was deceived by the serpent's cunnin', yer' mind may somehow be led astray from yer' sincere devotion to your husband-yer' Dominion, as you have submitted to the Lord, my daughter. Yer' have betrayed both, and yer' Angelic duties with that Trough, that you say you, an Angel of God, designed." Momma added, resisting the offer to comfort her any further than the lifeline of her hair that would keep them closer to God, inside Texas.

"I've really confused myself, Momma. My fetishes Momma. My Paraphilia. I've done so wrong to myself and Noah. Noey is my gift from God. I have known that since the day he put me in my place years ago-he is a powerful Dominion. He is my soulmate, Momma. I really do know that. And I'm scared I made him into an Outlaw. He ain't talkin' to me. I ain't knowin' where he is. I know he loves me and our babies. We never waste seed, Momma. I can't get pregnant again and I keep tryin', Momma. I don't know what is wrong. I'm so sorry. He only responded to my text a few times...pushin' me away...It wasn't in his heart by God's programmin'. Somethang went

wrong, Momma." She broke down more. "MY GOD WHAT IS WRONG WITH ME? We tricked him into rapin' me." Jay sobbed in her confessions and their hair. "I threaten to break our Accord if he did not do it." She pulled her eye patch up on her forehead so she could tend both leaking eyes.

"1 Peter 3:3-6, Momma. My behavior shan't win over my husband. I'm failin' him and my duties as an Angel." She buried her face in their hair to continue cleansing her soul to God, through Momma. "I was screwin' around with Andrea all these years. I violated Noah's rights with Rachael. I need him. I want him. I want to have more babies with him. And I still need him to..." She failed herself not finishing this sentence in her confession. "I just don't understand why an Angel needs this much pain and abuse. I'm losin' to sin Momma...again-Momma-College all over again. I can't help what I am and what I need, Momma. I love you Momma...and Daddy." Jay hugged herself shaking and Momma reached out and held her hand that was holding their tear-soaked hair together, and put more of her long salt and pepper hair over Julian's hand, as she held it. More lifeline was necessary.

In a soft motherly voice, "Julian Michelle." Momma leaned in. "Bless yer' heart, Deary. Bein' a woman is complicated. Being an Angel is more complicated. Being a Texas Accord woman is actually less complicated. Being a cheater with guilt is a circumstance only you delivered and more complicated. Us women tend to favor drama...favor emotional roller-coasters. Damn men, even keel it through life but, us women need somethin' more. Our emotions at times are more important than logic and common sense. Men live on common sense because evolution had them doin' the hard work, and common sense developed to make work easier for them-less

drama. We had time at home, and needed stimulatin' so we evolved our emotions. Yer' a modern woman fishin' to battle evolutionary instincts for both sexes." Julian leaned over and cried as her mom gave her a shoulder to shelter on.

"I'm goin' to give you some advice Julian, stop lookin' to lettin' Rachael satisfy yer' husband's duties. Get Emily under control again. Get what you need from him...he is the soulmate you chose to fulfill yer' womanly needs. A good southern woman never asks for it yet, she survives by gettin' her needs met...even if she has to do it herself. Share yourself with your gal-friend but, hold-fast the rights of yer' husband and the boundaries set-forth. You gave him Dominion through Accord. Let the Bible guide you, and give yerself to him again. Ephesians 5:24. Give yerself to God again. Restore your Angelic responsibilities to which you were bred. Don't be sayin' no to Noah or God...EVER! God gave him all yer' rights and you affirmed them to him when you Accorded. Sounds like you have taken ownership of yer' crown, body, and conjugal from him, and that is not our way. This is why yer' so confused now. Get what you need with yer' southern charm, not yer' prescriptions. Give yer' fetishes to yer Soulmate. 1 Corinthians 11:10. That is why the wife has the symbol of authority on her head." Gently, she dangled their hair together to make her point.   "You must submit to him faithfully, again Julian, and follow the words of the Bible and the music. Let him love and own yer' fetishes and manage them with the rules of the Bible. Brang him into them so that he sees everythang, and have his approval or disapproval? Yer' Daddy managed mine as I got...well let's say when I got wild. He knew his duties of a husband by Accord and an Angel. Noah is a confirmed Angel of God, and a husband-let him do his duty to

198

you." She hugged her as Julian sobbed and Momma went on to finish. "You never feel like an honest Brenley until yer' are an honest Brenley. Ask yerself my Angel, why has God denied you another Angel child? Figure that out, and maybe you will see another Angel in your birthin' belly. He knows when it is right and when it is not." Momma snuggled her as she cried out her frustrations and fears.

"When you were younger. I saw you-Emily and Jenna in the barn, naked, kissin', touchin'. You were about sixteen, I thank, and Jenna was floggin' yer' heart of Texas with a long stick. She was smackin' your Texas gift and I panicked. I thought she was hurtin' you. Emily was screamin' the sounds a woman offers when she is gettin' what she needs. I knew then you were one of us Texas women, and it didn't stop there. You abused yourself physically...got others to abuse you. Emily humiliated yerself with yer' public nudity everywhere gettin' what you needed. That bein' said, I know you need pain and humiliation to enjoy things without guilt...It's what you need for yer' fetishes to continue them. It's what Noah can provide you if you guide him properly. You have gal fetishes because it guilt's you into needin' more pain, and that gives you more pleasure. You cannot have one without the other, Deary-and you enjoy both. And that is why yer need Noah to manage them." Momma looked up at the Lord for courage before finishing her story, and snuggling her daughter, "Yer' like yer' mother in every way, Bluebonnet. Gettin' pleasure from yer' man-we want pain in our pleasure to drive the guilt out of our heart. Pain just came to be the way we gifted Longhorn women paid for our sin, and o'how we love to pay for our sins."

♫ Text Alert

"Momma, I never owned those toys you found-when you took me to the Pastor. I was hidin'em for Jenna. They were not mine, Momma. I thank you for savin' me from the sin, Momma. I never told you that." Jay got it out through her tears feeling as if the peak of the misdirection had been corrected.

"I know they weren't yers' but, Pastor Davis sure saved you from shamin' yerself to God, and yer' future husband." She remarked candidly.

Momma nodded remembering that day. Julian listened, cried, and hopefully understood, she was not alone in the mess, only she had violated the fine lines everyone has in different locations, and forgetting where she put her own lines. "Trust in the Bible as yer' guide. If it ain't in the Bible, you can do it. He can do it for you. You must study the Bible and note what yer' fetishes can and can't do and take them to Noah. That gives you many a ways to enjoy the pain, Deary. But, give yerself back to your husband-yer' owner. Put him in charge of yer' needs as prescribed in the Bible. Stop tryin' to be the only horse pullin' that longhorn ass. You tied yerself to another horse and two little wagons sleepin' on yer lap, and without askin' it, you have to get the other horse to do what you need as a team. Even I have rid'in' this rodeo a few times and maybe yer' not the only Longhorn here who paid for her sins with my Emily."

Julian's eyes opened wide to that honest comment, and looked up at her Momma in shock. "O'how the eyes of spawn open to the whispers of truth and sins bared by her Momma." Momma muttered. Julian quietly responded, "Yes-um. Thank you for tellin' me that Momma. I don't feel so alone in my confusion now." Jay contemplated ignoring her phone but, hoped it was Noah.

Text from Noah: Divorce me. I raped you. I hate you. I am going to rape Andrea for fun. I am on drugs. Marry Andrea again. Get away from all men. They are Rapist pigs. Remarry Andrea. I know your real identity now, Emily.

Jay read it and her mother watched. She was sobbing again. "NO NOAH! NO BABY! HE WANTS TO QUIT ME MOMMA! HE KNOWS ABOUT EMILY NOW!" Julian buried her face into her mother's chest and their hair blended together as they cried. Looking up again to the heavens, Momma said, "I have provided her with comfort, patience, salvation, unconditional love, purpose, and now protection." She smiled at the Spirit above, "My Angelic duties fulfilled, now it's yer' turn Lord."

Chapter 14

-Spy a One-Eyed Black Snake with Milk

Rachael held the phone to her ear comfortably, as she updated the case to the District Attorney's office. "It's strong circumstantial evidence. She is lying for him. Covering it up."

"Yes."

"He has made violent threats to her that is why." Rachael scooted down for a more comfortable position.

"Text messages. He threatens her daily. Says he is on drugs. I'm telling you. His next rape-HE IS THREATENING TO RAPE ME NOW! Let me talk to her some more. She is very afraid of him and wants to testify against him. She will do a deal, I promise."

The big black cock slid in and out of her pussy but, she just ranted on and on to the District Attorney.

"Fine. I can get the digital evidence done." And she hung up the phone. Rachael sat the phone on the end table of the vacant hospital room, and pressed record for the video.

"'Nothing like big black cock when you're having a bad day, said every white girl with a racist daddy," she said to him with a half-grin. She waved for the Black woman in her hijab to come over and tell her. Her husband, gently slid all nine inches in and all the way out at a pace that kept them both hard.

"What you got, Girlfriend?" Rachael said to her. The Muslim woman began removing her scrubs, and watched her husband fuck the curve-less white girl with a flat chest. "Jenna, the Dr. Stevens and Dr. Oronitz, they both send inquiries to Administrations for a full history of the ICE Patient this morning. Since you

have him cuffed and no guard, they want the police to check him out. I think is more safely concern. If you get guard, they say to be concerned." Her large brown breasts shook as she got her arms out of the sleeves, and she started working her bottoms off.

"Harder Cucky. Lower yourself. I want your dick to come up under my bone here and glide along it behind my clit...there you go. White girl like that. Hit the bone with your dick. Make sure it hurts me." She looked back at the Black beauty, and pointed to her bush. "I didn't know you had a hairy pussy. I don't eat hairy pussy. That is nasty. The bacteria buildup up is too much for my pretty face. Go wash our pussy in the shower and dry it good." The Black woman wearing her hijab, turned for the shower stopping to remove her socks. "You have a very pretty ass. You are built like my wife." Jenna said to her watching her walk away. "Shave that nasty hair off before tomorrow. I want to see that black beauty, not gag on the hair. I only gag on black dick." The husband smiled, seeing his future.

Her lover, slowly ground the head of his penis into her pelvic bone trying to keep it guided correctly. Taking it all the way out and nearly all the way in, he missed and slid into her ass.

"Whoa big boy. Slow that up. You can fuck my ass another day." Waiting for him to pull out, he started to push it in. "GET OUT OF MY ASS! My ass has special plans today. I need your cum for my wife. She needs to drink it with my seed."

Nodding, the dark bull slid it back out and went deep in her pussy again. She grabbed for his scrubs and pulled him close and held his dick in her and scooted closer to him. She jerked him to her right and squeezed him. Squat a little. "NO! Hold on, she put her legs onto his chest and crossed them putting her left

ankle up to his right shoulder and her right ankle on his left shoulder and adjusted her hips. "THAT'S IT! RIGHT there boy. That is my favorite white girl spot. Feel that? Pound that big black dick right there. Make it hurt. Right there!"

Slowly, he smiled and started moving it in and out and jamming the head deep into her uterus. Slow thrusts with a hard last few inches. "OH YES! I could get fucked like this all day." Her eyes rolled back and she just laid there letting him activate the nerves that carried to her reward system. This was the best life a woman could have, she thought. When she began moaning, she had to cover her mouth in the hospital.

His wife returned from the shower and showed Rachael her pussy. She felt her meaty labia and Rachael slid her fingers between her black Somalian curtains and into the pink warm center. Feeling her large clitoral hood with her thumb and she slid her white finger up to the base of it and dragged it along the bottom of her warm, swelling clitoris. The woman shook and Rachael smiled and winked at her. "Everyone has bigger tits than me. I love how round they are, they hang so sexy, like my wife's tits. Your nipples are thick and black. I like that. Smooth and dark skin is nice. I wish my wife was African." Rachael pulled her to sit on her face.

"Black African pussy taste so much better than white girls," Rachael said as the wife climbed over her and gently worked her pussy over Rachael's chin leaving it wet and sticky as Rachael parted her thick bush and licked at her big clitoris hood. Naturally, she put her hands over both her dark ass cheeks and smothered her mouth in her tastiness. Instantly, the Muslim woman smiled, and put her weight down onto Rachael's mouth and leaned forward on all fours and

closed her eyes. Rachael worked her up to pace with her husband fucking her.

"I need black pussy." She said, flicking her lover's pink clit with her tongue to get it fully erect. "My bitch is white and her pussy is pale white, brown, and black on the outside. It's really very pretty how it goes from white mound to a brown pussy that turns black. Black pussy is so beautiful and inside is so pink." Bumping her wet opening against her chin a few times, Rachael's slowly began to suck on her big black clit and felt the little dick pulsating in her mouth.

Her dark female lover started driving into her as Rachael sucked it like a small dick. Her husband's thrusts got harder and drove the pussy deeper on her face. Rachael reached up and squeezed her lover's tits and pinched her thick nipples. Instantly, she began lactating on the bed. Rachael worked to milk them as the woman fucked her face harder.

He kept that dark dick pounding deep into her cervix. She couldn't' take all of it but, her pussy tried to swallow every inch and he tried to give her every inch. Her sweet spot was getting its morning work-out, as her mouth worked on her little friend. His wife dropped her head and quivered her orgasm into Rachael's mouth and she slurped it and swallowed her repeatedly and again and again.

"I never give a White Woman before. I like it. My sister has white girl lovers. Eat my pussy. I shave tomorrow if husband can fuck you tomorrow. I milk for you." She kept in rhythm with her husband, and fucked Rachael's face. The milk was running down the bed and puddling in Rachael's very short hair and under her back. The more she felt its warmth, the wetter she got in her pussy and on her back.

He slammed it inside her and she squealed with each punch of pleasure shimmering up her body. The

wife smiled when she thought about her Black husband coming inside a White Woman, and plotted to make sure, she got more Rachael sex.

Rachael was where she always wanted to be. Getting pain and giving servitude pleasure at the same time to a couple that deserved her reparations. She fantasized about picking men and women off the boat and being their own nude welcoming committee in America. Much like she did minority neighbors that moved into her old Brooklyn neighborhood, and everyone got to have a feel. She was rather popular boyish-girl back then. Everyone was allowed to be welcomed in her book and her legs. She has gotten picky since Med School-honing in on her favorite flavors-anything not white male.

He picked up his pace and pounded her as she watched his wife thrusting onto her face. The three of them moaned out of sync, which added to the sexual atmosphere. The wife's recently pregnant belly roll shook with each of his thrust and Rachael held it with one palm and her breasts with the other. Holding a fat roll during sex was something she enjoyed, and picked at Julian for not having. Her big round butt cheeks shook forward and helped drive her little cock into Rachael suction and tongue flickering as she came again. His wife's vaginal opening just drenched the back of her throat and she created a suction every time she swallowed her juice, and wasn't distracted by having to lick her hole dry and back to the clit. Natural Black pussy juice was her favorite and her foreign lover was exceptionally wet and pouring graciously to meet her needs. Rachael bit her clit between her teeth gently and quivered from her own orgasm that drew, her alright small abdomen, in tight. Her Muslim lover began to get louder and louder from the intense pleasure of her clit pulling between her teeth. Her

pussy gave quake to his long, thick member and squirted inside her pink world as he moaned out to her in a different language. He pounded every drop out of himself to stick to her cervix letting his moans make his wife even wetter. Banging a white slut added a few extra drops to her punch bowl. He pushed Rachael's legs off him and leaned down and started licking his wife's sexy black ass crack.

She jerked and the wife began sliding forward and back for both their mouths until she screamed out again, satisfying words in a language Rachael was familiar with, thanks to the man seeding her. From the shaking, her breasts dripped onto the sheets and slid up under Rachael.

He pulled out and she slid down Rachael's chest and stomach, Rachael instantly began sucking milk from her breasts and spraying the other breasts all over her face and chest as she drank the nectar. Her lover reached down and fingered herself to another orgasm and Rachael felt harmony with her. Her lover came again on her and the warm, oily, milk flow increased. She sat up on Rachael and her nipples still sprayed on their own passed Rachael's head.

"Get up. YOU!" and she pointed to the husband. "Get that shot glass. The wife got off of her, still spraying milk without squeezing her breasts, and Rachael sat up on the edge of the bed and drained his cum into the shot glass. The wife's thick pussy juice was dripping from her chin and she lifted the shot glass up and mixed it in. From her mouth across her face and down, was soaking wet. Scooping up as much of his and her juice as she could Rachael reached for her big black breast and sucked more of the milk in her mouth and spit it into the shot glass nearly filling it. Rachael reached over and grabbed his dick and pulled him closer. She used her fingertip under his dick

207

to push any semen out, still inside his urethra. He smiled when the pain was worth that last big drop dripping into the shot glass. Without a word, Rachael handed it to her husband and pulled his wife back down on her and to feel her breasts on her chest again.

"I'm going back down on this real sweet, dark pussy again," she told her new friend. "I want to go down on you every day. So bring me a report about my Illegal friend, every day."

Chapter Fifteen

-Fat Pussy to Eye Patch Sees Bipolar Winky

In the late morning Jay held the mirror up with conviction, she was determined to get IDentifY, since her voice was becoming a louder whisper, she was enjoying hearing her own voice again. "I love the pigtails with this eye patch. Who knew an eye-patch could look good." She said to herself for fun. "I wonder if Noah would like me to wear it…in bed. I wonder if the Bible forbids me from wearing it." She reached for her phone and started asking it about the eye patch, blind, and Bible. She could not locate anything and steadfastly searched her own memory on scripture. Finally, she texted her man.

Text to Noah: Would you like me to wear my eye…oops. I have an eyepatch for seven to ten days. Would you like me to wear it when we are making love? I think I look cute. Let it be your command my husband and I shall follow. Please talk to me. I miss you. I miss your touch. Wooden cross missing. I am leaving DoctorLands West today or tomorrow. Where are you? I love you so much. I submit to you. ♥ We shall never part ways under God. Mark 10:8-9 Will send nude selfie if you command me? I hope you do. (O)(O) included. Please talk to me.

Jay took to her Bible and held it on her lap with his spurs in her straight, long hair. She inserted her hair into her vagina, in her mouth, and took it back out to spit Copenhagen juice into her empty soda can and placed the rope back in her mouth and clenched it

between her fingers to pray. "Nasty habit." She said to herself.

Rachael walked in carrying a warm shot of someone's semen, and dressed like her old self in a summer dress and heals and a purse to match. Oddly, she was wearing some makeup and her hairstyle was more feminine. She leaned over and quickly pecked Jay on the lips with a rope of hair in them, before she said anything.

"Well, look at you. My how the sun shines where you walk, my beautiful Lady." Jay said it to her with big smiles and even glowing a little. Rachael sat the semen down on the tray table and smiled at her warmly. Even offering a curtsy and a twirl for real effect. Jay was beside herself seeing the old Rachael, back in action. Things were definitely improving for both of them after a harsh talk.

"Did you find a Michael that would marry you or a Michelle perhaps? You look lovely, Rachael. I would love to wear dresses like that only I don't have your beautiful petiteness. You really do look beautiful and dashin'. Nice to see a bright smile on your face." Jay pounded her New York glow.

"I am feeling much better today, thank you. I stopped by the house and what have we here, my former wild friend but, a lovely specimen given by the nectar of man...all for you...his bride." Rachael said with a huge smile.

"I am dyin' here without the regularly two a day. I've been tossin' myself at any male nurse willin' to let me have his juice. I'm serious. I feel the withdrawals...depression, flirtatiousness with just about any man...even lettin' them see my boobs when they walk by. I'm bein' bad but, I can tell when I am havin' withdrawals. I would happily Witness if a guy offered. Noah said in his text, I needed to do what I needed to

do." Jay said with a huge smile through her hair and was happy to drink.

"Hold on there, my Hillbilly Hussy Angel, I think this shot, sense you are leaving today or tomorrow, should go to sweet Fat Kitty. She has struggled and come so far to be...kindly jested...less bovine vulva, even if she is still the biggest set of labia curtains I have ever abused. She has had intense husband therapy and deserves a shot." Rachael said. "Besides, 'might want to go home pregnant. Winky."

"How did you know I was leavin' today or tomorrow?" Jay asked curiously. Rachael, held back the hostage without offering an answer. So Jay assumed, she assumed, it was happening. Jay loved that she was getting back to her old self and wanted to encourage her more. Perhaps the transition conversation put a halt to the shot and medicine. Perhaps it saved their friendship. "Okay. I like that idea." Jay announced. "Can you pour her into Fat Kitty for me...my short chubby arms can't really get the right angle beyond my escape button or under the mountain."

"Sure Sister." Jay scooted forward and pulled the blanket to the side off and when Rachael got close to pour. Jay stopped her. Let me get on my back to make sure it gets deep and every swimmer gets a chance." Getting off the bed in the buff, her spurs rattled at Rachael, and she hopped back on it leaning forward to keep her hair out from under her. Laying back across the bed in her familiar missionary position, she pulled her knees up to her chest and spread herself wide. She tossed her hair down over her groin and moved it to the sides as her breast dangled over onto her arms. Her boots offered some visual protection, yet she got excited thinking some prying eyes would find her in such a sexy, inviting position and hoped they would

peek at her. Rachael smiled as she parted her black-tipped, heavy curtains to expose her opening with her fingers and slowly poured it inside her.

Jay's eyes rolled back into her head when she spoke. "Oh my Gosh. I can feel that. It's cold then it gets hot. WOW! Kitty is thirsty. I can feel my anxieties simmerin' away and my mood risin'." She was smiling at Rachael when she said it. Rachael kindly blocked the nurse's view of any witnesses. Jay started to get up to get back on the bed and Rachael pushed her back down with attitude.

"Don't you dare, Texas Hussy. You need to give it time…maybe even masturbate so your uterus sucks it up. If you want, I can just rub it out with the shot glass. Just a little sisterhood help-nothing to get us crazy about. Some maintenance for your pussy therapy." Rachael smirked and turned her head to the left and shrugged her left shoulder. Julian's mound began to leak down her divided labia, giving both of them a tingle down below.

Nervously, Jay agreed and held her knees back as far as she could so her back stayed flat, and Kitty could get to work getting her another baby. "Rachael Marie, do not be kissing on her. As well as you do it, and I will definitely miss it. Don't do it. Please? Oh and make sure you use the open part of the glass, I want to make sure it all drains onto my clit so it burns a little. I can lick it clean when you are done." Jay's louder whisper inflected her excitement.

Rachael looked around and started gently parting Jay's dripping dark labia apart farther at her bottom opening and slid it up under her huge vulva mound. The entire shot glass vanished under her mountain of Venus. Only the bottom could be seen from Rachael's direct view. "I need to shave her. I'm sorry" Jay offered. Slowly, her finger vanished under

212

the mountain to grip the glass and her thumb went on the other side between her wet, now swollen from the semen, labia. Rachael started working it up and down and getting herself wet in the process.

Jay laid her head back and put a rope of hair in her mouth as her snaffle bit, as she enjoyed the feeling of fertilization through orgasm with her children's Godmommy and former lover. Jay wrapped her hair around her head so she could pull on it from each side to pull the bit deeper into her mouth. She immediately remembered Jenna fingering teenage boy's semen into her when she was a teenager, and both the snaffle bit and Jenna touching her, made her wetness flow more. Rachael started pushing harder but, slowing down the grinding. Jay instinctively widened her legs for her to get more pain and Rachael started talking to her helping get the orgasm there. "Your fat cunt is sucking up his warm cum right now." Jay smiled and her nipples got hard as she held her breath concentrating. She pulled her snaffle bit of hair tighter to feel restricted.

"Your fat pussy gets so wet. Cattle pussy, Jay. You have a huge fat slutty brown pussy with black on the tips like a longhorn steer. You are so fat you cum so much out of your pussy. Guys in college came on your fat pussy lips trying to get into your fat girl hole. You always fingered it in and licked it. Say it to me. You know what to say."

Her chest was panting up and down as her pussy got manually abused, her mind stimulated, and she said it for the humiliation. She had to moan the words of psychological pleasure to make her pussy purr. "I'm a fat fuckin' slut. I let men use my fat pussy. My fat cattle pussy. I love being used hard. Cum inside me Stranger. Make me your fat cunt. I'm a fuck whore."

Jay whispered with her eyes closed feeling her juices flow.

"Strangers fucked you, Emily, and you wore a pillow case...they put their hot cum inside your slutty pussy Emily...they came inside your big Texas ass, Emily. Stranger-danger sex story of an Angel. People watched you get Strangers dick inside you, Emily. They are watching now. They will rape you and let your enjoy the cum." Jay jerked instantly and her tits bounced across her chest and back down onto her upper arms. Rachael kept slowing down and pushing harder until the orgasm died down.

"I'm a whore. Whore-" Jay held her breathe and shook her thick body like an earthquake. Rachael ground the smooth glass into her clit extremely hard. Wetness seeped out of her warm pink hole onto the blanket, and Rachael's mouth watered. She gently reached down and got her fingers wet to taste her as Jay finally let her breath out, exhaling forcefully from the pain and pleasure.

"Oh praise Jesus." Snuffling. "God Bless Texas." And now wheezing. "Thank you, Wyoming." She panted again for enough breath to speak. "YOU SLUT, ANDY! You slowed down and got harder. OH my Gosh, that was huge. Making me humiliate out loud always works." She kept panting but, it was subsiding. "You should be so jealous that was really huge, Rach. Oh my Gosh, it was huge. Semen is like Fat Kitty's crack." Jay looked over her separated cleavage to see Rachael smiling. She immediately felt it leaking and sat up fast. Rachael shoved her back down on her back again, and Jay got nervous quick. She could not see what she was going to do, but felt her touch the glass to the bottom of her vagina's honey spot, and Rachael used it to divide up her labia and fill the shot glass with mixed seed.

214

When she held it up to her lips to drink, she stared at Jay, and asked, "May I Witness for you, Emily?" Jay stared and slowly nodding, reminded her, "It is God's word that you not waste it as my Witness." Jay sat back up and when she dropped to the floor in her boots, a huge spill of thick, white wetness strung out of her pussy and dangled down her right inner thigh. Chuckling with glee, she wiped it off and sucked it off her fingers, happily letting Rachael admire her. Rachael, toasted her back before shooting Jay's seed to the back of her throat.

Wearing only her boots, Jay shuffled to the bathroom. Her ass jiggled and dipped each cheek the entire way and her spurs shook in her hair. The cute eye patch look was still working for her. Her long hair flowed behind her lifting into the breeze her body was making. With a Kitty full of cum, she was getting back to her old self. She liked the feeling of the atmosphere and sitting on the toilet, she started talking to Rachael again. "My thighs are finally rubbin' together again. I really missed that...a lot more than I thought I would. I love my thick thighs." She finished peeing and came back out glowing from the semen intake.

Naked Rachael kissed her again and said, "I really do hope you get pregnant from that. Imagine the possibilities. We can tell everyone how we did it." She laughed and skipped around the little room twirling. Jay just stood there, wondering why she was naked.

"Uh Rachael, maybe you should get dressed from now on. I'm really embracin' this public nudity again because my fears of Simon are gone. I am goin' to let Noah see my nipples...my entire nipples from now on. I was just hidin' from Simon and I thank that fear has passed in my life." Jay was smiling proudly at

her own self-progress and honesty. "Please move that chair to the left a little. It is driving me insane."

"Not today Jay. I'm not nude for you. You were right. I love the public humiliation of my ugly boy-body. I need people to see me get turned on and humiliate me for my little tits and 'SLUT' pussy. It gets me wet and I shaved Indigo to make sure everyone could see her." She through her arms out like she was going to say 'Welcome aboard.' "So what. We are both naked. I want Noah to see my Slut tattoo. And...I have a big surprise for you before I leave. You are going to adore this." She pushed the chair off center, even more, and looked back at Jay to gauge her.

"I guess...okay then. Not goin' to make any difference after three days here. People expect you to be naked. If you're okay with it Rachael, I am too. Now...IDentifY." Jay demanded immediately.

Jay shuffled back to her tray table and held up the mirror to Rachael. "IDentifY now." Rachael pinched her long nipples and pulled them really hard as she walked up to the mirror and obliged.

"IDentifY Rachael." Jay leaned her head back and looked down her nose at Rachael.

"Okay. That is you." She whispered in her raspy pirate voice.

"Now you. IDentifY." Rachael demanded and somewhat playful as she bopped up and down on her toes excited.

Jay flipped the mirror around and looked at herself. "IDentifY Julian." It didn't sound confident and the name was spoken slowly.

"Okay." Rachael said, so wrapped up in her rebellion she failed to notice, Julian was not an IDentifY personality but, the real personality. Julian looked at her, recognizing the bipolar switch from just the day before, she questioned herself whether it was

216

lack of medication, or mixing of other drugs with the
real medication.

Chapter 16

-Melting Tramp-Stamps Have No Alibis

Julian climbed back into her bed and reached for her can of Copenhagen Straight Long Cut chew, and packed it for a pinch. Rachael watched her flip it and listened to the packing sound of her fingers smacking the medal lid, combined with the spurs rattling. "I'm quitting again as soon as I go home Rachael. Don't judge me." She said with a friendly smile and took a pinch to her bottom lip. One of the nurses at the station saw her, and chuckled, as she picked up her phone to send a text about it.

"I have never under why a beautiful rodeo queen like you, would chew that nasty stuff." Grabbing her phone to text Noah, she answered, "I'm a country girl."

Text to Noah: Notre amour livrera nos circonstances ensemble. ♥♥♥

Julian put it next to the coconut oil perfectly placed, and grabbed the jar making sure nothing else on the table moved out of place. It was time to oil up her body, to keep her pale skin, with blue undertones, perfect. When she started spreading it across her chest, Rachael cheerfully offered to do her entire body and asked if she would rub her down, too. Julian climbed back out of the bed and walked to the doorway naked in her boots and looked around. She smiled at the ten or so nurses staring...admiring her

218

country gal sexiness that she could pull off so well in a pirate patch, and with a smile, she curtsied them.

"Okay Rach. Do me first and I will do you. I be feelin' dry on my Texas ass from sittin' these past days."

She walked back and spread her front against the wall and let Rachael begin. Julian pulled the rest of her hair around the front and roped all of it and put it her mouth...as usual. This was a morning ritual that Rachael had the responsibility of doing in college, and then it became Noah's job.

Rachael immediately dug a handful from the jar and started spreading it across Julian's lower back on her tramp-stamp. "Are you going to get anymore tattoos? I think I might start my sleeve I have talked about forever more." Rachael asked and stated.

"Yes. I really want to get some barbed wire...just haven't decided where yet. I have to be getting' Noah's permission first. I don't thank he wants me to get too many." Rachael worked her way up Julian's back and spread it across her shoulders. "Noah makin' me get tattoos, saves me at the Pearly Gates."

"A woman who thinks she is an Angel, is really a lesbian slut with tattoos...at the Pearly Gates." Rachael said to poke at her without poking too hard. Julian completely ignored the snide comment.

"Don't be forgettin' my back fat roll...both of them...need them to be adorable, as well." Julian said it playfully speaking the truth from years of wearing a bra. Rachael's hand rolled right across them happily.

"You are such a Midget, Jay." Rachael poked again. Julian did not like the joke she had heard her entire life.

Efficiently, she got back down to Julian's lower back and slowly worked her jiggling right ass cheek, and slowly worked her jiggling left ass cheek, and

around on her satisfying hips. Rachael suddenly stopped.

Julian glanced over her shoulder and saw Rachael fingering her own vagina, and Julian stared back at the wall thinking. *Her gettin' wet rubbin' me is natural. I'm goin' to get wet rubbin' her...natural, and nothin' else.* Rachael put another handful of cured coconut oil on the center of her 'Pull My Hair' Longhorn Steer skull and horns tramp-stamp, and let it melt against her skin. Julian instantly felt herself get wet when it melted down the crack of her ass, and made her smile.

Also smiling, Rachael's fingers followed it down between her cheeks and Julian's knees got tremors. She was instantly aroused and Rachael reached under and rubbed it between her low labia and thigh, and down her legs. Julian was thankful that didn't last long. When Rachael started again, Julian felt the wetness grow and as her hands rubbed against her brown and black labia. Julian realized this was not a good idea. She was swelling, tingling, and starting to drip. Rachael stepped back and looked at her Julian's ass and dangling labia.

"You have so much pussy, it looks like a big dick hanging down from behind." Julian immediately turned around and Rachael got another scoop in her hand and splattered it across Julian tits before Julian could speak. Julian rolled her eyes and put her arms up to get it over with. Two hospital staff stood in the hallway enjoying the scenery. Rachael started to speak as she rubbed down her breasts, her underarms, and right up to her chin. "Julian, do you remember anyone special we used to...you know...have double penetration with back in school? Like anyone special you remember?"

Julian looked at the nurses, who were listening. "Yes Rachael. Not the time. Not the place." Julian kept

her arms up in submission position as she urged her. *Getting rubbed nude and an audience,* Julian thought. *Drip. Drip. Drip.*

"You had this one guy, he gave you anal most of the time when you wore the pillow case over your head. His buddy would get under you and he did you in the ass from behind." Rachael continued.

"RACHAEL! Not the time." The nurses smiled and stepped away from the door. Julian felt her tension ease a little.

"What about it?" Julian asked through her teeth.

"Did you have a favorite guy who did you in the ass?" Rachael insisted.

"May-be. Get to the point, Sister." Julian was watching the door for listeners.

"I need to know, did you have a favorite guy? You couldn't see him but, you could feel it was him. I did. I got to the point where I could feel each guy and imagine him." Rachael noted. "What about you?"

"Yes. There was one guy. He had a nice...uh tool and always got up on me sideways and shoved it downward into me. He could make me scream easily. What about this? I don't like talkin' about this." Julian reminded her anxiously and hiding her face away from anyone that might look at it.

"Do you miss getting fucked in the ass?" Rachael asked politely, and confessed "I do."

"Some...times." She answered her delicately while watching the doorway.

Rachael bent back up and slammed a melting hand full of coconut oil into Julian's pussy knocking her back to the wall. Rachael looked down at her smiling and fingered it into her pussy, making sure she hit the sweet spot over and over. Julian took a huge deep breath as Rachael fingered it into her pussy opening and swirled around and up over her clit and swirled it

221

around the button. Rachael grabbed one of her thick, meaty labia and kneaded it between her thumb and fingers and Julian's knee gave way but, didn't resist. Rachael kept it going and Julian's knee started shaking with her hand shaking on the wall. The pain made her mouth instantly water and her vagina seep. Rachael switched to the other steak and kneaded her making her knees and both arms shake before the chill ran up her spine. She would get kneaded all day, if she could. She quivered against the wall with her eyes closed fighting back the orgasm. Until slowly, she found the strength and reached down to push Rachael's hand away. And Rachael instantly pulled it away for her before getting it smacked.

"You are all done." Rachael said with a nude, joyful curtsy.

"You were gettin' a little long there on my clit, Sister." Julian said to bend the tension.

"I was getting you aroused up and stopping. Just for fun, Julian. Don't worry. I still have my surprise for you. Go sit on the bed and I will show you. You will love this." Rachael said playfully.

Julian climbed back up on the bed and reminded her, "I still get to rub you down."

Julian looked over at Rachael and waited. She stared at her with her one eye and looking like a mighty fine nude pirate. Rachael sat back in the chair and started with her legs crossed and a deep breath.

"I just want to talk about a few things and I promise. NO arguments. I promise I will keep my temper down. No Alibis. No cold meds." Julian got uncomfortable inside as she shifted and got comfortable outside. She started to pull the blanket up for protection and realized she was already sticking to everything. Simply, she pulled her hair around, and

covered her Southern Lady parts, and roped it into her lips and waited.

Chapter Seventeen

-Adjourn thy Love, Hence, Pleasures Test Faiths

Piercing her lips nervously, Julian nodded from her hospital bed for Rachael to start speaking her gentle mind. "You really needed me after Simon. We made promises. We got married." Rachael reminded her of the key points and went on, "We broke promises. Promises that I held onto hoping they would survive but, we have gotten to the point where you have another life and I respect that. I just want you to realize, you are hurting me and I love you. And I hope we can get passed this AND...it will take a while for me to stop hurting so I may say things or do things like touch you or flirt with you...I am still a person whose true love walked away from them...and I still have to follow her. Am I making sense?"

"I need you to IDentifY for me, Rachael. This is not a conversation that you should be havin' with me. Give me Andrea, please?" Julian demanded and then asked. Rachael got up to use the mirror, and directly in front of Julian.

"IDentifY as Andrea." Almost thanking Julian with her smile, she sat back down in the chair to get back to topic.

Julian nodded a thank you, and dropped her defensive position feeling safer but, still reached for her missing cross to twist. Not finding it, her OCD flared, and she quickly spoke to distract it. "I do understand. I love you Andy and I am very sorry I dragged you through this...this therapy of time. Until Noah rap-did what he did, to me, I was scared and hidin' for nearly ten years, and you and he were my

saviors. But, since Noah did what he did, to me, I feel like Simon is gone from inside me. Yer' really be soundin' like yer' startin' to understand how I feel. Thank you for that love." Rachael began rubbing her clit to tolerate the pain, and Julian understood she needed reward for the misery she was feeling.

"I never meant to hurt you, Sister. I love you. I just am ready to get on with the life I have chosen, now that Simon doesn't haunt me anymore. That life Andy...is with Noah and my children. And kudos to you, maybe our next child." Julian smiled when she finished speaking. Subtly pulling on her hair and trying not to let Andrea see it.

Rachael started again, keeping with the cover, that she was Andrea for the moment, "Even though you told me you loved me and we would always be together. I feel the ending. I thank you for being honest and for so many years letting me be your Cuckquean Bitch." Rachael said with a little bite and crossed her legs and arms.

"Cuckqueanery just became us Andy. Rachael used Emily as her Cuckquean...behind my back." Julian shrugged her shoulders. "I don't know how. It just did. We got really confusin' as Rachael pushed for Emily. I want to tell you what I haven't said to you, about the night we tried our pharmaceutical hypnoses at my house." Rachael leaned back and waited to here this one. She uncrossed her legs but, oddly kept them side by side. Zero humiliation availability, and Julian picked up on it.

"I will be Envelopin' Jordan soon. You know she is accentin'-fragmentin', and Simon raped her in my livin' room that night-in my mind. I saw it. She lost the war with him and Emily. Noah won it. Jordan was always about protectin' me from Simon and helped me control Emily, and I don't need that protection

225

anymore. I have been thankin' of a new DIDC just to put Emily back in my mind, and I need it. Jordan is exhaustin'. I don't know when or who will replace her, but her time has come." Rachael nodded at Julian and spoke. "I thank it is probably time to retire Rachael as well, and get a fresh new IDentifY."

Rachael muttered, "They are good women. Fighters. Bitches. One sexy dumb country girl and one Modern Progressive woman. I am proud to have helped create them." Tears started in Rachael's green eyes and Julian nodded with her reaching for her missing wooden cross on her missing necklace, again.

"Jordan took Julian into the basement that same night and used Simon against her. She choked me. Put Simon's confessions into my ears and raped me listenin' to his instructions...in his voice. She is a tenacious monster at times. She fisted me much worse than you ever did. And Noah found me lifeless. He beat my chest and gave me CPR to save me. He had to save me not just from Simon but, from Jordan. I can never let him go. He really is my Angel." Julian said it with tears streaming down her face. "I need him to own me completely, and I need the Bible to guide my life." Julian wiped her tears from her one good eye, and finished. "I can't do this without God, and I don't know how I will do this without you."

Andy shared her tears as well, as they dropped onto her chest when she nodded. "I hate that stupid book." She uttered and then laughed at herself. "Religion is just like marriage-Stockholm Syndrome all the way. Instant, easy diagnosis." Sniffling, she asked her an important question. "Do you think you will ever be with another woman...if it is not me?" Andrea needed to know.

"I could never love another woman as much as I love you Andy. Jenna would be a close second Andy,

but I need to get with God. I need to get with my family. I need to take them back home to Texas...I love you Andrea and Rachael...Please don't be comin' to Texas, Andy. I'm sorry. I need to heal and Crash Jordan, and all my secret Alibis. You need to heal and Crash Rachael. We are goin' to finish this Operation as friends, and we will counsel and use the time to make sure we end thangs posivi...positvy...positivity...posletivity... DAMN IT! I want you to remember me as the woman who loved you the most even if you are petite sluttin' whore who loves sex with everyone." Julian nodded and gave her a warm smile of kinship in that department.

"And I fell in love with a fat cowgirl pain-loving slut who loves Stranger-Danger rape. I will never Cuckquean for anyone else, Julian. I promise." Rachael offered it back with love before asking, "Is our friendship over too or just our love?"

"I have to let our intimate relationship go, Andy, and I have to let Rachael go completely. I do not want to let you go." Julian confessed honestly.

"Are you lying to me again, Master?" Andy needed to know to protect her heart and her sobs were getting in the way of her words. "Rachael knows you lied for Noah raping you, and you're lying to everyone about having a rape fetish. She is concerned what lies you have told Noah that she may have to tell him to end their friendship with a clear conscious." Andrea tilted her head and smiled with love and affection, and lack of a sob. The silence took hold of the room as educated minds began to read the unspoken words that grew the tension.

The Master read her body language, and she tugged at her hair faster to stop Jordan from whipping her skinny ass. Without responding prematurely, she

took several long breaths and stared at her until the verbal gun was unloaded, and the hands were empty.

"Andy, tell Rachael, I plan to repent my sins with you to my husband, and most of our love makin' was not a sin as defined by the Bible, but when I let you inside me, it became one, and I let it keep goin'. This violation of Noah's rights is what got us to this point now. I was wrong, not you, my Love. I was the Woman and you the Cuckquean with a lot of lead-way I gifted you out of love and thinkin' you were an Angel in need. And you abused Emily, and turned her against me." Julian hoped her calm spirit would tread easily with her honesty.

"I will never, never divorce my Master, and I fear Rachael will tell him the truth about Ally." Stopping herself from stammering, Julian organized her words cautiously and tried to set her emotions aside. She would not let Jordan speak either.

"Mathew 5:38 Andrea, I will slap your ass back into tomorrow. Savvy?" This was the most subtle of words she could do, compared to the hail of verbal bullets her mind was loading into the gun clips as they sat silent. The tension in the room needed a saw to cut it before those present began to aim their weapons.

"1 Corinthians 7:2 Julian, let every man have his own wife, and every woman her own wife-me. I will never divorce you, or forget your real identity that Noah doesn't know about." Rachael said it harshly, and her body language read it was only minutes away from needing vast amounts of oxygen. Both women had leverage...and we call it blackmail. Julian rubbed her chin delicately, holding her firm expression, without being demeaning as she sucked on her hair to rid the emotional tension.

Julian didn't fight back her tears and she didn't stop looking Andy in her windows. "Your 'Mutual

Agreement' marriage with Emily ended long ago, Andy. This affair. This affair must stop. I'm sorry. I was wrong, not you." She made sure she spoke softly when she offered the final parley, "You turned on me and my fetishes. My fetishes control me, the Bible controls me, and you took control of some of my fetishes, control of Emily and condemned my religion, and now you want to take Noah away. Noah controls everythang that controls me. This has put me as the monkey in the middle, and I have to choose a side. I'm sorry and I love you with all my heart. There will never be another woman I love as much as I have loved you, Andy."

Andrea did not dispute the blaring honesty, and with tears dripping on her chest, she continued to stare back before her face slowly tighten up and she cried for her woman. Julian began sobbing and shaking from her sobs as well. There was a time when Andrea, was her Angel. The war was over painfully but, peacefully. There is a time for every purpose, under heaven.

Neither one spoke after the truce had been made. Only the whimpers and tears and sniffles filled the room. The nurses, the Alibis, Noah, and rest of the world never knew things were changing...until Rachael felt Andrea was losing the kind argument.

Julian eyed Andrea's pussy when she put her legs apart and relaxed to finger her clit. She smiled at her to give her approval of Andrea enjoying the pain of the moment, and stimulating opiates in her brain to ease the emotional pain. She would Witness for her out of love, kindness, and the understanding that pain came with reward. Rachael smiled back and stopped shedding her tears, as her skinny vagina curtains began parting and a huge, thick cucumber slid out into the seat of her chair. Julian's eye grew wide, even her

eye patch was lifting as the other eye widened. Julian's mouth watered instantly as did Kitty. "Oh my Gosh, Andy."

"I see you met my big friend, Julian. I thought maybe...you know...we could have one last thing together." Rachael smiled shyly as she held her vegetable toy at the ready against her clitoris...smiling and inviting.

Julian had a God-fearing look on her face, staring it down like it was a monster in the night, coming after her. "You know I can't have that. 1 Corinthians 6:13, I shall not masturbate with food," Julian uttered her words as she stared, searching for her faith for strength. Her Kitty was already preparing herself. Julian and Kitty were panting, just for different reasons. "I cannot Andy, and you know that."

"Want to test your faith again, Julian?" Rachael smiled as she rubbed her clit gently with the phallic symbol from Julian's faith. "Maybe just a little feel inside your fat slutty cattle cunt. Maybe the only thing that has never been inside you, Julian." Rachael was beginning to sound cantankerous and with a weapon.

With her strength in God, Julian spoke to her from her imposed position, "God would never let me, Andy. Never! 1 Corinthians 6:13." Julian stared at it like it was a Satan. It is the one vegetable every woman has had the pleasure of making love to...except Julian.

"You have told me since I've known you Julian, how much you have wanted to know what it felt like. 'That you should just do it once and you will know that God's fruit, could pleasure you...just this once." Rachael leaned toward her to get her words incepted. "Well, I could help you, my Love, after all, it is not the forbidden fruit of the Garden of Eden." Leaning back, Rachael slipped it in and out of her pussy getting her

pleather seat wet when she would drag it out and drag it back in. "It really feels good inside this pussy, Julian. Perhaps, think of it as a Stranger." She said carrying an evil after-laugh through her voice.

Julian's mouth watered as she saw it leave trails on the seat. All of it was true. All her life, even watching Jenna masturbate with it, she fantasized about it repeatedly rubbing her clit. She has even begged Noah to use it on her and he refused because her faith forbade it. This wonderful masturbation toy the world over for women, had never been allowed to be one of her toys. It was always her personal test of her faith, to deny it.

"I shouldn't Andy. God would never forgive me of the sin. I can't. I...I. Does it feel good?" Julian slowly reached down and felt her wetness seeping through her brown and black labia lips. She had never seen another woman up close using it. "Not usin' the cucumber is a symbol of my strength for my faith, Andy. You know that. I have fought this fight every month alone at home when I ovulate, with one in my hand, in the nude, and the Bible in my other hand."

Julian shifted in her seat to get farther away from the pleasure it was giving her second favorite pussy. "I can hear her slurpin', Andy. Please don't. I will never let myself enjoy it. God's will that I must seek escape of my pleasure with my clit. And...I...I...I...I wouldn't escape sin if I just did it once...on my clit is a gift from God and I could just rub it a few times."

Watching the magic cross Rachael face was breaking through to her desires as Kitty soaked herself. Maybe. 'Not insert it. Maybe let you rub it a little in me." Julian couldn't help separating her labia and digging deep under her mound. Her hand instantly drown. "It could fit inside my Venus hole and not my

231

pussy, Andy. Oh my Gosh. You look beautiful fuckin' it, Andy. And...And...And I want to fuck it so bad. It could be therapy for Deep in the Heart of Texas." Her tears came back to her and her red eyes glistened with fear and wanting to feel full inside.

"Oh my God Andy. I'm gettin' so wet for you." Julian whispered as Andrea slid it deep and back out and all the way in until it disappeared. Rachael laid her head back to hear the sound of her juices and feel the sensations glide up her innards. "I need it for my pussy therapy. I'm a doctor. I know I should use it...I can't sin of God. I can't if you just use it on me this time. It won't be a sin...will it?" She fought it off for the moment pleasuring herself again as Rachael invited the green, natural dildo into her body and moaned.

Julian couldn't stop watching the gliding wetness it was giving her pink Goddess. Julian knew it better than her own sometimes. She could smell the wet essence as it carried the familiar smell of Andrea to her. She could see ridges cut into it all up and down the shaft...that very thick shaft of power waiting to fill her now aching void, pulled on the sides of her vaginal opening with wet ease. Slowly, Julian put her soaked fingers into her mouth tasting her sweet essence, and spoke fast to herself with the seed still thick on her tongue.

"1 Corinthians 6:13. I cannot masturbate with food-even my Venus mound. 1 Corinthians 10:13-my clitoris is my escape from urges. My husband owns my pleasure-1 Corinthians 7:4." Slowly, she closed her eyes and swallowed her wetness as Fat Kitty began to burn with decision, and Julian's fingers found their way to rub her. She had to taste more of her dripping wet seed and used two fingers to gather it from her lower lips and rub it around her mouth and onto her upper lip. She felt the urge deep inside that had to be

touched. The Heart of Texas was chanting for a Stranger...again.

"Genesis 38:8-10, I shan't waste seed." She said it softly as her own pheromones absorbed into her senses. Her eyes closed and she was fingering herself to climax. Her nipples began to rise as her body temperature did from the blood flow to her thick, horny pussy. Her eyes recorded the wet reflections from the lights as it vanished and returned for her. "Let me have strength Lord...and just once let me know thy enemy inside me." She heard Andrea's pounding schlick inside and out of her skinny, little pussy that Julian drank from for a dozen years. Julian recognized the familiar schlicking sound with Andrea's moans remembering her hand getting soaked as it slid in and out of her lover. Holding the cucumber tightly, she pounded it in faster, as her head leaned back farther and farther throwing her moans of pleasure into the room. Rachael was close and Julian knew every second of the stretch to her orgasm. 'Knew her signals. 'Her breathing. 'Her wet sounds. She had kissed her wetness. She knew her taste. Her smell and how wonderful it was.

Julian felt the moisture under her ass now, and fingered her burning, wet opening and rubbed it on her nipples and then sucked her nipple rolling her eyes back. "My fat slutty pussy. My fat slutty pussy. Fuck my fat slutty pussy, Andy. Push his cum deep inside me, Andy. Fuck my fat pussy, Andy. Fuck me, Andy." Julian moaned for her Cuckquean one last time fingering herself. One of the nurses signaled to the others and they watched through the door as the happy lesbian couple battled their pleasures together.

Julian finally, looked down at Andrea and watched her pussy struggle with her pounding friend and in response, Julian used all her fingers to scoop up

her wetness and rub it all over her face and into her mouth. Nurse Theresa was brave enough to come to the door to watch and when the other nurses told her to move away, she slid inside and into a corner where the other nurses could not see her. She watched Rachael fuck Andrea for her woman, and Julian rub herself. Theresa reached down into her scrubs, fingering through her thick, wet bush, she slid her finger under her clit hood and joined in.

Rachael began moaning louder and held on to her right nipple twisting it hard. Her panting got louder and louder and her moans escaped care. She knew she was holding out for the really wet, big one. Julian began moaning and panted her prayers to stop, her fingers danced on her escape button as her thick curtains held onto her hand tightly. Rachael jerked back letting out her screeching moans of pleasure as the cucumber crashed into her clit and slid deep inside her. The red pleather was soaked in front of her personal entrance. The room echoed their moans of wet, painful pleasure to all three women. Rachael fingered her clit and pounded down into her hole over and over never having any mercy for Andrea's pussy. It was close. It was win Julian back now or never. Julian moaned out Andrea's name and Rachael screamed into orgasm spraying her seat as she forced the Green Devil into her with everything she had left in her arm. Julian started to feel the shock and jerked her hand away and bit down on her soaking wet fingers and bucked in her bed. Her expression was intense, as the wine dripped from her fingers onto her chin. Julian bit harder and her sin backed away from her angry Heart of Texas. She stopped herself before she came.

Theresa jerked her sexy chubbiness against the corner and bent over as her orgasm soaked her fingers

and panties. Her knees rocked against each other and she quickly pulled her hand out of her private entrance and sucked her own juices and then rubbed them all over her face. Experiencing group masturbation with other women, she was hooked for life now.

Julian bit all four fingers growling her urges away and inhaled the pheromones floating around the room as she sucked the sweetness onto her palate crying her anger out. Theresa leaned into the corner still licking her fingers dry and slipped them into her love tunnel again and refreshed her taste buds. Julian washed herself with guilt as she kept her eyes closed and recited scripture in her mind to keep the orgasm away. She finally stopped biting her hand of sin and won her freedom from Rachael.

Her scripture was working until the wet cucumber rubbed across her lips. Julian jerked and opened her eye to the Devil close to her face in another hand. Rachael was grinning like a bitch drunk on power. Julian closed her eye again and let her rub the wetness on her face and slowly, maybe accidently, put her tongue out to taste her friend's juices for the last time. She could not allow her seed to be wasted.

Rachael worked up and down her mouth giving her every drop of her essence. With her licked clean cucumber, she took it in her left hand and jammed her wet fingers into Julian's mouth like she did her pussy so many times before. Julian sucked it clean and her pussy trembled for attention, and Julian refused to open her eyes to the daring moment.

Julian felt the cucumber divide her labia from the hole of essence and it slid up dividing the clinging, swollen lips as they tried to anchor to it. Started to shake, the stimulation made her beg, cry, and plead for Andy to save her from sin. Julian's head pushed back farther and farther into the mattress to escape,

235

as she opened her legs even farther, expressing her disapproval with only her face. It was rape time again at Julian's very public entrance. Her expression was a pro-longed wince as she succumb to her Cuckquean Angel doing the Devil's work. Her moisture strung across her black labia tips as the light glistened on it as they parted. The Green Sin delicately ground against the inside nerve endings of her thick, wet, deep labia and Julian started to scream in pleasure making Rachael's evil wetter. Slowly, it drove up into the deep, dark, drowning canal under her swollen wet mound and Julian screamed and quivered as it hit her impatient, throbbing button of joy. Rachael slid it into under her mound slowly until the Green Demon got sucked in against her clitoris. Less than half of it could still be seen. Andrea let go of it and stared at Julian wincing in her pleasure. Cattle Kitty was fighting to hold it in place with muscles that didn't exist, and begging for pain to reward her pleasure.

Theresa was already rubbing herself again, this time with her pants down to her knees and trying to get as many fingers inside her as she could. Rachael noticed her with a smile, and spoke to Julian without taking her eyes off a possible Cuckquean for her to abuse.

"I will be back my beautiful Angel. Keep it right there for me and test your faith, you FAT BITCH! YOUR GOD IS WATCHING YOU!"

Chapter 18

-Country Girl Tomboy Beauty Queen Angel & Devil

Rachael walked away from Julian as she laid there, stabbed under the mountain of Venus by a huge, almost throbbing Vegetable Monster that had crashed onto her clitoris. Every time she shook, so did her Venus, and the Green Sinner ground against her pulsating clitoris, that she Edged to orgasm just minutes ago. She was near dead with fear as her hands curled up on each side of her face in the surrender position, and shaking as she squinted. If she moved, her clit would explode into spasms and God would know she let it happen. She felt herself twitching in her gifted Texas loins as her mound tried to swallow the green dick...like so many dicks before it. She barely breathed, and her Kegel exercises started on their own...by accident of course.

Rachael slammed Theresa into the corner and began French kissing her violently and pulling her hair. Their tongues battled and Theresa could not escape her roughness or the chemistry she was feeling. Rachael viciously grabbed her by the pussy, and jerked her into the wall with her other hand on her neck. Theresa moaned with fear and pleasure, which is what she needed. She spread her legs as much as she could and put her hands down like a good Cuckquean. Rachael rammed all her fingers into her pussy and stood over her and lifted her up by her pelvis bone onto her toes. The poor nurse screamed in pain and wanted more.

Theresa jerked and screamed and another nurse came in to watch, then another, then another, then another. Rachael ripped her scrubs down to Theresa's

ankles and got on her knees naked and drove her face into her hairy pussy and Theresa slammed back into the corner again and fell to the electrifying orgasms smacking her in Rachael's face. It wasn't the first time her face had met Theresa's hairy pussy. She ripped her own blouse up to expose her impatient, tubular breasts with thick, pink nipples. Humiliation was just a glance away and she took it. Rachael licked through her hairy snatch and sucked her little clit hood, nearly taking it from her body. Theresa screamed in pleasure from the instant pain-driven climax, and quivered to her new Master.

Rachael got off her knees and slapped Theresa's fat pussy with her open hand three times until she bent at the waist conceding, and then the Fallen Angel fingered her way back into her pussy opening and lifted her up by the pelvis bone again jamming her thumb into her clit. Theresa yelled out "Fuck me, please." Rachael squatted and shoved her fist, fingers first, into her pussy and lifted her new Cuckquean onto her toes. This was power.

Instantly, Theresa began shrieking in pain and grinding herself into her fist. Her loud cries were everything Julian desired as her mid-section jerked and shook her belly as the slowest orgasm ever, drew on her. This Cowgirl's gifted Longhorn pussy had met its outlaw match. She was going to cum on the Green Monster, and nothing she could do to stop it. She had passed the point of no return. Grabbing it would just send her into fucking it. Her only strength was not moving it and asking God to help her escape her sin. The sounds of pleasure rape going on next to her...the sounds of the pain...the smell of sex...the screams of exhausting orgasmic rewards would be her tilting point to sin.

Watching Theresa collapse to the ground like Rachael did in the shower to her Master, Rachael stood over Theresa like a female fighter over her opponent. Her fist dripped, and she tasted her fingers before reaching down and slapping the wetness across Theresa's young face. Rachael stomped over to Julian and smeared Theresa's pussy juice all over her face and finally into her mouth. She scooped her own dripping wetness up and slapped Julian across the face hard, bringing out more tears from her lanced victim. Rachael stopped to finger Andrea's pussy and leaned over to Julian's ear. Julian's was shaking and her midsection cramping to orgasm.

"Repeat every word I say as loud as you can BITCH! OR I will shove it up your fat, ugly cunt!" She gleamed at Julian fighting off the home-stretch to pleasure. "I am a fat slut. My name is Julian. Say it loud." Julian repeated it and Rachael barked at her to say it louder and she did with ease. The nurses just watched and listened. "I want to be raped by Strangers and I'm a fat slut." Julian repeated it. "I think I'm some kind of Angel, and I let strangers fuck me in the ass to save their souls." Julian whispered it and Rachael cut her off to make her say it louder and she did as Julian began to cry. "I wore a hood over my head so Strangers could rape me and I could never tell who did it. Say it LOUD JULIAN!" Julian began bobbing her head as the orgasm began to pick up burning speed.

"I drink Strangers cum. I let Strangers cum inside me and I will let any man cum in my SLUTTY FAT TEXAS PUSSY!" Julian screamed it at everyone crying and jerked in pain, as God watched her.

Rachael grabbed Julian's left tit and jerked her nipple hard into the air as her hand flew behind her demonstrating the huge explosion inside her God

fearing friend. Julian quivered and screamed and grabbed the Green Goblin and ground it into her clit as the orgasm took her away from her faith. Again, she screamed for her Cuckquean.

A defeated Julian, jerked it back and forth with both hands and finally pounded it into her huge labia and mound making her explode again and again. Rachael, could only see the red of her blue eye as it rolled back and Julian's chubby tits shook for everyone watching and tingling. Rachael smiled for her former lover and screamed loving encouragement at her, "CUM YOU FAT BITCH!"

Rachael spun her naked behind, behind the bed as Julian jerked off in it in the upright position, and grabbed Julian's long beautiful black hair and hung from it with all her ninety-five pounds. Julian was just starting to shove the Devil deep into the Heart of Texas when her head reared back and her scalp began to pull her face upward.   Instantly, she began screaming in unsatisfying pain and flailing her arms for her gifted Angel locks. Rachael dangled her feet off the ground while screaming, jerking, and laughing at Julian in pain. This was her reward with pain.

'GIVE ME YOUR CRASH KEY YOU FUCKING LYING BITCH! I HATE YOU JULIAN! GIVE ME YOUR FUCKING CRASH KEY MUSIC AND NUMBER! YOU FAT BITCH! WHOEVER YOU ARE EMILY!"

Julian was screaming with her hands trying to hold her hair from being ripped out. And each time she franticly waved and whispered at the nurses huddling around Theresa's pleasurable bout, they didn't really notice. Julian tried screaming and winced from the pain and finally the nurses realized this was not a sexual ritual and ran to stop Rachael.

"I HAVE TO BASELINE YOU JULIAN! YOUR HELIX IS FRAGMENTING! GET OFF ME! GET OFF ME! I AM

240

TRYING TO SAVE EMILY FROM JULIAN! GET THE FUCK OFF ME! GIVE ME THE KEY JORDAN!" Rachael was still screaming as they dragged her away from behind the bed. She would not let go of Julian's four feet of hair.

"GET OFF ME! I HAVE TO SAVE HER IDENTIFY! I NEED HER CRASH KEY! GIVE IT TO ME JORDAN! EMILY? TESSAAAAA? PLEASE! ONE OF YOU GIVE IT TO ME! ARIZONAAAAAA PLEASE?"

Security came running in to help the nurses. Theresa was standing in the same corner she was groped in. Being one a those woman who just realized Cuckqueaning was a demand she would forever have to meet, at the cost of feeling the pain first.

"-HELIX IS FRAGMENTING! -CRASH WITHOUT HELP SAVANNAH! RAPE FRAGMENTED YOUR HELIX! SAVE YOUR ALIBIS EMILY! GET OFF ME!" Julian was crying and her naked body twisted up on her boots in the bed and her head was being pulled through the top of the bedframe behind her. She was screaming but, only making small sounds.

"GET THE FUCK OFF ME! NO! I'M A FEDERAL OFFICER!"

Her hands found their way outside the bedrail to her hair and now in a tug of war with Rachael. One of Noah's boots fell to the floor as Security and Nurses dragged Rachael around the bed toward the door, and Julian's hair pulled her the opposite way. "LOWANA YOU'RE FRAGMENTING! WAKE THE FUCK UP! GIVE ME YOUR FUCKING KEY EMILY! LOWANA? CASEY? CHEYENNE? GIVE ME THE KEY ID! ALIBIS HELP ME!"

Security finally got what was left of Julian's locks out of Rachael's hands, and got her to the ground as she kicked at them and screamed at Julian, in the nude. 'STOP IT! I'M A FEDERAL OFFICER! GET OFF ME! SHE IS FUCKED UP! I AM HER DOCTOR! GET OFF OF ME! LET ME GO! I'M A FEDERAL OFFICER!" Nurses and

Security kept yelling at her to calm down. As they held her down, a naked, large Longhorn ass with a short body to match, landed on top of her and started beating her in the face with her thick fists.

Rachael screamed as Julian repeatedly punched her, and got control of Julian's hair again with a spur and tried shoving it in Julian's face but, it landed on her pirate patch and rolled up her forehead tangling the spur into her hair. Security began separating the two former, disheveled lovers, and Rachael clung to one of Noah's spurs tied in her hair and held onto as much of her hair as possible. Julian kept her one-hundred and seventy-five pounds of thickness on top of her ninety-five pound ex-woman to hold her in place for the Texas beating.

Rachael held tightly to the locks as Security got them to their feet and finally separated but, Rachael was still screaming and using Julian's hair for tug of war. The entire nursing staff and some patients were staring through the door and window. Cell phones were recording and Rachael's screams carried across the halls of the hospital. When a Security Officer let her arm go to get the hair away from her, she took after Julian again as a Cowgirl size five wide boot kicked her in the face. Another Security Officer, pulled Julian to the side by her hair to get her out the door and Julian jumped up and kicked him in the chest knocking him backwards into the hallway. Still holding her hair, he jerked Julian to the floor on her face in the doorway as Rachael's screaming and struggling continued with the other Security. Now two people on opposite sides of her were pulling her Angel locks. Her Daddy told her the work of an Angel would be painful.

Julian jerked her hair away from Security as another one laid on top of her to calm her down. She was already pissed, when she pushed him back onto

the floor and wrapped her legs around his neck and under one arm, and clamped down with those big girl, country thighs. His face went right into her wet, angry vulva. Her hair was everywhere, even pinned down under herself. Security and nurses stepped on it and pulled her away from the Security Officer in the leg lock as he dragged along with her. Country girls don't play when they get a hold of you.

One Officer got down on the floor behind Julian and flipped her over on her chest and sat on her wide ass. She would not unlock her legs from the other Officer. The Security Officer on top of her was sitting on the most, well-padded nude ass of his life and it still jiggled. The Officer she kicked into the hallway, got back into the room to help his friend sitting atop Julian's rear when three Officers lifted Rachael over their heads holding her jerking feet and arms as she violently twisted and screamed. One Officer had her up under her arms and across her flat chest. Julian reached out and tripped one of the officers trying to carry Rachael to the door by her feet, and she fell into the officer sitting on Julian, and knocked him off, as Julian unlocked her legs to roll away. Rachael landed on Julian still kicking and jerking.

She landed with a screaming face onto Julian's shaking breasts and immediately started trying to punch her and bit Julian's left boob on her areola. Julian's scream was finally heard as she tore away the soft repairs her vocal chords had achieved over the past week. Julian immediately started pounding and punching Rachael on top of her head with her knuckles as Security picked Rachael up off of her and Julian's breasts was still in her teeth. Julian's choice words were of an angry Bi-Cowgirl nature.

Julian, jerking and screaming in pain heard Rachael growling as she tore her teeth through her

areola, the Simon scar, and jerking her head back and forth growling. Quickly, Julian grabbed Rachael's short hair on the back of her head and jerked it as she hammered away at her face with the other hand. Blood spilled out all over Julian's breasts, chest, and belly, instantly. Rachael's feet hit the ceiling tile above Julian and only her bite kept them connected. Security continued pulling Rachael upward to unstick them, and she would not let go of Julian's nipple in her teeth. Julian growled back in her scream as she pounded her face and jerked on her head again. Finally, she tore away and blood dribbled everywhere from Rachael's face.

Julian held her left breast as she clamored to rise to her knees for more scrapping. Rachael was carried out the door over everyone's head bucking and kicking and screaming and naked and bloody. She was still screaming IDentifY, Helix fragmentation, and Crash keys. Hopefully, the sexual humiliation she felt being carried through the hospital naked in front of everyone, met her fetish. Security Officers were still holding onto Julian on her knees, and she jerked her thick arms away and coddled her left breasts in the nude. She was swaying back and forth on her knees to manage her adrenaline and maintaining her fierce expression of a pissed off woman with Texas capabilities and many Alibis.

As she realized about ten teeth bit through her areola and Montgomery glands, her nipple was still there, and she exhaled with a growl. As a wife who openly admits she loves giving blowjobs, this position should have been comfortable to her. She stared out the door daring the bitch to come back. None of the blood was from her, except her areola bites leaking and oily, white prolactin from her nipple, her hair clung

244

to her sweaty body and the blood-soaked floor around her. Thankful her nipple was still there.

The tension began to fall, as she sat back on her boots and knees gasping for a breath, and still staring at the door through her hair, for her enemy. Slightly bent forward at the waist and sitting on her Texas ass with her boots spread outward, she was only about two and a half feet to three feet tall. Her hair went in every direction spread across the floor around her in Rachael's blood. Those red sclera glared with her blue eyes through her dark hair as she panted her anger; staring intensely. Her mouth was open, her teeth clenched with her lower jaw pushed forward. She was damn sure going to make changes in her life, even if she had to go Cowgirl on someone's Twig-ass.

Julian sat there occasionally coughing and wheezing through her dangling hair that moved away each time she breathed. Her body was rushing oxygen away from Kitty and prepping for another go round. She was waiting, Texas style. As Nurses tried to help her up, she jerked her arms away from them without a word and never taking her eyes off the doorway. Her fists were tight and her arms were hanging over her thighs ready to throw down. She sat on that large ass comfortably, and waited. The Cuckquean was driven away by the woman who was still the Master, just not for Andrea anymore.

The very shortest person in the room, though thick and of unimaginable cowgirl sexiness, just made her point and sealed it with a bark. "YOU DON'T MESS WITH TEXAS, BITCH!" She screamed it at the door to make sure the world heeded her warning. Her vocal chords did not appreciate it and the room drew silent and stared at her.

Security started asking the nurses what happened and Theresa kept interrupting, stating Julian

and her were being attacked. Julian finally, let the nurses help her get up and they hugged each other in a circle with Julian in the middle. No one could tell with her lack of height that she stood in the circle. Most of them were crying with Julian. It was really over. And she did not get caught with her boots off this time.

A Black Nurse wearing a hijab, grabbed Rachael's phone sitting on the window ledge recording the incident and scooted over and took Julian's phone from the tray table shoved behind the head of the bed. After picking up Rachael's dress, purse, and heals, she quietly left the room. Someone's mission was accomplished.

DoctorLands West Nurses Notes:
Patient Doe, Jordan 626   Duty-RN Sheila Walker

11:16AM - Fight between patient and spouse occurred.
Security Incident Report 223145A3DW.
Patient bitten on left breasts by spouse. Patient accepted care for breast wound. RN Theresa Woods attacked by spouse. Pulled her scrub pants down in struggle. No immediate wounds.

11:38AM Patient 125/67 BP- Psychologist Dames, L. Contacted for visit.

4:14PM - Three male officers visit Doe, Jordan 626
Officers closed door. HN RN Sheila Walker verified credentials.

Texas Rangers- Austin Beauchamp, Chadley Bartholomew.

Wyoming Ranger -Samuel Taylor. All hugged patient.

Chapter Nineteen

-Cunniling-Us Calls Begging Giddy Bag

Jenna was all insolent smiles when she stormed into Noah's room, and smashing the door into the wall. He was peeing into the bed pan sitting off the side of the bed. He was still naked and had his right hand still cuffed to the bed rail. Jenna wiggled her stick figure as she pulled her top off over her head and sat down to remove her shoes and then her shorts. He watched as she bared her skin to him, and he appreciated her sexy petite-ness, a little more after yesterday.

Finally looking at her face, instead of her sore, petite Hoo-Ha. "Who fucked you up?" He asked grinning big for someone else's team. "'Rape the wrong co-worker and he tagged that eye? There is no white left in it. All the blood vessels-"

"SHUT UP! It's just as bad as both Emily's eyes. Fuck you, shut up!" she demanded and somewhat appearing to be frazzled.

"Rachael I have got to get out of here. You can't keep me locked up forever. I have told the nurses you are holding me against my will. When they brought the food I convinced her to call 911 for me and gave my name and DoctorLands West. She told me they were coming. You are going to be arrested for kidnapping and rape, Rachael." He was stern about it and stood up to look into the bathroom and pretend like he was stretching. He mumbled IDentifY Jon, in the distant mirror.

"What did you say about Jon, Noah?" She chlicked at him twice like he was a horse, to get his attention, and remind him that Jenna was there.

"I said Jenna scares Jon, Jenna. Don't know how Julian fell in love with you back in Texas or why she felt she had to hide it from me." He said to re-direct. "A lifelong affair for you, and maybe she wants to live as a straight woman to society?"

She came off firm and upbeat, "Did you enjoy fucking me, Noah? I really enjoyed it. More than what I thought I would actually. And today, you get a special treat. You get to fuck me in the ass." She smiled proudly at him and chlicked again. "I'm going to give you what Julian never would give you. 'You filling my ass. Real men never complain so I don't think you will. Julian never complained." She said it just to poke his frustration since, all of us women know, angry sex can be wonderful. "Now tell me really, what's your thought of my pussy? 'Since it is very different from Julian's fat, cow pussy. Is hers better or mine?" He figured she was just rambling to distract him, as he had done her but, she waited glaring at him for an answer.

Jon sat back down and just laid on the bed ignoring her inquiry. His defensive play was already in motion. Jenna walked over to the other side of the bed to cuff his left wrist and he ignored her innuendo. "I do not want to have sex with you, Jenna. You have a little ass."

Giving him a sigh before she spoke. "Noah. I plan to let you go today, after you fuck my ass-AS LONG as it is fruitful and multiplies my orgasms." Jon looked over at her and she was bubbly with her black eye. "Seriously Noah, I already have your sample from yesterday. 'Not going to get a clean sample from my ass. Think about it. You get to butt fuck me and punish me as hard as you want, and I get out the door and toss you the key. Simple as that. I swear. I have what I need to ruin your life. I just want to give you

something I know you don't get at home. Unlike Julian, Emily and I can admit we like it in the ass. You should be grateful, Noah."

"How can I fuck you in the ass if I am on bottom?" He asked hoping to get cut loose and open up a can of whoop-ass on her like the person who blacked her left eye.

"So you want to fuck me?" Jenna inquired. "I would let you go if I believed you would actually fuck me without running out the door. I promise you, you will not get out of here or my deal, if you don't fuck my sweet, petite ass."

Jon just stared at her. Like most men, he was hoping his dick would think for him and give him an answer. "Let me show you something. She walked back to her shorts and pulled out a phone. I will show you some very dirty pictures of Emily, if you let me ride your cock. I will show everything I got. I assure you, it will be shocking. Interested?" She opened up a picture of Emily nude and masturbating while lying in the grass in a Park with men standing around her jerking off to her.

Noah was shocked, and looked closer. "That is Julian. Why do you keep calling her Emily? Bring it closer, and let me-"

"Not until you let me cuff your other wrist." Slowly, he put his wrist over and let her cuff him. "Do you need duct tape on your face again or are you going to be a good boy...besides I liked hearing you moan from my fantastic pussy yesterday. I'm very good in bed."

"Why do you keep calling her Emily? Is that an IDentifY or something?" He asked with much intent.

"It's funny how much I told you yesterday and you don't remember that your wife's real name is Emily." He looked at her, not buying the bullshit. "I

As she fingered herself, she tasted it and licked her fingers clean and his dick jerked, and she smiled proudly at him.

"I want to snowball with you also, Noah. I can do that for you." She lovingly offered.

"Thank you. NEVER!" He responded. She fingered herself more as he watched and started faking her moans and his dick moved around as the blood began to fill it. With her dirty smile, she got her fingers soaked and got up to offer it to him to taste, and he didn't open his mouth. "Taste me Noah, our wife does...more than you will ever really know. Emily likes to eat my pussy...like Julian." His dick started standing up against his will and she held it close to his lips as he unknowingly sniffed it. Finally, he opened his mouth and she put her fingers in and he sucked them dry. "You will taste my seed but, not your own." She said rhetorically.

"Don't swallow me...let it sit on your tongue. Rub it on the top of your mouth and let it sit. Taste me like wine, Noah. Drink what your wife drinks...from my vine." Giving him a wink, "Who is the real Angel now, Boy? Let the fresh essence back into your throat." Noah actually followed her instructions and the uncut foreskin on his dick peeled back as it got long and hard for her. She watched the smooth dark head pull through searching for its prey.

She smiled at him validating her magical power, as the plan worked. She was hot, and Julian's man's dick confirmed it. She needed him to be attracted to her-for the plan. "Your dick is really pretty for me, Noah. I hope that this is everything you thought it would be. I love pretty dick, Noah." She fingered her pussy again and he sucked off her essence coyly. "I will give you a choice, Noah. Do you want to fuck me in my ass or in my pussy today?" She sat her phone

down on the small table next to the head of the bed and aimed the camera at his rising dick and pressed the screen to record. "I hope both," she whispered to herself.

"Your ass." He confessed with his erection standing by for some attention.

"Be honest, Noah, have you masturbated thinking about me before?" He shook his head.

"Have you wondered what it would be like to fuck me?"

"I guess." He confessed, again being coy.

"Do you like my tits?" She reached up and pinched both her drooping, long nipples for him. He nodded, quickly.

"REALLY? Are you just lying to me? I am flat chested, Noah. Only Jay likes me tits." Noah nodded and spoke.

"I like your nipples very much. They stick out so much...like a bend down barn hook. I like very small titties, too." He confessed hard as a rock, making her tingle from his words.

"Men always ignored my chest." She confessed.

"Really? Why?" But before he could speak, she had to insult him.

"Is it because of your gay past, with flat-chested boys, Noey?"

"I hate being called Noey...like being a kid. Call me Noah or James. And I like little tits. I don't know why. Julian has a nipple fetish and so do I. She told me." He looked down at his dick standing at attention. He really did want to fuck her up the butt, and he didn't understand why because he never offered it to any other women.

Jenna leaned over and gripped him in the center of it. "That is rock hard. You really do want to fuck me in the ass." He nodded impatiently and she added.

"You can really get thick. I can't get my fingers all the way around you. It is so warm." She squeezed it really hard and felt her arousal grow instantly.

He spoke up now that she had his gear shift. "I need you to stroke it a few times to flow the blood. It's so hard for you and it hurts." She stroked it a few short strokes and his eyes closed to enjoy the relief. Jenna got up and got another phone and sat it next to the other one.

"Be honest, Noah, have you ever sucked another guy off? Be honest? I love gay men-Especially Alpha males with gay fetishes."

As she came back she climbed right up on his face and sat on his mouth without waiting for an answer…her own way of being coy. He immediately started eating her pussy without resentment. She chlicked at him and rolled her head back to slowly grind with him as her knees slid off his shoulders and onto the mattress. She could feel she was still sore, and that added to the stimulation. "I just came back from Cleveland. Julian is losing one of her eyes. Her left eye." He stopped licking. "NO YOU DON'T BOY! EAT ME! What's done is done. EAT MY PUSSY GAY WIFE BEATER!"

Jon swallowed her juice and she kept grinding into his face and he started licking again. She leaned forward lifting her pussy up over his mouth and winced over and over as she poured her natural wetness into his mouth. Jenna pushed her cervical walls up and squirted into his mouth. Slamming down, her orgasm splashed her pussy with fresh, impatient juice as she fucked his mouth forward and downward moaning his name. She jerked back exhaling and sat on his chest enjoying the wonderful sensations releasing in her brain. Her wetness seeped onto his chest muscles, and Jon wanted more of her seed.

"Have you ever taken an inhibitor to enhance your orgasm...not Viagra? A brain inhibitor." He shook his head. "Got some pussy juice all over your mustache and beard. Lick me up, Noah James. I think we really can enjoy each other today. I need anal as much as I need semen." She smiled with a giddy bag of self-confidence. "I once had twenty-five orgasms in one night. Fucking some chick back in Med School. My, was she determined to get me to thirty in one session. Best bi-racial pussy I ever had. I felt like Emily the next day. You know. My pussy was swollen. I let Emily eat me the next morning and the pain was wonderfully intense orgasms." She chlicked at him. "I need more of that from your ex-wife."

She turned around on his chest to suck his cock and slid back to let him sip her wine and once she got it back on his mouth, he licked her ass instead. She squealed and jerked forward and pushed it back into his mouth with a real smile. She was enjoying that because of all the men she had slept with, none ever licked her ass. She was actually too short to deep throat him and have her ass licked, so she kindly stroked him a little and let him please her as she squealed from the sensations.

"Emily told me, you were an ass man. I didn't know she meant licking ass. THIS IS SENSATIONAL! I WANT TO SCREAM! She laid on his body, rubbing her face against his warm tan belly and licked his six pack. Her pussy dripped onto his chin and neck as her eyes kept rolling back. She jerked as the intensity tickled her fancy. She could feel her vagina burn from the constant rush of fluid. Sparingly, she jerked her entire body and slowly turned her head to her shoulder and licked it. Noah could not see anything but pretty, tight butt cheeks, and ceiling. She laid her face down on his firm belly and talked to him warmly as she picked up

255

his scent and oils. She felt like a princess sexually trying to tame a bad boy.

"Emily is so addicted to Stranger-Danger Rape, Noah. Julian, your multiple personality wife, loves to have sex with Strangers and a blind-fold. She can't be with you anymore without constantly having rape in her eroticism. She wants my logo tattooed on that big ass. She has kept me around all these years to cuck for her...to sexually abuse her. I fucked her with a cucumber yesterday to help her pussy swelling. She loves it when we share dildos...especially cucumbers." She jerked his cock and then stroked him good and hard for a response. "She likes to suck them clean...I'm sure you know that. Remember the cowgirl dildo I bought? She can take every inch of it in both holes. I can get it all in my ass, just not my pussy yet but, I'm working on it for her." Her words came out as rough as her strokes, and she slid back and let him drink her thick, clear string of grool as it strung down into his mouth.

"All this time, I wish she had been sharing you with me. I have tried to get her to share you, but she never took the hints. I always got her what she needed-Stranger-Danger sex when she was tied up. I used it to keep her with me in college. I was her manager, I guess. I set it up, got her fucked by complete Strangers. 'Even watched, and licked her clean afterwards so we could snowball. She is the most sexual Goddess I have ever fucked, Noah, and her semen addiction is really the problem though. I encouraged her to show herself naked in public and she just started masturbating for anyone and everyone and the semen kept coming in. She felt right at home being nude in public." She sat up on her elbows and rocked back into his mouth to tease Indigo.

256

"I tried to use it as positive reinforcement, but guys came from everywhere, every day. I know I need semen but, she was like an alcoholic with it. She was so short, thick, sexy, cute, and guys would line up to see her nude, and jerk off for her at her Bible Studies. I remember one evening in or dorm, she drank nearly twenty guys who jerked off on her pussy. She had me finger it off the floor and put it in her pussy. She fingered it off that fat pussy and worked it in. Then she started letting guys put the head of their dicks in her to cum. Then she started letting them fuck her to cum inside her. I couldn't control the flow to her. She just had guys lined up outside the dorm room. Keep licking, Noah. Savor my wetness on your tongue." She started sliding her both holes across his mouth and he licked it like warm caramel.

Jenna finally stood up and stretched her legs, and rubbed her lonely nipples, before stepping over to his dick and putting her leg against it. You really do have a good size dick for being White...must be part of your White Privilege. That is really thick, Noah." She offered him a big smile of appreciation. *If she didn't speak, this would be great,* he thought.

She got down and took some close up photos of his stiff manhood, and then ripped a piece of duct tape off the role and he got nervous. When she curled it inside out, long ways, and made a long sticky tube, he got curious, instead of nervous. Putting her thumb and finger under his smooth sack, she lifted his balls all the way up his shaft and held everything with one hand, then wrapped the sticky tube of tape around the base of his shaft, and sack.

She climbed over his waist and smiled at him, and slowly sat down until the head of his cock was just inside her pussy, instantly, chasing her juice down his manhood, she dropped all her weight on him and

rammed it in and jamming his balls against her boney
ass. She screamed with him from the pain and let her
nerve endings continue to signal the wonderful
impulses to her brain. Her pussy instantly grabbed
hold of his base and the bucking Non-Binary opened
the gate. He was still wincing with his lungs filled but,
experience told her to grind it in, just to make it hurt
more.

Chapter 20

-Darkness Wants the Pale Euphoria

When the Nurse Cecilia walked into Julian's room, she immediately saw her sobbing alone in her bed, jerking her hair viciously, and she rushed over to console her. Julian immediately accepted her hug and cried harder.

Nurse Cecilia hugged her again, and used her lanyard radio phone to code another nurse. Julian had latched on to her and was not letting go. She needed a friend, and it was going to have to be Cecilia. The nurse she paged came to the room and it was Samira. She immediately latched on to Julian so Cecilia could escape the interruption of her rounds.

"What is wrong, Honey?" Samira asked hugging her again and kissing her on the top of her head through the twined rope of hair in her own mouth, as Julian clung to her scrubs with her hands. She pulled Julian's face to her chest and Julian sobbed and shook, jerking her head with her hair to try and regain control of her anxieties.

"My hair arguin' me. Emily is coming." She sobbed to her. "My life is messed up. I had control over it and it hath turned on me for my sins." She looked over at her Bible resting beside her and placed it between her legs. "Momma knew what she was talkin' about." She surreptitiously joked. "I'm so sorry 'bout the fight. I...I...just not sure how it happened. I forsake my husband. Forsake my best friend. Emily is comin'. OH GOD! DON'T LET EMILY GET ME!" Samira looked around for anyone, and told herself to talk to

Security about a visitor named Emily. "I got myself put in this lyin' mess. My weddin' ring is gone. My Daddy's cross in gone." She reached for her near empty box of tissues. She had been crying so long, her eyeliner and mascara was on her chest and blanket but, the red still filled the whites of her eyes. With her other hand, she clung to Samira top.

"Well Jordan-"Julian cut her off.

"My name is Julian. Jordan is...is...a long story. My name is Julian."

"Julian, we all make mistakes. I'm sure your wife will come-" Julian was shaking her head to correct the story.

"She is my ex-wife. Mutual Agreement Marriage, in college at a bad time then and we ended it the same year. We have just been best friends and co-workers." Samira stood back as Julian's tears subsided, and because Julian had said she was her wife. She was re-applying it to what she had absorbed since she always thought they were a Lesbian couple.

"You are lesbians right? Both of you? Right? I saw some things that-" Julian interrupted her, unlike her usual Southern etiquette.

"Sometimes we were lovers...I'm Accorded to Noah. Andy...We needed each other. I'm Accorded with two children." She sniffled her cries to stop herself. "And she ain't, and that has become the problem." Julian looked at her hoping not to be judged through her tears. "Can you please fix that chair for me?" She pointed to it, and Samira glanced.

"I see. Does your husband know about...her?" Samira raised her eye brows and waited for an honest answer. Julian nodded as the tears rolled down her cheeks, unevenly because of the eye patch, and her body shook from the cries trying to get out.

"Help me. Would you mind bein' with me?" Noey and Andy kept me safe and saved me. I need my Noey and my Andy. I need-" she crumbled again into her tears. "I need my Babies and my Momma."

"Julian. Julian. Please. You are...are...are going to make me cry. I can stay with you for a few minutes. I promise." Samira reached up and wiped her tears.

"Everything will be alright, Julian," as Julian clung to her scrubs again, pulling her closer to her, and Samira finally, just hugged her.

"You are going through so much. I'm sorry. I am here to talk. I...I...I...can get the Counselor in here as well, Julian." As she sobbed, Julian shook her head staring at the crooked chair, and Samira looked at the spurs and boots on the bed with her. "Okay. Okay. Let me go for a second. Julian please let go so I can-" Julian let her go, and when Samira stepped back to finish her sentence, Julian scrambled out of the bed onto the floor on her chest screaming, and scrambled to straighten out the chair.

Samira's eyes could not get wider as she stepped back in fear. When Julian, still laying on the floor, got the chair corrected, and just balled to herself.

"OCD! I see." Samira said, as she got down next to her and helped her get up and helped walked her back to her bed. She was still crying about Noah, missing. After getting her back into her recliner bed, she quickly went back to the two chairs, and made them even and rushed back to Julian's bedside to hold her hand.

"I...I...I...like your boots. Are you a real Cowgirl? You are very beautiful." Julian's sobs slowed to a crawl, and nodded as she wiggled her boots for her.

"Thank you. You are very beautiful. Thank you for helpin' me." Her eye was swollen from crying, and

her makeup was on her cheeks blending with her black-eye. Samira reached over and pulled her hair out of the way so she could see her clearly.

"NO Julian! I mean it, you are very beautiful. Really, really beautiful woman." Julian smiled and squeezed her hand.

"Thank you. I thank you are so beautiful, Samira. Thank you for helpin' me."

"Are you feeling better now?" Julian nodded and Samira looked around, and lifted her hand and kissed the back of it. "You are...are...are...a real Cowgirl?" Julian nodded at her.

"Cowgirl, like you ride horses and attend ro...rod....rodeos?" Julian nodded and started to smile as her fears subsided. "I like that. I have never been to a rodeo."

"We have to go out West for a real Texas Rodeo," Julian said.

Samira looked around again, and told her, "The Nurses are talking about you and your Wife....sorry...BFF and seemed to be entertained by all the nudity and messing around. Julian sniffled her snot, and it wasn't pretty, and Samira got her a tissue from the tray table and handed it to her.

Julian quickly pulled the other tissue out of the box, so that it was just right, and blew her nose, and tossed the tissue into the trash can, as Samira giggled.

"Your wife, I mean BFF, said you were very religious, and it requires you to have her naked with you at all times. Is that true?" Before Julian could answer, she added, "She didn't tell me that, I...I....I hear...hear...heard the nurses talking.

Shaking her head, Julian explained. 'She is just gettin' turned on by people seein' her naked. We both have that problem." Samira looked down at Julian's

262

exposed body, and admired what she was seeing. She wanted to pull the blanket and cover her, but waited.

"Do you ju...ju...just like people watching you? Is it a religious requirement or are you just enjoying the people watching you? Everyone is tal...ta...ta..talking about they have seen you nude and touching yourself in here...and...and...sex." Julian looked down at her boots on her feet and finally responded in kind. "I must have a Witness as the Bible prescribes, and yes, I do enjoy people watchin' me...I like people watchin' me I guess. And I am doin' physical therapy down there. I'm sorry." She began to realize the embarrassment at the end of her words, likely from being out of her normal elements.

"Does more people make it better or one person?" Julian nodded agreeing with her.

"More people, I guess."

"Well, everyone is peaking, and chatting. Perhaps you should stay covered up." Julian nodded as she reached for the blanket and Samira helped her pull it up to her chest, and then pulled her hair out from the bed, and admired it.

"Would you like me to get some nurses in here to chat with you? It might make you feel better." Samira asked feeling uncomfortable about what to say, and looking for a way out for the moment.

"No. No. You are wonderful. Thank you for helpin' me. My fears got the best of me. I like chattin' to you. I feel safe with you here."

"Wellllll, I like talking to you." Samira told her with a big smile.

Julian shook her head, and said, "I really want you to stay with me...alone. If you want to? I thank you have a good heart and I would like to share smiles." Reading Samira's mannerism and minor social

inadequacies, she suspected they shared somethings in common.

"And what religion are you if...you don't m...m...mind me asking?"

Julian stammered a little, "I'm a Christian. Is that okay? Are you Islamic? Your name is Arabic?" She still shook but, she was no longer crying.

With a hint of disappointment in her voice, she answered her. "Muslim and I am not practicing my faith right now. I have bott...bott...Secular at this time. Long story. I am not to judge yo...yo...you. I like th...that you seem so tolerant...more than I should admit." Julian's smiled grew warm, as she kept eye contact and hand contact.

"I just wanted to know. Is...is...is...is that okay?" Samira nervously smiled at her with warmth and real curiosity, and started to look away from Julian when her stuttering came but, merely glancing in between.

"Don't. Please don't look away when you stutter. Please." Samira stared at her in shock, and glanced away nervously, and looked back at her.

She tried to speak, but had to pause. "Really? You see that?" Julian nodded and squeezed her hand.

"Don't feel that way." Julian said, and Samira's eyes grew wider as she stammered. "Don't feel that way." And Samira stammered again to respond.

"You think you know how I feel?" Samira said, actually being somewhat confrontation, instead of trying to sound curious, which was her intent.

"My Texas accent, Samira. I get judged for it and people treat me like I am uncultured. 'Treat me like I am stupid for bein' a very short, Country Girl with an accent." Samira slowly drew her head back as the light-bulb in her mind lit up, and slowly, she nodded in agreement, and smiled at Julian, and Julian smiled back.

"I like that." Samira said, and then petted Julian's head. "I like that."

"I shan't view you that way, Samira. I know you are carin', beautiful, and bright. Thank you for carin'." Julian said with her sore larynx.

Samira smiled really big looking over her, and her shoulders lowered as she put down some of her social defenses. When Julian read them, she pulled her hand to her lips, keeping her eye on Samira's brown eyes, and kissed her hand softly. Samira blushed and smiled at her and naturally looked away embarrassed.

She had to redirect her feelings, and told Julian. "We were told to contact Security if yo...yo...yo Rachael returns. Does that make you feel safer?" Julian nodded and let go of her hand to make herself more presentable and Samira began checking the IV still in her arm, but not connected to an IV bag. "Everyone gossips about you and her...friends have the st...st...staff on every floor talking about you and your wife...I'm sorry...fr...fr... fre...friend Rachael, having sex in here?"

Julian smiled, and whispered, "Long story, also. We had to do thangs to figure out how to end thangs. It wasn't pretty, and...just...just I ended it and our relationship, and that fight happened. I'm very sorry but, she attacked me. I would have never thanked she would do that." Samira started straightening the sheets and moved on to the tray table and pointed at Julian's can of tobacco.

"What is that?"

Smiling, Julian picked it up and showed it to her. "It is Cowgirl tobacco." Julian packed it as Samira watched with curiosity, and opening the can, Julian pinched some and put it in her lip. Samira's eyes got wider and wider and she watched her very closely as her mouth slightly opened aghast.

When Julian put it back, she made sure it was symmetrical, and Samira was still looking at Julian's lip. When Julian smiled, Samira walked toward the end of the bed. "OH WOW! That is sexy." She burst out laughing, and her right hand covered her mouth. "I...I...I...oh my! I have never seen that before and...and Julian, that is really HOT!" Samira kept glancing at her, but too shy to maintain eye contact. "Sorry."

"So are you, Samira." Julian whispered.

With a deep long breath, Samira looked directly at Julian with a look of trepidation on her face, and slowly pulled her hands up to her wide hips nervously and whispered. "I like Men...and Women Julian...and please don't repeat that." She looked around, and back to Julian for a promise. She even looked over her eye patch and back to her eye, waiting. Julian nodded to her with a big smile, and confessed.

Calmly, "I do to, Samira. That was part of the problem with Rachael. She hates men, but likes messin' around with them, and hates my Angel husband, Noah."

Julian smiled and slowly peeled her patch off her head, and fustled with her hair to look prettier. Samira stared at her eyes and Julian offered to let her look into her windows. Samira actually moved her head to the side, never breaking the stare. She was not confrontational, she was reading her or making a decision. Julian opened her windows and wanted her to see everything. As the clock began to tick on them, both of them stared and worked through their feelings and consequences.

Slowly, nodding her head and her gentle, bright smile, Samira let her know what she was thinking. "Can I see you before you leave the hospital?" Julian nodded gently making sure she did not break the

stare. Samira took a long breath and dropped her hands from her hips, and looked away to ask her another question. "Can I see you after you leave the hospital?" Julian nodded and kept the windows open for her. She glanced and Julian watched the tension drop in her manly shoulders, again.

"I'm Black and Muslim. That doesn't bother you or your religion...in any way? BE HONEST!" Samira did not glance away this time.

Shaking her head without losing eye contact, Julian told her the truth, "No."

"What about your family and friends?" Julian shook her head and repeated.

"In public, Julian?"

Shaking her head again, Samira wondered, as she read her windows. But before speaking, she took a long breath and slowly let it out.

"I see your Alibis." Julian's eyes got really big as she choked up being caught off-guard and she sat up, nervous and her expression showed it, and Samira kept reading her. Holding their stare, Julian sat back, nervous and evaluating Samira's choice of words that included, Alibis. Her body language did not fit one who knew about IDentifY.

"I thank you be very beautiful and very shy, Samira?" Samira slowly nodded. "I thank yer' heart is good." Samira offered a small smile. "I thank you fear a lot of thangs...especially yer' hidden desires." Slowly, Samira nodded in agreement, and Julian told her out right, "You have no reason to fear mine."

Samira puckered her lips as she worked up the courage to swallow and take a chance on a new friend. After her hard swallow, she smiled and flipped her hair, and Julian smiled and flipped her hair back, making both of them smile really big.

267

"I have goosebumps, Julian." She looked at her left arm and offered it to let Julian see, and smiling, Julian held out her right arm, and Samira could see her goosebumps, and they giggled nervously.

"When I go home, I hope you will come to my house and brush my hair for me and meet my family." Samira turned to catch up on her duties, and stopped at the door.

"I can't wait to brush your hair." Samira said as she walked out the door as Julian admired the thick, muscular rear view.

Chapter Twenty-One

-Black-eyed-Green-eyed Asterisk

Opening her eyes from the wonderful pain, Jenna continued telling him Emily's story as they shared the warmth from his pole. "Emily was like that in high school too, Noah. Those God-awful tits of hers." She leaned forward putting her palms together on his tight stomach and slowly rode him as she spoke.

"You married a used-up Ho who tells everyone she is an Angel to cover it up." Jenna got up and got her feet behind her to enjoy him more. Enjoying his thrust, he kept his eyes closed to roll them at her when she spoke.

"I tried using orgasms to manage her anxieties, when we were in college, but her anxieties got terrible, the more she read the Bible and the fearing God-shit, she needed more semen to soothe her. I would pull her hair but, semen became the real pill for her. Starbucks of semen, college was for her. She makes me sick with that stuff. I hate the taste of it, and her anxieties are the worst I have seen since I have known her-"

"MY GOD WOMAN! Do you talk this much with everyone you fuck? How does Julian put up with you? And this duct tape hurts my balls." Jenna stopped riding him, and just gave him the stare until he closed his eyes again.

Clearing her throat to continue. "Like I said, her Alibis are fading and or bleeding into each other. Jordan can't speak without accenting. Arizona is a fade into Casey and ditzy Lowana. She is more dangerous

now, to herself, than your man-brain can understand."
She followed it up with a smirk at him as he focused
on her warmth, all over his throbber. Gently, she
rocked him and he just quietly listened and watched
her fuck him. His eyes would roll back a little more on
the down thrust. The back of his penis seemed to be
the most sensitive, she remembered.

She shifted trying to get that perfect angle to hit
her favorite spot, and finally spoke when she got it.
"Her crazy Hillbilly Bible upbringing gave her all those
anxieties, you know. Her Daddy probably raped her or
her brothers and beat her over the head with the
Bible, like mine Father did. Whatever it was, she is
most comfortable feeling raped, Noah. I have seen it.
It is her drug of choice. STOP STARING AT MY BLACK
EYE!" She stared him down with it until he looked
down at her nipples, and went back to pleasing him.

"I wish I could feel them." He said, making her
feel desired-with an Instant problem solver strategy
that almost always works.

"Like I was saying, she wants raped...raped by
Strangers. I have been visiting her and getting friends
to come giver her their semen. She was having
withdrawals. Shakes. Ticks, paranoia that you would
rape her again. Nervous signs of withdrawal,
depression. She has called the suicide hotline twice
since your raped her, Noah James." Jon gave the
smirk back, when she said that.

"I hooked her up with a couple male nurses' too-
BLACK male nurses at the clinic to go in and jerk off in
her mouth daily." Now he rolled his eyes with the
smirk, and she didn't notice.

He stopped thrusting with her and spoke up.
"Why the fuck would you say shit like that? She would
never do something like that without asking me about
it. She is not a Slutbag, like you. I don't believe that at

all, Jenna." Jenna stared at him and continued to please him slowly, with her green-eyes locked on him, she smiled at him.

"She did ask you, Noah." She created the silence for just enough time for his male brain to try and catch up to her. "In your text, you told her to get as much as she needed and to ask Rachael to Witness." One would never think her smile could get wider on her skinny face, but it did. "Thanks to your wonderful guilt-confessing texts to her that will help convict you."

"I don't have my phone you bat-crazy..." His brain caught up to her. She had his phone, and was telling Emily, everything she needed to hear from him, to hate him. Checkmate.

Jenna started going farther up and down on him to indulge her victory. It was way too early for him to need to release that pent up rage. She wanted it long, she wanted it slow, and she wanted it to hurt when he planted his seed. "Women should redesign men to get a second little dick on top of their dick to hit my clit when they fuck...that would change the world. Talk about world peace." She chlicked at him again and laughed.

"Maybe if men had two big dicks, it could solve Climate Change, too." He added facetiously. Jenna ignored him, except for his eight inches scratching her itch, of course.

"You know, my clitoral hood is big compared to Julian's. Her clit is smashed between her huge, fat labia. I wish her clit was larger. I think her clit is so small because her pussy is so fat."

"I don't have any problem with my wife's clit, Jenna...maybe you just aren't man enough. Wink, Wink." He suggested. She looked back down to him from her high-horse and gave him the look.

271

Let me tell you, "Today, Emily dumped some guy's semen in her pussy and told me to masturbate her on her back to raise her pregnancy percentage. I am finally going to get my Black baby. Isn't that sweet?" Jon just nodded...and quietly stirring his anger and plotting her death.

Staring him straight in the eye, like old friends chatting, "You were supposed to knock her up one more time so we could run off together as a family. Hopefully yesterday, you got me pregnant." She spoke up with glee now, "I really hope you did. I want to breastfeed my baby with her and I hope my friends got Emily pregnant. I want my tits full of milk and the size of Julian's tits. Not her dinner plate nipples."

She sat up and started riding him harder to change the pace of the conversation. Jenna asked him "Does my pussy still feel good, Baby?" Jon nodded, enjoying the change in pace as well, and gave back to her with thrusts.

Mocking Emily's young voice, "You sure are quiet, Baby. Maybe I should duct tape your mouth again so you will make some noise, Baby. Humiliate me, Stranger."

"STOP IT! I'm concentrating on not cumming for you. I want you to enjoy it too, Rachael. And I never claimed to be an Angel." He said pushing her button, and not the special one either down below.

"You are a real dumb ass. Only an Angel can Accord another Angel, Noah and I married Emily first." Jon chuckled at her stream of rhetoric.

"Jenna. I am not an Angel. Julian claims we are, but I don't believe that stuff." He reminded her as she stopped and got confrontational.

"But, you use your religion to control her through her anxieties and mental disorders. Lying-ass

pig." She waited a second, and sat back on him, staring.

He started riding up into her harder and she sparked up a little and squeezed him in appreciation. So much so, she focused on her left nipple and fingering her clitoris. Trying to tighten her ass repeatedly and bouncing on him, she worked herself close. Moaning out her words, "That's good I like that. Keep it coming and keep me cumming." He actually pounded her a little harder and she rolled her eyes back and her mouth drifted open as reward leaked into her brain.

"Uh HUH! I'M CUMMING! I'M CUMMIN'!" She jerked forward bending his dick with her as she threw herself onto his chest and began French kissing with him, finally, she jerked away to breath and pant. "Oh that was huge. That cucumber has me sore inside." Panting her words, "I love it."

"I'm ejaculating right now." He said softly and she jerked up to look at him. "Your pussy is so good, when you laid on me, I felt it leaking repeatedly inside you. I want you to have my baby too, Jenna." She smiled slowly at him, warmly coming out of her panic mode.

"You are a Bad Boy, Noey. I can see why Emily picked you to try and father our children." She said it, cooing him. She squatted up releasing him and guided the tip of his dick into her ass, sparking his erect curiosity. She stared at him with all the confidence of a sexual Goddess and him, the trainee.

"Jenna, you sound like a fuckin' idiot, Emily, Julian, Emily, Julian, Emily, Julian. I ain't buyin' this stupid shit of another personality taking over Julian. You are on drugs, and I can see it in your eyes. Um...your black eye."

273

"DON'T!" She barked. Getting it passed her muscles, she dropped her weight on him and slammed it in. She screamed, and so did he. She jerked a little to the amazing rush of pain that settled in. His eyes were huge as he leaked into her ass with small pulses of amazement. She slowly came to a smile, and just sat there with her eyes closed, as he discovered a new fetish, he had. She could feel the thickness of him and him flexing or pulsating inside her.

"WOW! That is very different...better different." He confessed.

Deliberately, she leaned forward and dragged him out of her ass to reset the muscles, to feel more stimulation than pain, and to breathe. Jenna smiled at him and nodded before reaching for the phone laying behind her, and slowly slid back down. She started checking her text messages and pulled up a few pictures to show him.

"Recognize that battered pussy, Noah? On your Battered ex-woman?" She showed him a photo with the cucumber sticking out of it from below Julian's mound. With her zooming in, he could see it. Jon's concentration left his face as he recognized that bovine size labia.

She moved on showing him picture after picture of her posing completely nude in the hospital bed for Jenna. "Stop! Are those her nipples? She actually let you photograph her nipples? I'M GOING TO KILL HER!" He said as he drove his cock into Jenna's tight ass as retaliation for showing him. "That fucking CUNT...has been lying to me. FUCKING PLAYING ME!" Jenna smiled really big as she finally got a wedge between them that she could work.

"This is an oldy Noah, but a really goody." She flipped the picture around and he was somewhat confused trying to recognize her. Looking at her curves

and finally spotting the tramp-stamp, he knew who it was.

Two guys were fucking Emily on her knees as she wore a red pillow case over her head. Her wrists were bound to her ankles with duct tape and her ass was up in the air and her tits smashed onto the guy under her. The Black guy under her, was driving his cock into her, and the White guy was behind her, up over her round hips and driving his cock down into her ass. He had his arms up showing his muscles. "See the guy jamming it in her ass? That is Simon. He is doing to her what you never could. He is doing to her, what you are doing to me right now."

"See the blue bandana? That is the one hanging on your bed in your bedroom right now. That was Simon's choker for your innocent wife who claims to be an Angel. I proved her wrong. Thanks to Special K." Jenna smiled and started fucking his hard cock really fast. Her stimulating pain level needed to match his emotional pain level as her punishment for the pleasure of giving him pain and pleasure and avoiding the guilt of wanting the painful pleasure.

Jon was dumbfounded and not moving. His face was bilious, and she kept riding him watching it spoil. She leaned down with her elbows on his chest and he stared at the ceiling as she laggardly grinned when the tears fell from the sides of his eyes. She was not letting this dick get soft over his psychological state. The tears fell out of the corner of his eyes, again and he did not say a word.

Taking herself to the limits of the pain, she had to stimulate him verbally. "You could have had me, Noah. I always wanted to use you for my satisfaction, like with Simon. Did you know, Simon raped Emmy for more than a year before stabbing her? I never told her. He was her favorite." She picked up the phone

and played the video of her rubbing Emily down with coconut oil that morning. "Listen to her talk, Noah. She will tell you in her own words."

Playing the video, Julian described the guy in the picture, and his style. Jon continued to let the tears flow yet, he stayed hard from her tight stimulating rear. He didn't even look at the video but, recognized her whispers. He knew now, that he knew the truth about his wife.

"Look at the bright side, you are fucking me in the ass and I'm married to her-kind of a Munchhausen by proxy." She waited a few seconds before acknowledging his lack of acknowledgement. "Nothing, huh?" She shifted herself by putting her feet under her and bounced up and down on his dick harder and her painful expression showed the difference, she was looking for.

She had to pause until her eyes rolled forward again before she could talk. "So the fake Angel wife liked to pray with two dicks in her and a pillow case over her face. Eh? You can thank me. I worked my little ass off to prove she was not a real Angel and pimped her Angel ass. I got her into double penetration. I pimped her fat ass to anyone and fed her the right chemicals. Some Angel, Noah."

She leaned in to him, and spoke softly and from her heart, "There is no God. I proved it and I proved it being raped by my own father for ten long years. God never rescued me. A CHILD! HE COULDN'T RESCUE A CHILD, NOAH?"

"You know, Men are just too stupid to know we cheat on them almost daily. We Women always have someone waiting their turn. We are meant to have anyone we want, Noah. The best part is, if the Patriarchy complains, we just cry, and you believe us." She leaned back up and enjoyed the freedom to fuck

him against his will, because it was her will. It would be sexist for him not to agree to have sex with her, when she wanted it.

"So we know the 'Angel' likes rape, likes to let Strangers fuck her, never goes to church and wears the pants in your house, has affairs, and..." she chuckled at him, "...you wear the panties." She busted out a short laugh to sweeten the pain of his emasculation.

Not finishing her chuckle yet, she still spoke up. "She hates your oppressive religion, Noah, but uses it to keep everyone from knowing who she really was and is. It's part of her DIDC lie, Boy. And she never let you enjoy fucking that ass of hers-AFTER all those men in college and Med School. I am flabbergasted. But, you are only part of her Emily cover-up. Emily saves herself for me and our trips to the Holiday Inn with other men. This is why I have to Crash Julian, Noah." He glanced at her, stirring in his anger.

She grabbed her phone again and showed him pictures of his shy wife, posing nude in the hospital room, and smiling while doing it. "This is Emily fucking a soda bottle in her bed today. See it. She invited nurses into the room to watch her...like Emily did in college. Are you picking up on the connection here, Floridian Boy? Yet, Julian's-"

"WHY?" He barked in his anger, "WHY...do you keep saying Florida to me? I'm from Wyoming." She went right on sliding on his pole, and talking.

"That's what we told you, Danny-man." She went right back to her rant. "Julian's religion says she cannot insert anything into her vagina, and here is a soda bottle." He looked up and recognized that ass and saw the bottle swallowed up in her labia. "This is what I have been telling you, Noah. She is bleeding memories into other cover blankets and her Diddy

277

meds are no longer working for her real personality disorder. Julian is a DIDC for Emily. JULIAN is not a real person and she is going to Crash the bad way. I have to Crash her properly with the key to save her real identity. She is Emily, but thinks she is Julian. Tessa, Arizona, Casey, Lowana, Cheyenne...all her Alibis are in there blending and as it does, the Helix fragments and Crashes, altering the original person- Emily. We will lose the Julian you know and love, and you will be stuck with...with...zombie Julian as a Mommy." She changed to a condescending tone, "Not a good idea, Noah."

Jenna started really working his dick harder. The more pain she gave, the more pleasure she got, and the more his dick wanted to punish her. She slid her feet down the outside of his legs and rode it up the bottom of the shaft and down. It pushed between her Venusian dimples and loved that painful rush. Instantly, his eyes rolled back and she glowed with Girl Power.

"I need her Crash key, Noah. You know it. You have it. If you don't give it to me, she will Crash to a Zombie. Fuck my ass, Noah." She tried to squeeze his thick meat and spoke, "Feel that...feel it deep in my ass." He leaned his head farther and farther back into the bed and as she watched for him to hold his breath, and she stopped, and got up. He was edged. "No key- No reward, Boy."

Mildly panting, he looked up at her standing over him nude. "I need the key to finish this, so I can Crash her today, Noah. You have to understand, she is miserable fragmenting." He looked away and gave it up easily.

"Eric Clapton, Can't find my way home. 2:32 marker." He mumbled and she repeated it for him and he nodded.

Sounding joyous, "Now was that so hard, Noah?" She will be back to being Emily Cuckquean by tomorrow night. And uh...I will be moving in with her tomorrow, too. Thank you for helping her." She bowed her head slightly when she thanked him.

"Really Noah. Thank you. You sacrificed your fake marriage just now, to rescue her. I don't think she knows how much you really love her, even though she did shoot you once. By the way, I set that up, too." He immediately looked at her with fire in his eyes.

"Yes. I set all that up. I used old triggers, suggestive counseling, and a few strategically prescribed meds to Emily. Worked her fears like a charm. Damn, Men are so stupid." Shaming him with her finger, "SHAME ON YOU for surviving, Noah James." She looked at him glowering. He was more along the lines of WTF now, and argued that one.

"That did not happen that way. We both know that...you inferior species." He was shaking his head at her, utterly annoyed, and mansplaining. "Julian was having severe problems after her undercover work. She panicked out of fear." Jon said, responding to the soap opera with good sex.

"I worked the false memories hard on her to curve her double penetration addiction. I actually made some progress. I admit, I could never stop her double penetration fetish, but I curved the others with Special K. No one should ever stop a Woman from double penetration, Noah. She crashed after Simon raped her-Crashed bad. We used psychotherapy, meds, synthetics, you name it, and IDentifY to create her Julian personality and revive her world. Rape fucks up the memory blankets, Noah. Adderall was a good maintenance stabilizer for the memory blankets. If

279

you're on it long enough. But, keep the vitamin c away though. Fucks up the stable."

He looked right at her with his eyes wide, and spoke fast. "Julian always tells me to stay away from vitamin C. Am I on a stabilizer, too?" He asked in a non-confrontational tone of concern.

Nervously, she informed him, "Yes you are, Noah. You have been for years now as Noah and Jon, both are Alibis." She said it as a kind matter of fact. She even stopped riding him to answer.

He maintained his stare after putting more and more pieces together that had gathered into routine through the marriage with Julian. He took a deep breath of anger and began thrusting into her and those green eyes glowed at him with teasing lust, as her head went forward and enjoyed the rush of intense pleasure and pain. He was past it for the moment. She was going to get a good ass fucking now driven by rage...the best a Man can give a Woman.

Her eyes were rolling back as her words blundered. She had provoked him into giving her, his best sex. Unbeknownst to him, he found the perfect way to make a Woman shut up. She leaned back and let her body push into him more and pulled on both her nipples with exciting intensity. Holding her breath, and her teeth clenched, she let him give her the pain, and her painful expression deepened as she got the point of no return, and he stopped. She was edged.

Her eyes opened wide at him with anger, rage, and desire for the pain he stopped providing this cute, petite blonde, Masochist. "You son of a bitch. I fucking love feeling used in the ass." Panting, he chlicked at her and winked. She got down on him for a breather and loved how his bare skin felt against hers.

She took a few deep breaths before talking again, "I use Emily's coconut oil idea to keep me

lubed, and it works great for us gals with needs back there. Most of us women do need it back there...don't let us lie to you. Emily though, can cream back there without lube. Cream like milk, I tell you. Why do you think she takes so much magnesium? It lubes her on the inside for ritual butt-sex."

"You know, I used the same breath-mints trick on men to rape Emily back in Med School. PCP and sildenafil works like a charm, Noah, and it worked on you." She offered up a wink from her black-eye. "I believe I gave Simon too much PCP in his breath-mints drink, and that was what brought on the stabbing. When I worked out the plan for him to rape her in public-her ultimate fantasy by the way, it was perfect, except for the stabbing, and we never knew real rape would Crash the Dissociative Identity Disorder Cover Julian, back then. Crash isn't the correct term though, because it doesn't really Crash, it...it just bleeds them into each other. Knocks the hell out of them Alibis by chemical differences in the receptors-most trauma alters the chemicals of the brain. PTSD alters the mind, and that is what happens. Simon went to prison never knowing he was under a DIDC until they took away his stabilizer in prison and BLEED! His calliope crashed to the ground."

She pulled her knees up to her chest and started dragging him all the way out and sliding him all the way in. "Ever notice your wife's addiction problems, Noah? She is prone to addiction easily. Semen, hair pulling, Adderall, tasting her herself, breast milk, pills, tasting women, sexual humiliation, hillbilly chew, fisting, pain, boots, sucking on her hair, her hefty morning rituals, praying ten times a day, her no panties policy-all that is part of her OCD and she is OCD on her fetishes. And now, she doesn't understand any of those because of her psychosis."

"I call it her spices of life." He offered and stared.

He watched her eyes close as she stimulated herself deep inside. Each time she took the last inch of him, she winced in pain rushing her concentration, and made sure she bounced on it three times before taking the long slide up his pole. "Since we tricked you and drugged you into raping her. I just push a fetish with a trigger and her OCD grabs onto it, and I have instant control. When she masturbates, she imposes some sense of rape into it-ALWAYS! Hell, she never lets me do anything sexual to her, unless she feels forced into it. That makes me wet thinking about it, Noah. I have triggered her for years." She paused to bounce six or seven times on the pain, and her lower jaw dropped as she enjoyed the extreme stimulation.

"Rape is a lifelong fetish addiction claimed by her OCD, Noah. She can't want it because, she needs it. And you can't do it because it fragments her Helix, which proves Men having sex with Women, might not be natural and the Patriarchy. Therefore, to fulfill her needs, I will be raping her, for her-SAFELY!"

His whisper sounded like defeat as she leaned in to hear him, "I let her accept other's seed because it's NONE OF YOUR FUCKING BUSINESS BITCH and if you show me another picture, I will stop this SHIT! I won't give you my seed-JENNA WANNA BE!" Her eyes widened as she jerked back. "You have proven to me what's really going on. Don't keep putting salt into my wounds or so help me God."

She sat up on him again, "Did you know, Simon grabbed her in the parking lot and started fucking her and people watched and cheered. They actually thought it was just more of her religious crap...until he knifed her. Emily doesn't even know the truth about it

anymore. She only knows the false memories I attached to it."

Done with the conversation, he worked that dick hard and long into her dark surround, forcing her off balance and she only used one hand to stretch her nipples. She was getting the impression he wanted this over with. She struggled to stop the stimulation, and climbed off of him for a break.

"I CAN'T TALK WITH...you ramming your dick up my ass so hard...I can't talk when you do that." Flailing her arms into the air, "Scream me to the heavens anytime during sex, but conversing, is asking a lot." She walked over to her purse and pulled out another caplet, and popped it into her mouth and chewed on it.

"Let me show you some more pictures of this proven-to-be-a-fake, Angel." She suggested, and he rebutted her.

"I don't want to see any more, Jenna. Why are you showing them to me still?" Jon insisted, growing very agitated again.

"This is her in Med School, after you were married. She is having a Bible study, see." Jenna held the picture up and put it close to his face. He didn't look away and took it all it. Emily was lying in a chair naked, showing her scarred tits, with her hand fingering someone's cum into her vaginal opening. He refused to look.

"That is the only reason she wants the Bible...perfect cover for a Ho, Danny-boy."

Holding onto the phone, she climbed back on him and worked her gaping rear door down on his cock head and slid it back in with ease and an exhale of satisfaction. He was in a blank stare again...dwelling in emotional pain. She sat down on him gently, not to disturb the emotional pain that was to become her mind-control over him, and she started to reel him in

283

slowly. "Daniel...oh that is your real name by the way...YES keep moaning the pleasure of my sweet, tight ass, Danny."   Bearing her evil grin, "Daniel Jose Gonzales, Illegal from Florida State." She started working her hips forward and back, instead of up and down. "I have been pleasuring you because, you must be attracted to me Danny, to reach the natural inhibitors I need, to Crash you." She got his attention with that remark, and he looked at her.

"I am going to tell you about the Crash, Danny, and when you cum in my ass I don't want you to fuck it while your cumming. Let me feel you throb in my ass. Now, think about the Orbitofrontal Cortex...for present uneducated men that would be the area behind your left eye and-" she stopped short.

"HOLD ON! I'm cumming. HOLD ON! Jenna sped up and fucked him up and down losing her rhythm and shoving him deep enough hit the extreme pain in her colon. "OH FUCKING GOD! FUCKING HURTS! FUCKING GOD FUCK ME DADDY! FUCK ME DADDY! Her face crushed into itself as she bounced on his cock along the full shaft and with each pounce, pounded her chaw-bone ass into his pelvic area moaning wonderfully into orgasm. He instinctively, began thrusting her as his hands reached for her chest, only to be held back by the cuffs. Finally, the Big O took her, and she screamed with empty lungs as her legs shook and she squeezed his cock like a vice. Her left hand pulled her nipple nearly six inches off her chest. Jerking in her bounce, she fell backward between his legs onto her back and he howled as his cock went with her. She laid there, enjoying the after effects of her reward. Her head stopped moving, and she was lifeless. "You are really hurting my dick, Jenna. Jenna you are hurting me. JENNA! Jenna?" In so much pain from the top of his shaft getting stretched, he tried to

sit up to find relief and couldn't get away from the cuffs. He tossed his right leg over and could not completely get it to his other leg because her lifeless legs were bent over his. He pulled himself up using the hand rails and his dick shot out of her ass and stood back at attention with relief. This was not his first time fucking a woman into unconsciousness, with her wearing a black-eye.

He looked at his dick in a sense of accomplishment and had a clear view of her pussy and flat tits. Her pussy was actually very pretty, very well kept, shaved clean, the word "Slut" had a ring of sexiness to it and her chest was rising and falling. He wanted to fuck her...and fuck her hard but, with her on the bottom. He had never actually had sex as an adult, with a skinny, white Woman. He was attracted to her now, and that was what she needed.

"Jenna? JENNA? WAKE UP SKINNY BITCH?" When she didn't respond, he used his feet to roll her toward the far end of the bed. He hoped it would wake her, but her legs dangled off the side and whipped her body off the bed and onto the floor, lifeless. She never made a sound. He was not sure what happened, yet his male ego felt stimulated. One of the phones had slid down to the base of his erected penis and he couldn't dial a call with his wrists cuffed, and grunted at the situation. He tried using voice command but, the phone did not respond to him.

Exhaling dramatically, "What a freakin' way to get blue balls. Fucking Julian has lied to me all these years! 'Lied to me about everything in her past. I married a fucking tramp lesbian dick drinking fucking whore cumbag. And...WHO THE FUCK AM I?" He just laid there stirring, wondering if letting her have Julian or a person named Emily, really was the solution...for everyone. "Am I really from Florida?"

When his crying began, he felt distance growing between him and his children already...if they were his children.

Chapter 22

-Bend the Crash with Venus Dimples

Jenna woke him up by pushing on his chest. "Hey Cowboy, want to ride a thin Cowgirl." The chlicking sound woke him up faster and he saw her standing beside the bed. Her pretty nipples staring down at him as her hands rested on her narrow hips. She bent down and French kissed him warmly and kissed him all over his neck. "Are you okay, Cowboy? Looks like your saddle horn got a little tired." And she gestured toward his limp dick.

Noah slowly cleared his thoughts, when she grabbed his balls, and ripped the squished duct tape off, and started kneading them right away. Instantly, he felt relief. She started talking as if nothing had happened. "I started pegging Julian back in Luckenbach, then she let the guys. I got really good at it. I actually like pegging men. It turns me on for some reason to hear their virgin screams. I love hearing men scream like a woman from the pain I know is really pleasuring them. It's like draining a man of his toxic masculinity and he is fighting it screaming and he is losing to the pleasure of being a Woman. The more men get pegged, the more chemical changes in the brain that feminizes them. Real Feminist never turn down pegging a man. It detoxifies their masculinity. It defeats them."

His dick started responding to her touch and she smiled with pride at her goal being met. "That's a good cock, Dan-man the Wife Beater." Gently, she reached down and fingered his ass hole. He jerked and squeezed his legs and cheeks together to stop her.

Yet, his dick started rising faster. "I told you, you are Queer and lived the life of a Gay man. 'Proves Julian wrong again that you are an...an...'" She sighed at herself, "What is that stupid man-word for a Male Angel?" She waited but, she had no clue. "We reprogrammed your pretty face, Danny." She was breaking into a friendly chuckle to the friendly poke he was not so friendly about. Noah, finally realized, he reset his IDentifY from sleep, and tried to get up to see the bathroom mirror again. She jerked away and chuckled at him when both sets of cuffs held him down.

She stood over him next to the bed smiling, and pointed toward his dick as it noticeably rose to the occasion. Feeling the wonderful firmness of his shaft and urethra, she stroked it to full attention feeling her own tingles. "I already know about your gay past, Daniel. I helped Julian design your personality with false memories-false memories is my specialty on the team." He tried to get up again and his cuffs held him back. Staring at each other as she investigated his odd behavior, she turned and looked up to his direction of intended travel, and back down to him, with a shocked look. His eyes showed how desperate he was, and how he had been moving the chess board, instead of the pieces. She dashed over to the bathroom door, as she frantically tried to get up again. Slamming the door on his escape mirror before he could IDentifY Jon, she won.

As she turned around seductively wet by the win, he finally felt the fear of it. He was trapped, even from IDentifY escape. She began talking to him as she stepped one foot in front of the other toward him making sure her seductive powers were at their highest levels.

"Do you want to fuck me in the ass tomorrow before I peg you, Noah? I would like that myself. Maybe...tease your orgasm and then I can work it in your ass and milk you and I can play your Crash key music as I raise your level of estrogen giving you anal." He feared her evil moves as they closed in on him. "To Crash, I need the inhibitor pill, your anal orgasm, IDentifY, a video recording, and your song with time key. And since Rachael designed yours so long ago, we already have the file."

As she got close to the bed, he started scooting back as much as he could. "Emily picked the song out for you years ago. It is the Biblical song, Seasons in the Sun by Terry Jacks. Rachael says it has to be old music that one doesn't hear being played randomly today. Stupid religious song."

"Why did you pass out, Jenna? What the fuck? Scared me to death. What the heck is wrong with you?" Noah demanded.

"You were a floating Soy-Boy, when Julian met you. But as all of us women do, we want to change everything about you...except your looks. And as long as we have control over your life, our life is perfect. Emily befriended you, moved you in with us, and we went to work on you. We flipped you from IDentifY to IDentifY trying to get her what she wanted. You were to be her Cover-boy that provided daily semen and babies and money. I think Noah is your fourth identity, actually. I can't remember. Another stupid Bible preceptor, for the Julian Bible lover cover crap. Well...A few pills here, a few there...false mems here, backtail stories, and 'finito. Emily had her perfect cover couple, Julian and Noah. Only Emily didn't really want to keep you because, well to be honest, we really don't want permanent men. Emily whipped you pretending to be

Julian, and she got bored with you. Time for a new dating app."

She walked away and washed her hands in the sink and stepped back to get the phone off the bed. "We women are complicated like that. Damn if you do, damned when you don't. Live with it. We do, Danny." She started drying her hands with the sheet. "Danny, did you know your wife has aborted several babies since you got married? She just wasn't sure if they would come out your color. Rachael says she had about five or six every year in college. She thinks Emily would get pregnant just so she couldn't get pregnant. You know? Did you know Rachael kept a reminder on the calendar for testing and aborting, just for Emily?" She flipped through her text messages as he spoke.

"Let me ask you something Jenna, since this is such good pussy." His eyes rolled around after he said it. "When is mine and Julian's wedding anniversary? Just tell me that." Jenna gave him the stare...and she tried to remember. Noah waited her out and the longer he had to wait, the more he infected her mind.

She pulled up a picture and showed him fucking her from behind. He was fucking Jenna. His eyes got really big. He looked younger, about twenty-five in the picture. He did not respond to her. But his mind truly felt fucked by that one. She smiled as he stared at the ceiling again, searching for himself. He knew he had never had sex with Andrea or Rachael or Jenna until now. *Or had he?* He thought.

"Here is one of Emily sucking on a huge dick." The image was of a younger Julian, her mouth wide open with some guy's dick in it. She was looking up at the camera with those beautiful baby blues and so happy. "That was about the time Emily used the double-dildo on me in front of one of our Med classes

290

at the Holiday Inn." Jon smiled, remembering when he took the picture in the second or third year together, in Texas. When he chuckled to himself, she got quiet and stared at him.

Jenna climbed back on him and worked his dirty cock back into her ass and once she got the head passed the sore muscles, she slid home making him feel like a champ again. "Pretty sweet Angel ass, isn't it?"

She worked herself back up and took him out for a few seconds, and worked it back inside. "I need to tell you that you have to Crash too, Danny. Tomorrow. I have to Crash you and Julian. You have learned way too much, and if I'm going to send you to prison for so many rape victims, and well, I can't have you knowing your Alibis." She chlicked at him, again.

"Let me finish telling you, the pill is awesome. It helps the mind reboot in a 'classified' order. I guess that is the best way to describe it." She finished her air quotes and went on, "The orgasm shuts things down and alters your state of consciousness naturally, like I just did, yet the pill reorganizes the booting sequences and alters that to an extent. It is like shooting heroin every time. It fucks with your limbic system, hypothalamus to manage that unconscious body control the mind provides-sneaks in right under its little function and acts like a digital virus...like a computer virus. There you go. That is a cool way to explain it to you...Men are too stupid for medical terms anyway." She smiled, watching him try to listen as she beat his mind down and pumped his penis up.

"Understand how this works. The Lateral Orbitofrontal Cortex shuts down during orgasm. It is used for encoding in our brain. Music is a digital code, Danny. We must incept the pre-programmed numerical code value within the prescribed song, prior

to an orgasm, to incept it. So many functional regions of the brain during orgasms activate, and we have to stimulate them without the LOFC functioning to Crash-from the orgasm. This will affect your memory long and short and quickly the pre-coded numerical value key already programmed into her and your little brain, becomes the baseline. Hearing the numerical music value must back up in being coded, in the system in your brain...so to speak. In order for encoding to Crash in the LOFC when it wants to reboot and latches onto the new artificial numerical value from the song, that matches baseline. Once I get it to shut down in you through orgasm and the magic pill, the system functions but only part of it, this incepts the code and back-ups begins. The code just bounces around the brain a while until coding values begin again...and the fun part is, with a sweet magic pill, the coding shuts down for much longer and poof-Crash of the Identify DIDC." She put her right hand up and waved, "Bye-bye Alibis. We will curve your inhibited responses. Alter behavior through somatic markers and...the best part...it feels so good. Like heroin. It is that wonderful."

When he started to speak, she began thrusting her hips forward and back as she worked the soreness out from earlier. "I don't do drugs...I don't even do prescription drugs, Jenna." He fought her pleasure, "This sounds like typical Rachael hogwash. The typical sounds of a woman who slept her way through Med School...and a woman, who you are trying to kidnap, said to me." Noah smiled as that knife sliced into her thick skin. It did not have any effect, since his penis was thinking for him part of the time.

Laughing as she rode his cock softly now so she could speak, "You do drugs Danny, only you don't know it. Stabilizer REMEMBER?" Winking at him with a

chlick, she tagged it with an extra this time, "Julian kept you on certain inhibitors...you just didn't know it, Danny. And I did sleep my way through Med School...with your wife and a few hundred friends."

"The good thing about Crashing Danny, is you have to get it in the ass. Tomorrow, I'm going to Crash you and I get to fuck you in the ass like you are doing me, today. Damn, that is hot, Danny."

He responded with a non-believing crude look of sincere doubt and she gave him that girly smile that glowed. "I actually like pegging, remember. And I like getting it, remember?" She looked down at herself to indicate his dick was in her ass right now...again. "Don't worry, I will bring an entire jar of coconut oil for you. I haven't Crashed you in a few years. Unless...does Emily peg you?" She gestured down again, to the fact his dick was inside her. "I love to Crash. Well I do a partial Crash. You saw it."

"Masturbation has its limits, Danny. So someone you are attracted to, must give you the orgasm and we know you are attracted to me, again. Getting an orgasm from me increases your hormone prolactin, to like five times its masturbation level. One cannot masturbate and Crash...even with the pill. If we could, we could be Crashing daily for fun."

"I will certainly enjoy pegging you, again, Danny. STOP rolling your eyes. You really do have to be probed through the anal cavity. LISTEN TO ME STUPID! I have to use the hypogastric nerve and stimulate it via your prostate along with your pelvic nerve to pop that reward circuit in your reward system of your brain. STOP LAUGHING AT ME YOU WIFE BEATING RAPIST!" Jenna slapped him across the face while sitting on his dick. He looked at her with shock and then started smiling again...and eventually shaking

his head with the smile and growing dangerously close to a laugh.

"Girls like Emily and I, we can actually near Crash from anal sex because we can orgasm from anal sex. NOT MANY WOMEN CAN! WHAT ARE YOU LAUGHING AT?"

Noah, was rolling his eyes and chuckling with a shaking jolly at her story and it continued in his tone. "You have no fucking clue what you are saying." He roared up at her to ask her with a laugh in his voice, "I have to get butt-fucked to crash? Butt-fucked by a Man-hater, none the less?" He was speaking through his chuckles, as he laid back down. "Hell Rachael, peggin' will Crash any guys party." And without warning, his demeanor shifted. "You stupid fucking New York CLAM! YOU AIN'T FUCKIN' ME IN THE ASS BITCH! IF YOU HAVEN'T NOTICED YOU FUCKING SUCK-CUMMING WHORE! MY DICK IS UP YOUR ASS NOW! AND...IF that is true that rape Crashes, why didn't Emily crash every time she was raped in college you stupid fucking TWIG CUNT COWBOY WANNABE! AND! AND! AND! IF Julian could have butt orgasms, I GUARAN-FUCKING-T YOU-she would be begging me to butt-fuck her every night."

Losing her sweet smile, and raising her voice a little "I do fuck her in the butt every other night, Danny. That is why I recognize who she is now and that you partially Crashed her Alibis." She punched him in the face. And punched him again. And again. Getting laughed at by a man, was her biggest button...even Jordan never pressed that button. She tried punching him again, only he moved his head quick enough and she fell onto the side of the bed dangling with his cock up her ass. He booted her off and onto her face, and she busted up laughing at him, lying face down on the floor.

He started smiling and broke into a nervous laugh about the entire situation and the stories, until he felt the cold steal of her barrel lean against his right temple. Instantly stopping his play, only his eyes moved to confirm what cold metal he was feeling and hopefully, no sound would follow. Even his pee shooter stood without moving for her pee shooter. The stand-off of 'whose dick was bigger' had finally arrived.

Speaking delicately to her, "Rachael, you have lost your FUCKING CRASHED MIND! Anal fucking to erase memory? Really? Just say you want to peg me to emasculate me. It's your thing with men. IT WETS YOUR BONEY CUNT, BITCH! Julian has told me how much you hate me...especially Mustangs, like me. And this drinking semen shit didn't start until after we were dating. Come to think of it, are we Accorded too, Rachael...just so I remember to get you an anniversary card you PUSSY BITCH WITHOUT A DICK! YOU AIN'T NEARER THE BALLS TO PULL THE FUCKING TRIGGER ON ME! B-AAAATCH! I ROCK THIS FUCKING WORLD! I ROCK JULIAN'S WORLD! AND WHEN YOU PUT MY COCK BACK IN YOUR ASS TOMGIRL, I AM GONNA ROCK YOUR FUCKING WORLD! WHAT YOU THINK OF THAT...IN THE WORDS OF DENZEL 'KING KONG AIN'T GOT NOTHING ON ME, BITCH!"

CLICK! The sound of cold steel shook his confidence when she pulled the trigger on his mind with her 9mm pistol resting millimeters from his brain.

She stood up and walked closer to him and stabbed his leg with a syringe and her thumb injected the fluid without concern. She kept her eyes locked on his, along with her gun pointed at his face. She dug the syringe in deeper and jerked it around to remind him who was the boss. She did not look at her needle work. "A little Ketamine for your anger and memory MOTHERFUCKER! I'VE BEEN SEDATING HER WITH IT

SINCE OUR SECOND YEAR IN COLLEGE! I KEPT HER ON HER HANDS AND KNEES AND PIMPED HER MENTALLY HANDICAPPED ASS TO THE PIGS TO PROVE THERE WAS NO GOD!" She ground it in again, even though it was empty, and tried to rid herself of her anger.

"Shot her up this morning again. Your move now BOY!" She raised her eyebrow with a smirk and jerked it out of his leg flinging it behind her. A final release of her anger, perhaps.

He started calm, but it wouldn't last. "Are you out of your fucking mind, Rachael? Drugging me? Cap one bullet in me and good luck explaining a dead cop's body to the hospital. Trace evidence all over that round you used-up Slutbag. WHAT THE FUCK IS KETAMINE? Drugging my fucking wife so you could have sex with her? SLAMMING HER TO ME! I AM GONNA KILL YOU RACHAEL BRIGGS!" He paused for control and started again, "You just don't live enough reality to realize it. I am gonna' murder yer miserable, fucking life, BITCH!" His words were likely the most honestly spoken of the entire conversation. He felt it. He decided it. He was going to rid his happy life of this woman, permanently. "SERIAL KILLIN' AIN'T NEW TO ME, BITCH!"

"Hey stupid," She whispered, and reminded him of the facts...again as he refused to calm down. "I'm an MD, Boy. I will remove the bullet from your brain when I am finished with you. Drop you downstairs into the freezer with a Mexican toe-tag as an Undocumented. Into a body bag you go, on a plane, and enjoy your permanent vacation. Tax dollars don't get wasted on dead Illegals YOU FUCKING RAPIST! Don't you ever talk to me like that again. I have been your wife's lover for twelve fucking years. I own her."

Jenna started pushing the end of her gun against his temple really hard and he resisted her. His dick was still hard, and so was her clitoris. Enter the standoff, again. One has the thick ramming rod, the other needs rammed by the rod.

"How do you think I got her to do all those fucked up things in college? Drugs-Special K. How do you think I got her to let those men rape her? Drugs. How did I get Simon to rape her? Drugs. How do you think I got you to rape her? Drugs. Why did you rape me? Drugs. I used her to prove the truth. SO FUCK YOU RAPIST! FAT BITCH PRAYED FOR GOD EVERY TIME THEY RAPED HER AND I SAT BACK AND JERKED OFF TO IT! DRUGGED HER FAT ASS THE NEXT DAY AND TIED HER DOWN AND PIMPED YOUR GOD'S LITTLE ANGEL TO THE PIGS! THAT MOTHERFUCKER LET ME SUFFER FOR TEN YEARS AND NEVER RESCUED ME! FUCK HIM AND FUCK YOU!" The stand-off, became the silence of stand-off.

After a very long exhale, he finally tried to talk to her softly. "Julian and I talked about her college sex, JENNA! She already told me everything. I know about her and guys and Bible studies. BUT SHE WAS ONLY A RAPE VICTIM BECAUSE YOU DID NOT PROTECT HER FIVE-FEET TALL ONE-HUNDRED AND SEVENTY-FIVE POUND THE-SIZE-OF-TEXAS ASS LIKE ANY TRUE FRIEND! INSTEAD YOU DRUGGED HER AND LET YOUR FRIENDS USE HER? YOU BATTERED HER BITCH! I VOWED TO KISS THAT ANGEL'S ASS THE REST OF MY LIFE! YOU ARE A FUCKING IDIOT THINKING MY WIFE LIVES ON RAPE! TAKE THE DRUGS AWAY FROM HER AND SEE! YOU SHOULD HAVE SEEN THE LOOK-!" Jenna pulled the trigger again on his manly brain and pulled the gun back. He immediately started pleading for Julian softly and almost in tears. "The look on her face when she thought Simon was

coming to get her in the back of that car. If I had to sacrifice my life at that moment to save her from irrational fears I would have...I would do it again. I would kill you for her, Jenna. I would certainly butt-fuck you. Now get my cock back in your ass, BITCH!"

Chapter Twenty-Three

-Steel & Boney Ass to Confessions

CLAMP! Jenna loaded a full magazine into her pistol, and locked and loaded. The next trigger pull would now fire the bullet. He instantly shut the fuck up. I guess she figured out how to shut a man up. "You are like any other man. Completely clueless..." She put the gun back to his head. "...Too ill equipped to think on a level women can think. You will all be slaves one day. All you men." Her tone got really mean now, "White men will be bred out and every woman will have a wife and a Cuck-preferably Black with a huge, chocolate dick to please us with. Women will rule this fucking planet, Daniel. You are just outdated hardware. We have big plans for Emily in the future, Danny. We will make sure all her future rapes never end up this fucked up. I will rape her and control the semen until she is off of it, and addicted to anything else. Let MY DNA live in her mind and I will OWN her again. 'Fucking man DNA fucks women up, she needs female seed to infect her mind. When I stop the male seed, she will adapt to needing my seed." Seeing him trying to speak, she poked his head with the gun, and reminded him it better be liked.

"Jenna, Julian has worked very hard to repent for her sins. I cannot judge her for that. She told me that. She will have to face God one day and explain to him why she did all those things you claim she did. When I tell her how you drugged her, and tied her up to be raped by your friends, because you hate God, she is going to let me kill you. She is trying to be like her mother and be a guide for our children and a

loving parent. Please Jenna, why do you hate that so much? Why tarnish the memory of her so badly, Jenna?" He took a quick loud breath, "Just because you had a miserable life, you want everyone else to have one. Your nuclear family failed, ours hasn't. Change it by making your own family and find the love of your own child."

Noah looked over at her rubbing the pistol on one of her nipples and she seemed to blur into the background of the room. He blinked his eyes harder to gain control of his vision but, a dreamlike state was rushing in his veins and making things better...for her. He saw her Alibis dancing around her, encouraging her as the dizzy feeling grew and grew, he knew he was going to Crash.

She pulled the pistol down and rubbed it on her vagina as she spoke. "How can Julian repent for Emily's sins, when Julian is not a real person, Noah? Marriage and the Bible, created by men to use Stockholm Syndrome on women. That is the foundation of Patriarchy itself and you infected Julian with it and she got control of Emily." She said it with sincere inflection. "Leave her now and the kids and run back to Florida or go to prison or let me kill you right here. THAT! Is my offer. It is not negotiable, Boy." He looked at her, realizing he wasn't making a dent.

But, she was not finished. "You will either die Daniel, or go back to Florida, and sell your tail back on the street to your paying customers. I know you can't Pitch but, I see you as a fine Catcher. You only like Bottom for the men Danny, and after you Crash, the first thing you will ask for is BBC. I promise." She checked the phone on the table next to him recording, and grabbed Julian's phone to review her recent messages.

300

"Men who take it in the ass tend to be less toxic. It stimulates their estrogen growth. One of the ways us women are defeating men is by pegging them regularly-instantly that testosterone level drops and boom, we have control. Feminize the planet makes sense if you're a woman, Noah. I get to abuse Emily...and you will stop being their Cuckold. This is why marriage has me owning her, and she put me in that position and demands I be in it to provide her with satisfaction in all her wonderful fetishes." She said it viciously while still rubbing her clit hood with her loaded semi-automatic pistol. Frustrated, she slapped her palm to his forehead and jammed his head back, and jammed the pistol into his mouth laughing. When he froze in fright, moaning, she seductively lent him a whisper to his ear. His eyes held wide open trying to see the blurring above him, and she looked at the phone recording, and winked at it with a hidden smile.

"You know Danny, I have a strong case against you. Drug abuse during the rapes. Multiple rape cases linked to you via DNA, thanks to your donation inside Indigo yesterday. You raped me for days in here and blacked my eye." She punched herself in the face with her fist and screamed into his ear. The gun rattled in his teeth as she made him suck on it.

Hyped up now from abuse, her tone got really mean. "You blacked both my eyes raping and sodomizing me...thank you." She grinned with her teeth together at him. He knew that was a read of instability, and she did too. *Intentional or unintentional?* He quickly thought. "Suck my dick, BOY! SUCK IT! SUCK MY DICK PISTOL!" She pushed the pistol in as far as it would go, and his eyes grew brighter and brighter as his face expanded. "You would have been better off asking me if I wanted to be

raped. I would have brought Emily's pillow case." She joked harshly and got closer to his ear to make his neck hairs rise and lowered her whisper. "Emily already filed rape charges on you Boy-as Julian, and I'm going to arrest you. Your DNA is everywhere for us to use against you...again. THE WOMAN WINS AGAIN, BITCH!" She pulled the gun out of his mouth and turned it toward his leaning tower of thick manhood, and held it at gunpoint, and spoke to it.

"You can't understand that I just love her more than you, AND want us to be happy, again. I need her. She needs me. I will arrange the guys like you to rape her, and then she will need me, again. See the fucking cycle of life, Dick? I've held her down and they fucked her over and over against her will...just like she needed. She came hard every time with all the different guys that paid me for her...yes Dick, my wife." She began laughing at it, and said, "Don't talk back to me, MOTHERFUCKER!" She poked his cock with the end of the barrel. He was speechless. She stood up and looked down at it like a fighter looking down at it, and flaring her shoulders. "Get hard for me, and you can give me some pain."

"The entire university fucked her, Danny, and I loved watching her crying face, and her crawling to me afterwards...needing me. Holding me. Giving me unconditional love. I would masturbate watching her cry and beg and pray for her God, only to have her find salvation and safety in my arms afterwards, and she never knew, I was the one drugging her and setting her rapes up." Putting her arms up to the sky, she proclaimed, "I became the God who saved that child, over and over." Turning to him with the gun somewhat pointed at his chest, she got angry, again and he jerked and leaned his face away from the gun, in real fear.

302

"The pillow case was the perfect rape fetish and this went on for...SEVERAL WONDERFUL YEARS! SHE FANTASIZED IT WAS ME FUCKING HER PUSSY WITH MY BIG DICK! ME FUCKING HER ASS! ME GIVING HER SEMEN! SHE CRIED FOR ME WHEN THEY WERE RAPING HER! SHE CRIED FOR ME TO HELP HER! AND THEN YOU PUT THAT FUCKING BIBLE IN HER FACE AND TOOK HER AWAY FROM ME! I HATE YOU!"

She started shaking and glaring her eyes as she seemed to be pulling the trigger but, fighting herself. His eyes glanced at her and then he squinted away, hoping she wouldn't shoot.

Jenna started sobbing to herself and dangled her arms down to her side with the gun and Noah waited. He watched from the corner of his eyes, hoping his castling move worked. As she dangled her body looking for what it was she needed to do while sobbing, he started reading her. *That was not planning. She was losing to her own emotions, her own guilt. She is talking to her own guilt,* he thought. He was slowly moving the chess board.

Between her short breaths and tears she tried to explain, brought one of her hands to her face, and covered her crying eyes. "Simon...He wanted to marry her. He...he...he...started demanding they get married. I had to cut him off from her...he was a Bible thumper too...'Said she was God's gift." She started sniffling and wiping her eyes as they poured down her face, And...said he had to get his semen inside her as much as possible." She wheezed and gasped into a full blown cry and flopped her tired self into the chair and began to ball like a toddler.

Noah slowly turned letting his eminent fear, fade a little, and searched for what to say. Maybe she was turning the chess board, too. "Semen inside her...is her illness. She uses it to treat her anxieties because it

works so well. There was never enough and I couldn't make any for her." She laid down on her thighs and cried horribly into her hands and gun. "I was JEALOUS OF THEM! Why me? Why did I have to born the wrong gender?"

Finally, she slid her snot along her arm still holding the gun and struggled to continue. "Emily was Simon's long time victim before he did what he did to her. She never ever knew she was...He hated my body and worshipped her. I told him I could hook him and his roommate up to fuck her if he stayed with me." She kept sniffling and sobbing through her words. "I never took money to let people have sex with her. She...she..." Jenna sobbed so hard, she could not speak for a few moment.

"Emily wasn't into Strangers until I fucked up and drugged her and tied her down. I hate myself for it. I HATE MYSELF!" She screamed. "I never knew I would fall in love with her later." She squalled again unable to speak, and smacked herself on the face with the gun angrily and whimpering to let it out, "I put the pillow case on her because she cried so much. She cried through it every time and I pushed more strangers to keep the rape going longer to punish her for being so into the Bible and so beautiful and I HATED HER FOR BEING PERFECT! She pleaded for me to stop them each time they raped her. They fucked her for hours...one group after another. I thought she would get used to it and enjoy it. I didn't realize how bad the rape fucked up the minds chemicals. Rape become her pathology."

She was confessing so much, Noah didn't know what to start with to calm her down. "Emily discovered a fetish she never knew existed and got addicted to it and all I could do was stand on the side DICKLESS and watch her get all the attention. If I can just get her off

of you and addicted to me, we can work this out. I can make her happy. I owe her so much. I owe her so many apologies, Noah. I will keep her happy, Noah. I promise. Please just go away and let us be happy."

She wiped her snot across her other arm again, and balled out the rest of her confession into her face buried into the knees. "Simon liked both of us, until he knifed her, and I set that up and I hate myself for it. I HATE MYSELF!" I would hold her afterwards and she cried the entire night holding on to me-Thanking me for being there for her awful need that she had no clue I was making happen. I just kept drugging her and sending her back to it, just so she would crawl back to me. I never knew what unconditional love felt like until then. She said I touched her spirit like nothing else had by taking care of her after. I kept telling her she asked them to sleep with her. I have to Crash her today and erase all of that, so she will never know what I did to her."

She fell onto the floor and sobbed on her right side with her arm stretched out and still holding the gun. Snot and saliva ran down her face as she lifted the gun and dropped it and lifted it and dropped it again, sobbing. Noah just watched. He knew she was trying to decide if she should just end her guilt and the truth that she attempted to destroy the only person who ever really loved her, and was actually trying to destroy her again to feel less guilty.

"She told me yesterday it was over between us. And it is because I can't be a man for her. I can't let her go because she will realize I'm still drugging her to get Emily in bed. I am the wrong gender, Noah. That has been my struggle in life all along. If I was the man, I would have never let other men rape her. I would have been doing it for her. Cuckqueaning for

305

her was my only way to be with her." She burst out sobbing again to the reality of her plight.

Noah fought back his own tears now, but not for Jenna or Rachael. Realizing they really did love Emily or Julian with all their hearts but, did everything to destroy Julian, to just have Emily. He truly felt it, and understood why she was making a play for her after his recent rape. Guilt could defeat anyone, he knew. Andrea's opportunity had come to get him out of Julian's life, and she made her move. Now he really wanted to give her the only thing he could to make her feel better...fake unconditional love.

"Andrea Baby, leave your gun over there and come hug me. I will make love to you and punish you with my seed...just like they did Julian. I will try to show you what Julian feels inside when I make love to her. Maybe you can try and learn and appreciate feeling like a real, appreciated woman. It's all I can do. Shake off the Tomgirl, and be a beautiful Princess with a man who will give you the right feelings." He said it lovingly to her, so she didn't believe he wanted to escape.

She left the gun on the floor and laggardly got up and dragged herself over to him sobbing and wiping her face off. She stopped at her shoe, and picked up the key to the cuffs, and un-cuffed his wrist and dropped the key on his chest so he could un-cuff his other wrist. Will you hold me, Noah? For real, hold me?" For the first time, she laid her naked soul upon his and with her arms around his neck, cried her real story, foretold.

He quickly removed the other cuff, and with deep thought, slowly put his arms around her as she cried. His masculine warmth had compelled her to reach out for him. She let every inch of her nude body rub against him and kissed him passionately. She held

306

his face in her hands and caressed him as she offered her warm saliva into his mouth. Her heart raced to meet his and she inhaled his warm, wet breath, and began to feel like a woman who was desired. No need to fight vulnerability. No need to resist vulnerability. No need to manipulate vulnerability.

Never had she felt the attachment to a man like this before. She embraced his aura and felt her body shiver for the first time. She couldn't offer herself to him fast enough. She panted for her breath and moaned at his kisses as her heart rate grew fast. He licked up her neck and the tingle raced down her spine as she opened herself up to his touch. She had to have the moment as her tears fell to his rescue and jerked her flat breasts up to him like a woman in need and he inhaled her nipple. Noah sucked it in in a man's way as his hands explored her narrow, flat rear. She felt her wetness tingle in the lips below as his tongue rounded her small areola. Every caress crashed her internal wounds and she cried as she felt more vulnerable to him. She dragged her nipples through his teeth and he forced her areola into her chest with his wet tongue. Letting the vulnerability to him come was all the pain she needed for this moment. She felt like a real woman having her ignored breasts, the center of his desires. She reached down and gathered her wetness upon which her fingers lie, and forced them into his rushing mouth while still kissing him. He accepted her four fold as his cock rose against her leg.

She had always felt used, only now, for him, and with the right feelings, the right moment, the right timing, the right man to make her feel it was without judgement and unconditional.

"Noey touch me all over please. Make me your country woman for the moment. Fuck me. Hurt me. Please Noey. Punish me. Make me feel you deep inside

Julian like Simon did to her. Like you did to her. Let me feel my soul get your stain on it. Let your semen drift inside me and live in my brain, Noey." She looked him in the eyes and commanded him, "Rape me, Noah. Punish me for what I have done." She slid down his chest keeping her fingers of her left hand inside his mouth and her essence left a wet line down his stomach. She instantly rubbed her face in it and licked it off his muscular abdomen, as her legs spread and his thick cock slapped her wetness. His male scent invigorated her and she would finally feel like a real slutty Goddess getting punished for her sins.

He sat up, picking her up, and slammed her down on the bed, next to him, and forcefully climbed on her as she rolled onto her chest and offered herself to him, unconditionally. Using his left hand, he guided his cock slowly into her back door and she fingered herself with all four fingers as he took her breath away. She started hard and kept it there. He reared his big dick up at her and slammed into her bottom and coconut oil squeezed out onto his balls as she moaned out her pain. She began to pant with her moans and grasped the sheet with her free hand. Leaning forward as he pounded her sins, she used his thrust to push her fingers all the way inside her wet center, and finally, she began to cry. It was necessary for her. His thick dick grinded against her colon and pushing it into her pelvic floor muscles. His level of concentration and muscle memory would cost her dearly.

His foreskin pulled up and down the shaft with each thrust shocking him with sensations he had only experienced with her. She was his first time experiencing anal sex and he was getting into it. She lowered herself to get every inch of him and began her screaming as her ass felt like it was tearing apart and

her fingers worked to tear her vagina apart. He pounded her even harder when she started screaming in agony and purging her guilt. He punished her intolerable boyish sexiness. He punished her to reject her. He punished her to ease her guilt. He fucked her to give her what she really needed; the seed of a man who could care enough to hurt her. Her scream echoed into silence as she stopped breathing and shook rocking to his cocking. Andrea exploded onto him squirting onto her fingers, as she continued to grimace in pain and turn blood red. The pain twisted up her spine spreading around her body as guilt burned her.

She reached forward pulling the sheet sobbing and panting and shaking uncontrollably as she whimpered one word over and over, 'Daddy.' She tried to scoot away from the pain he forced her down by putting his hands on her back to support his weight. Her moans and cries told him she was getting what she wanted and he fucked her little as like a piece of ass from the bar. She raised her head and slammed her face into the mattress, and slammed it again as she winced over and over, unable to breath. She leaked down her fingers and pulled her hand out and sucked her own wetness. Her eyes rolled back into the darkness of her many Alibis as the red on her face got darker. He fucked her even harder for contrite. Noah was almost there and she was near lifeless again. He was not going to give her a break for what she did to his Soulmate. He wanted to kill her for Julian. He kept his dick in her ass and violated his vows to the woman he worshipped, to punish the woman who violated her life.

As his facial expression turned to pain and short bursts of agony he felt it coming. He was almost there. The round, thick head of his cock forced its way through her and pushed and dragged her colon toward

her intestines and her brief high-pitched screams escaped her with each deep touch. Her most precious gift, shared so often, to so many, for so little, meant everything to her in this one moment.

His last pant took into a long scream as he thrusted to tear her apart and as hard as he could, and suddenly, he stopped, deep in her darkness. The drugs she had injected rushed through his veins, as the room blurred on him. He held his breath and pinched his eyes closed as his assumed blessed seed shot into her bowel, sticking to her guilt and anxieties. She cried hard as she felt the pulsating penis violate her with its milky syrup. His teeth gritted together and his closed eyes tightened even more. His cock pulsated and squirted inside on her soul making her clitoris burn and her reward system defeat her. His entire body took the spasms and fought for her need. He took the brunt of it trying to give her the motionless squirt she asked for. He squirted again and she sobbed with her cheek against the sheet. She was lifeless and letting him have his way for her benefit. He kept his word as his thick ejaculate interred her body to live inside her mind with so many others. The squirts of passion shot into her again, and again, marking her forever as a desired woman. He kept his word to Jenna, for Andrea. Maybe because of compassion. Maybe for lust. Maybe with the truth. Maybe because he was really an Angel, and so was she. With his last throb, he spit as she finally let his lungs escape their capture and he screamed as loud as he could in anger.

His heart pumped the life blood through his system briskly, as well as the drug, and as he collapsed next to her with his cock still in her, he Crashed. His Crash key Song Code continued playing, as she her satisfied smile slowly glowed. Jon is dead.

Chapter 24

-Brown & Blue Twist Fate & Flavors

Julian stuffed her hair between her labia and leg, shook her spur, roped her mouth, laid out her bible on her lap, and twined her hair through her fingers and closed her eyes to Morning Prayer. She asked to be forgiven for the sins of her soul and her family, and that Rachael find guidance in God and someone who she could fall in love with. She prayed for a speedy discharge since the paperwork was due back this morning, so she could go, and for the children of the world be saved from the evils of starvation and rapist. She smiled for baby Emma being accepted back into heaven and hoped one day to see her and hug her. She asked for a safe return of Noah, free from any prosecution. Finally, she thanked God for Texas, and the gifts they have bestowed upon her. And may her Daddy's wooden cross rope necklace and wedding ring somehow magically appear and if a miracle could happen, and make her hair two feet longer before Noah sees it. She closed with Genesis 2:17 in regards to her lost friend Rachael.

When she opened her eyes, before her stood a beautiful thick, taller than her woman, with hair brushed outward and laying upon her wide shoulders, dressed in stretchy blue jeans, a bright white shirt taught across her breasts, and of the most beautiful brown skin she had ever seen. She even had on high heel boots with a very thin heel. They were not real Cowgirl boots but, Samira wore them well. Leaning in the doorway with a bag in one hand and her keys and

phone in the other, both of them smiled at their arrival.

"My, oh my how you glow with beauty. You be a fine Cowgirl in Texas." Julian told her.

"Well thank you, Julian," she said making her way to her bed bearing gifts and a big smile. "I might say, you are looking better than yesterday. You are all smiles Cowgirl," Samira told her, putting the bag on the tray table.

"I'm buckin' this rider. Home to my kids. I am loco sittin' here. I have so much laundry and cleanin' to do. I had to go to the store weeks ago, so I know I am short on everythang at home by now. Momma don't say 'no' to her grandbabies in the kitchen." Julian put her arms out to display her 'thick self' as an example of Momma not saying no in the kitchen.

"That is a very pretty 'self' you have there, my...my...my...my..." Samira did not finish her sentence and nodded to her with a smile. Gently, she pulled out a wrapped breakfast burrito and presented it to her. Julian's eyes flared with anticipation and held it with great care.

"OH my Samira! A woman after my heart. I am starvin'." When Samira pulled out a box of bakery brownies. Julian melted with her mouth full and grunting as she somewhat danced sitting in the bed. She through her head back showing the victory of every morsel consumed by moving her head back in forth and wiggling.

Unable to use her occupied mouth, she handed Samira the kitchen box of brownies and tried to get her to eat some. She smiled watching Julian and shook her head. She was seeing the happy side of her, instead of the anxiety ridden woman of the day before. Julian signed a thank you, and Samira responded in sign language. Julian was taken aback shortly, while

312

still inhaling her burrito, and asked her in sign language if she spoke sign. Samira answered her back in sign, that she could speak some of it. Julian's eyes lit up with bonding desires. She had been looking to have someone to practice sign with since Noah didn't care to learn, and it was really only practical for her occasionally.

"Would you like me to brush your hair while you eat, Julian?" Samira offered anxiously, and got up before Julian could even answer. Julian covered her mouth nodding and chewing fast. Quickly, her friend pulled out a bottle of diet soda and a can of Copenhagen Long Cut Straight out of her bag. Julian went back to dancing in her bed giggling and chewing. Samira felt warm and fuzzy inside.

As Samira walked around the bed, she pulled on her friend's long hair and held it out to admire it. "That is some long hair Girl. How do you manage it?" She held it up to her nose and smelled it and without letting Julian see, she rubbed it across her face gently and enjoyed it. "I recognize that smell, hospital shampoo." Julian was nodding trying to finish her burrito as not to be rude to conversation. Twisting the top off her soda she took a big drink to answer her.

"'Tis much work but, I enjoy it. Longer the hair, closer to God, in Texas." How long did it take you to get it this long?" She asked as she pulled the scrunchie off the top of her head and gathered hair from around her shoulders. When the spurs rattled, Julian immediately stopped sipping and took them out of her hair. Samira could now touch one of Julian's most precious Texas gifts, and play with it freely.

"I cannot recall not havin' hair to the ground. All the women in my family have it. It was longer but, the EMT team cut about a foot of it to untie me during the accident." I will treat it and have that foot of hair back

313

on me faster than you can snatch a rattler with a lasso." Julian took into the brownies, that is just a given, and Samira pulled the rest of her hair out behind her and began to brush...not so well.

"I really want to brush your hair, I'm just unsure how to do the full length of it." Samira was a little embarrassed and wanted to make her new friend happy.

"Just start at the bottom with your hand under the brush and work up. Thank you so much for the brownies and gifts. I will be happy to pay you the-" Samira stopped her right there.

"I DON'T THINK SO! I bought those for you because I wanted to. Please accept my gifts without any...any...any...any..." Julian waited patiently, gathering her Intel on her new friend. "Let me gift you Julian, please?"

"Thank you," Julian said again. "How you doin' back there?" Julian took another sip to wash down the moist brownies.

"These be the same brownies Rachael brangs to work-same Brooke's Bakery." Jay slowly milked the bite in her mouth and sent it to her palette for testing. "They taste a little different." She worked her tongue around thinking it was the texture. "New baker, perhaps? These brownies taste different-better different. Thank you again Samira." Julian said it to her, while working that analytical mind of hers.

"I think I am getting this. I love how it feels. I would love to have long hair as it is empowering to see a professional woman still display her feminine quality and wear manly boots. My hair is a hybrid mess. African American mother and my Middle Eastern father hair. I would love to have it longer it just gets to be so much work." She said, trying to be gentle with Julian's locks of love.

"Do not be gentle Samira, please. I enjoy havin' my hair pulled, especially when it is brushed. Very soothin' to me." She kept her hand over her mouth as she spoke, and it actually reflected her raspy whisper backwards toward Samira. "At home, Noah usually brushes my hair every morning and night, or my daughter Ally. She is goin' to be eight this year. Her hair is down past her tushy. When I am alone, I have to bend over and work it. If you ever get married and yer' partner has a hair fetish, it comes with a lot of power, Girl."

Samira laughed and nodded as she brushed. She didn't want to tell Julian, she was getting tingles each time she held her hair. "May I ask you?" Julian nodded her hair.

"Why do you sleep with Cowboy boots on and a pair beside you in bed and with spur-thingies in your hair?" Julian chuckled because she heard the nervousness in her question.

"I'm from Texas, you never want to get caught with yer' boots off in Texas. The other boots belong to my husband, Noah. I must give my devotion to him as I would God. I have God's book here, thus I need somethang of my husband's here to feel I am fulfillin' my duty to him. Somethang I be guilty of not doin' for a long time now. And I love the smell of leather, especially bein's after Noah has sweated on it for years. The sound of his spurs stir me in many ways. My Momma always sat in her rockin' chair after my Daddy died, with one of his boots on her lap, and me on the other side of her lap. She wore his spurs in her hair-still does after so many years. I was in high school when he passed away-Brain Cancer."

"I'm so sorry. Does your Mother wear an eye patch, also?' she asked to be silly.

"Only when she comes to see me here." Jay said smiling. "My Momma ain't a normal, Cowgirl."

"Where are you from?" Julian asked as Samira started making her first pigtail.

"I am from Ohio. My mother is American, my father is Middle Eastern and still lives there...I do...do...do not recall knowing him. Only photos." Samira said honestly.

"I am sorry." Julian apologized.

"No. No. I was raised well. I have a wonderful mother I still live with."

Julian didn't think that was odd, only unexpected. "How old are you?" Julian pried kindly.

"I will be twenty-seven this year. You?"

"I will be thirty-three this year. Husband, Two kids, Momma, and a mortgage here and back home."

"Wow! Two kids? Two mortgages?" Samira added while starting on her second pigtail, and bumping the tray table.

Everything knocked out of place on the table and Julian quickly adjusted them symmetrically and labels facing appropriate directions. Samira stopped to watch her, and used her own analytical mind.

"Are these too tight, Jay? I'm sorry, can I call you Jay? I just figured-" Samira stopped to hear her.

"As wonderful as you are, you can call me anythang and get away with it." Samira smiled and blushed and appreciated it. Samira smiled back at her nodding.

"Husband? Children? Samira?" No, I have yet to find a partner who wants such responsibilities. I will remain hopeful as the world turns."

"You go, Girlfriend. You will know when you find the right person. Don't kid yourself. Believe me you will know. The trick is to ask yerself' if you can live

316

happier without them." Samira walked around front to look at her work.

"Oh my. I am not doing a good job." She chuckled as she hunched over to fix it before anyone else saw them. "It is not centered." Julian immediately adjust them correctly and asked Samira to come sit with her. She assured her, the pigtails felt even. As expected, Samira pulled up Rachael's chair and nervously sat down.

"Samira, just to clear up a few thangs. In my family, it is customary for us to go by different names sometimes. Often times you will hear me referred to as Jordan, the name I am registered under, and Julian. Occasionally Michelle, and any number of cute names my country Momma can muster from the barn. I just don't want you to feel uncomfortable when you hear such names and feel I have hidden anything from you. My name is Julian Michelle...and Jay for short." And Julian Michelle and Jay for short, smiled as she packed her can of Copenhagen teeming with excitement.

"Can I call you Jay, sometimes?" Samira asked, feeling the conversation was abnormal. Julian nodded to her.

"Can I call you Sam or Sammy?" Samira nodded, feeling the give and take.

"And...don't you ever worry about stuttering in our conversation. I was in love with a Stutterer once, and Jenna and I managed fine. I will always give you my patience with it." Julian added. Samira looked down at the floor embarrassed but, felt more comfortable immediately.

"Thank you. Was it your wife...sorry, your Rachael friend?" Julian shook her head. "I really would prefer Samira over Sam, from you I think I like

Sammy when we are not here. Do you follow me?" Julian nodded when she spoke.

"I certainly do Samira. And uh...you didn't happen to see a cell phone back there in my hair did ya'? I lost it yesterday when thangs got Wild West, and I thank someone be stealin' it." Julian looked around again to lead a search. "I have searched this bed and room completely. I had a nurse call it and nada. I thank it died."

"You really do look cute with an eye patch. It almost...almost blends into your beauty...I guess is the way to say it...since your shiny black hair blends into it. Very cute. I think your husband will like it." Samira finished and reached out to touch the end of Julian's hair on her leg. Julian reached out and held her fingers in her hand, and they both smiled at each other warmly. Words were not necessary for this.

Julian would be the first to speak, "I want to get a quick shower before I leave, would you mind waitin'? I will only take a few minutes because I'm not washin' my hair."

A Doctor in his long white coat knocked on the door, and entered. "Hello Mrs. Briggs, I'm Dr. Dewitt, I spoke with your wife on the phone this morning regarding your desire for breast reduction surgery and areola reduction. She said you are not happy with your breasts and asked us to provide you with a consultation of how our services could help you. Do you have a minute to discuss the options?" He was very polite and professional Samira thought. Julian was bitter about it.

Julian and Samira both stared at him...for different reasons. Finally, Julian smiled at him with a quick nod and spoke. "I'm an MD as well, Doctor. I am sorry you had to come here under false pretenses, as another MD claimin' to be wife, has misguided you in

yer' inquiry. I do appreciate the work you do for the needy men and women. I apologize with respect, I will not be needin' your services." Julian wait impatiently, to get up and get her shower.

"I'm very sorry, Please, I will leave a pamphlet for you if you have any questions regarding future procedures." Thank you for your time. I wish you well in your recovery Doctor." He laid the pamphlet on the tray table and turned to leave.

"Thank you Doctor, Bless you." Julian said as he smiled at Samira and went out the door politely. Julian looked up at Samira and shook her head with a growl and explained, "Rachael."

Samira did not respond to the situation that she knew very little about. She continued on subject. "I can get your clothes ready for you if you like? Are they in the locker?"

"Noooooo." Julian dragged out the exhausting word as she took the pamphlet that was not balanced with everything else on her tray table. "I am gonna' have to wear a hospital gown and a blanket. I am not sure where my clothes went or bagged into evidence. All I need is my boots." Julian tried to lean up but, her rear anchored her to the bed-recliner again, Samira quickly got up, and helped her out of bed.

Julian shuffled in her untied hospital gown to the bathroom and Samira snuck a peek at her nude rear view, and smiled shamefully with delight. Watching Julian stop and bend over at one of the chairs and place the pamphlet perfectly in the center of the seat, she admired her tattoos and voluptuous pale caboose. Storing the image into her long-term memory, as Julian shuffled on into the bathroom, Samira grabbed her phone and walked out of the room to solve the problem at hand.

When Julian finished, she peeked out of the bathroom with her towel covering her front. It wasn't big enough to cover the Texas longhorn rear, so she didn't even try. Samira was not in the room so Julian flung the door open and finished drying her hair from the shoulders down and Samira walked into the room carrying a pile of scrubs. Julian closed the door partly to finish, and after a brief interlude and covered her front up again, before walking out.

Samira announced she had gotten her some scrubs to wear home so she would not have to wear a blanket. "We may have to cut the bottoms off of the pants, I can't recall having seen them short enough for you. Please don't take that offensively."

Julian smiled as she walked around her to get her Coconut oil, and thanked her as she took the lid off at the tray table. "I can stuff the pants in my boots like a good Cowgirl."

"They are not pretty. We donate them to the ICE Ward. Julian stopped herself from heading to the bathroom and asked her.

"I'm a Doctor, what is an ICE Ward." Julian inquired.

"It's the Sanctuary City section to hide Illegals from ICE-Immigration. The hospital donates excess and worn material to that Ward.

"Are they hidin' Illegals from ICE or for ICE?"

"I think from ICE? The hospitals make a bundle from Government Healthcare for them. Julian looked into the distance with a thought. Clothes, boots, coconut oil, and Copenhagen...she had everything she needed, and Samira could show her the way.

A knock came to the door again, and Julian turned and used Samira to lean her naked bottom on her to hide it. It was another Doctor making his rounds.

"Hello Mrs. Briggs, my name is Doctor Hutchinson, and this is my assistant, Chloe van Hauson. Your wife called this morning asking us to stop by for a consultation regarding Weight loss surgery. We would like to show you our brochure that could help you decide if Weight Loss surgery, is for you. If you like, I see your showering, we can come back later.

Samira leaned down and whispered into Julian's ear, "Rachael?" Julian nodded and Samira stepped up her game and stepped in front of Julian, completely. "Thank you Doctor, please just give us the brochure and should we find further ques...ques...ques...questions necessary, we will contact you for further information. Thank you and Chloe." Samira reached out and took the pamphlet with a smile and thanked them again. She recognized Chloe from when she worked her floor years ago.

Julian rolled her eyes at Rachael, even though she wasn't there, and headed back to the bathroom to put her coconut oil on her body. She stopped before entering the bathroom door and turned her head around to look at Samira, she flipped her hair at her, and thanked her.

Samira stood there alone, trying to read the clues she thought she saw. She was not good at this, she told herself. She took a second look at Noah's cowboy boots and Julian's tray table, and made her best guess. Samira closed the door to her room as one of the nurses gave her a dirty look from the station, and Samira smiled and avoided eye contact.

She quietly walked over to the bathroom door in her three-inch spiked heels and observed. Julian was completely naked and rubbing her breasts and chest down with the oil. Samira could see her scars in the reflection and Samira took it all in seductively without

sharing her aroused opinion. With her sexy eye-patch, Julian glanced at Samira in the cracked doorway through the mirror, and continued rubbing herself down with a warming smile and her hair roped and in her lips.

Samira slowly pushed the door open nudging Julian back into the corner, and not against her will. They had made eye contact and started reading each other. Quietly, she shut the door behind her in the well-lit room. Neither one spoke a word. Neither one moved. Neither one stopped staring. Neither one wanted to stop the other one.

With her hair through her lips, she stood there nude with her jar in her hand. They stared quietly, without movement, and both feeling their hearts race a little. They were reading each other, and offering clues to one another. Flirts that only one looking for could read. Julian's mouth watered generously and she delicately swallowed without losing eye contact. Samira swallowed and stepped towards her without imposing herself on her and reached for the jar. Julian slide herself to the corner of the room and let her take the jar from her. Her shoulders seemed to lower, as Samira rose up.

Samira looked down at Julian's scared breasts, and pushed her lips together and nodded slightly, and back to her blue eye. Feeling subtle fears of the past, Julian slowly lifted her forearms to hide her battle scars.

With a simple click of her heal on the tile, Julian froze, and Samira stepped up to her slowly and took in the beauty she brandished. To her, Julian was breathtaking and her scars added to her real character. Watching Julian closely, Samira slowly put her left hand up to her neck near her own shoulder, and briskly flipped her hair behind her with her hand

keeping eye contact. Julian stared into her eyes before finally, Julian nodded to confirm her question.

Samira reached up to Julian's forearms and gently pulled them down. Julian looked down when her arms went down, breaking the stare. Samira slowly reached under Julian's chin and pushed her head up offering permission. Samira looked deep into her blue world, to see the pain that came with those scars. Julian kept her hair tightly in her lips until she had permission to remove it as Samira slowly leaned in to see her soul.

Julian looked at her, and Samira watched her pupil dilate farther. Julian slid her hands behind her own big rear and pinned them to the wall, as her breathing got shallow. Samira carefully peeled her eye patch off and rested it on her pigtail without losing sight of her blue world. She watched her pupil close slightly from the light and delicately open back up completely to absorb Samira's beauty. Julian gracefully tilted her head to the left never breaking eye contact. Samira admired her, and assessed her feelings about whether she should, or should not. All the clues were there. "Winsome." Samira whispered to her, still reading her soul.

Samira leaned in slowly keeping her lips just inches from Julian's lips and let Julian feel her warm breath onto her lips, as Julian pinched her rope of hair and inhaled it. Their eyes stayed locked, absorbing the sentiments of their natural desires, and both understood the opportunity being presented. Samira's chest was rising and falling as they stared into each other's worlds for answers. As their chemistry blended in front of them, their bodies responded to desire, speeding up the blood flow within. Samira placed the jar on the counter never breaking eye contact, and Julian slowly began to pant in anticipation as she

looked up at her. Samira looked down on Julian and gently brought her body closer to her.

Slowly, Samira lifted her shirt off over her head exposing her bra. They read deep into each other's eyes as they read into their souls. Both their chest rising. Fat Kitty dripped on Julian's leg and she kept her butt pushed against the wall keeping herself pinned down. Samira's hands vanished behind her back and Julian panted harder watching just the eyes. Instantly, her bra came loose, and slid down her breasts, stopping at the nipples, to be enchanting.

Grabbing her straps, she let the bra fall to their feet. Neither woman moved from the fright their eyes held. They let the burn fill their carnal senses, and struggled to keep their breathing from becoming harsh. The first touch was only moments away. They could feel the heat of their bodies blending between them. The dark skin of her breasts moved up and down as she respired. The pale skin of Julian's breasts lifted to meet hers repeatedly. Keeping their eyes locked, their breaths met as Samira gently pulled Julian's rope of hair from her mouth removing a key vulnerability from her. That terrorized Julian delightfully and she began to shake and leak for this dominant, dark woman.

Gently, Samira pushed her large brown breasts against Julian's chest, just under her chin, to let their bodies intimately touch, for the first time. Jay stared up at her feeling vulnerable, and wet, and that was her appetency. Samira's chocolate skin melted into Julian above her lowering breasts, and pushed against her against the wall more. Samira moved her mouth around Julian's mouth without touching her. She spent her moist warm air onto Julian's swelling lips and softly Julian's lips parted to taste it, setting her clitoris

on fire. She could actually feel the pulsation and burn of the full capacity being met.

Samira held the moment with her domination, as she was eight inches taller in those heals. Samira taunted her with the promise of a kiss, and Julian pushed the back of her hands harder into the wall giving to this tall, dark, beautiful woman, who wanted to dominate her desires. Both their hearts raced against each other's chest for that first kiss. Her dark full lips waited to meet Julian's rosy red ones. Slowly, Samira reached up to her hair and twirled it around her finger. Holding her breath, she delicately put it to Julian's lips, and slid it deep into mouth. Julian's lips embraced it, and held the finger, and softly curled the curl around her tongue, while staring at her. Wetness spread across Samira's cotton thong, and she shivered from the blood flow.

Softly, Samira slid her finger out of Julian's rosy lips, and slowly leaving her curl in her mouth. Julian closed her eyes as feeling of ownership took hold. Speaking in the slightest of whisper, Samira said, "I love your ghost white, blue skin." Julian shivered with her eyes closed as enjoyable anxieties pounded inside her. And she did not speak, because permission had not been granted.

Samira blew into her face gently and whispered, "Tu es si belle." Julian slowly opened her eyes as she interpreted the beautiful words. All four sets of lips were swollen and yearning for the first kiss, to each of them. Their breasts pushed against each other's bodies, offering the limit of their moment. The meeting of White skin and Black skin, in the incarceration of chemistry, burned their fires. They so needed their desires...their lust...their passions to be tasted. Julian did not want to let go of her first spoil of flavor and gently swirled it around her tongue. Samira stared her

down as she slowly moved her head around to take in her own spoils. Offering ownership of Julian, Samira savored her precious Texas gifts.

The chemistry had met, mixed, and burned without a single kiss, without a harsh touch, without tasting their seeds. Samira gave Julian a pain she longed to feel, a forbidden fruit from the serpent she had so much desired to taste. Julian gently lifted a small lasso of her hair up to Samira's mouth without closing her window, and rubbed it across Samira's dark, full lips. Slowly, she opened them and with great care, Julian slid her finger between them with her lasso on the tip, and without a sound, Samira sucked her finger against her tongue and took control of her curl, and softly Julian pulled her finger out.

Samira closed her eyes and shared her flavor with the rest of her senses. As Samira's eyes slowly opened, Julian jerked when Samira's finger touched her scar on her right breasts, and slowly slid it down over her areola. Samira's hands were like ice as she trembled. Her cold fingertip absorbed Julian's body heat. Julian gently jerked again with Samira stared her down and touched her left breasts scar underneath and slowly followed it up to her nipple and across the areola to the scar tip.

Now that ownership had been established, Julian could speak. Whispering softly, "Ta beaute m'accable." And tried to stop herself from kissing her. She needed that urge touched, and remembered, she was not in control anymore. Both their nipples poked each other and absorbed their warmth and tasted the oils from their colorful skins. Julian wanted to get down on her knees to her, and Samira did not permit it.

Samira gently pulled her hair out of Julian's mouth and fingered it slowly into her own lips and then slowly pulled Julian's hair out of her mouth and

slowly lifting her head to rise and look down on Julian, and placed Julian's hair back in her mouth. Together they tasted each other's saliva. Their essence, their seed, would have to wait her turn.

"Pas ici mon cher." Samira whispered softly and demanding.

Julian gently nodded back to her eyes agreeing, "Oui pas ici mon cher."

Samira stared at her vulnerabilities. Read her desires, and conquered her with only a sample of her taste. Samira slowly stepped back pulling her large black nipples away from Julian, with one click of her spiked heal, and without breaking the stare, Julian nodded her submissive role in their relationship. Both were still panting as Samira saved the moment. Julian felt how cold her hands were, and them under her breasts to warm them, and waited to be commanded.

Samira did not break eye contact when she reached for the coconut oil, and stared at Julian with it in both her hands. Both felt the pressure in their chests to breathe as Julian waited and Samira held the reins. With two clicks from her spiked heel on the tile, Julian smiled with a curtsy, and she turned around and put her hands up on the wall. The moment was over, for now.

Samira smiled at her warmly with a hand full of coconut oil, and both women took a long deep breath as Samira dug the coconut oil from the jar.

Chapter 25

-Curves of Duos Derrieres Escape

Samira refused her blissful rub down from Julian, as she had refuted Julian's desire for warm kiss. Samira was not comfortable exposing herself, her sexuality, in a bathroom, at the hospital in which she worked. Even if she was off the clock. Julian however, needed her daily bath in oil, and intimate touch that reassured fears.

Samira laughed heartedly when the third pair of scrubs could not fit over Julian's seat saddler and hips. The top crushed her loose breasts enough and, crushing Fat Kitty was necessary in clothing but, her ass and hips was just too wonderfully big for non-stretchy pants. "A punishment for thick women who dared have such luscious curves," she said to her new friend. Samira smacked her on her Noah's Ark tattoo and said, "It's hard to appreciate a flat stomach, when you can't get your pants over your hips and rear. You are so short and thick and lovely. Let's do this, instead." She kicked off her spiked boots and peeled her stretch jeans off, exposing her sleek, red thong with a big question mark on the front, and offered her jeans up to Julian. She stood there admiring her thick dark legs and curves, and Samira smiled shyly watching Julian take it all in. Gently, she turned her hips, just enough to show Julian her ample rear curve. Julian glowed with a smile nodding her approval of what she was hiding behind there. Samira, in her cute, shy way, twirled slowly for Julian and won her approval all around as her face got rosy. "I like the

question mark on the front? Certainly is my question, Samira."

Julian rushed to get her feet through the pants, and without socks or panties, drove one back into her boot. She quickly did the same with the other leg, and Samira helped her struggle to get them over her voluptuous rear. Of course she touched it a few times and wishing she had rubbed the coconut oil in every hidden place. Julian finally, got into her friends pants. The jeans did fit, only they were about six inches too long, and six inches too short in the back but, scrubs top covered her crack when she was standing. Samira was still standing there staring at her dirty thoughts about her friend going commando in her pants. That was Hot! Julian was straightening the remaining items on the tray table, before her head exploded.

Samira graciously donned a pair of scrub bottoms and shamefully put her spiked heels back on. The two were far from fashion, but a mere trip around the ICE Ward would be tolerable to help her friend. Wearing a pair of scrubs between them, Samira's legs led the way, and her Pirate lover followed her direction.

"We are lookin' for a brown country boy, brown beard, age thirty-two, Samira-Mexican lookin' guy. Just so you know. He looks Mexican with his dark skin but, with brown hair and a short beard." Stopping to speak at the Nurse's station in the ICE Ward, none of them admitted to having any males in the Ward. Everyone was Mexican, South American, or Middle Eastern Women patients. Julian cared not for their whimpers of Political Policy drowning the minds at the nursing station, she headed down the corridor to look in the rooms. Samira followed behind her quickly as she ran on her toes, and the nurses alerted the Head Nurse that visitors were pushing their way into the

Ward. Without a badge, M.D. Julian had no authority to be taking a look in a restricted access zone.

Samira clicked her way up behind the manly sounds of Julian's boots and with a snap of her finger, she pointed to the left side of the hallway for Samira to check. Julian wasted no time peeking through the windows of the closed doors. An M.D. she was, appreciative of hospitals, she was not. Being said in truth, she got lost in them constantly, and that frustrated her enough to want to NOT work inside one.

"Jay. Hey Jay. Tan guy, beard. In this one." Julian shuffled over quickly and eased through the door with intention. He was not Noah. After a quick curtsy to the older man, she rushed back out into the hallway, and kept looking. Samira called for her again. She whispered to her, "This gentleman kind of looks Mexican-Whiteboy-ish. The door plate says, his name is uh...Daniel Gonzales."

Julian burst into the room and there he was. Laying on the bed, covered with a blanket fast asleep, and cuffed to the rail. She curtsied as fast as she could and whispered his name as she rushed to hug him. He was startled but, her voice and tears woke him up fast. She climbed on top of him like a saddle and through herself into his arm sobbing and showering him with her love and kisses. She squeezed him as if her life depended on it.

Samira, a woman of passion and respect, stood back with her arms crossed on her chest in respect and jealousy, and quietly wiped the tears away before they could run. The sounds of happiness filled the room as Julian's joyous sobs echoed into everyone's hearts. Julian rubbed herself all over his face in short bursts and his tears were as plentiful as hers. Her tongue, desperate for a reunion, circled his and she tasted his saliva seed again and again. She thumbed

his tears and rubbed her cheeks on them as she shook and cried holding his face to hers. Samira slowly dropped her defensive stance, for admiration, and appreciation, yet jealously brought them back up to her chest, only not as bearing. She was happy to see their love was real, and not a fake happiness of so many couples today. She worried how this would affect Julian's feelings for her, now that he was back. She kept fighting back the tears of joy for a friend she had only met days ago but, who she knew, had a good heart. Her eyes now saw what so many people talk about, but never really experience, real love.

"Get me out of here, Julian. Use your cuff keys. MY GOD! Rachael has been telling me you hated me. 'Didn't want to see me. She has lost her mind, Julzie. She came in here naked and raped me-" Julian shut him up with her hand smashing to his lips and nose, as her ears listened to someone else. She sat up on him and slowly turned her head through her hair to see who the voices were, as her fight mode shoved flight mode aside. Without looking, she slowly put a rope of her hair into his mouth and prepared for battle. Samira's stepped back when she saw Julian flare, and her arms fell to her side, in momentary fear.

"IDentifY." She commanded him as she assessed the situation in the hallway. Staring like a bull ready to charge a Matador's waving cape, her body began hording oxygen as she prepared for a Texas-style fight. An older Nurse came pushing through the door threatening to call Security. Cowgirl was getting ready to get mean, and with her clothes on, this time. Her stretchy jeans had worked their way down in the back, and she didn't notice. This was the first impressions to a Head Nurse standing behind her as she sat on her man.

"You are not allowed in here! Why are you people violating visitor policy? I am calling Security right now! GET OUT OF HERE NOW! GET YOUR CLOTHES ON!" The Virago was daring Julian to put a size five boot across her wattle, in her best Anne Bonny impression.

Julian rattled off to her in a plea. "Por favor no llame a la policia. El es me esposo. Padre de mis hijos por favor cinco minutos? Por Favor Senora? Cinco minutos por favor?" Julian screamed her whispers at her through her real tears, and wearing her eye patch in clothes that didn't fit her. Noah, grabbed Julian by the neck hole of her shirt, to keep her from attacking. He knew his wife, well.

The Head Nurse looked at Samira for translation, and Samira honestly shrugged her shoulders stalling for an answer. "I know that...that...that...that...that is her husband. Look at her crying. She was in ICU from an ac...ac...ac...ac...accident. I think he...he...he was in the accident as..as...as well. I guess. I couldn't understand her. I think they are both...both Illegals. She has children with him, I do know...know...know this fact." Samira put one hand out to gesture for the Head Nurse to read the situation. "The pants do not fit her very well," Samira offered as a last ditch effort of omitting certain parts of the story, via opportunity distraction.

"I love you, Baby. I missed you." He whispered to Julian, who was not on her mind that moment.

"That is her husband. Father of her children. She is begging you to let her have five minutes with him. He is an Illegal to be deported." Said a nurse in the doorway behind them. Both women turned and looked at her.

"Well. I am calling Security in five minutes." The Head Nurse said to Samira, and put her hand up to

332

gesture the number minutes. Samira nodded in agreement and appreciation, and responsibility to have them gone in cinco minutos.

"I will get her back to the ICU, she is checking out today. Five minutes." Samira promised, as the Head Nurse told the others to get back to their stations and call her if they were not gone in five minutes.

Julian went back to hugging and crying on her man as laid herself upon him. Her soulmate. Her gift from God that keeps her in her place. "Julzie get off me. Five minutes, Baby. Get your keys and un-cuff me." Julian looked up at his arm that did not embrace her, and saw the cuffs violating her hug.

"I don't have my keys, Noey. Or my badge and gun. Do you have yours?" she said recognizing the situation for what it really was, and trying to jerk his hand through the cuffs.

"NO!" he screamed jerking his hand away from his wife. It was sore enough after days of lying there and trying to get his wrist through the cuffs. Julian got herself airborne and landed on her boots to look at the bedrail and see if she could get it off. His blanket went with her and Samira admired his shaved equipment, before looking away, and glancing a few times.

"Where are your clothes, Noey? Your panties?" Julian asked, kneeling down to view the bolts on the side rail. Her hair laid on the floor below her, while the back of her stretch jeans was caught under her bulging rear, leaving Samira to read her 'Noah's Ark' tattoo again. This time however, she got the joke. Samira smiled when she looked at her his equipment again, and looked away hiding it.

Noah quickly sat up and put his feet on the floor to cover himself and reached for the blanket on the floor. "Who is your friend, Julian?"

"WHAT?" She answered before it completely registered in her brain. "Oh uh...um...that is Samira, my girlfriend." She went right back to studying the situation and so did he.

"Riiiight. Hello Samira, nice to meet you. Got a Tylenol on ya?" he said, nodding at her with an expression of burden. "Welcome to the family?" he said sarcastically. "Like, are you a girl friend or a Girlfriend?" *Julian never called another woman, other than Rachael, her girlfriend,* he was thinking. He immediately suspected there had been some changes and liked it.

"We just met the other day. Nice to see you, Noah. We did not know you were here at DoctorLands West. I hope the staff has pro...pro...pro...provided well for you. Julian wanted to come looking. She has been in ICU for...for...for a week...maybe."

"Noey. Noey look." Julian jerked his wrist down when she shift the cuffs up the bottom of the rail. "If we get your hand in there, I thank these two bars will scissor your chain. This is an electric bed isn't it?" Julian pushed the bottom and went down on her knees to get a better look. It was not functioning.

Noah watched Samira walk over and plug it in before he could mention it to Julian. Instantly, the bed jerked downward and Julian saw the bars cross. "Yes, Noey. We can do this, get under here and be puttin' yer' arm through there and I will put the bed down to cut it."

Noah tossed himself to the floor and jammed his arm up inside the forest of square bars and Julian climbed up and pushed the button. Samira got another eye full of his cock and scrotum, and looked at his eight-pack abs flexing, and then Julian's long hair, still on the floor. Her ass shook with her jittering bounces, and Samira giggled at the twerk. Only she was

professional enough to admire assets and not market them. She could not understand if it was the color of her pale skin, the shaking of her ass, or the large perfect shape. Either way, when it jiggled, she felt tingly.

The bed pinched down on the cuff chain and did not break it. Noah put it up again and back down. It did not break. Again. Again. The bed motor did not have enough strength to cut the steal between the two bars as one rose up and the other rode down. "Pinch it and hold the down button Noah. Momma's got an idea." She pulled Samira's pants back over her ass and walked over to the bathroom. When Noah pinched the chain between the bars and held the motor on the downward glide, he looked over at Julian, fixing her hair in the bathroom mirror, and herself. Samira thought the timing was very inappropriate, and vain.

She walked out and toward the entrance door calmly. Even Samira looked at her no longer able to read her, as she put her hair behind her in a ponytail without a tie as she glided with professional stride. When she past her, Samira immediately felt the difference. Something about her had changed. This was not the woman she planned to satisfy very soon. Noah waited for her to look at him before he asked, "Jordan?"

Jordan nodded slowly bearing her strong jaw to the situation. This problem would now be solved with Jordan solving it. Samira looked back and forth between the two of them communicating without speaking, and picked up the scent. She quickly asked herself, *What in the hell is going on?*

Jordan held onto her hair with her fist and came running full speed and tossed herself into the air at him. She landed toward the backrest of the bed on the mattress with her right shoulder and all one hundred

335

and seventy five pounds jammed down tearing one of the cuff links apart. After days of rape and torment, Noah was a free man...for the moment. Those Days were still ahead of him in Julian's bedroom. Quickly, they wrapped him in a blanket and Samira blocked the door stopping them.

"Julian STOP! He is a prisoner. You are breaking the law." Samira warned her stepping out of the situation, but not from blocking the door.

With a solid look in her eyes, she spoke to her firmly, "My name is Jordan. It is nice to meet you. Please, you go first and meet us at Julian's room-626. He needs a pair of scrubs and his boots. Gather Julian's personal thangs and we will meet you at the main exit. You have a car? Right?" Jordan asked as Julian's anxieties stood back, fearful of Jordan's bite.

Samira was very confused and tried her best to locate a common sense explanation for what was happening before her brown eyes. "Yes. But...Okay....I will get your things. But, you didn't tell me you were Illegals, Julian." Samira said as she stopped leaning on the door and prepared to depart the situation permanently.

Shoving Noah toward the bathroom, she barked orders. "Noah, get to the bathroom, IDentifY NOW! WE ARE OUT OF THIS HOSPITAL!" Her short, thick arm was immediately pointing to the bathroom snapping her short, thick fingers. Jordan was very curt and dominant in her position. Noah did not talk back to her-maybe even curtsied, before he dashed. Jordan ruled his roost as well as Julian's, and now for the moment, Samira's roost.

Samira had both her hands up in front of her to stop the attack, when Jordan commanded her. She sensed she was a complete stranger now...for some reason. "We are not Illegals. We are Federal Agents,

and Noah has been locked in here by Rachael, Emily's ex-wife-." Jordan could not bite her tongue fast enough to stop saying the secret. She waited for it. And here...it...comes.

Noah barked from the bathroom, and Samira glanced, confused at the conversation. "Who is Emily and was she really married to that raping cunt?" As he stepped out of the bathroom and appeared dizzy to Samira, he walked without confidence and holding his head with both hands. Jordan quickly shooed Samira out the door, and taking a last look at him flashing his pretty tool as he adjusted his blanket, she took her chance to escape the situation. Feeling as if she was jeopardizing her job, she opened the door and ran away on her toes.

"Noeeeyyyy. Julian loves you." She said like talking to a child. Jordan knelt down on one knee behind the doorway to gain a tactical advantage. "Now shut up about Emily or I will have Noah jerking off on the side of a hospital bed." She was piercing her lips and sporting Julian's sexy eye patch that offered a momentary bribe of distraction to him.

He spoke up to her, like a child to his Momma, "I can't get Jon? I...I can't IDENTIFY!" She quickly turned and looked into his eyes.

Slowly, it dawned on her, "Oh my God Noey, she crashed you. SHE CRASHED JON!" Holding a pause and the question of what to do expressed on his face, she blurted, "FUUUUUUUUCK!"

She turned and peeked out the door to see Samira pressing the button on the elevators and running in place. Jordan counted to herself up to five as she timed the distance and elevator time, and dashed out the door with Noah wrapped in a blanket behind her, holding her hand. Blazing past the nurse's station, her hair filled the air behind her as her pants

fell down her ass again. She grabbed the front of them with her only free hand and crashed inside the elevator going down, and then down to the floor. Samira watched them from outside the elevator as Jordan crawled to the buttons and her pants inching their way down to her knees. Barely tall enough to reach the close button, Jordan pushed it over and over staring at Samira, and finally reached out for her, and the door closed, as Jordan screamed for her.

"*They needed to go up, not down.*" Samira said to herself in a panic, as her anxiety levels climbed and Nurses stared at her.

Starting to get up, she barked the orders, "Fuck it Noah! We are goin' out the front door. Bring yer' Alibis...uh, if you have him. Sorry." Jordan stood up quickly to get dressed again, and instantly her head jerked her backwards and to the floor on Julian's Noah's Ark.

"GET OFF MY HAIR NOEY!" After he rolled to get up, she rolled over and struggled getting her hair under control and out of the way. Back on her feet, she pulled her pants up again, growling at the complications. The lobby was only a few floors up and Noah helped her get the back of her jeans back over Julian's rump. The plan was to walk right out the front door without style, until the elevator stopped and the doors opened.

Both of them stood there, looking up to the ceiling like posed mannequins, and hoping the people would not think anything out of the ordinary was going on. Looking out the door, they realized no one was there. Jordan quickly hit the button for the lobby, and blamed him for it.

Samira dashed out of the main doors and made her way to the employee parking garage with Noah in a white blanket, and Jordan still holding the front of

her stretchy jeans up and mooning anyone behind her. Employees and patients alike could feel the tremors as her but twerked in stride, but they did not stop puffing on their smokes. From a distance, witnesses saw Samira running away from a half nude couple chasing her with their fetishes.

'Love is the Rainbow'

In the next Book:

Chasing Her Fetishes

Dark Pleasures &

Enchanting Pains

SEXUAL PLEASURES from guilt works

when punishments fit SEXUAL NEEDS.

Buy it today at Amazon.com